I0687115

Irene Ayo Asuen

Not Quite Imperfect

a novel

QuietlySpeaking™
www.ireneayoasuen.com
www.quietlyspeaking.com
https://www.facebook.com/iaasuen/

Copyright

Imperfect - The Poem

His eyes light up whenever he sees me.
He is a simple kind of guy.
What I like best about him?
Him. All of him. His person.
He is simple and imperfect.
Yet, he is my perfect person.

His smile is genuine and infectious.
His heart is honest and sincere.
He makes many mistakes. He is flawed.
Some days, I don't even like him.
Yet I love him all the time, every day.

His emotions are deep and real.
He is open about his insecurities.
He is not afraid to share his feelings.
Sometimes he is uncertain,
and he gets mad and frustrated.
But that's okay. He is human after all.
And his imperfections are also his qualities.
They make him uniquely him.

His gestures are also endearing.
Unexpectedly, he presents me with quirky gifts.
And every time, I squeal in delight at
his innocent display of affection
We are not perfect together.
We have our ups and downs.
But in our hearts, we are in perfect sync.
We are each other's perfectly imperfect persons.
We just fit like answers to the puzzles of our lives.

What I like best about him?
Him. All of him. Just him.
Simple, human and not quite imperfect.

- Destiny's Voices ©2015 by Irene Ayo Asuen

Not Quite Imperfect

"We all have drama in our lives, some more than others…"
Just My Opinion But … ©2024 by Irene Ayo Asuen

Chapter 1

It was a beautiful Sunday evening in September, but thirty-three-year-old Kendra Mercury could see nothing beautiful about the evening as she waited anxiously for Ian Sharp, her boyfriend of eight years to come home from playing basketball with his friend, Julian Capers. She was fully dressed in black jeans and a light grey sweater as she lay down on their king-size bed in their large bedroom. For the umpteenth time, she mentally went through what she was going to say to Ian. She had just received the confirmation that she had been waiting for. She knew Ian would be upset when she broke the news to him but she could not keep it a secret any longer, especially as she hoped to keep it this time. Besides, he was going to find out sooner or later anyway, so now was as good a time as any other to tell him. She was optimistic that he might allow her to keep it this time. After all, this was the fourth time, and she felt that God was giving her one last chance to perform this miracle that she was brought to this earth for.

Finally, after what seemed like forever, Ian, wearing a hooded Nike tracksuit, entered their third-floor, one-bedroom apartment on a Hundred and Twenty-Eight Street near Ninth Avenue in New York. Their apartment was such that the front door to the apartment immediately led to the foyer, which in turn led to the living room where they had set up a dining table and chairs. The apartment was partially carpeted with area rugs and tastefully furnished with beautiful paintings and other home furnishes thanks to Kendra. The coat-closet was on the right side next to the main entrance and the kitchen was on left side. Their large bedroom and bathroom were at the back. He had his earphones, which were attached to his cellphone firmly plugged into his ears as he sang loudly off-key to Kanye West and Jamie Foxx's Gold Digger song. He was apparently in a good mood. Once inside, he locked the door with his keys and then opened the closet door to put the basketball he had brought with him along with his gym bag on the floor of the closet. As soon as Kendra heard him come in, she got up from the bed, took a deep breath and made her way to the living room to give him a kiss and a false bright smile.

"Hi babe, how was the game?" she asked with false cheerfulness.

"It was cool. I feel great and my thirty-five-year-old body feels younger," Ian replied in his raspy voice as he kissed her back warmly and he returned her embrace. "Wow, babe, I love it when you kiss me like that!"

"I missed my man," Kendra smiled sexily.

"And I missed my woman," he responded equally sexily, passionately kissing her all over her face.

"Hmmm…nice," Kendra said when he stopped for air. "Are you hungry? I made your favorite meal; fried rice, fried ripe plantains and red snapper."

"That's a nice surprise! What's the occasion?" Ian asked happily, his mouth watering at the thought of his favorite meal. Besides being fantastic in bed, Kendra had always been a really good cook.

"Can't I do something nice for the man I love, just because?" Kendra asked brightly while secretly dreading the conversation that was about to take place. Ian could be the most charming, romantic guy that a woman could ever want, but at the same time, he had the ability to cut you off emotionally and without warning if he did not get his way.

"Sure, you can babe." Ian turned her around so that he was embracing her from the back in that warm protective way she loved. She always felt secured when he hugged her like that.

"Good, let's chow down!" She was anxious to talk to him about what was on her mind, even though she was also very nervous about what direction the conversation could go. You just never know which Ian you were going to get by the end of a conversation. Either way, it was time to roll the dice.

"Thanks, love but I need to shower first," Ian said, as he released her from their embrace and then headed for the bathroom, taking off his tracksuit jacket as he walked toward the direction of their bathroom. Kendra decided to wait till he was ready to eat before telling him the news.

After Ian had showered, he put on a pair of black and white-striped pattern cotton pajama pants. He did not bother to put on the matching pajamas shirt before coming back to the dining area, bare footed. Kendra had already set the food and put some bottled water on the dining table, along with a bottle of red wine. She let Ian sit down before proceeding to prepare him a dish of food. She set the plate before him, before preparing hers and then sitting down opposite him. She watched him enjoyed a couple of bites and smile at her in satisfaction before she took a bite of her own meal. After he took a third bite of his meal, the words suddenly seem to fall over each other from her mouth.

"Ian, honey, I am pregnant. I am sorry. I did not mean for it to happen but the good news is that we are going to be awesome parents," Kendra said in a quivering voice hoping that his reaction would not be the same as three other times before.

"What?" Ian barked angrily, his whole demeanor instantly changing. Kendra got up and went over to stand behind him. And then she wrapped her arms around his shoulders not even sure why she was doing that. Maybe if he felt her love for him, he might calm down? Instead, he shook her hand off him violently and visibly backed away from her. His voice was cold and his face was very stern as he turned around to look at her. He could not imagine how careless she had been yet again, never mind that it took two of them to be responsible.

"I swear I took my pills, I did," Kendra said in a diminutive voice, trying not to let the tears at the corner of her eyes roll down her face. She felt very small…almost ashamed, as she felt the full burden of birth control was hers and hers alone. Ian had a way of making her feel like a badly behaved child when he was upset with her. His scold was worse than that of a parent.

"Well, you are just going to get rid of it," Ian said without emotion.

"I've done that three times already just to please you, Ian, because I love you," Kendra replied in a brittle voice.

"Well, one more time won't hurt, now, would it?" his voice was hard.

"Ian…" her voice trailed off.

"You did it before because you love me, so do it again," he repeated in an even harder voice.

"Why can't we keep this one?" she dared to voice her feelings.

"Because like I said many times before, I don't want children!"

"Ian, be reasonable," pleaded Kendra.

"You knew that about me when we first started dating, I haven't changed my mind!"

"Please, listen to me. I really…"

"Really what?? Want to keep this thing in your stomach?" he asked harshly.

"You don't have to be so cruel," she said now angry. She hated that she loved him so much but right now she did not like this person standing in front of her. This person was mean and selfish and could care less about how she felt.

"Ken, you are just going to get rid of this one like you did the others," he repeated with finality as he got up from his partially eaten meal and made a U-turn away toward the direction of their bedroom. His appetite was suddenly gone.

***

As Ian lay on the bed in their bedroom, all those childhood memories of his relationship with his father came flooding back. His father, a retired army sergeant had always told him that it was a good thing that he was an only child and that children were nothing but expensive brats and there was really no point to them. Growing up, whenever he did anything wrong, his father had beat him senseless and had drilled into his head that he was an unwanted child after each beating while his mother watched helplessly. According to his father, children made a mess, they cost a lot of money, they got into trouble and they always made the parents look bad when the parents tried to discipline them in public places. Ian must never have children, he cautioned. They were a curse he added, after each beating and lecture. Ian never forgot those lessons. He had vowed from an early age after a particularly bad beating for accidentally breaking a drinking glass in the kitchen that he would never have children. His father was right, children always got in the way of life and since he could never do anything right in the eyes of his father, he believed his father when he told him that he would never be a good daddy either.

Kendra knew about his abusive past because he had told her early in their relationship about his childhood and his lack of interest in having children. The thought of having children did not sit well with him. They were little brats as far as he was concerned. He was not cut out to be a father and he accepted that as a fact of who he was. He had been very clear to Kendra at the beginning of their relationship that he never wanted children and told her many times during the course of their relationship. She had given him the impression that she understood and seemed okay with not having children. Yet during the course of their relationship, Kendra had tried several times to change his mind about having children without success. His mind had already been made up; he was not having any children and that was that. She could either deal with it or leave. She knew this about him yet she deliberately got pregnant again to hurt him! How could she be so stupid?

***

Kendra took a sip of water and then sat on the long sofa in the living room area, leaving her barely touched meal on the dining table. Once again, she decided to resign herself to Ian's decisions in order to keep the peace in their home. It did not matter that they both knew the pill was not a hundred percent effective and that Ian simply refused to take any precaution himself because he did not like the feel of a condom on his skin. As far as he was concerned, it was completely her responsibility not to get pregnant. She had tried many times to talk him into taking precautions as well but he always said that they made him uncomfortable and he wanted to feel close to her without any barriers. The last time she had brought up the topic of precautions and had warned that unless he used condoms if he did not want children, she would stop using any herself, he almost struck her in anger especially when she would not drop the topic but had stopped himself just in time as his father's face flashed through his mind. He did not want to be like his father. That was the first and last time that he had ever tried to physically strike Kendra and it was the first time that Kendra had ever seen that kind of behavior in Ian. Her own father had always been nothing but loving to her mother, her sister and herself. Ian had felt ashamed when he saw the look of fear in Kendra's eyes for the first time in their relationship. He realized what he had almost done and it had hurt him for making her feel that way. He had immediately apologized to her and had actually cried claiming he did not mean to strike her and he would never, ever hit her. He was not his father. He would never hit someone weaker or smaller than he was. He did not hit women. He had never stuck a woman before and he was not about to start with the woman he loved. He disagreed with her about having a baby but he loved her and would never cross that boundary of striking her.

Kendra believed him and she forgave him. The topic of him using protection was dropped and everything seemed to go back to normal except that a cord had struck in Kendra that she could not explain. She forgave him, yes, but she also wanted to help him heal his emotional scar. She felt that a child would bring them closer together and once Ian felt the effect of having a child, he would understand that his father was wrong about assuming he would be a bad father. Also, for reasons, she could not explain, that incident of Ian almost hitting her and then crying triggered her maternal instincts for the first time in her life. She had always thought that she was fine about not having children with Ian and that their love was enough until that moment when she did realize that their love was not enough. She wanted a child born of her and Ian.

Yet, despite it all, Kendra loved Ian unconditionally and she knew he loved her too regardless of everything they had been through as a couple. So as far as Kendra was concerned, a child would make them complete. A child would heal Ian and a child would make her whole. It would seal bind them as a single unit forever. So as long as they were together, she would keep trying to convince him.

***

After about half an hour, Kendra went to the bedroom to check on Ian. He was watching Family Feud on TV and did not look as angry as he had been earlier when she first broke the news to him.

"I'm sorry Ian," Kendra said from the doorway.

"Sorry enough to get rid of it?" he asked hopefully.

"I want you to be happy," she said instead.

"I'll be happy after you agree to get rid of it."

"Okay," she replied with resignation. For now, she would try to appease him yet again but until she actually went through the procedure for the fourth time, she was not so sure what she would do.

"Okay?"

"Yes, ok, I'll call the doctor in the morning."

"Thank you, baby. Let's go finish dinner." Ian got up from the bed, walked toward Kendra and took her hand as they went back to their dinner. The meal had gotten cold so Kendra heated it in the microwave and they resumed their meal. They talked about everything but the pregnancy, a topic, which though they had come to an agreement to get rid of, still hovered in the air.

Later that night, Ian poured on the charm and they made love passionately, and for Kendra, a little more desperately because sometime in the middle of their lovemaking, something changed inside her. She suddenly knew that nothing would ever be the same again between them.

Chapter 2

The next day was Ian's day off from work. Kendra had come back from work a little later than usual because she had spent a couple of hours in the shopping mall window-shopping to 'clear her head' after last night's emotional conversation with Ian. She had purposely left their apartment much earlier than she usually did to avoid seeing him this morning. She left before he woke up and had not seen or heard from him all day since she had also turned her cell phone off. After killing some time at the mall after work, she finally went home.

When Kendra got home, she took off her shoes and jacket and carefully put them in the coat closet by the main entrance. She washed her hands in the kitchen faucet, got out a bottle of water, took her time drinking it in the kitchen before making her way to the bedroom where she found Ian stretched out on the bed in sweatpants watching a Yankees versus Cubs' baseball game on the television with a frown on his face. From the way he was intensely focused on the game, she knew he was not really watching and he had heard her come in. He did not look up when she entered the room. She walked toward the bed and sat crossed legged in a meditating pose beside his stretched form on the empty side of the bed. She knew he was thinking about the note that she had left for him on the bedside table before she left the house that morning. The note had simply said, I'm sorry, honey, but I changed my mind. I want to keep him or her. Please understand. I love you, Kennie. Sensing the invisible wall around him, she knew that he had read the note and his response was to shut down from her. His demeanor toward Kendra was devoid of emotions. His eyes had that cold, dead look that she had come to recognize and dread whenever things were not right between them. Ian's cold twin was in the room. She wanted the charming, understanding guy who made love to her last night. The one who wooed her from California to New York in the name of love many years ago.

"Hello Ian," Kendra said calmly, refusing to be drawn into his darkness. She wanted to play it cool.

"Hey Kendra. By the way, I am going to spend tonight and the next couple of days at Julian's place," Ian did not look at her as he made his announcement in an emotionless voice with that frown still on his face and his eyes still glued to the television.

"Why? Are you leaving me?" she asked wondering if he was leaving her because she decided to keep the pregnancy.

"I just need some space from you to think about our relationship, that's all," he replied still not looking at her.

"Why?"

"Are you seriously asking me that after the note you left me?"

"Please try to understand."

"What I understand is that we agreed to terminate the pregnancy, Kendra and you decided not to do that after we agreed."

"I really feel we should keep it this time. I think the time is finally right for you to discover the joys of being a parent and what a wonderful father you are going to be, Ian."

"Kendra, I am not cut out to be a father. I will not be a father against my will. I thought you understood that," Ian replied looking at her for the first time since she entered the room. There was a mixture of pain, hurt and anger in his eyes. He wanted Kendra to see what he was feeling. He wanted to get to her. He always knew how to get to her. He was banking on her giving in to him like she always did.

"Ian, baby, I am sorry. You are right," replied Kendra, once again waffling under Ian's influence and resenting herself for letting him get to her after changing her mind and being strong all day in her resolve to stand her ground.

"I know I am. We are enough for each other, trust me."

"I should have been more careful in the first place. I shouldn't have forgotten to take my pills," she said.

"Yes, my sweetheart," agreed Ian. "I love you so, so, so much. Please don't hurt me by doing this. Get rid of this pregnancy."

"I'll call Dr. Madrin tomorrow to make an appointment to get rid of it," Kendra said in a small voice as she wondered yet again if she was one of those people destined not to be a mother.

"You do that, baby. I don't want to share you with anyone, not even with a baby. You are mine and mine alone. I love you baby. Only I could ever love you this much, my love," Ian said with a charming smile as he stretched his arms toward Kendra to pull her on top of him. There was suddenly nothing in his expression or behavior that showed his unhappiness a moment ago. At age thirty-five, he still looked very boyish and like Kendra, he could easily pass for someone ten years' younger. His job as a Personal Trainer at Thomas Louis Gymnasium in Manhattan's downtown area allowed him to maintain his lean athletic features. Ian, an African American man, was six-feet-three-inches tall, handsome, bald-headed, dark in complexion and had a physical appeal that could match or even surpass most men. From the first time that Ian saw Kendra as she was crossing Sunset Boulevard in Los Angeles, California where he had been visiting a friend eight years ago, he had chased her shamelessly until she agreed to be his. They had been perfect together since then except of course when the topic of babies got in the way.

***

Ian had been driving to a friend's place when he first spotted Kendra wearing tiny braids, dressed in skin-tight dark blue jeans and a form-fitting white tank t-shirt as she was crossing the street in the opposite direction. He immediately made an illegal U-turn, so he could catch up to her and talk to her. When he finally had her attention, he turned the charms on her. After that, it took her only three weeks before she decided to quit her job as a Systems Analyst and move to New York to be with him. There was just something about Ian that she could not explain. Her friends and family had tried to talk her out of her impulsive decision to move cross country to be with someone she barely knew but it was all to no avail. Good or bad, Ian had gotten to her. She could not explain what it was about him. She barely knew him but the pull to him was too strong to resist. She was meant to be with him. Kendra tried to explain to her family and friends that Ian was her person but they did not understand. They had always known Kendra to be a smart woman, not prone to hasty decisions, but after she met Ian, 'sensible, responsible' Kendra had morphed into, well, someone else. But the way Kendra saw it, no one felt Ian like she did.

Unfortunately for Kendra, her relationship with Ian turned out to be more than a tad complicated. A few months after she moved to New York to be with Ian, he began keeping a close watch on her every move without her knowledge. Her only escape from his watchful eyes though unbeknown to her, was when she was inside Tedon Financial Firm's building where she had found work as a Systems Analyst after moving to New York. Even then, she was only free from his prying eyes for a short time because her office building was just opposite the gymnasium where Ian worked. He knew the exact time she left work, when she had her lunch break, who she had it with and how long it would take her to get home. When he was not on the gym floor training a client, he was at his office, which happened to have a window overlooking her office. One could even say that Ian was obsessed with Kendra. Though he had slept with other women since he and Kendra had been together, in his mind, it was not really cheating because he only slept with these other women when he and Kendra had arguments, and he wanted to punish her. It was not as if he had promised these women anything. They always understood it was purely a physical thing and no emotions were involved. These affairs usually lasted a few months and then it was over.

Now, Kendra was the special one, Ian had always reasoned to himself. She was his woman. His heart. Still despite Ian's claim to Kendra, he had 'loved' her possessively for the last eight years though not enough to marry her. The institution of marriage was another battle he constantly struggled with. He was not sure he believed in marriage. The way he saw it, most people divorced within a couple of years of marriage. And even more people opted to live together before marrying. Funny thing was that these same people who wanted to live together before marriage, ended up breaking up after moving in together, and just as many others didn't even bother to get married at all because as far as they were concerned, marriage was archaic and they were happy the way they were. In fact, Ian noticed that society had re-written 'the rule' about relationships and the new norm was to live together before marriage or just live together as a couple without the paperwork of marriage or the expensive headache of divorce, should one become necessary. Certainly, his parents' marriage had done nothing to strengthen his belief in the idea of marriage either.

***

Ian's parents had been together for twelve years before his father, Evans Sharp, left. All Ian could remember when his parents had been together were the constant tensions and arguments between them until one day his father had simply announced that he was leaving the family for another woman. Instead of being angry, his mother, Sadie, had actually been relieved. In fact, she seemed much happier after her husband left. Three weeks after Evans left, Sadie was served with divorce papers, which she signed immediately with great relief and actually rushed down to the courthouse the same day she signed the papers to file them. The sooner it was official, the quicker she could carry on with her life. After his father left, Ian saw him only once or twice a year until his death from a heart attack.

After his father died, Ian had felt sad, angry and even a slight sense of relief. No more beatings, no more put downs and no more sense of obligation to see his father once or twice a year anymore, but there was also a small sense of regret of what could have been, had they ever gotten a chance to mend their relationship and grow close, which they never did. It ended up just being him and his mother whom he had a fairly decent relationship. She had remarried a year after her divorce and was clearly happier with her new husband. Unfortunately, she too had died three years after his father died from a brain aneurysm. His maternal grandmother brought him up after his mother died and his relationship with his grandmother had also been decent at best.

"I love you, Ian. I didn't mean to hurt you," Kendra said breaking into his thoughts and snuggling up to him. Ian put his arm around her. She would do anything to make him happy. She loved him so much. He was everything to her. His words were gospel. Everything he said was right. A baby would mean divided attention. That could not happen. She was thirty-three years old. She still had a few years left in her biological clock. Maybe he would change his mind next time. He might even marry her then, who knows. Ian often told her he was still very attracted to her and that marriage was just a piece of paper. As far as he was concerned, they were already married in his heart. Kendra had always accepted his view on marriage because she herself had always been ambivalent about it until she met Ian and she became more open about the idea but only if it was marriage to him.

Unfortunately, he was not on the same page with her when it came to marriage. She did not push the issue too much because though she wanted to marry Ian, she often wondered how much more demanding he would be once they were officially married. When she was absolutely sure within herself that Ian, and all the challenges that came with being with Ian, and she was absolutely sure he was the man she wanted to spend the rest of her life with, she would insist that they set a date. For now, she was content the way things were. Besides, their love life was still very active. Not just lovemaking but romance. Ian could be very romantic when he wanted to be. He had this ability to make women feel special and beautiful no matter what age, race or size they were. Kendra always felt special just knowing he was hers. The only bone of contention was him not wanting to be a dad and of course those times when he got into his dark moods when he did not get his way. That was when 'Ian's evil twin' appeared like a mean petulant child out of nowhere.

Not Quite Imperfect

Kendra knew she was still a beautiful black woman with a body most women would die for. Younger men hit on her all the time some of them as young as nineteen but her heart belonged to Ian. Never mind that her family and friends thought she was a fool in love.

***

Kendra's father, mother and sister had each made it a point of duty to call her at least twice a week to see how she was doing when they could not stop her from going to New York. When they found out through conversations with her from what she did not say, they knew that Ian could be very manipulative and were concerned about how he treated her. They tried to get her to leave him but she refused to listen.

Ian knew Kendra's family disapproved of his relationship with her and so he convinced her to reduce her contact with them. Eventually, Kendra told her family to stop visiting or calling her. She did not want to upset Ian because she loved him too much. She told her parents and sister that if they loved her, they would go along with her wishes and not call her unless she called them. And whenever her mother came from Los Angeles to visit her without warning, Kendra would make her stay in Hoboken, New Jersey, with her sister, Piper, a nurse who was two years older than her, and married to a French, Real Estate Lawyer, Cain, before going back to California.

And because of her relationship with Ian, Kendra had no friends in New York. Her life was with Ian and he made sure that she was completely and totally dependent upon him.

"Honey, I am all the love you will ever need, please get rid of this thing in your belly and don't change your mind again," Ian's deep raspy voice broke into her thoughts as he gave her a kiss before proceeding to make love to her, the baseball game he was not really watching, now forgotten. They made love passionately pleasing each other in ways only they could understand. Ian was once again the passionate considerate lover and Kendra, a willing participant, giving her body to him completely but somewhat urgently because this time, unlike last night and other times before, somewhere in her soul something died inside her. She knew she would never look at Ian the same way again. Yet because she still believed that Ian was her world, she decided not to allow a child ruin her relationship with him. She would go ahead and get rid of it like he requested but her feelings for him would never be the same again. Yesterday, she had felt something shift in their relationship. Today, she felt something die inside her. For the first time since she and Ian had been together, she recognized that she was in this relationship alone and had been for quite a while.

***

The next day while they were having breakfast together, Ian insisted that Kendra call Dr. Madrin in his presence and schedule the appointment. So, like three times before, feeling resigned, she called Dr. Madrin, her gynecologist to make an appointment to terminate her five-week-old pregnancy.

Chapter 3

A few days later, on the day of Kendra's appointment, Ian got up very early as usual. He had enough time to gently nudge Kendra awake so he could make love to her before going for a run and coming back home to take a shower, have a breakfast of cereal and coffee, and then heading for off to work in a good mood. Kendra had listened to him. All was well with the world again.

After Ian left for work, Kendra called in sick at her job so she could go see Dr. Madrin. The whole process would be over before she knew it.

As soon as she got to Dr. Madrin's private clinic, she signed a few papers at the receptionist's desk and then a nurse by the name of Courtney Florence, came out from another room, retrieved her file from a cabinet behind the receptionist, looked at it, and then told Kendra to follow her to examination room one. She gave Kendra a loose disposable hospital gown to change into, checked her blood pressure, asked her a bunch of standard questions to verify her information on file and then told her that the doctor would be with her in a few minutes. Kendra smiled weakly at her and said thanks but the nurse did not return the smile or say anything else. She simply nodded back at Kendra before she left the room leaving her alone. She had been polite to Kendra but not friendly. Kendra was sure the nurse did not like her because of what she was about to do yet again.

***

"Are you sure you want to go through with this?" Dr. Madrin asked Kendra with concern in his eyes. He was a short, average-looking Korean man in his early sixties, with a head full of salt and pepper hair. He had kind fatherly eyes and a soothing voice. He was also the same doctor who had performed her last three abortions.

"Well, Ian does not want this baby. I love Ian, I want to do what's right by him," Kendra said simply, trying to separate herself from what she was about to do. She was lying on the bed inside the examination room of his private practice.

"Well, this is your fourth trip here for this procedure, you are doing damage to your body," said Dr. Madrin, concerned.

"Will this affect my chances of having another baby in the future?"

"Well, for some people it does, for others not necessarily but as you get older it might be more complicated."

"I see," Kendra said without emotion as though she was in a trance.

"Do you want to reschedule your appointment to give you time to think about it?" he asked kindly.

"Ian does not want it. He is not going to change his mind. He expects me to carry out his wishes."

"I don't mean to interfere in your relationship with your husband but…"

"He is not my husband," Kendra interrupted without thinking while interlacing her fingers in a nervous gesture.

"Sorry, I mean your boyfriend but don't you have any say in this?"

"It's what Ian wants."

"What do you want Kendra?" he asked her pointedly without being judgmental.

"Ian wants me to get rid of it so I am getting rid of it," Kendra replied evasively. She knew he was genuinely concerned about her.

"Why don't you talk to him again?"

"It won't do any good. He is very clear about what he does not want," she responded wondering why the doctor was asking her all these questions this time around. He was getting a bit too personal and it was making her uncomfortable because she did not want to deal with her own feelings. She just wanted this to be over. He didn't ask so many questions the last three times she came to see him. It was one of the reasons she kept him as her doctor. Why couldn't he just do what he was supposed to do so it could be over with? She did not want to think about it anymore.

"So, you are sure you want to go through with this?" asked Dr. Madrin again He could feel her desperation not to go through with the process this time. He felt compassion for her.

"Well, Ian wants me to," Kendra replied again trying her best to distance herself from the situation. She really did not want to think about it anymore.

"I'll tell you what, I'll have the receptionist reschedule you. Let me know what you decide in two weeks. Ian does not have to know why you didn't do this today. If he calls my office, they'll tell him I had an unexpected emergency and you had to reschedule," Dr. Madrin said kindly to her as he squeezed her hand in a comforting manner. He suspected she did not really want to abort her child and quite frankly, he was hoping that she would change her mind and not go through with it. Dr. Madrin also wondered what kind of man Ian that was would scare and control the woman he supposedly loved like this. He wondered why Ian was not even here with Kendra for her appointment. From his experience, many of his patients regretted their decisions after they went through with the process and many of them always had their significant others with them for support. Kendra always came to her appointments alone. He could not help but feel protective of her. She could easily be his daughter.

"Thank you," Kendra responded gratefully, breaking into Dr. Madrin's thoughts. There was relief in her voice. She was not even aware that she had been holding her breath until she spoke those words.

Chapter 4

Kendra was grateful that Dr. Madrin had come out of his professional self to be a supportive friend. He had sensed her silent struggle and helped her understand what she needed to do. After that fateful day at Dr. Madrin's practice, she finally resolved to keep the baby and deal with Ian's wrath, whatever that might be. No more waffling for her.

Once Kendra finally made up her mind, she made many secret follow-up appointments with Dr. Madrin to monitor the progress of her pregnancy. He had given her a list of instructions on how to take care of herself, what to eat, what types of exercises were safe during her pregnancy and pre-natal vitamins, which she hid from Ian. Though she was now four months along, she was still not showing yet. Kendra had always been one to take really good care of herself. As a result, no one could tell that she was pregnant, not even Ian who thought he knew her so well. Ian usually left in the mornings for work before she did, so when she felt the need to throw up because of morning sickness, he was almost never around, except once or twice when he nearly caught her and she dismissed it as something she had eaten. Luckily for her, pregnancy was wearing well on her. Unlike many expectant mothers, only once did she have to call in sick from work. She told Ian that she was having really bad cramps that day and thought it would be best if she stayed at home. He had agreed but had called in twice to check on her. Thinking she had done as he had asked, he was once again the sweet, loving boyfriend with the occasional mood swings that she was used to.

As for Kendra, she hated Ian with all her heart for making her go through what should have been a joyful time in their lives alone, but at the same time she loved him with all she had to give. Right from the moment they met many years ago, Ian had had a strong, unexplainable effect on her. He brought out all kinds of emotions in her that she never knew she had. He was the only person she had ever met in her life that had the ability to evoke emotions that embodied such intense hatred and love in her at the same time. He was like a drug she couldn't quit. He was so good for her yet he was just so bad. He made her feel small and yet on top of the world at the same time. In order to stand up to Ian or to quit him if and when the time comes, she would need something extra. And she knew deep down in her heart that she would eventually have to make a choice between him and her unborn child. She also knew that though she did not voice it aloud to the universe, deep within her heart, that choice had already been made. Their unborn child was the extra she needed to stand firm in her decision.

***

Today marked the fifth month of Kendra's pregnancy and she was finally beginning to show signs of pregnancy. For one thing, people at work noticed that she had gained a few pounds even though she was still quite slim, and they had also noticed that there was a 'certain glow about her.' The nosy ones pointedly asked her if "there was a bun in the oven?" Others closer to her asked; "should we plan a baby shower?" "Do you know whether it is a boy or girl?" "Are congratulations in order?" At some point during their inquisitive questions, Kendra had responded with a "yes, I am having a baby." The first time she said it out loud, she felt a sense of empowerment. Finally, she had openly owned her pregnancy even though she had done it to her boss and colleagues and Ian.

Kendra's mannerisms had also changed without her even being aware of it. She was a lot more sensitive to things emotionally and she was always rubbing her stomach unconsciously. Her appetite had increased and her cravings were all about grapefruit juice and potatoes in any form; fried, boiled, mashed or baked. If she did not have these when she craved them, she felt she would kill someone.

Just the other day, Ian had commented that Kendra was getting 'curvy' but he loved her anyway. Kendra had laughed his comments away with an excuse about just being bloated from her period. But then yesterday, he remarked again that her breasts were looking bigger and certainly much softer these days when he touched them. Kendra had gone on the defensive to distract him by demanding if he was calling her 'fat'? Ian backed down immediately pouring on the charm and telling her he meant she was glowing and looked beautiful. If Ian suspected that Kendra was still pregnant, he did not comment, or he simply thought she had ended the pregnancy as he had requested because despite her obvious changing appearance, after all, 'Kennie would never go against his wishes. She knew better.'

After Ian's last remark about her breasts, Kendra decided that the time was approaching for her to tell him the truth. She had had enough time to brace herself for his reaction, whatever it was going to be. He could either deal with the fact that they were going to have a baby or not. Either way, she was already mentally preparing herself for single motherhood if it comes to that.

Chapter 5

Some days later, Kendra was preparing a dinner of grilled salmon, vegetables and baked potatoes when she heard Ian come in from work. She had come home from work a few hours earlier because she had taken a half day so she could keep an appointment with Dr. Madrin, who had assured her that she was progressing nicely.

"Hey, sweetie," Ian said as he dropped his gym bag on the living room floor and walked up to stand behind her in the kitchen. He wrapped his strong arms around her waist and gave her a kiss on her neck as he nuzzled her.

"Hey, babe, how was your day?" she asked in her sweetest voice while at the same time momentarily turning away from the stove to face him.

"It was all right, but I couldn't wait to come home to my baby," he replied nuzzling her neck.

"Good. Dinner is almost ready. Since it looks like you already took a shower at work, do you think you could set the table after you wash your hands?" she asked pleasantly, no hint of what she planned to tell him during dinner.

"Sure, not a problem," Ian responded good-naturedly. He kissed her again on her lips, before going to the bathroom to wash his hands. He came back to the kitchen after he was done and then started searching the upper cabinets on the opposite side of the kitchen where Kendra was making dinner, for the dishes. He took out two flat, square-shaped, China plates to put on the dining table. Then he returned to the kitchen for cutlery, drinking glasses, a big bottle of spring water and a carton of Tropical grape juice. He had noticed in the last couple of months that Kendra had been drinking grape juice as though the product was about to disappear from earth and she was eating French fries like no man's business. It was as though she had suddenly discovered a special secret taste in potatoes and could not get enough of it. He knew Kendra ate junk food occasionally but not like this. She had even put on a few pounds but he was not complaining because he liked her new voluptuous body much better than the really skinny self she was once. He was zipping his mouth about her weight gain because the last time he mentioned the change in her body, she almost bit his head off. Women were so sensitive about their bodies, he thought. She was not fat by any means, just…well, fuller. Thoughts had flashed through his mind once or twice that she might still be pregnant, but he quickly dismissed those thoughts. Kendra would never dare disobey him; she knew better. This must be something else. Anyway, whatever her sudden cravings for this kind of food, he figured that she was just dealing with the recent abortion she had had to go through. After all, he had read in some magazine that many people tended to turn to food for emotional comfort when they were going through things although he was just not one of those people. He usually just worked out like crazy when he was upset. Sometimes, if he was angry with Kendra and had had an argument with her, he would have sex with other women just to punish her. He never turned to food for comfort. As far as he was concerned, food was just an excuse for people to pig out. Anyway, she would get back to herself soon enough, Ian thought despite that nagging feeling that something might be up with her. Anyway, there was nothing a little loving in bed could not cure. He would make her feel better about the decision to discontinue the pregnancy soon enough.

Ian set the table nicely before he remembered to get the tablemats. Kendra hated it when he put cups or food directly on the table without any coasters or tablemats. 'Damn, now I have to set the table again,' Ian grumbled silently in his mind as he went back to the kitchen to retrieve tablemats and coasters from one of the kitchen drawers. 'Why can't women just let things be? Why do they have to fuss over silly little things like coasters and tablemats? I don't hear the tables crying to be dressed up every time somebody put a simple glass of water or plates of food on them,' Ian thought as he reset the table. He was standing over the table mulling over anything that he might have left out when he heard Kendra instruct him again.

"Ian, baby, could you come take the veggies and potatoes to the table?"

"Sure." He came back to the kitchen and took the bowl of mixed vegetable from the counter where Kendra had put it along with a dish of potatoes and placed it on the center of the dining table, followed by the dish of potatoes. Kendra brought in the salmon and the sauce and they settled down to eat. At first, there was comfortable silence as they helped themselves to the food and began eating. Ian looked very content as he enjoyed the food. When Kendra saw that he was enjoying the food, she put her fork down on her plate, took a sip of water and then broke the news to him.

"Ian, I have some news, which you may not like," she said softly but firmly. This time she was not afraid. She had already gone through a wide range of emotions and had had enough time to prepare herself for his reaction. She was quite sure he would leave her but she was ready for that too. She would move into one of those rooms that people advertised on the classified sections at a weekly rate as a first step. She could afford a fairly nice neighborhood for now. Plus, she still had her job and it came with good benefits. She had already been looking casually at rentals and had stepped up the process within the last couple of weeks without Ian's knowledge. Two places looked promising so far. She was ready. The time was now.

"What is it, Kendra?" Ian asked her expectantly. When he saw the look on her face, he realized with sudden self-honesty that not only had he been lying to himself but Kendra had been lying to him too. She had dared to defy him. He knew what she was going to say but he wanted to hear the words from her mouth. There was no emotion on his face as he waited for her to speak. It always amazed Kendra how he could shift from one mood to another in a blink. And his voice always fitted his mood. Right now, his voice was impersonal. No emotion, no anger, nothing. It was worse than being angry.

"I didn't get the abortion. I changed my mind. I am keeping the baby, our baby." She stared at him without blinking; waiting for the explosion she was sure would follow his impersonal attitude.

"You did what?" Ian asked in a tone that Kendra had never heard before. It was dangerously soft. He helped himself to some more salmon as he spoke, shifting his gaze from her to his food.

"I am keeping the baby. I am getting older. My biological clock is ticking, and you have no plans to marry me. I need something. I need to feel like I have achieved something."

"So, you lied to me." Ian paused eating for a moment and proceeded to stare Kendra down, trying to intimidate her, make her feel small like he had done many times in the past when they had had arguments. This time Kendra did not flinch. She stared at him right back. She was determined to have this baby.

"I need this for myself. I need something for us ... of us."

"You know how I feel about fatherhood and yet, you have decided to do this selfish thing, anyway…you have decided to keep it after all?"

"It is not an it, Ian. It is our baby, a human being … our miracle of love. With or without your support, I'm keeping this baby." There was a stubborn edge to her voice that Ian had never heard before.

"Kendra, the choice is up to you. Get rid of it or we are through," Ian said and then calmly continued eating.

"First of all, I am too far along to consider getting rid of it. And secondly, even if I was not, I would still want to keep this baby."

"Give it up for adoption," Ian said through clenched teeth as though he was talking about an inanimate object.

"I can't do that," Kendra said with quiet determination.

"I'll give you till the end of the pregnancy. If you still refuse to see things in a sensible way, then there will be no 'us' anymore."

"Is that a threat, Ian?"

"No sweetheart, it's a fact."

"Is that right?"

"It is what it is. You always knew that I did not want children. This is not the first time we've had to deal with this matter."

"Well, I was hoping…"

"Hoping what exactly? That I'll change my mind this time? That I'll suddenly want for children? What exactly where you expecting, Kendra?"

"After all these years together, you know how I feel about children. Don't you want me to be happy?"

"I want you to be happy, Kennie, baby. You know no one can love you like I do," Ian said, suddenly pouring on the charm hoping Kendra would just be a 'good girl' and get rid of the baby like he asked her to do previous times and she had obliged.

"This baby will make me happy Ian. I bet you'll make a fantastic dad despite what you think about yourself as a dad." Kendra did not want to be sucked in by Ian's charm again.

"I don't want a child, Kendra," Ian said in a hard voice as memories of his childhood with his dad flashed through his mind. The charm he was displaying a moment ago suddenly disappeared.

"Let's sleep over this and talk about it again tomorrow. I don't want to have an argument with you." Kendra was suddenly tired of all the fighting. She loved Ian but she did not want to miss the opportunity to be a mother. This was too important.

"Kennie, my answer is still going to be the same tomorrow. Being a dad is not what I will ever want. I don't understand why women meet men the way they are and then they think they can change them once they are in a relationship."

"Are you serious about us breaking up if I have this child, Ian?" Kendra asked instead, ignoring his comments about women.

"Yes, and it'll be your fault."

"I see. I have tolerated every crap from you in the past. This time, I am standing my ground. It is not something I will mull over anymore now that you are crystal clear on your position. There is just no way I am giving up my baby this time,

Ian. Not even for you. I am sorry." Her voice was very strong. She found strength in her unborn child to stand up to him.

"Well, I guess you have decided to break us up then," he said without looking at her.

"No Ian, I decided to have something for us, or maybe for me. To have someone who could love me unconditionally without judgment. I already feel bonded to this child…our child," Kendra replied. She could not believe his gall. He had the nerve to say she was breaking them up. As usual, this was her fault. He was never one to take any responsibility for his actions. She had given up all her other unborn children for him in the past. This time, something clicked. Not anymore. She was not giving up this one for Ian. She had already sacrificed everything she ever was to be with him and yet he still could not love her unconditionally. It was suddenly all too much after all these years with him. All she could see was that she was bringing a gift born out of love to this world, yet all Ian could see was that she was hurting him.

"Whatever," Ian's cold, emotionless voice broke into her thoughts. This was not his lover. She was the person that was deliberately hurting him.

"I'll be out of the house by the time you get back from work tomorrow."

"Like I said, your choice," Ian said as he resumed eating. He did not believe for one second that Kendra would actually leave him. He owned her, body and soul. He called the shots in their relationships. Now that they had had this talk and he had given her an ultimatum, he was sure she would see things his way like she always did, despite her last comment about her leaving him. Ha! Like really? Where would she go? Back to California like a looser? No worries there. He knew Kendra like the back of his hand. By the time he came back from work tomorrow, she would have come back to her senses and agreed to get rid of this pregnancy like she had done with the previous ones in the past. The only this is that she might have to give this child up for adoption since she claimed she was too far along to get an abortion. He should have known…all those changes in her body; weight gain, sudden craving for certain foods ... it was not his imagination! Maybe he had just not wanted to acknowledge to himself that she had not done as he asked.

"Ok, Ian," Kendra voice broke into his thoughts as she looked at him long and hard with a clarity that she did not have before. Suddenly the voices of her family and the friends she once knew in LA began ringing in her ears; they were right. They had always been right. She had just been so stupidly in love that she did not see the truth all these years. Ian was one stubborn, self-centered son of a bitch and she had had enough. Kendra suddenly got up from the table without finishing her meal and without another word to Ian. She went into their bedroom and closed the door. She lay down on the bed fully dressed and stared at the ceiling for a long while until she fell asleep.

***

Ian slept in the living room on the sofa that night. He could not bring himself to sleep on the same bed with Kendra after their argument. After all he had put into this relationship, she had decided to break them up. It was pretty obvious she did not love him like he loved her. Well, he was tired of her ass anyway. He was still a handsome, strong brother who had it together. He was It. Women threw themselves at him all the time, much younger women for that matter. Kendra was getting too old for him anyway. Besides, she had become one of those women men ran away from; constantly nagging: "do this, do that," "Ian, baby, bring this on your way home," "don't forget to do so and so..." like he was some damn child! And she wondered why they were still not married! It was all her fault. How many times did he tell her he did not want children?? Anyway, didn't she know how to use birth control pills? Maybe she stopped using them on purpose to trick him to becoming a dad! That must have been it! She wanted to trap him into marriage. Well, he was the one laughing now. Her plan had backfired. If she wanted to have this thing in her stomach, she was going to have to do it without him. By the time she came back to her senses it would be too late. He would be with someone else. Her loss.

Chapter 6

The next day, Ian woke up much earlier than his usual time. He sat up on the sofa, rubbed his eyes and then stretched for a few minutes before getting up and walking quietly to the bedroom where Kendra was asleep still wearing yesterday's clothes. For a few moments, Ian stood at the doorway and looked at Kendra silently as she slept. Even after many years together, he still loved this woman so, so, so much. He had never felt anything this powerful for any other woman in his whole life. And then suddenly, the love and softness that he was feeling for Kendra turned into a wave of anger, betrayal and disappointment as yesterday's conversation replayed in his head. She was willing to defy him and break up their relationship for some kid! Well, she would regret it. She needed him and she was going to be sorry for not abiding by his wishes. Ian shook his head as if it would help reduce the wave of emotions he was feeling and then tiptoed around the bedroom to avoid waking Kendra up while he gathered some clothes to wear for the day. After he got what he needed, he quietly made his way to the bathroom to take a quick shower and then got dressed in a pair of black jeans and a black sweater before leaving for work without having breakfast. He planned to get a buttered bagel and coffee from one of those mobile commercial food carts on his way to work. He had skipped his usual morning run to save time. He wanted to be out of the apartment before Kendra work up. He could not leave the house fast enough.

***

When Kendra woke up, she was relieved to see that Ian had already left for work. Her first instinct was to rub her stomach before heading to the bathroom to brush her teeth and take a shower. She took her time taking a long hot shower; letting the water sting her as she tried to wrap her head around what she planned to do after her conversation with Ian last night at dinner. She actually felt relieved and secured in her decision once she had made up her mind about following through with her plans. After she had finished taking her bath, she had a breakfast of oatmeal and green tea, took her vitamins, checked in with Dr. Madrin and then called in sick from work. Next, she called the landlords of the two rentals she had on her list that she thought was promising and made an appointment to look at each of them again the next day after work. Luckily, she was able to get a one of the places, settled the first couple of months' rents and was back home before Ian came back from work, none the wiser of what she had done. By the time he came home from work, Kendra was feigning sleep to avoid any further confrontation with Ian.

***

The next day Kendra and Ian continued the pattern of avoiding each other. In Kendra's mind, keeping this pregnancy was the blessing that would make their relationship even stronger than it had ever been, but in Ian's mind, this baby was the curse that would ruin their relationship. As far as Ian was concerned, Kendra was trying to hurt him while Kendra thought her decision to have a child was too important to give in to Ian's demand to give up the child once it was born. She wanted a child and nothing Ian said or did was going to convince her otherwise. Both Kendra and Ian were stubborn regarding this child issue. Neither was giving an inch. It was definitely a messy problem. And so, they avoided each other with Ian thinking that Kendra would eventually give in to him in a matter of days like she always did, and Kendra already checking out mentally from the relationship. This was the biggest test of her life but carrying this baby had also changed her into a woman she never knew existed within her: a strong one determined to carry on as a single mom without Ian.
***

Not Quite Imperfect

On the third day of their silent treatment to each other, just like the two days before, Ian who had slept on the living room sofa again, woke up very early, quietly got his clothes from the bedroom while Kendra was 'asleep,' took a shower and left their apartment for work before she 'woke' up. As soon as Kendra heard him leave, she jumped out of bed and began packing. By mid-morning, the movers had arrived and Kendra was out of the apartment. She did not leave a note. There was no need for goodbyes. Eight years of her life with Ian was now over. It was time to begin a new life. She intended to make it one way or another with or without Ian Sharp.

Chapter 7

When Ian got home from work later that day, before he even walked inside their apartment, he immediately sensed that something was different. He felt emptiness, an uneasiness that he could not explain. He nervously inserted the house keys into the keyhole of the front door and turned open the door, slowly pushing it wide open. As soon as he stepped into the living room, he immediately knew that Kendra was gone. There was finality about the atmosphere that he had never felt before when he and Kendra were still a couple. Kendra was actually gone. Not gone to the supermarket or gone to run errands or gone to work but gone as in really gone. She had actually left him for good. He had threatened to leave her but she had actually beaten him to the punch and he did not even see it coming! Kendra had chosen the baby over him and without even so much as a word she left! He dropped his gym bag on the floor in the living room, took off his jacket, flung it over one of the dining chairs and then walked briskly to the bedroom he shared with Kendra.

He opened the door quietly, slowly and peeked not sure of what to expect. The bedroom was neat and everything was in its place. The bed was well made as usual by Kendra, no shoes lying out of place, no belts, scarves, or any random item lying around carelessly. Kendra had always been a neat freak. Everything always had to be in order. She was OCD about neatness. For a second, he was relieved before remembering that there was of course no sign of Kendra. He pushed open the door wider, walked to their large walk-in closet and opened the double closet doors with more force than was necessary. He immediately noticed that Kendra's clothes and shoes were all gone and so were two of the four suitcases that they kept in the closet.

A tad annoyed and anxious at the same time, Ian walked to the chest of oak double-sided drawers and mirror combo dresser standing against the wall on the left side of the bedroom facing one side of their bed, where they kept their underwear. He frantically pulled out one drawer after the other only to see that the first six drawers where Kendra kept her underwear items were empty and the bottom two where he kept his, still had his boxers and undershirts neatly folded in little squares, just how Kendra liked them. But her things were gone! All gone! How dare she leave him! Or would she? This was not the Kendra that he knew. When did she grow a backbone? If anyone was going to do the leaving in the relationship, it was supposed to be him. He was not even sure he meant it when he threatened her. He just wanted her to come back to her senses and follow his wishes. Maybe he took it too far this time, or did he? Damn Kendra. Damn! Damn! Damn!

***

Heart pounding, Ian paced furiously back and forth in the bedroom, his emotions were mixed; he was angry, sad, and scared of being alone…without Kendra. Did Kendra really leave him? He loved her more than anyone ever could, didn't she know that? All she had to do was get rid of the baby and listen to him. He knew what was best for her and he was the only one that could ever love her…ever…she had to have known that! Ian suddenly walked to the kitchen, not sure why he suddenly thought she would be there cooking when there was obviously no one in the apartment but him. Of course, the kitchen was empty. Yesterday's leftover dinner of stewed potatoes and lamb sat on in the pot on top of the gas-range four-burner stove. The dishes had been washed and neatly racked. A couple of glasses stood upside down on paper napkins on the surface of the granite counter. Ian opened the refrigerator, which contained two large bottles of Poland water, fruits, a plastic container of half-eaten chicken salad, half a dozen eggs in a bowl, orange juice and a 12-pack-can of Heineken beer, which he had bought the day before on his way home. Kendra did not drink beer. Ian grabbed a can of beer, ripped open the can viciously and drank it in one long gulp while standing up with the refrigerator door opened. After he finished it, he took another one from the fridge, opened it just as angrily as the first but sipped it more slowly as he used his leg to push the fridge door shut and made his way to the living room. As soon as he entered the living room, he flung himself on the sofa, grabbed the remote control from the center table and turned on the television to watch the New York Knicks play against Miami Heat in a basketball game. He did not turn on the sound of the television nor was he able to concentrate on the game. After a few minutes, he stood up and began pacing the apartment again. Finally, he grabbed his gym bag from the living room floor and fished out his cell phone. He dialed Kendra's number. Maybe he was just over-reacting. Kendra did not answer her phone. Instead, he heard her voicemail instruction stating that he should leave a message. He left her several messages in rapid successions until her phone was no longer accepting messages. Next, he tried texting her but his texts were rejected, leading him to the conclusion that she had blocked him.

After several pointless efforts of trying to reach Kendra, Ian went back to the kitchen, grabbed a third can of beer and then headed back to the living room where the soundless television was still on and the basketball game was coming to an end. He flopped down on the sofa again, dejected and feeling like a little boy that had been betrayed. He needed to find her to make her see the errors of her ways and come back to him.

After he finished his third beer, he went back to the kitchen to retrieve the remaining cans of beer. He came back to the living room, once again threw himself on the sofa and proceeded to get wasted. Ian passed out after the eight can of beer. The last thing he thought about before he passed out was the first time he met Kendra in California.

Chapter 8

Kendra had rented a room on Twenty-sixth Street and Lexington after leaving Ian. The next thing she did was to change her phone number after he had bombarded her phone with text and voice messages, which had ranged from angrily ordering her to; "get your behind back home now!" charmingly coaxing; "baby, you and I are a team. You know I love you so, so, so much," and finally tearfully pleading with her to; "please come home, Kennie so we could talk. Lover, I need you." The last three of his messages sounded as though his voice was slurred but Kendra could not be sure. She had never known Ian to be a heavy drinker. He was too obsessed about his health to indulge in no more than a couple drinks once in a while and not excessively. Anyway, regardless of his messages, she intended to stay at the room she had rented until she could get a proper apartment and sought herself out. Going back to Ian was no longer an option. It took many abortions and years of intense sadness at the loss of each child, to make up her mind to leave him. She still loved him; he was her first true love but it was different now. It would take time to get him out of her system completely but she promised herself that she would try. However, one thing she knew for sure was that she was keeping her baby. Her mind was made up. He gave her an ultimatum, her child, or their relationship. She chose their child. In her mind, she got to keep her child and a piece of Ian through the child that they had made together. She was not going back to Ian. She had taken the first step to her new life.

After two months, Kendra was able to leave the one-room rental that she had initially rented and get a two-bedroom apartment in the northeast section of the Bronx in Co-Op City. It was exactly what she wanted. Her salary as a Systems Analyst was enough to get her qualified for a mortgage loan form the bank. Everything was within walking distance of each other; several laundromats, three huge shopping malls, medical offices, a few banks, convenient stores, a few parks, public transportations, and various grocery shops. Plus, the building management gave tenants the options to buy their apartments if they wanted. Her credit was good and within a month of applying, she was approved to buy the two-bedroom apartment. She chose to buy instead of renting because it was cheaper and made good investment sense. She knew it would take her a while to furnish her place but she did not care as long as she had a roof over her head. Her only other immediate purchase was a bed and a baby's cot. Everything else would come later. When she lived with Ian, he bought almost everything in their apartment except for some high-priced paintings, which she had bought with her own money through lay-away plans. Ian did not care much for art but Kendra did. She had taken these paintings with her when she left Ian. As Kendra reflected back on her life with Ian, she realized that she had never had a home because everything had always been about Ian; the furniture, which he chose, the way everything in the apartment was arranged, what she wore, how she did her hair, who she saw (thanks to him, she did not have any real friends), the direction and pace of their relationship. It was all his way of controlling her. The only good thing was, aside from her contribution toward household groceries, he let her keep the rest of her money from her job so she was able to save a little. And yet through it all, she loved him unconditionally. To her he was not a mean, controlling man as her parents and sister pointed out every chance they got. To her, he was simply flawed and imperfect like any other human being but they got each other in more ways than one.

Despite her savings, Kendra realized that she would need more financially as she thought about the baby she was about to have. She planned to finish the computer degree program she had started in LA at some point after she gave birth so she could boost her income. After all, she only had one more semester of college to finish before she had dropped out of college to move to New York to be with Ian many years ago.

***

As the months progressed, Kendra began to have difficulty doing certain things by herself due to her pregnancy. By her eight months, she knew it was time to reconnect with her family not just to make amends for the way she treated them during her relationship with Ian but also to tell them that she was pregnant and no longer with Ian. First, she called her sister, Piper, who lived in Hoboken. She readily forgave Kendra for treating her badly during her relationship with Ian and immediately came to visit her that evening. Piper promised to check on her every day and come see her as often as she could.

Next, Kendra called her parents a few days after reconnecting with Piper. When she spoke to her father, as expected, he immediately demanded that she come back home to California so that they could take care of her, never mind the fact that she left California a long time ago.

"Kennie," Leon, her father, a math professor at Maryon College in Downtown Los Angeles, said, "why don't you come to your senses and move back home to LA?" He was a lean, bespectacled, dark-skinned, man who stood at six feet and two inches tall. At 67 years old, he still had a head full of salt and pepper hair and a strong, commanding voice, which sometimes made it difficult for Kendra to argue with him when she did not agree with him.

"Daddy, my life is in New York despite what happened between me and Ian. I still love New York. It is where I make home. Besides, the doctor said I could not fly until after I have the baby."

"Honey, you need someone to take care of you and my grandchild," her father said gruffly with affection.

"I can manage and I have Piper. Hoboken is just a stone's throw away. I spoke to her a few days ago and she's already been here a couple of times. As a matter of fact, she is coming over again tonight for dinner," Kendra said half-convincingly.

"Kennie, you need more than Piper, you also need the rest of your family. I knew that guy was a scumbag all along but you wouldn't listen to me."

"Daddy, I guess I found out the hard way and you were right. But I also want to finish out college here after the baby is born."

"And how do you intend to do that while raising a child by yourself?" he asked without accusation. She was still his daughter and no matter what, he still loved her.

"Dad, Piper will help out. We are not far from each other," Kendra reminded her father again about her sister's close proximity.

"Hmmm," her father grunted unconvinced. "Hold on while I get your mother to pick up the other extension." After a few minutes, her mother, Kate, picked up the other extension from the kitchen where she had been making a cup of tea and preparing a snack.

"Hello, Kennie, honey, how are you? I am so happy you called, I missed you," her mother said in her soft, calming voice, which Kendra always felt soothing. Piper and mother always took turns playing peacemakers in the family whenever there was an argument going on between any of the family members. She was a 65 years old, slender woman with medium-length thick graying hair, which she wore in two heavy braids. Like her daughters, Piper, and Kendra, she looked several years younger than her age.

"Hi, Mom, I'm so sorry for cutting you off when I was with Ian. You were all right. We broke up, and...and..." Kendra's voice broke as a tear rolled down her face. She had not allowed herself to cry since she and Ian broke up but as she spoke to her parents, she felt like a little girl, and suddenly her suppressed emotions began to overwhelm her.

"Honey, tell me, what's wrong. Talk to me Kennie, I love you," her mother tried to comfort her. Unable to hide her pain any longer, Kendra told her everything. By the end of the conversation, her mother had decided to come to New York to stay with her until the baby was born. Her father could not come with his homemaker wife until much later when school was off and he could take time off. For now, her mother would come and help her. Piper would also check in on her occasionally. Since Piper's own husband, Cain, was away for two weeks on business, it would all work out well.

Chapter 9

It was a cool Fall Saturday morning in late September. Ian had just come from a five-mile jog through Central Park and was looking forward to his date with Charlie later that evening. Charlie was 22 years old, five feet, seven inches tall and French. She had a beautiful smile, long jet-black hair that fell straight to the small of her back and a lean athletic body. Ian had met Charlie at the 86th Street subway train station on his way to work earlier in the week. As far as he was concerned, she was a welcome distraction from Kendra at just the right time. Since Kendra left him, she had occupied his thoughts day and night. Everything reminded him of Kendra. He needed a mental break from anything Kendra. She did not come crawling back to him like he had expected but he still held out hope that she would eventually come to her senses and come back to him. After all, what woman wouldn't want all of him? He looked good and he knew it. Even better, his charms could get him anywhere and he knew that too. Charm and good looks had worked well for him all these years. They were his gifts to women and his passport to getting out of life's sticky situations. When Kendra first left a few weeks ago, a small part of him wondered whether his looks and his charms had worn thin but after meeting Charlie, he realized he still had it. As far as he was concerned, Kendra should count herself lucky that he had shared his beautiful self with her all the years they had been together. The pregnancy issue with Kendra and her stubbornness to get rid of it was just a small hiccup in their relationship, as he preferred to think of it. As soon as he could find out where she was staying and actually speak to her in person, she would come crawling back soon enough. If only she had appreciated what a catch, she had in him and did that 'small' favor that he had asked of her, their relationship would still be ok today. They had been 'separated' for just a short while and already the universe was throwing 'thirsty' women toward his radar. Take for instance, the beautiful Ms. Charlie.

Not Quite Imperfect

Charlie, a fine young thing that she was, noticed him at the subway station and made no secret of appreciating what she saw in him as he did, he in her. Yep, he still got it. So just because Kendra decided to be a stubborn fool that he wanted back nevertheless, it did not mean that he was blind to other beautiful women in the meantime. Besides, he needed to feel the warmth of a woman's body next to him in bed, however temporary that may be. After all, he was not made of wood. He was still a red-blooded American male and he had needs.

***

With Charlie, it started with a quick glance in her direction as she boarded the number 5 Lexington Avenue Express train at 86th Street subway station. She caught his glance through the windows of the train car that he was already in, as it slowed to a stop. Once the train came to a stop, she smiled at him and walked quickly to sit on the empty seat next to him before an aggressive always-in-a-hurry New Yorker could grab that seat. She had lived in New York City long enough and used the train often enough to know the drill by now; stay close to where the car doors of the train are expected to be when the trains stopped but not so close that you accidentally fall into the tracks, and then keep your eyes on any empty seat as the trains rolled to a stop. As soon as the doors opened and people start coming out of the trains, create enough space to walk through the crowd without obstructing movement out of the train and claim 'your' seat or else you will be standing all the way to your stop. Gentlemen were few and far between these days so do not count on a guy already sitting down to give you, his seat. Anyway, once Charlie was seated next to Ian, they exchanged "good mornings," complained to each other about how slow and crowded the trains were during rush hours and then decided that their mutual dislike about the subway system and her "sexy" French accent (according to Ian) was enough to warrant a dinner date and get to know each other under more pleasant and relaxing circumstances. With that, a dinner date was set.

***

When Ian got home, he was still sweating from his run as he made his way to the fridge in the kitchen for a cold bottle of water. The fridge was empty except for four small bottles of Poland spring water, a small carton of half-eaten week-old Chinese food and a crate of eggs, which was half-empty. He took out a bottle of water and took a long gulp until the bottle was almost empty. He took another gulp before he surveyed the kitchen. His mind drifted again to Kendra as he took in the rather dusty and somewhat dirty kitchen. He had taken to eating out since she left him because cooking and cleaning was just not his thing. Kendra used to do all that because she liked cooking and more importantly, she loved a spotless kitchen. She did not like to see the slightest food crumb on the counters or dirty dishes anywhere. She always said they made her 'itch.' If she saw the kitchen now, she would probably more than itch, she would have rashes, Ian mused as he looked at a couple of dirty dishes and tumblers from three days ago still in the sink, a small pan that he used to boil eggs a couple of days that ended up burning the eggs along with the pan, which still sat on the top of the gas stove, and the somewhat dusty counters. The kitchen certainly did not smell like food, more like a barely used room in need of cleaning. The apartment as a whole was clearly lacking a woman's touch since Kendra moved out. Initially, he had missed her terribly when she left him. Actually, he still missed her terribly despite his eagerness to meet Charlie.

Despite feeling the finality of Kendra's absence after she left him, Ian still held out hope that she would come to her senses and beg him to take her back and of course promise to get rid of the child once it was born. At one point, for a brief moment, he actually considered calling her parents so he could convince them, well, truthfully, beg them to tell him where she was. He stopped short at the last moment when he remembered that they hated him. He always knew what they thought of him and he knew what they would have done if he had spoken to them on the phone. They would have scolded him in a condescending manner and tell him how unhappy he had made their daughter when they had been together and then at the end of a long, tedious phone conversation they would still not tell him where Kendra was. As far as he knew, Kendra did not have a close relationship with her family while he and her had been together. He had seen to it that he, Ian, was her only family and only friend. So of course, it would have ended up being a total waste of his time and energy speaking to her parents. So no, he would rather eat glass than speak to Kendra's 'nasty' parents. And so, days turned into weeks, and slowly but not completely, Ian began to accept that Kendra had actually left him for good. Yet here he was; still wanting her more than ever and suddenly developing an even deeper attraction to the Kendra who had developed a backbone to stand her ground and leave him wanting more of her despite Charlie and other women, and despite the fact that he did not get his way with his demands. Feistiness and stubbornness was surely working for her.

Chapter 10

Charlie was nothing but a fling for Ian…a much-needed distraction. Their first date was nothing to write home about but at least the weather cooperated for a night out in town. The evening weather was slightly cool in the mid-fifties with light winds. Their conversation during dinner was rather forced, and both Charlie and Ian seem to be circling each other, each with their own agenda.

"So how long have you been in the United States?" Ian asked Charlie in his most seductive voice. They were having dinner at Carmine's on West 44th Street. It was an Italian restaurant that Ian had chosen and Charlie could care less about but since he was paying and he said it was one of his favorite places to eat and insisted they go there regardless of her less-than-enthusiastic response, she went along with it while mentally deciding it was strike one against him. She only decided to give him a chance because Ian was a) good looking, b) he could fulfill her pressing wish: marriage to an American who could take care of her and of course either get her a green card or file for her to become a US citizen since her student visa was running out fast and c) quite frankly, she needed to get laid. She was single and it had been a while since she had been with anyone, so why not him?

"Going on four years now. I am now in my final semester as a Business Management student at NYU. After school, I will be going back home to Lyon," Charlie smiled wistfully as she drawled her response making sure to thicken her accent because she heard somewhere that Americans, well, many Americans, had a thing for accents.

"Nice thing about school. Why do you have to go back to France?" Ian asked politely, not particularly interested. He did not care much for school. He never went to college and had no desire to. High school was good enough for him. He had always been interested in athletics. After high school, which he struggled to complete, he tried his hands professionally as a boxer, made a decent living before quitting out of boredom to take a job downtown as a physical education teacher at a small private learning institution for teenage boys. After he got tired of their bratty behaviors at the institution, he got certified as a Personal Trainer and began working at Thomas Louis Gymnasium opposite where Kendra worked. They paid him a decent salary with good benefits and his schedule was flexible enough to allow him to offer private training services during his off-days when he needed the extra money.

"Well, my student visa will expire in a few months and then I have to go back home unless I get a job with a company that agrees to sponsor me or otherwise," Charlie responded as she took a bite out of her Shrimp Parmigiana and then a sip of the white wine that she had ordered. Ian had ordered Rigatoni with sausage and veal and water to drink. He did not feel like drinking any alcohol today. Charlie did not add that "otherwise" meant she needed to marry an American pronto.

"That's a shame. Pretty girls like you make the good old USA a better place to live in," Ian replied, touching her left hand longer than necessary. Charlie did not brush him off; she was enjoying flirting with him. "Now what can we do about you staying? It would be my pleasure to get to know you better."

"Perhaps that can be arranged, qui? Je vous aime, vous semblez être une personne agreeable," she flirted back, leading him on.

"I don't know what you just said but it sure sounded nice in French. Ian liked the way she spoke not particularly caring what she was saying. Her voice was soft and low and her accent added to her appeal. Her green eyes complemented her slightly crooked nose. He wanted to feel her naked body next to his.

"I said I like you: je vous aime bien. You seem nice."

"I am nice, especially to lovely girls like you," Ian whispered back seductively. He liked the direction their date was going, at least from his perspective.

"Hmmm. So, tell me more about yourself, what do you do for a living? Are you married?" Charlie asked, lightly, taking a slow bite from her food.

"I work as a Physical Trainer," Ian swallowed some water as he stole a couple of glances at her size 34c breasts. He imagined his hands gently cupping them as they made love, which he hoped would be sooner rather than later.

"Ah, now that explains it. You have such a nice body," Charlie said putting down her fork and reaching across the table to touch Ian's muscled right arm while thinking Ian's job meant he probably could not afford her champagne tastes. Strike two.

"Why thank you. Ms. Charlie. I am all yours for the feel," Ian could not help adding, daring to go a little dirty despite the fact that it was their first date. Charlie's French accent turned him on and the sound of her sultry voice was taking his mind to places he wished they both were. He could not wait to take her to bed. What she was wearing only made him want to skip the obligatory polite phase of their date. She was dressed in tight dark blue jeans, five-inch stiletto thigh-high boot and a body-hugging black sweater, which revealed a sheer, V-neck, cream-colored, sleeveless blouse, and a black lacy bra underneath when she took off the sweater to make herself more comfortable at the restaurant.

"So, are you single?" she asked with curiosity blushing at his response and withdrawing her hand from his arm to take a sip of her wine.

Ian hesitated slightly before responding. "Well, I am single at this moment." She did not need to know that he wanted Kendra back. He quickly stirred the conversation back to her. "You must get hit on a lot by many men…you are a beautiful woman," he complimented.

"Thank you and yes, I do get my fair share of attention. So, what kind of things do you enjoy doing?" Charlie was already thinking of how to ditch him after she slept with him. She was not sure if he was really single judging from the manner in which he responded. He sounded married, taken, or emotionally invested in someone else but more importantly as far she was concerned, trainers did not make the kind of money she wanted a partner to make in order to take care of her, which meant he was not of any use to her, well, maybe except for the sex part and that was a maybe. That was yet to be determined. He was dangerously close to strike three. Maybe she would test his bedroom skills before ditching him, hmmm.

"Well, you know, basketball, boxing, running, and other sporty things," Ian smiled as he answered her question. "What about you, what do you like to do?"

"Many different things really. I like sports too but things like bowling, tennis, and soccer. I also like to travel a lot, go to live concerts and the theatre."

"Really, that's nice. Perhaps we should do those things together on another date?" Ian suggested while thinking her tastes in hobbies would require a lot of money. The girl sure sounded like she had expensive taste. He was not a big traveler and good live concerts cost quite a bit of money and let's not even talk Broadway shows.

"Yes, perhaps. I have been meaning to catch Mama Mia! for some time now," Charlie smiled. Maybe this Ian guy could afford her after all, hmmm. Her gig as a waitress and a French teacher off the books, could barely pay her share of rent for her Queens apartment, which she shared with a roommate, much less a Broadway show.

"Yes, that would be a good one to go to together," Ian faked enthusiasm. He had no intention of seeing a Broadway show with this chick. At least not before he tasted the goods. Kendra used to drag him to Broadway shows back when they were together. Most times he made excuses not to go or suggested that they do something else. The very few times he went with her, he always got bored in the middle of the show. He preferred to hang around sports bars or do something more sports-oriented or outdoorsy activities. When he went to cultural events with Kendra, it was mostly to please her and stop her nagging. Truth be told, Kendra was a worldly, sophisticated, cultured woman who was always ready to try new things, and Ian, well, not so much as worldly. If he was completely honest with himself, he knew she had been a great catch and he had been lucky to have had her, not the other way around. Even though he never admitted it to her, he had always been slightly insecure for some reason when they had been together; he had always felt that he was always trying to catch up to her standards and any man could steal her away from him at any given time but of course he never told her that. Instead, he asserted himself by telling her no one could ever love her like he did, which as far as he was concern, was true anyway.

"Good. We can get to know each other even better then," Charlie smiled at Ian breaking into his thoughts, her eyes twinkling as she spoke. He was such a cutie. She just wished he had a better paying job. Oh well, he was still a choice for option A and C: legal status and sex.

After their meal, as they walked down the street, Ian suggested that they go somewhere for a nightcap but Charlie declined politely.

"Perhaps, next time. I have to complete a paper for my final exam for one of my classes," she lied. She had had dinner with him. That was enough for now. She had no intention of going home with Ian after their very first date. Much as she wanted to get laid and to move things along in order for her status to be legal after she graduated, she still barely knew him so she had to play it cool on the first date at least. Perhaps if they went on another date, things might progress from there. Besides, beneath his apparent easy-going charm, there was a certain edge about him. He had been slightly guarded during dinner and not really giving much about himself. For all she knew, he could be a serial killer. She had to play her card rights, take it a little slow. She had other things to do for now, none of which included finishing up a paper for school. She was supposed to call a rich married guy she met at the restaurant she worked at that she was seeing to set up a date for tomorrow. She had bills to pay.

"That's a shame, Kennie," Ian said. He had been looking forward to feeling her warm body next to him later.

"Kennie? Who is Kennie?" Charlie's eyes narrowed a bit but her tone remained polite.

"Did I say Kennie?" Ian was not even aware he had accidentally mentioned his pet name for Kendra.

"Yes, you did," said Charlie coolly, not smiling. She was right…he was still hung up on another woman.

"No, no, no, no, no. I said what a shame, Kitten," Ian lied, hoping she would bite.

"Comme un chat?"

"What?"

"I said, like a cat?"

"Yes. But I mean it as a term of endearment in American culture. You are pretty and sexy. You are a kitten and I mean that in a nice way."

"Ah, I see. Sometimes, I hear people use the term foxy lady to mean sexy. I have never heard kitten before."

"Ah, well, that's my word for you," Ian laughed lightly. "But I would love to spend more time with you," he added hurriedly moving the conversation along.

"Then perhaps, we can do this another time? Qui?"

"Yes, how about tomorrow?" Ian asked eagerly.

"Tomorrow is no good. Between work and school, my schedule is a mess. Let's talk on the phone and plan for some time next week."

"Ok, Ken-kitten, sounds like a plan." Ian could have kicked himself. Damn Kendra! There was nothing worse than calling a date, another person's name.

"What?" Charlie was puzzled. This guy was a trip. She was glad their date was over for today. She was not a fan of guys calling her terms of endearment the first time they go out on a date. As far she as was concerned, only couples that know each other well and were comfortable with each other should refer to each other that way. She barely knew Ian. Normally, she dated richer, older, cultured men. Unfortunately, most of them were either married or looking for a mistress on the side. She needed a ring to stay in the US.

"I said it sounds like a plan," Ian cut into her thoughts.

"Good. Now I must go home to do some schoolwork."

"Let me get you a taxi."

He hailed a taxi for her, kissed her on her cheek goodnight, gave her money to go home and she was soon on her way. By the time Ian got home, his mind once again returned to

Kendra. He had slipped and called Charlie, 'Kennie,' a couple of times at their dinner date. He hoped that she bought his excuses and did not read much into it.

Chapter 11

Ian and Charlie went on a few more dates during the following weeks. They had coffee and lunch a couple of times, went to the park, and even went to see Mama Mia! the Broadway show, which made Charlie happy but not Ian since it dug a deep hole in his pockets. As far as he was concerned it was too expensive for his pockets and not particularly his thing but he also knew that if he wanted to sleep with Charlie, he needed to play along and make a good show of enjoying himself when they went out.

Of course, by this time, Charlie soon discovered that Ian was a struggling heartbroken American who was a player on the rebound. He had mentioned this person "Kendra," at least six times during their subsequent dates and conversations. He had even slipped and referred to her as "Kennie" a few times just like he did during their first date, thinking she did not notice that his excuses for the slips were lame. Eventually, she asked him point blank who Kendra was and he was forced to acknowledged that she was his ex, but quickly added that "he had moved on and Kendra was kind of 'crazy,' so he dumped her," which Charlie did not believe. She had had enough experiences with men to know that they were usually the crazy ones when they complained of an ex being crazy.

Finally, a couple of days after seeing the Mama Mia! Charlie agreed to visit Ian at his home, something she had been holding off with one excuse or another because she was no longer 'feeling' Ian particularly as he really was of no use to her, except maybe in bed, which she was about to find out just because she wanted to get 'laid.' She had mentally decided to keep looking for the 'right' person to fulfill her most important check box (the green card issue), hopefully sooner rather later. As far as she was concerned, Ian was a charismatic, handsome, less than average-earning American who was still stuck on his ex, Kennie, or Kendra Somebody. But at least maybe he might be good for one thing: sex, which was why she finally agreed to visit him at home just to satisfy herself that he may not have been a complete waste of her time.

***

As for Ian, he had already gotten already bored with Charlie. They were not on the same maturity level but 'damn!' the girl had a great body and she was young and fresh. He needed to taste her body on his bed at least once especially after have spending all that money on her in such a short time for things he could care less about like some 'stupid' Broadway show. After they had slept together, he could dump her ass and look for less expensive fish to fry, until, of course, Kendra came back to her senses and begged him to take her back.

***

On the day of her visit, Ian had taken the time to hire a cleaning service to spruce up his apartment for their dinner date at his place. He also made dinner, which really meant ordering dinner from a nice restaurant, and bought some good red wine at the liquor store around the corner from his apartment. He planned to finally romance her to his bed by the time they were done with dinner. She was going to be his desert.

***

Charlie and Ian had a good time at his place. The food was good and after dinner they settled down to listen to some music and sip on wine. This led to bed, which they both knew was coming. They made love to each other most of the night, both thoroughly enjoying themselves.

Charlie could finally check the 'third' box as a 'yes' with Ian. His chiseled body was not a complete waste after all. He sure knew how to please a woman in bed. Though she did not plan to see him again, she was one happy woman on this particular night.

As for Ian, he decided that Charlie had been worth his time and money. The woman was a sex goddess! She made him go places he needed to. She was his physical therapy for the night however temporary that was.

At least on that level, they could both agree. The sex was worth it to both of them. But Charlie and Ian both also knew without talking about it that it would also be their last time together and they would probably never see each other again after that. They had met, had a good time and left it at that. Besides, Kendra was still very much on Ian's mind no matter how hard he tried to forget her. She consumed him more than he liked to admit even to himself.

Chapter 12

Kendra message came in a simple text through a number Ian had never seen before. It read: Hello Ian. Our daughter, Liana, is due in two weeks at New York University hospital on First Avenue. Please text me back if you want to be involved in her birth. Hope you are doing well, regards, Kendra.

Ian's first thought was that Kendra had finally come to her senses for her to contact him, and then he thought about the implication of her message; first of all, why was she so impersonal with her message? Was he now some damn stranger to her? That thought was quickly replaced by the meaning of the message itself; Kendra was actually having the baby! She was actually 'forcing' him to be a father! The nerve of her! Well, she was just going to have to wait long and hard for him to respond. She had finally deemed him worthy of her new number, did she? Of course, he missed her when she left him and despite feeling the finality of her absence after she left, he was still hoping that she would come back to him and they would be together again. But he had heard nothing from her and finally accepted the fact that he would never hear from her again ... until this text!

Ian mulled over the text message for a while, almost dialed the number it came from but then changed his mind before going out for a run. After he came back, he called his friend, Julian, and they went to a sports bar to shoot pool. Ian did not mention to Julian that he had heard from Kendra. Later, he went home, showered, and went to bed. He had decided not to contact Kendra for now. He was not ready to deal with all this 'mess.'

Chapter 13

Kendra gave birth to Liana Flowers Mercury at New York University Hospital in Manhattan. Her family members were present for the miracle of her birth but Ian was not there. Dr. Madrin was the doctor who delivered her baby. Kendra trusted him with her life and she considered him a good friend not only because of the way he took care of her during her pregnancy but also the way he encouraged her to open up to him about her problems regarding Ian's attitude toward her pregnancy. He had been there to listen to her and advise her to follow her heart. When the baby was placed in Kendra's arms for the first time, Kendra knew it was the most joyful pain she had ever experienced. She never knew love for someone else could be this empowering. She felt truly blessed. This baby was worth it. She felt an immediate intense bond with her child.

Kendra was so overwhelmed with the display of love from her family that she wondered how she could have cut them off from her life for so long during the time she was with Ian. She had chosen him over them and yet they had forgiven her without hesitation, welcomed her back to the family with open arms, and supported her completely when she was pregnant. Everyone "cooed' and "ahhed" about the baby and exclaimed how beautiful Liana was. According to Kendra's mother, Liana was destined to be a singer. Of course, her father, Leon declared that she would have a gift for numbers, become a mathematical genius and discover something important to the world while her Auntie Piper said she would be a great actress and win several major awards and if not, then she would make a great doctor or nurse. Kendra was amused by her family's comments of love and silliness. She realized she still had a lot of making up to do with them. This was the beginning of a new life. This was her little angel whom she was bonded to for life and made her life worth living. Her purpose in this world was now fulfilled. All those years with Ian were now worth it. Unwillingly, Ian had given her the best gift of her life. She felt a slight pang of regret that he did not want to know what a joyous gift he brought to this world but more than that, she felt relieved that she would have Liana all to herself even though it was selfish and not exactly in the best interest of Liana. For now, this was where things stood

***

Kendra never heard back from Ian after she had sent a text about Liana's due date. For Liana's sake and to ease her conscience, she tried to reach him again through another text message three months after Liana was born to tell him about his new daughter. This time she sent the text along with three pictures of Liana at one, two and three months' old and the number to reach her so they could set something up if he wanted to meet his daughter. Still, she got no response from him. Kendra decided not to hold her breath waiting for his response, she knew Ian well enough to know he was probably still expecting her to come begging him to take her back and to tell him she had given up Liana to an adoption agency or something. As if! She had done what she needed to do for the sake of Liana by reaching out to him and offering him the chance to get to know his daughter. Now, she was just going to enjoy being the best single mom she could be to her. They were now a package deal.

***

Liana was growing into a beautiful, energetic child. Kendra knew without a doubt that Liana was worth all the hardship and unhappiness she had had to endure with Ian. Sometimes she wished Ian would make an attempt to get to know his daughter and develop a relationship with her. She had purposely let her number be shown on the first text she sent him before Liana was born and sent it again in her following texts after she was born so he knew how to reach her. She did not want him back but she wanted her daughter to get to know her father. She only hoped Liana would understand that she had tried when she grew up.

Not Quite Imperfect

***

Kendra's mother stayed with her in New York for a while after she gave birth. Sleep was now a luxury for Kendra as she nursed Liana while trying to work and go back school to complete her studies at the same time. Sometimes, Liana would wake up in the middle of the crying because she was restless or hungry or needed a diaper change and Liana would have to feed her or change her and coax her back to sleep. She had never felt so determined in her life to succeed. She was also grateful that her mother was there to help. She had everything to live for and in another month, she would get her degree in Computer Science. The last thing on her mind was a man's love even though she had told herself that she would not let Ian have the last laugh by giving up on love. However, anytime any of her family members asked her if she was interested in meeting anyone new, her response was always the same; "I am not quite ready yet," or "I just want to focus on Liana for now." Her sister had tried to set her up a number of times but Kendra was not interested. Kendra knew that even though it was now over a year since she and Ian had broken up, her heart was still a little hardened but more so, scared. She was scared to allow herself to be vulnerable with any man again after she and Ian broke up. So, she hid behind Liana, behind school and behind work. She had tried and failed at love so until she was ready again, her child and her family were more than enough. Family stayed the same. Despite her imperfections, they loved her anyway. They were her safe haven. They loved her unconditionally.

***

After Kendra graduated, she quit her job downtown, and got another one as a Senior Systems Analyst at Trans Computer Management consulting firm at Fifty-Ninth Street and Lexington. The salary was several times higher than what her previous position had been paying her and the benefits were exactly what she needed. Also, Liana was now a little over a year old and Kendra had established enough stability in her life that she was able to develop a routine with a baby-sitter she hired while she worked. As the days went by, Ian became a distant memory. Kendra no longer expected to hear from him. She and Liana were doing just fine without him.

Chapter 14

Today after a particularly stressful summer day at work, Kendra decided to stop at Nell's café on her way home. It was around six in the evening. She wanted to have a couple of hours to herself and read her novel, Destiny's Faces before going home. Liana, now two years old, was out with her Grandma Kate, who was visiting them for the month. As a result, Kendra could afford to indulge herself for a few hours before heading home. At the café, she ordered a crushed raspberry ice drink and an oatmeal cookie, paid for her order, and then settled down at a two-person table by the window near the front of the I. She did not notice another handsome African American patron come in and order ice black coffee. He was five feet eleven inches tall, lean, athletic-looking and looked to be in his late twenties. He was clean-shaven and his hair was cut very close to his scalp, almost bald. He was dark in complexion and he wore a pair of wire-rimmed eyeglasses, dark blue jeans, a light gray, long, sleeve button down Oxford shirt tucked neatly into his jeans and black converse sneakers giving him the appearance of a smart hi-tech, preppy guy. He noticed her immediately. After debating with himself and assessing his rejection factor while making a show of looking for where to seat, he went over to her to say hello.

"Nice day today, isn't it?" he said politely. His voice was distinctly modulated in a rich, cultured way as though he was raised in many different cities. The sound of his voice caused Kendra to look up from her novel.

"You could say so," she replied looking up briefly with a slight smile before returning her attention back to her book. Though he was quite easy on the eyes, she was not immediately taken by him and did not want to be bothered. She just wanted some time alone. "Is there something else I can help you with?" she asked with a hint of annoyance since he was still hovering around her.

"Actually, yes. Do you mind if I share your table with you?" he asked politely choosing to ignore her tone as he glanced at the empty seat opposite her where she had rested her handbag.

"Well, there are other vacant tables," she said politely without attempting to be friendly. She came here to be by herself for a few hours not to make small talk with some stranger. She refused to be deterred by his cute smile and charming tone.

"Please?" he asked smiling at her with a twinkle in his eyes.

"Okay," she said wondering what it was that he wanted. It did not immediately occur to her that he was hitting on her. It had been a long time since she had had any desire to be with another man much less notice any attention from the male gender. She took her bag from the empty seat and hung it over the arm rest of the chair she was seating and then gestured to him with the wave of her right hand to have the empty seat opposite her.

"Thanks," he said before placing his coffee on the table and then sitting down.

"No worries," Kendra replied before pointedly returning to her novel, hoping he would get the hint and leave her alone or at least be quiet.

"So, what are you reading?" he asked smiling at her looking quite comfortable while ignoring her hint.

"It's a book called Destiny's Faces," she replied indifferently not looking up at him as she spoke.

"It must be really good; you look like you are enjoying it." He really wanted to know her despite her resistance.

"I am. Perhaps you might have heard of it?" Kendra replied resigning herself to his company for the evening as she took in his comfortable position.

"Actually, I haven't. I tend to read a lot of magazines instead of books but only because I am a lazy reader. When I do get around to reading novels, it usually takes me weeks to finish reading them."

"I see. You must know that reading novels are a nice way to get away without being physically away if you know what I mean," Kendra said smiling slightly again. Despite her initial reservations, she was beginning to warm up to this stranger.

"I'll take your word for it," he responded as he took in her features; medium-brown skin, dark-brown hair done into tiny, twisted strands that fell just beneath her shoulders, almond-shaped brown eyes, long eyelashes, crooked smile that revealed a slight gap between her two top teeth, and slightly flared nose, which complimented her natural beauty. She wore no makeup, not even lipstick, yet to him, she was strikingly beautiful. He did not even think that she was his type until he saw her and something hit him; he liked what he saw. However, he could sense that she had a wall around her. After a few minutes of silence, he spoke again. "By the way, my name is Peter Rite," he said extending his hand for a handshake.

"Kendra Mercury," Kendra replied shaking his hand. It was strong and warm, and enveloped hers comfortably. Kendra noticed his nails were clean and well-trimmed, which pleased her.

"So, what do you do for a living?" he asked as he studied her with discrete interest.

"I am a computer systems analyst and you?"

"Well, I am a children's book jacket designer for Mory Publishing House."

"Interesting. Do you enjoy your job?" Kendra asked, putting her novel down and looking directly at him. It was the first time she was giving him her full attention since it did not look like he was not going to be quiet.

"Actually, I do. I studied Graphic Arts and Literature in college, so it's an opportunity to do something I truly enjoy. I relish the creative outlet."

"Good for you, Mr. Rite."

"Peter. Please call me Peter. All my friends call me Peter," he said. When he spotted Kendra, he thanked his lucky stars that he had decided to come to the café to kill a little time after, Ridge, a friend that he was supposed to meet up with, stood him up.

"Well, I'm not your friend, I just met you," Kendra replied bluntly, though not unkindly.

"Ouch," Peter said clutching his heart as though he had been hit.

"Sorry. I didn't mean for it to sound like that."

"Then call me Peter, please."

"Okay, Peter," Kendra said with a small smile and then asked, "so where are you from?"

"I am from New York City. Brooklyn to be precise but grew up an army brat all over the world, wherever my pop was posted at the time."

"So, you have been around the world, huh?" observed Kendra.

"Something like that. My father is a retired army doctor. He was never posted at one region for longer than four years while my brother and I were growing up. He usually brought his family along wherever he was posted, so we got an opportunity to see the world and meet many interesting people."

"Lucky you," said Kendra.

"Yes, but I was a kid then so I am not sure I appreciated other cultures or my travel opportunities as much as I do now as an adult. The world is so much bigger than New York; so many amazing people and cultures to learn from."

"In other words, the world does not revolve around New York as New Yorkers would like to believe," Kendra laughed at her dry sense of humor.

"If you put it that way, yes, but can you imagine a world without New York? Less spicy, less character!" Peter replied joining her in her laughter. He liked the way she laughed. It sounded like a giggle with a hint of shyness. "So where are you from?"

"Los Angeles, California but I moved to New York many years ago."

"Must have been a huge culture shock for you when you moved."

"It was. Especially the weather."

"So, what prompted your move?"

"Love," Kendra said simply and took a sip of her drink without further comment. Peter sensed that she did not want to talk about her love life but he hoped she was single, nevertheless. After a moment of awkward silence, he stirred the conversation back to a lighter tone.

"So do you like New York more than California?"

"Well, circumstances brought me here, there are good parts and there are bad parts, but overall, it is not a bad city to live in. New York is not sunny California but it is very special. The people are as real as they come and there is always someone ready to give you his or her opinion on just about anything." She did not want to share her story about why she came to New York with this person, even though he seemed nice. In her mind, men were usually nice the first few times and then the monster in them come out.

"Hear, hear," Peter nodded his agreement as Kendra spoke and then lifted his cup of coffee to his lips. Kendra noticed for the first time that he wore no ring. In fact, he wore no jewelry except for a nice, expensive, black, leather Kenneth Cole watch. As Kendra discretely observed him, she briefly thought in mild amusement that if she were a casting director she would cast him in a soap opera. He could easily play the part of the good doctor turned bad that everyone could not help but love. He had that chiseled handsome soap opera pretty boy look. Though he was not a particularly tall guy, he could easily hold his own with the quiet confidence he exuded. Kendra noticed a few female patrons smile flirtatiously at him as they walked by their table and a few of the men that walked by give him a slight nod of acknowledgement as a way of polite greeting. Kendra could see why. Peter commanded the room by his mere presence. Not bad at all. She quickly shook away the thought. She was not going to delude herself that he was interested in her in any way other more an evening conversation before going home to his woman. At least, she thought he had a woman. Men like him were usually not single. There was always some woman or partner in the background, assumed Kendra. Besides, she was not sure she was ready to enter into a relationship with a man right now no matter how charismatic he was, even though she and Ian had been broken up for a little over two years now.

"So, what do you do during your spare time?" Peter asked Kendra, looking at her with a smile, revealing a nice set of teeth. His lips and nose fitted his face perfectly. Kendra liked his crooked, easy smile, which added character to his handsome face. He also had a comfortable way about him, which she noted silently. Kendra was not sure she liked the way he looked at her. It made her feel as though he could read her mind but on the other hand, he also made her feel as though she was the only woman in the café and she kinda liked that feeling too.

"I take care of my daughter and read a lot of books, magazines, whatever. Sometimes, I go to the movies, museums, flea markets, bookstores, the parks…you know, here, there and places that are child-friendly when I am with my daughter, which is most of the time."

"You have a daughter?" Peter asked with surprise, hoping she was not one of those women with 'baby's daddy' drama. Maybe she was married but then again, he did not see any wedding ring on her finger. He wondered what her story was.

"Yes. I have a daughter, Liana, whom we like to call Lili," Kendra said proudly, breaking into his thoughts.

"Wow, how old is she?" Peter asked surprised. He wondered who "we" was.

"She turned two a couple of months ago. Why so surprised?" she asked correctly reading his expression.

"You just don't strike me as a mother."

"Am I supposed to be amused or offended?" she asked slightly annoyed. He was beginning to get on her nerves just as she was starting to like him.

"Sorry?" Peter was confused about her reaction.

"How is a mother supposed to look like?"

"Oh, I'm sorry. I didn't mean it the way it sounded. Forgive me?"

"Well…" Kendra hesitated not sure if she wanted to continue talking to him. His comments annoyed her considering how hard she fought Ian to have Liana. Motherhood was everything to her.

"Hey, I'm really enjoying talking to you. I can see my comments ticked you off. I'm really sorry," he said again, sensing her withdrawal from him.

"It did annoy me," Kendra admitted.

"I am sorry. Can we start over again, please?" Peter looked at her hopefully.

"Well…"

"Please?"

"Okay," Kendra responded forgiving him only because she was enjoying his presence more than she cared to admit to herself. In all fairness, there was no way he could have known about the circumstances surrounding Liana's birth.

"Thanks." He was clearly relieved. "So, are you married?"

"No. I'm single and not exactly looking for a relationship," Kendra replied taking a bite out of her half-eaten cookie.

"I see. You are a very direct person, aren't you?" He refused to be daunted. She intrigued him. He definitely wanted to know more about her.

"No sense beating about the bush," she shrugged.

"I guess that's one way of putting it." There was something about her that drew him to her and he would not let her scare him off.

"So how old are you?" Kendra asked, changing the subject before taking another bite from her cookie. "

"Twenty nine."

"Very young," she commented softly, taking a sip of her drink.

"Dare I ask your age?" asked Peter, daring to ask the question that women would prefer men don't ask even when they, themselves feel free to ask men that same age question.

"Thirty five years old," Kendra did not hesitate to respond since she felt that they would not be seeing each other after this evening anyway.

"Wow!" whistled Peter. He could not mask his surprise. "If I had to guess, I would have said you were twenty five, maybe twenty six but not a day over twenty nine."

"Flattery will get you everywhere," Kendra laughed.

"Really, you do look good for your age. You could give the twenty-something-year-olds a run for their money, any day!"

"Thanks. Keep piling on the compliments…they suit me," Kendra could not help but sass. Peter had a very likeable character.

"Sassy! Love it. And confident ... not afraid to reveal her age."

"Should I be?"

"Should you be what?"

"Should I be afraid to say my age?

"No, no, no, I did not mean to offend you with the comment, I meant nothing by it," Peter said sincerely fearing that he had put his foot in his mouth again until he saw Kendra's amused expression and realized that she was teasing him. "Oh, you got me there for a minute," he smiled. This beautiful woman he was drawn to also had a sense of humor. Check.

"Yep. Having a little fun at your expense."

"Well, some women take offense when it comes to the question of age. Others don't like to reveal their age or they lie about it…even in the day of Google where anyone could check everything online."

"Actually, you are right, some women don't care for the age questions. I say, hey, whatever works for them. Aging is a natural process. It's what you've achieved and how happy you are at whatever age you are that matters," Kendra replied glancing at her watch.

"I can see my time is clearly up," Peter said a little disappointed noticing her gesture. He was enjoying speaking to her.

"I am sorry, I don't mean to be rude but I really need to go home now to my daughter. My mom and daughter are expecting me soon. I would like to spend some time with Liana before her bedtime," Kendra said as she put her novel inside her bag and started to get up.

"Can I call you sometime?" Peter's eyes pleaded as he rose from his chair along with her. A gentle man too observed Kendra despite herself.

"Look, Peter, you sound like a really nice guy but I don't want to lead you on."

"You can lead, I'll follow," flirted Peter, refusing to give up. He wanted to see her again.

"You know what I mean," laughed back Kendra.

"Yes, but I'll take my chances. I'd like to get to know you better," he said more boldly.

"You should be with someone your age."

"Why?" he asked a little offended.

"Well, I think you'll probably have more in common with someone your age," Kendra said.

"So, what you are saying is that people of the same age automatically have more in common."

"Well, maybe not," Kendra felt a little foolish. She was used to younger men hitting on her all the time and now was no different. She and this man, Peter, had a connection and they both knew it. Age was no excuse to run away from happiness or the possibility of it. It was time for her to jump back into the dating world. Ian was now a distant memory. She could just hear her sister or mother speaking these words to her.

"Ok, so we agree on that. Even my parents know that age mean nothing when two people connect."

"Sorry?" Kendra did not understand what his parents had to do with their conversation.

"Both my parents remarried people much younger than either of them or they could not be happier. So, I am thinking age should not limit anyone from whom they want to be with."

"I guess but I might be one those people that are bothered by that," Kendra said with a little hesitation. She always felt flattered by the attention younger men gave her but she never really thought about the possibility of a relationship with any of them. She was not against such relationships; she just did not care one way or another and not quite sure how she would actually feel about being in one with a younger man.

"Don't knock it till you try it. I promise you, I'm a nice guy," Peter said charmingly and then added, "unless you are already seeing someone?"

"No, I am not seeing anyone, and I am sure that you are a nice guy but…"

"Hey, age is just a number, nothing more. You can't help whom you connect with. I do feel a certain connection with you and I think you might agree with that?" He purposely made his comment into a question for fear of her assuming he was being presumptuous.

"Well … " Kendra still hesitated. She was not sure why. She liked him. He seemed nice. For some reason, though she only just met him, she felt like she had known him much longer. Maybe she was just afraid of being in a relationship again.

"Look, can we at least be friends?" Peter asked not all meaning it. He wanted more than friendship. He wanted to become the most important person in her life. He already knew she was special. There was just something about her.

"Okay then," he had worn her out with his persistence. Besides, it wouldn't hurt to get to know him as a friend, Kendra reasoned with herself.

"So, my new friend, can I have your number please so we can hang out sometime as…you know, friends?" Peter asked mischievously.

"Sure," Kendra laughed and gave him her number, which he added to his contacts on his cell phone.

"Don't you want mine?" he asked after he had saved her number.

"Well, I gave you mine, if you call me, your number will register on my phone."

"How do I know it's real? You are not trying to get rid of me now, are you?" he asked lightly.

"You can call right now and see for yourself if it's real," she smiled. It felt nice to be seriously pursued by a handsome man who was definitely not Ian.

"No, it's ok. I trust you."

"Here is my card if it makes you feel much better." Kendra gave him her business card. She intended to take whatever this was, very slowly.

"Thanks, friend," Peter smiled. As Peter took the card from her, he cupped her hand with both of his and kissed them lightly, politely but clearly sending a message that he wanted to know her better and not just as a friend. He felt as though she was the one, he had been looking for without even realizing it. He had never been one to buy into the notion of people claiming to know immediately when they meet 'The One,' but when he met Kendra, he just knew she was his 'The One.' He had barely spent more than forty minutes with her, yet in that short precious time, he felt every emotion he had never felt before for any other woman, for her. He wanted to protect her, impress her, fight for her, confide in her, hear her voice every day and be with her. He more than liked Kendra. She was a familiar stranger as though he had known her in another life. She made him feel comfortable and nervous at the same time. Kendra was his forever woman. He just knew it. Though she was a mystery who was clearly closed off to love, Peter refused to be deterred. He intended to break through her tough exterior. She was a woman clearly wounded; he was a man clearly in awe. He would teach her how to love again.

Chapter 15

Peter called Kendra a few days after they met to chat. Kendra was surprised that he actually called considering that she had done everything she could to discourage him. She found out soon enough that he was a man who was not afraid to go after something or in her case, someone that he wanted. As they talked, she grew to like him and eventually they became friends. She found out that his father, Andrew was a retired military doctor and his mother; Laura, had been a freelance magazine photographer until she became a mother to him and his older brother, Kenneth, who was an accountant and married to a British lawyer, Julia. According to Peter, Kenneth who was forty years old lived in London with his wife and two children, a ten-year old girl called Brea, and an eight-year old son called Jude. As for his parents, after over thirty years of marriage, they decided to go their separate ways. Within a year of their divorce, they had each met other people and gotten remarried. Their explanation to their children was that they simply stopped loving each other "that" way anymore. There were no hard feelings from either side, no cheating, and no big fight. Nothing. They had simply grown apart, becoming more like roommates than husband and wife. As a result, their divorce was quite amicable and they remained friends after their divorce, thus, avoiding any negative impact on their two sons. His mother now lived in Washington, DC with her second husband, Ellington, and his dad moved to Long Island with his second wife, Samantha after retiring from the army. Peter and his brother remained close to both parents and to each other by communicating frequently by phones, Internet, and travels. They did not let their different geographical locations, divorces and marriages get in the way of them remaining a close-knit family. Even their parents' spouses' children from previous relationships were close to Peter and his brother. It was one big Brady Bunch family, which turned out just fine.

It took Peter another couple of months to convince Kendra to let him take her out to dinner on a real date. She had chosen a day when her sister, Piper would be around to take care of Liana because her mother was in California. Her sister, like other members of her family had been encouraging her to go out because they thought it was important for her to start enjoying her life again in the company of men.

During the course of Kendra's friendship with Peter, her mother, Kate, met him once on the last day of a short visit to see her granddaughter, Liana. Piper had met him a few times. He had made a great impression on both Piper and Kate and so they were pleasantly surprised to hear that Peter and Kendra had decided to take their friendship to the next level.

Even Kendra was surprised that she was actually enjoying his company as a romantic prospect and not just as a friend. One date led to another and another, and soon Kendra found herself inviting him to have dinners with her, short weekend trips, picnics or just to hang out as long as they were together. She felt comfortable being herself around him and the big test, which was meeting Liana and seeing how they interacted, worked out perfectly.

Peter and Liana took to each other immediately, like perfect puzzle pieces as though they were father and daughter from another life. They bonded instantly and much better than Kendra had ever expected. This was good because she had already decided that whomever she dated seriously after Ian would have to be liked by Liana otherwise it was not going to work out. Liana was first in her life. They were a package deal.

Along course of their courtship, Peter learnt about Kendra's relationship with Ian and the circumstances surrounding the birth of Liana. He was appalled by Ian's behavior toward his own daughter but he figured that Ian's loss was his gain. Peter soon took Kendra to meet his parents and they had warmed up to her immediately. She was now their bonus daughter. She had expected reservations because she had a child and was older than Peter but she was pleasantly surprised by their attitude toward she and Peter's relationship.

Peter's parents were very open-minded and laid-back, and they could see how happy Kendra made their son.

Eight months into their relationship, Peter flew to Los Angeles with Kendra and Liana to meet her father. Kendra hoped her father would like him. After her disastrous relationship with Ian, she felt it was important to seek her family's advice on any future boyfriends. Although her sister and mother already liked him, her father was the big test. She knew how protective; he was of her. To her relief, he also took to Peter. During their stay in Los Angeles, Peter and her father had gone off to jog together, play golf, monopoly, and basketball. Kendra suspected her father was also telling Peter not to hurt his daughter or else there would be consequences to pay. Other than that, they appeared to get along very well. By the end of the visit Peter was already feeling like a member of the Mercury family. He knew in his heart that she was the woman he had been looking for all his life even when he was not aware that he was searching.

Chapter 16

Peter and Kendra got married a year after they met in a non-denominational church in Los Angeles. The wedding was small and intimate with just a few close friends and family. Peter's parents had attended with their respective spouses. His brother, Kenneth had also flown in from London with his wife, Julia and their children and so did Kendra's sister, Piper and her husband, Cain who came from New Jersey. Liana was the flower girl at the ceremony. Kendra was dressed in a simple, long, elegant sleeveless cream-colored Vera Wang gown and was walked down the aisle by her father who was dressed in a navy blue suit. He looked proud and happy to be walking his daughter down the aisle. He was happy that she was marrying a "good man," and not that "foolish boy, Ian."

It was a special and beautiful ceremony as Kendra and Peter each said their own heartfelt vows. There was not a single dry eye left at the wedding by the time it was over. Kendra was overwhelmed by the love and gratitude she felt for Peter. He had come into her life at a time when she needed him the most without her even knowing that she needed him that much. He was the man who taught her how to stop running and to open her heart to love again. Most importantly, Peter and Liana had bonded instantly and that bond had only grown stronger by the day. Liana had made it so easy for him to step seamlessly into the role of fatherhood and Peter had made it easy for Liana to trust him. With Peter, Kendra knew she had found her mate for life.

After the ceremony, there was a reception held at her parents' garden at home. The food was plentiful; there was something for everyone, from smoked barbecue steaks to salmon, shrimps, chicken, fried rice, yams and Liana's personal favorite; specially prepared Nigerian meat pies, and tiny fried dough called chin-chin. There were also soft drinks, beer and wine to everyone's satisfaction. When it came time to dance, Peter and Kendra took the first dance. They danced to Barbara Streisand's I finally found someone. After their first dance, everyone joined them on the dance floor and danced to all types of music. Afterward, Peter and Kendra left Liana with her grandparents in Los Angeles so they could enjoy a two-week honeymoon in the Greek Islands.

***

Peter and Kendra did not live together when they were dating but just before they got married, Kendra sold her apartment in Co-op City and Peter who had owned a loft in Greenwich Village also did the same with his place, after which, they bought a town house together in Brooklyn Heights, which was a short train stop from downtown Manhattan. Their combined income along with the right sticker price gave them their lucky abode and a perfect area for them to raise Liana and start life afresh as a married couple.

Kendra loved their new house and took delight in decorating it. A short pathway led to the stairway stoop, which in turn led to the main entrance of their new brownstone. One would have to walk up the short flight of stairs and buzz the main security-wired door before being allowed in. On the top floor of the house were four bedrooms, two full bathrooms, an extra room, which was used as a laundry room and a large hallway closet next to it. The master bedroom, which had a huge oak bed was very comfortably furnished and had its own ensuite bathroom that contained dual granite sink tops, stand-alone shower, a huge jet bathtub and brightly color tiles. Kendra had put a chaise in front of their bed and insisted that they have only a music box in the room for entertainment instead of a television because as far as she was concerned intimacy and connecting was more important than electronic distractions. Peter did not fight her on that; he wanted her to be happy. Kendra also took pride in decorating one of the bedrooms to suit Liana so she filled it with a lot of stuffed animals and Liana's favorites toys and decorated the walls with colors, patterns and furniture that Liana liked. The two other bedrooms were used as guestrooms for now until they had more children. Kendra had put up her treasured paintings and a few of Peter's odd collections from his travels in various areas of the house to give it a warm feel. On the first floor was a half bathroom, a den, which Kendra and Peter had converted into a study, and a huge white kitchen with an island, plenty of glass and white wood cabinets, granite top counters and stainless steel appliances, which included a large fridge and a six-burner gas range stove and double ovens that simply delighted Kendra who generally enjoyed cooking and testing out new recipes. The kitchen opened out to the dining area and large living room, which was tastefully furnished to reflect the Rites' eclectic, global tastes. The sofa, loveseat and coffee table had antiques flairs to them while the center table was as modern as they come. She adorned the floors of the house with area rugs so that part of the polished dark hardwood was still revealed.

***

Kendra and Peter complemented each other in all the ways that counted; they had a calming effect on each other and supported each other in ways where they were different from each other. They had established some kind of routine when they returned home from their honeymoon. Kendra registered Liana in a private school not far from where they lived in Brooklyn. She and Peter took turns to take Liana to and from school. Once or twice in the week the whole family would go out for dinner or an event and then go home in time for Liana's bedtime. Sometimes, Peter and Kendra would hire a babysitter for Liana and go out for date nights to keep their romance healthy.

Once in a while, when Kendra thought about how happy she was with Peter, her mind would drift back to her time with Ian and she would wonder how she could have been so drawn to these two different yet similar men.

When she and Ian were together, she was the much calmer and patient one, less impulsive and less prone to lose her temper in most situations. She had also been the more responsible one in their relationship. However, with Peter, the reverse was the case. Yet, Ian and Peter also had characteristics that were strikingly similar though reflected in contrasting ways; both men were handsome, take-charge guys who were confident and charming. While Peter exuded quiet confidence, charm and authority, Ian's confidence, presence and charisma was something that could almost be touched the moment he entered any setting. Before any of them had ever met Kendra, Ian and Peter had been used to doing little work when it came to meeting women because they were so used to women throwing themselves at them. Yet when each of them met Kendra, they were both undeniably attracted to her and knew instinctively that they needed to work hard to win her love.

And love her they did, each in his own way; with Ian, it was an all-consuming, passionate, noisy kind of love, which transformed Kendra from a girl to a woman. He was her first great love, which meant regardless of how or why their relationship ended, she would always have a certain soft spot in her heart for him and would always wish him well no matter the circumstances. With Peter, it was unexpected love, which dared her to be brave and not only to love again in unchartered territory but also to accept love in return with abandon and equal respect. With Peter she was not afraid to be vulnerable again. He made her feel safe. Peter was her adult partner in life. Her husband. The man she would always put first in all aspects of her life and consult before making any major decisions. He was also now Liana's father by all accounts even if not biologically. They had already taken legal steps to make it official. Peter gave her and Liana a family unit. He made her and Liana happy.

***

A few months after they got back from their honeymoon, Kendra and Peter discovered to their delight that they were pregnant with twins. Peter was extremely happy and had taken Kendra and Liana out to L'mai, a French restaurant in The Village to celebrate. Peter's other joy was further increased when the adoption papers for Liana, which Peter had filed with Kendra's blessing, came through a day before Liana's fourth birthday and he became her officially recognized father. Her name was now Liana Mercury Rite. Kendra could not be happier. Liana was crazy about Peter, and Peter obviously loved her to death. He was very protective of her. Liana had him wrapped around her little finger.

Though Kendra never heard back from Ian when she had sent him the text informing him about Liana's birth a few years ago and a few more texts after her birth, nevertheless, for the sake of Liana, she had also sent him several letters and pictures of Liana on each of her birthdays. Not surprising, Ian never responded. To the best of her knowledge, he still lived at their old address and his phone number had not changed. She was particularly cautious when it came to Liana and made sure that Ian had received information regarding Peter's adoption intention via registered mail. She knew he received the registered mail because he had signed for them and she got a receipt confirmation. He just never bothered to respond so she took his silence to mean he was still not interested in Liana. She could not believe that she once wished he would want to be part of Liana's life. His rejection of Liana turned out to be a blessing in disguise because she had gained Peter as a father. Truth be told, Kendra was secretly relieved that he did not respond to her regarding Peter's intention to adopt Liana. She had been afraid that he would put up a fight to spite her. Silence from Ian was good news in her opinion. It was just a pity that he was denying himself the chance to know what a special person Liana was turning out to be.

Chapter 17

Four years later, Kendra and Peter's lives were going better than they had imagined. Kendra was now the director of the entire computer systems' division at her job and with that came a huge salary boost. Peter had decided to branch out on his own and it was the best move that he had ever made professionally and financially as it allowed him to either work from home or travel to clients' offices on a flexible schedule. Liana was now a happy, smart eight-year-old girl, and the twins, Ryan and Easton now four years old were delightful and a handful like most children their age.

***

Today, it was a cold winter day in January and the Rites were enjoying an extended four-day holiday weekend. They had all gone ice-skating earlier in the day and then did a little shopping before coming back home happy but exhausted around 7.30 PM. Kendra was too tired to cook so they ordered Chinese food for dinner. By the time the food had arrived, everyone had taken a bath and was settled comfortably on the sofa, ottoman and couch in front of the television in the living room watching Small Time Crooks, a Woody Allen movie that they had ordered on demand from their cable service. Kendra dished out the food and everyone munched, chatted and giggled while they ate and watched the movie. A few minutes into the movie and dinner, the phone rang. It was 8.30 PM. Liana was the nearest one to the cordless phone so she picked it up from its base.

"Hello?"

"Hello. Is this Kendra's number?" came a deep male, authoritative, raspy voice from the past.

"Yes, it is. Who's speaking?" asked Liana, stealing a glance at her parents and siblings who were focused on the movie and laughing at comedic moments.

"A very close friend of Kendra. May I speak to her?" the person said, and then more curiously asked before Liana could respond, "who's this?"

"Her daughter but you called so I should be asking you who you are, so what's your name?"

"You are her daughter?" he asked again, ignoring her question. He sounded intrigued by Liana.

"Yes."

"Wow, so you must be Liana."

"Yes, I am. How do you know my name?" Liana asked curiously stealing another glance at her siblings who were still engaged in the movie, chatting loudly with each other and earning a light-hearted "sshhh!" from Peter and Kendra who were also engrossed in the movie and not paying attention to Liana.

"What kind of friend are you? My mom's best friend is my daddy. She says so all the time," offered Liana innocently.

"I told you; I am a friend of your mother."

"But you are not my daddy so you cannot be her best friend," replied Liana with a scoff.

"I didn't say I was her best friend, I said I am a friend."

"But you said close friend, so that means…"

"Listen, little girl, I am Kendra's…I mean your mother's special friend," he interrupted sounding annoyed. "Put her on the phone now or…"

"Who's on the phone, Lili?" Kendra asked suddenly realizing Liana was still on the phone.

"Mom, it's a man who says he is your special friend," Liana said to Kendra momentarily turning her attention away from her phone conversation to respond to her mother without saying "hold on."

"Really, what's his name?" Kendra was not in the mood to chat with any "friend" on the phone but at the same time wondering who was on the phone. She had a few male friends who were also friends of Peter and they never called the house unless it was for some event or another that they wanted to invite Peter and Kendra to.

"Umm…let me ask him," Liana said turning her attention back to the phone.

"What's your name again?"

"So, your mother is in then?" he asked instead of answering Liana, wondering what Kendra sounded and looked like after all these years.

"Yes. She wants to know your name, so what is it? I have to go back to our movie, we are having family time," Liana was no longer interested in talking to this person and was now getting bored.

"Family time? Hmmm…interesting. So do you have siblings too?" he asked still ignoring Liana's question about his name.

"Siblings? What's that?" asked Liana, pretending not to know what he meant. This person, whoever he was, was already annoying her. He would not even tell her his name.

"Little girl, don't they teach you the meaning of words in school? Siblings mean brothers and sisters," he schooled her condescendingly.

"Then why didn't you just say, 'do I have any brothers or sisters?'" shot back Liana a little rudely. She did not like this 'special friend' of her mother who was talking to her like this. He sounded mean.

"My bad. So do you have any brothers or sisters?' he asked in a more friendly manner thinking Kendra needed to teach Liana how to speak politely to adults. He was right; children were brats. He tried to warn Kendra but she would not listen; insisting she wanted children and children were a blessing. Well, Liana seemed to be a wise ass, talking back at him. What a brat!

"Well, I have a brother and a sister. They are twins. Why do you want to know?" Liana's curious puzzled voice broke into his thoughts. Why was he asking her all these questions, anyway?

"I'm just curious about you, that's all. You are an interesting child," Ian responded trying not to sound bored talking to her.

"So, what is your name so I can tell my mom and get back to our movie?" Liana clearly sounded uninterested in talking to this stranger anymore. She really wanted to get back to the movie now.

"Well, I am your…"

"Lili, you are missing the good parts of the movie, who's on the phone?" interrupted Peter this time while not looking away from the TV.

"Some guy who wants to speak to Mommy," Liana replied still holding the phone to her ear.

"Well, give me the phone then, Kendra said, getting up from her spot on the sofa next to Peter to reach for the phone wondering who it could possibly be.

"Hold on, I'll give the phone to my mom…" Liana said to the stranger on the phone but he did not let her finish her sentence before interrupting.

"Pumpkin, I was trying to say, I am your daddy. My name is Ian," he said suddenly sounding as though it was only yesterday that he spoke to Liana.

"My daddy is right here. You said you are my mommy's close friend," Liana replied in confusion. Kendra caught her daughter's expression and reached out to take the phone from her but Liana would not hand it over to her. Who is this man on the phone? How can he be her daddy? Peter was her daddy.

"Baby-doll, I am your real daddy," Ian said oblivious of the impact his words were having on Liana. As far as he was concerned, Kendra should have told Liana that he was her father regardless of whether he was in her life or not.

"No, my daddy is here. I think you have the wrong number."

"Nope. Your mommy, Kendra and I made you. I am you real daddy. She should have told you a long time ago. I told you I am your mommy's friend.

"You are lying! My parents said lying is wrong!!!" Liana shouted at Ian. Why was he telling her Peter was not her daddy???

"Little girl, it's rude to shout at your father! I want to speak to your mother now," Ian said with sudden stern authority.

Liana flinched at the sudden change in Ian's tone and almost dropped the phone. Who was this man and what did he mean by telling her he was her daddy? Her mother would never lie to her. So, what did this man mean??? Kendra and Peter glanced at each other before Peter got up from the sofa and went over to where Liana was still sitting clutching the phone to her ear and still refusing to give Kendra the phone. He pried the phone from her hand and spoke to Ian. Kendra, sensing trouble, wrapped her arms around Liana as Peter spoke to Ian. The twins, also sensing something was wrong, stopped watching the movie and playing with each other, and went over to hover around Peter, Kendra and Liana.

"Who is this?" Peter asked with authority.

"No, who is this? I asked to speak to Kendra," Ian responded sharply.

"My name is Peter; I am Kendra's husband. You called my house so I am asking you again, who are you?"

"You must be the guy she mentioned when she wrote me about my kid's adoption. So, you are the one who thinks he's Liana's father," Ian said changing his tone to sound as though he was having a conversation with an old friend.

"I just said I was Kendra's husband. And yes, I am Liana's father. And you are?" Peter asked with annoyance suddenly realizing that this was the Ian that had caused his wife so much pain and Liana's biological father. Still, he wanted to hear Ian say his name. Kendra had told Peter of her history with Ian the first few months after they started dating. She even kept a few pictures of Ian for Liana, which Peter encouraged for the sake of Liana.

"Oh, my bad. My name is Ian Sharp, Kendra's lover and Liana's father," Ian said very slowly, making sure he emphasized the word 'father' and 'lover.'

"I think you lost those privileges years ago," Peter replied very annoyed. This guy irked him just by the way he spoke and his assumption of legal relations to Kendra and Liana. They were his family, not this joker on the phone. He could not believe that after all these years, Ian had the gall to resurface from nowhere and claim ownership to his wife and daughter.

"I don't think so," Ian replied with slight amusement. "See, Kendra and I were lovers for the longest time and she conceived and had my baby. Since I am still alive, I want the right to my daughter," Ian said with as much force as Peter. He still did not care much for children so this fight was really to get Kendra's attention again regardless of how much time had passed between them.

"Ian, is it?" Peter responded in his most condescending tone.

"It's Mr. Sharp to you if you don't mind," Ian matched Peter's condescending tone with his.

"Whatever, Ian. Why did you call my house?"

"To speak to Kendra and my daughter," replied Ian nonchalantly now speaking as though he was having a normal conversation with Peter.

"Sorry pal. You got the wrong number. And just so we are clear, Liana is my daughter and Kendra is my wife," Ian said before hanging up on Ian. The phone rang again almost immediately. Peter grabbed it again.

"How dare you hang up on me?" Ian shouted through phone, all pretenses at nonchalance gone.

"You are not welcomed to call my house to speak to my wife or daughter," Peter said calmly, "Now I am going to hang up again on you. Good b…"

"I will take your ass to court to gain access to my daughter if I have to!" yelled Ian before Peter could hang up on him.

"What do you want from us?" Peter asked trying hard for the sake of Liana and Kendra who were both now straining to hear the conversation, to be calm.

"I want to speak to Kendra about Liana. My permission was not sought before she decided to let Liana take your name."

"I believe she wrote you a letter informing you of my intention regarding my adoption of Liana. We contacted you more than once. You signed the registered mail.

"Well, I did not respond to her letter, now, did I?" asked Ian meaningfully, "which in my opinion means you adopted her without my consent."

"Or maybe you got it but did not respond because you never really cared in the first place," Peter replied.

"Look, Mr. Whatever-the-hell-your-name-is…"

"My name is Mr. Peter Rite," Peter cut him off sharply.

"Well, Mr. Peter Rite, this is between me and Kendra, you know, my baby mama, not between you and me. She gave my child your name without my permission and that's not acceptable by me."

"So why didn't you stop the adoption if you were so opposed to it?" Peter challenged him while glancing at Kendra with a slightly worried look. Her worried expression showed that she realized it was Ian on the phone. His eyes questioned hers to see if she wanted to speak to Ian. She shook her head 'no.'

"See, I was thinking about it the other day, Mr. Smarty Pants. That should have clued you in that I was not happy about it."

"You needed four years to think about it?" Peter scoffed. This guy was a joke!

"Big decisions need a plenty of time," replied Ian smugly.

"Well, too little, too late. I am the only father Liana knows. I love her as though she is my flesh and blood. I adopted her fair and square, legally.

"Here is the thing, Mr. Rite. We can all talk like adults or we can fight this thing in court however long it takes, your choice," Ian's tone was suddenly hard. He was pissed that Kendra was there and this Peter character she called a husband, would not hand the phone over to her so he could speak with her. How dare he!

"I guess we will have to settle this in court. Please don't call my house again. Have a good night," Peter said and hung up the phone before turning it off. He looked at Liana who appeared very confused and frightened, and Kendra who had a look of sheer terror on her face having picked up most of the conversation from Peter's side of the phone. Peter put his arms around his wife, the twins and Liana and hugged them tightly.

Chapter 18

"That was Ian, wasn't it?" Kendra asked Peter in disbelief. Her worst nightmare was coming true. Ian was back for Liana even though he never wanted her in the first place. All these years there was no word from him and suddenly he was back like a bad rash.

"Yes, it was. But don't worry, honey, he can't hurt us. I'll make sure of that," said Peter, trying to alleviate Kendra's fears.

"What does he want, Peter? After all these years, what the hell does he want from me???" Kendra asked tearfully not really expecting Peter to have an answer.

"Honey, we need to have a talk with Liana now," Peter said, not wanting to say too much in front of Liana who was looking back and forth from Kendra to Peter in confusion. Kendra immediately understood. Her hand flew to her mouth and tears immediately began to stream down her face.

"He wants to take Liana from us, doesn't he?" Kendra asked as her worst fear was being confirmed. Ian would have to kill her to get to Liana. She would spit fire at anyone who tried to take her child away from her.

"We are not going to let him take her away from us, she is our daughter! Peter said fiercely. He loved Liana like she was his own flesh and blood. He would fight tooth and nail for her.

"Daddy, Mommy what is it? What did I do wrong? What did that man want? Why would he take me? Why did he say he was my daddy? I heard you say something about adoption on the phone, Dad." Liana began to cry as she saw how upset both her parents were. The twins also started crying because their sister and mother were crying and their father looked very upset.

"Sweetheart, your mother and I need to talk to you," Peter said ushering his wife and children to the couch. Peter sat next to Liana on one side of the couch and the twins sat on the other side while Kendra sat on the love seat. Their dinner and movie now forgotten.

"Daddy, you are scaring me," Liana said as soon as they were all seated. Kendra was still crying. Liana held Peter's hand tightly sensing her life was about to change but not sure how. "What is it?"

"First of all, Lili," said Peter, "I want you to know that your mother and I love you so very, very much. I hope you understand that what we are about to tell you was something we planned to tell you when you were a little older so you would have a better understanding of your birth."

"Daddy tell me already! I know you love me. I want to know what's making you and Mom so upset. Why did that man say he was my dad? You are my daddy, aren't you?"

"Of course, dear, I am your father and nothing will ever change that. I love you with all my heart. Don't you ever forget that" Peter responded to Liana fiercely, as he drew her close to him.

"So, what did that man mean?" Liana asked Peter, her big brown eyes wide with questioning and confusion. Kendra gestured to the twins to come sit on the love seat so she could sit next to Liana and Peter. Liana now sat between her parents while the twins looked on curiously, chin on their hands, not really understanding the kind of conversation that Peter, Liana and Kendra were having. All they knew was that everyone looked serious and upset and that made them feel sad too.

"What your daddy is trying to say is that he loves you very much and, and" Kendra was struggling to finish her words between tears, "and, but…"

"The man that called on the phone is my real father," Liana finished for her in a shaky voice.

"Yes," Peter said, "but that doesn't change how I feel about you in the least. The minute I met you, I loved you so much that I wanted to make you mine legally so that no one would take you away from me. You and I became father and daughter once I laid eyes on you. I wanted the world to know that too, so I adopted you. Legally, I am your father. And as far as I am concerned, you are my flesh and blood no matter what anyone says." He would not let anyone tear his family apart. Not if he could help it. Liana was his and Kendra.

"I love you too, Dad, but what was it about me that my other daddy did not like? Why was he never around so you had to adopt me? Why is he coming back for me now?" Liana was very confused. As much as she loved Peter, she wanted to know about Ian, why he had rejected her. She looked from Peter to Kendra and from Kendra to Peter and then without waiting for an answer, she suddenly demanded angrily, "and why didn't you tell me that I was adopted before? Why did that man have to call and tell me? I am a big girl. I am eight years old. I know what adoption means!! I am smarter than most people my age, you know!"

"Honey," Kendra said, "we were going to tell you. We really were, just not this early." She and Peter had planned to tell Liana the circumstances surrounding her birth when she was sixteen. Except that it was not going to be the way they planned anymore. Ian had come from nowhere to make sure of that.

Liana looked at her mother and then at Peter with such a hurtful expression that it broke Peter's heart. Then she said quietly in such a small voice that her parents could barely hear her; "I think I need to be alone." With that, she ran off to her bedroom banging the door shut.

Chapter 19

Liana was lying down on her bed staring at the ceiling in shock. She could not believe what her mother and Peter had just told her. She was feeling angry, betrayed, sad, hurt and rejected all at the same time. The man she thought was her father was not her real father but her real father did not really want her and her mother did not think she was old enough to understand all this. And the man on the phone who was her real father did not sound like a nice man and might take her away from her mother and Peter who was her real daddy, kind of, because he was the only father she ever knew and he loved her very much and she loved him right back. After all this information, what was she supposed to think? Who was she supposed to trust? Even her grandma, Kate, whom she was especially close to, did not think to tell her the truth about her real father. Liana's thoughts were interrupted by a knock on her door. After a few minutes, Kendra and Peter let themselves in without waiting for Liana to invite them in. The twins followed right behind them and started playing around in Liana's room while Peter and Kendra sat on the bed on either side of Liana. She started crying again as soon as she saw her parents come in.

"So why didn't you tell me I was adopted?" she demanded tearfully, again, sitting up to prop herself against the headboard of her bed after a few minutes of crying. She did not look at either of them. Instead, she stared down. Peter reached out and put his hand under her chin and gently moved her head up so that she could look at him as he spoke.

"Sweetheart, we wanted to tell you when you were a little older," Peter said. He attempted to put an arm around Liana but she flinched and shook him off. He was hurt at her gesture but did not let it show because he knew Liana was hurting even more.

"Just how old is old enough to you, Dad? Don't you think I would understand something as important as this? I am old enough to understand. How could you not tell me?" She did not feel like being reasonable. Her whole sense of self had just been shattered. Peter was her world. He made her feel special and secure. He taught her to be confident in herself and not be afraid to speak up to bullies in school. She and Peter were extremely close. She loved Peter! He was her daddy. She was daddy's little girl! She did not want another father.

"Honey, we really planned to tell you later," Kendra entered the conversation taking Liana's hand. Again, as with Peter, Liana pulled away as Kendra continued speaking while Peter looked on, wishing he could take the pain away from Liana. "My relationship with the man who put you in my belly did not end well. Then I met Peter, and he made you and I so happy and you made him very happy too so he became your daddy in every way that matters. He loved you right from the moment he met you when you were just a baby. You two got along so well right from the start. He loves you and would never, ever give you up. You will always be his daughter. I am lucky that he loves you as much as I do. No one can ever take that away, please believe that. He is the best father in the world. As for Ian, the man you spoke to on the phone, I wanted you to get to know him when you were born but he was not ready to know you. He did not want to be a dad. That's sad news for me to tell my little girl but it's true and his reasons are complicated but I promise you it does not mean that he did not want you either. He was just not ready to handle the responsibility of taking care of another human being and did not want to disappoint you as a father. You would not have understood if I told you much sooner. Can you at least appreciate why I wanted to wait until you were much older?" Kendra was pleading with her daughter to understand as she tried to soften the blow on Liana about Ian not wanting her.

"You should have told me sooner," Liana replied stubbornly in a small voice even though she was still confused as to why Ian did not want her. She did not know him and was not even sure she liked him from the short conversation they had on the phone, but she felt hurt, nevertheless.

"Baby, you are still too young to understand. The story of your birth and your other father, Ian, is too complicated for you to fully understand the details," Kendra reiterated patiently to Liana. She refused to refer to Ian as Liana's real father. As far as she was concerned, Peter was Liana's real father.

"All I know is that my daddy who is sitting on my bed right now is not my real daddy, and my real daddy, the mean man I spoke to on the phone, doesn't want me," Liana responded tearfully, looking very sad as she glanced from Peter to Kendra, and then back from Kendra to Peter again. It pained Peter and Kendra to see her this way.

"I know sweetie," Kendra said and then added, "this doesn't change anything at all. Peter is still your father in every way that matters. No one can ever break your bond with him. We will continue life as normal but if you want to meet with Ian and talk to him yourself, much as it scares me, I will find him and let you speak with him. "

"No! I don't want to see that man! This is my dad, I love him so much," Liana said to her mother while looking at Peter with forlorn eyes. "Don't let that man on the phone take me away from you, Daddy!"

"Lili, baby," Peter said, "I love you too...so, so, so much. No one is going to take you away from me. You are my daughter. I will always be here for you, remember that." He gathered Liana in his arms and this time she did not push him away. She felt safe in his arms. She trusted him. "There is no difference between the love I have for you and the love I have for Ryan and Easton. In my eyes and in the eyes of the law you are my real daughter. I will always be your daddy. I need you. Ian may not want you but don't ever let that hurt you. I am still and will always be your father. I am not going anywhere and nobody is going to take you away from me, I promise you. Always remember that you are constantly surrounded by people who love and want you; your mom, Ryan, Easton, your aunt, uncle, grandparents and me. You are very important to us. We are family, one unit. Baby, please forgive your mom and

I for not telling you sooner. We were only trying to protect you. We thought you were too young to understand but we forgot how much smarter and mature you are than children your own age." Peter was not one to tear up often but there were tears in his eyes as he spoke to Liana. He wanted the pain and confusion in her eyes to disappear. He did not want her to feel abandoned or rejected or let the fact that Ian did not want her, affect her relationship with men in the future. It was important that she maintained her self-confidence.

"Yes, Lili. We love you to death. We are sorry we did not tell you earlier. But believe me when I say, Peter, your daddy who loves you, and is the best thing that ever happened to you and me, would never, ever hurt or leave us," Kendra said looking at Peter with tears streaming down her face. She put her arms around her daughter and Peter as they and hugged them tightly as she cried. She never wanted to see this look of pain in her daughter's eyes again. The twins jumped on the bed and joined in the embrace for a short while before screaming that they were being "squashed" and everyone laughed amid tears.

Liana felt much better after the talk with her parents and hugs from everyone. This was her family and Peter was her daddy as far as she was concerned. As for Peter, he knew he would do anything to keep his family intact. Ian's sudden appearance of Ian in their lives was not going to change that.

Chapter 20

Today, Kendra came to work feeling much better than she had in a while. It had been almost three months since her family had heard from Ian. They had all been pretty shaken up when he called out of nowhere that faithful weekend; pretty much ruining what was left of their family weekend time. After their talk with Liana, Peter and Kendra had decided to wait and see if he would contact them again at which point they would speak to a lawyer.

As for Liana, she seemed to be dealing with the news of Ian in her own way; she was more dependent on Peter than she was before. Though they had always spent considerable amount of time together before Ian re-entered their lives, now, she was practically his shadow. She hung around him every chance she got. She followed him to get milk at the corner supermarket in her pajamas and a jacket, she went with him to the gas station to get gas for the car, she played basketball with him, went with him to the newsstand down the road to get the newspapers and would not go to sleep at night until she saw Peter no matter how late he came home when he went out. When Peter was alone in the study trying to catch up with work, Liana would insist that she could concentrate on her homework much better when she was there with him in the study. After she finished her homework, she would fall asleep on the couch in the study and then Peter would carry to her bedroom. On occasions, when Peter had to go out of town on business for a few days, Liana would become restless and panicky. She would call Peter at least twice a day during that time to know when he was coming back home. Peter had to re-assure Liana that he was coming home soon. It was as if she was afraid that Peter would leave her or Ian would come and take her away when Peter was not around.

Eventually, Peter and Kendra arranged for Liana to see a counselor to help her deal with her fears of abandonment. By all accounts, the therapy seasons appeared to work on Liana as she slowly adjusted to the fact that Peter was not her real father and was once again behaving like a kid her age with the typical growing pains. She still loved Peter as much as she did before the revelation of her birth and still considered him her father in every sense of the word even though every now and again, her mind would go back to 'the mean guy on the phone that was her other dad.' At one point, she even surprised Kendra by asking her what Ian was like. Kendra had done her best to paint him in a good light for the sake of her daughter and showed Liana pictures of Ian that she had preserved for her. Liana seemed satisfied with her mother's description of Ian though Kendra still expected Liana to ask more questions in the future and perhaps even a request to meet Ian somewhere down the line when she was much older, a possibility that Kendra was not quite comfortable with but would support Liana whenever she was ready. Regardless, Kendra was glad that her daughter was feeling better emotionally. She was also thankful that if anything, they were still a close-knit family and Liana did not shut everyone out and withdraw into herself.

In terms of her marriage, Peter and Kendra were closer than they had ever been before, if that was even possible. Peter still showered Kendra with affection as though they were still in their early stages of dating. As a couple they rarely argued and when they did, they never went to bed angry. Their parenting styles enhanced each other, with each person taking turns to play 'good cop, bad cop' with their kids when necessary. Kendra was thankful every day for her family. She was also thankful for her parents and sister who made sure they were around in person or otherwise to support her and her family without Ian in the picture.

Chapter 21

Kendra sat at her desk in her office and smiled to herself as she reflected on her blessings. Life could not be better. Her professional life just kept getting better. She had been hearing rumors that she was up for another promotion and a huge bonus this quarter. She had headed a team of analysts that had successfully worked on a huge project for a well-known advertising company and the project had gone really well. Her personal life was also blissful. The fact that Ian had popped back messily into her life out of nowhere after years of silence made her even more appreciative of Peter. She was not sure she would have been able to handle speaking to him again in a strong and mature manner when he had called that weekend, a year ago. She was just glad Peter had taken charge of the situation because she did not hear from Ian again.

She was jolted from her thoughts by the sound of the phone on her desk ringing. It was her private line. Only few people had this number, which by-passed the secretary. She grabbed the phone without looking at the caller ID thinking it was a family member.

"Hello," she said while playing with her pen absent-mindedly.

"Hello to you too, Sweetness," Ian said cheerfully. "It's been a long time since I heard from you.

Your voice still has that sexy twang that I remember so well."

Chapter 22

"How did you get this number? It's unlisted!" Kendra snapped as she instantly recognized Ian's voice despite the years that had gone by. For a second, she wondered what he looked like today.

"Why so hostile after many years, Kennie?" Ian asked, ignoring her question. "You didn't want to talk to me last year when I called your house so I decided to give you time. A whole year is enough time to adjust to me being back in your life, don't you think?"

"Correction, you are not back in my life. You've been out of my life for years. You are completely irrelevant to my family just so we are clear," responded Kendra in a hard voice. A voice she did not even recognize as her own.

"Ouch! Well, now, let's not be so nasty. That's not a nice thing to say to the father of your child," Ian replied slightly amused, which only annoyed Kendra even more.

"Peter is her father; he has been her father for most of her life. She has his last name," Kendra replied, enjoying the small satisfaction of hearing him bristle upon hearing that Liana was a Rite. Why did he have to come back after all these years? She had given him several chances to be in Liana's life but he had ignored her…until now.

"Really Kendra? You and I both know the kid has my blood … "

"Which does not automatically make you her father in the ways that matter. And by the way, how did you get this number?" she asked again. She could not believe his nerve. Kendra had not been expecting him to reach her at her office. In fact, she had not been expecting to hear from him again after Peter spoke to him.

"Sweetheart…"

"Don't call me Sweetheart," Kendra abruptly cut him short. Her day had been going so well until he called.

"Okay, Darling…may I call you Darling? Or would you prefer Hon ... "

"No, you may not call me Darling, Sweetheart or any other terms of endearment," retorted Kendra irritably.

"Jeez, you are so touchy!" Ian said, getting a kick out of annoying her. "One would think that after all these years and our history, you would at least be glad to hear from an old friend, well, lover, since we were definitely more than friends."

"Definitely not glad to hear from you," shot back Kendra

"Well, I am happy to speak to you again, regardless," he said smoothly just to irk her. "Are you having a bad day? You sure sound prickly!"

"Maybe I am sounding prickly because of you," Kendra said, not missing a beat. She could give as much as she got. She wished he would just go away…crawl back into the hole he came out of.

"Aren't you happy to hear from me?" Without waiting for her response, he added, "so when are you bringing Liana to see her daddy?"

"Never. She has a father that she sees every day and I don't mean you, Ian."

"Look, I helped you conceive her. Whether you like it or not, she is mine. She has my DNA."

"DNA or not, you are not the father she knows. Peter is her father in every sense of the word, deal with it, Ian."

"She has my blood. She is mine."

"You rejected her without a thought. You rejected me because I was carrying her. You broke us up because I wanted to keep Liana."

"I was not ready for a child then. Now I think maybe I am."

"You think??? You think??? You 'think maybe' you are ready??? Just maybe??? Even as you are making demands out of nowhere to see my daughter, you are still 'thinking maybe' you are ready to be her daddy???? Un-freaking-believable!!"

"Calm down. What I meant was I can try to be her daddy now, okay? So why don't you just let bygones be bygones?"

"Oh, you can try to be her daddy now??? Boy, are you laughable or what?" Kendra scoffed. "What a joke!"

"Now I am a joke? I am funny?" Ian was annoyed now.

"Yes, actually you are funny. You've got jokes today. So much so I am rolling on the floor laughing," replied Kendra with biting sarcasm.

"What do you want from me, Kendra?" Ian asked irritably. What was so funny about him suggesting that he wanted to take a turn at fatherhood? She should be complementing him for changing for the better!

"Actually, I want nothing from you. Liana has a daddy, Peter, who does not have to 'think maybe' he might be ready to be her dad 'now.' He just is. Unconditionally. You, on the other hand, should just go back to wherever the hell you came from."

"Well, I am here to stay, and I want to be in Lili's life…"

"When I sent you pictures after she was born years ago, I told you her name was Liana, not Lili," she snapped. God, he was annoying!

"Can't I just call her my own cute little name for her? See I happen to like Lili," he replied smoothly. "As a matter of…"

"Do not call her Lili!" Kendra interrupted him forcefully. Nope, she would not allow Ian to call Liana by the nickname Peter already used for her. "Her name is Liana to you."

"Okay, okay, okay…jeez! If that makes you happy, then I'll call her the kid…I mean Liana. Anyway, let's not get distracted by trivialities and focus on co-parenting."

"There will be no co-parenting between you and I, thank you very much."

"Not if I have anything to say about it."

"What's that supposed to mean?"

"Well, I've got rights and since I am not dead yet, we'll see what the courts have to say about that."

"So now you are dragging me to court for a child you did not want in the first place?" Kendra could not believe her ears. She tried not to let fear show in her tone.

"Well, I tried to be reasonable about it but since you think I am a joke, then I have to do what I have to do. Simple as that," Ian replied in a more authoritative tone sensing that he had gotten Kendra's attention now that he had voiced his intention to take legal steps. 'Who's laughing now?' he thought to himself in amusement.

"Why Ian?" Kendra asked trying to sound calm.

"Why what?"

"Why are you now pretending to want to be in Liana's life? What's changed? You gave me an ultimatum when I was pregnant with her because of her. I was carrying our baby, your baby. Yet, here you are, coming out of nowhere after many years, suddenly claiming to want to be her father. Why? Do you hate me that much that you would take the best thing that ever happened to me away from me? Or is it because I dared to move on and find my happiness without you? Why are you doing this to me Ian? Just why??" Kendra asked plaintively. Her voice had faded to a whisper as she recalled the loneliness and rejection she felt after Ian demanded that she make choice between their relationship and their unborn baby.

"Correction, I do not hate you, I just want what's fair…to be in my daughter's life or at least see her sometimes even though you dumped me." Ian's voice was serious. The way he saw it, Kendra left him because he had made a 'reasonable' request of her. Well, times have changed. She forced him to be a daddy…so even though the kid was a little bratty on the phone the day he called last year, he was somewhat curious to know what she looked like, nevertheless. After all, she was his creation. He may not have been there for her in the past but he was here now. Besides, he was not asking for any form of custody…yet. But he could use the kid to get Kendra to help him out financially. After all, life had been quite tough on him these last few years.

"No, you made me leave you," Kendra interrupted his thoughts, "because you left me with an impossible choice."

"No, Kendra, you dumped me. You left me. Let's be clear."

"Well, I had no choice. You wanted me to choose between you and our baby. You gave me an ultimatum. My chances at becoming a mom were dwindling and you had no plans to marry me, just empty promises. I needed something to show for all our years together. I needed pure unconditional love born of me, of us."

"Look, I was wrong, okay? I wondered about you all these years and the kid too. Maybe I didn't have the guts to reach out to you but I thought about you all the damn time Kendra," Ian said with sudden emotion, not even sure where the sudden burst of emotion came from.

"Well, I don't read minds and life goes on...with or without you, Ian," Kendra said tiredly. She was worn down with this conversation but she wanted Ian to back off any threats of taking Liana away from her.

"We can still get back together you know," Ian figured he might as well throw that suggestion into the conversation despite the long shot. He wasn't even sure how serious he was about the idea but whatever. Why not? Maybe, just maybe she might come back....

"Really? Are you serious? Hah! In what alternate universe are you living in?" Kendra scoffed. She was annoyed that Ian still took her for granted after all these years. "You must be joking! You actually think I put my life on hold for you all these years that we have been broken up? You think that I would come back to you just like that? Drop my happy life and come back to you because you snapped your fingers and demand I come back??? Wow, Ian, get a clue and get over yourself. Tone your over-inflated ego down a notch. And, oh, here's a thought...the world does not revolve around you."

"Tell me how you really feel, Kendra. Why can't I ask anyway? You loved me! We had a real relationship," Ian could not believe Kendra's response. He had been her world for crying out loud. Anyway, it wasn't like he was that serious about it...or was he?

"Wow, you actually sound like you believe what you are saying!" Kendra could not believe she was actually having this conversation with him.

"So, you never loved me?" Ian sounded hurt but Kendra did not believe he was being sincere.

"I did. So much so, I put myself through several abortions for you. So much so, I cut off everyone that loved me from my life just to make you happy. So much so that I was still willing to let you be a part of Liana's life after she was born despite everything, I went through because of you. I finally learnt to love myself more and realized that I was just not enough for you. I was never enough for you just being Kendra. Breaking me made you feel better about being you. That was how you thrived, Ian. Being in control and having someone grease your elbow despite what it caused that person."

"You are enough for me now Kennie, come back to me. I am a changed man."

"Really? I can't tell. You still sound like the same self-centered person I used to know, and totally disrespectful to me and my marriage."

"What??" He actually forgot for a moment that Kendra was now married.

"Yes, Ian. You assumed that I would just break up my loving, supportive family and destroy my wonderful marriage…drop everything and pick up where we left off?"

"Well, why can't you?" Ian asked completely missing Kendra's point.

Kendra shook her head incredulously at the audacity of Ian. He sure was obtuse. "Since you don't get it, let me break it down for you. I am extremely happy in my marriage to a wonderful man. After you broke my heart in more ways than one, I moved on. It took me a very long while to do so but I did. It's been many years now. I do not need you anymore, Ian. I do not want you. I am no longer in love with you. I love my husband, Peter. I love the family I created with him. I love my life without you, Ian. I am a renewed person. Stronger with a sense of who I am. I am happy but thanks for asking. Am I clear enough for you?"

"Crystal clear. And, since you don't want me, at least let me see the kid. I am her real daddy after all," Ian replied sulkily. He was annoyed that Kendra turned down his suggestion that they get back together even though deep down he knew it was a long shot. He was not even sure why he suggested it. Maybe it was to see her reaction or was it his ego that needed greasing like she said? Or perhaps he wanted to gauge how she felt about him after all these years? Or did a tiny part of him still subconsciously want her back? Well, he would make her see the errors of her ways for talking to him like this! What nerves. Liana was his and he had rights whether Kendra liked it or not. She needed a little shaking up for rejecting him like this.

"Sorry, you are just a sperm donor, nothing more," Kendra said cruelly, breaking into his thoughts as she recalled the hard choices Ian had presented to her when she told him that she would keep Liana.

"Kendra, why do you want to be like that? You are really starting to piss me off," Ian's tone was detached, matter-of-fact, as though he was having a business discussion…reminding Kendra of how he could shift from one mood to another in a heartbeat.

"Why don't you ask yourself why I am annoying you?"

"What's the big deal about me seeing the kid? I'm here now. You should be happy about that."

"Do you want the 'Daddy of the year award'?" Are you even listening to yourself?" asked Kendra.

"Look Woman, the kid needs a good male influence in her life."

"Her name is Liana, Ian, not 'The Kid,'" Kendra said condescendingly.

"Whatever. Anyway, the kid needs a strong, male influence in her life…like her daddy," Ian repeated deliberately.

"Well, Liana Rite," Kendra said very slowly allowing Liana's name to sink into Ian's head, "already has more than one strong positive male influence in her life; her father, my husband, Peter, her uncle, Peter's brother, her paternal grandfather, Peter's dad, and her maternal her grandfather, my dad."

"Interesting that this Peter, that weak man you call a husband who spoke to me on the phone her is a male influence," Ian laughed cockily but also somewhat jealously.

"He is more man than you will ever be Ian. More importantly, he is Liana's father. Her daddy. The only father she's ever known and the only father she loves. She is the apple of Peter's eye. You cannot beat their connection, DNA or no DNA," Kendra said slowly and carefully to drive home her point.

"Look, I suggest we come to a compromise," Ian was now completely irritated at Kendra. How dare she talk to him like that?!

"What do you mean by a compromise? Exactly what do you want from me after all these years, Ian? You made it clear years ago that you did not want a child so what's the real deal here? We could have worked something out many years ago. After I had Liana, we still could have worked on our relationship. Or at least work on being co-parents. There is nothing left to compromise on anymore."

"Okay, look, I lost my job, and quite frankly, my unemployment checks are running out and I have still not found a job in this crappy economy," Ian finally admitted.

"And?" asked Kendra unsympathetically.

"And I need your help."

"Why do you think you deserve my help?"

"Look we have many years of history between us…good or bad. And a child connects us forever. The least you could do is show some compassion."

"Like how you showed me compassion when I told you I was pregnant with Liana?"

"Ok, I should have handled it better," Ian conceded without a hint of remorse.

"I see. Now that we agree on that, we can move forward. I wish you the best Ian."

"That's it?"

"Yes, that's it. We have nothing left to say…"

"No, we have a lot more to say!" There was a sudden hard edge to his voice, which jolted Kendra. She regained her composure quickly, not particularly surprised at his attitude. This was so typical of Ian. You never know which Ian you were having a conversation with by the time you were done speaking with him.

"What do you want Ian?" Kendra asked in a measured tone.

"I want money to tide me over Kendra," Ian said directly, all pretense of being friendly gone.

"Now, we get to the real reason you called, you want money, not Liana."

"We lived together as though we were married. I need support."

"We were never married and do not share custody of Liana, I owe you nothing, Ian."

"Liana…hmm, what kind of name is that to call a child anyway?" Ian now sounded amused forgetting for a moment that he was asking Kendra for financial help. Kendra wanted to bang his head a thousand times with the phone as he mocked Liana's name.

"You don't get to debate her name, thank you very much."

"Okay, okay, okay…whatever. Anyway, look, I need money," Ian said, going back to being very serious.

"Then keep looking for another job. That's what normal people do."

"I am still looking for another job but, in the meantime, I need money to tide me over now. You know…to maintain my lifestyle and all that. Like I said, my unemployment benefit is running out. Since, you don't want me to bother you about Liana, I'm just saying…"

"What has this got to do with me? I don't owe you a thing." She refused to believe Ian would use Liana as a pawn to get money from her.

"Darling…"

"Would you mind not calling me any terms of endearment?"

"Okaaaaay! Jeez, touchy, touchy…"

"Well, excuse me if I am not feeling sugary and spicy toward you," shot back Kendra.

"And excuse me, if I really don't care," Ian responded in a hard voice, wondering where Kendra grew the balls to speak to him this way. She used to be quite the docile girlfriend back in the days when they were still together. Now she was all feisty and definitely not a pushover…hmmm…

"Well, since we both don't care about each other's opinions, I have work to do. I think I'll hang up…"

"No, you will not hang up on me," Ian said in such a forceful voice that Kendra flinched. She had a flashback of her time with Ian, recalling how his mood could change in an instant from charming to downright mean in a second. She always had to be careful around him.

"By the way, don't you or your husband have any phone manners?" Ian's words broke into her thoughts. "First, he had the audacity to hang up on me, now you want to try the same stunt? What the hell…phone etiquette down the drain these days! Anyway, as I was saying, I want some money from you folks. I hear you and your husband are doing very well these days. So, sparing a little change my way will not hurt you any."

"So, you have resulted to being a panhandler?"

"Call it what you like, my dear. Money is money is money. However way you look at it, money is a beautiful thing to have."

"And if we don't give you the money?"

"Well, I know the way to an attorney's office. I know Liana's school. I know what time she goes to school. I know her friends. I know she must be curious about me. She must have some questions. She sounded quite inquisitive when we talked on the phone that day I called last year, what do you think?" There was no trace of emotion in his voice this time.

"I think you are one sick bastard. You have actually degraded yourself to this. You truly are one poor excuse for a man." Kendra hated how Ian still affected her after all these years.

"Honey, I need to survive. I am down and out…so for old times' sake, it wouldn't hurt for you to be a tad generous to the father of your child, now, would it?"

"You are not asking me for help, Ian, you are blackmailing me."

"Who said anything about blackmail?"

"Well, you are insinuating it."

"Who? Me? Well, I would never! What do you take me for?" Ian asked innocently switching seamlessly to charm while still demanding what he wanted.

"So, you would kidnap your own child to get money out of me?"

"Oh, so now, we agree that she is my child?"

"Well, so much for claiming you want to be her father, yet you are willing to kidnap her and blackmail her mother for money," mused Kendra.

"Well, I never said I was going to kidnap her…jeez, woman, you are putting words into my mouth. Anyway, Honey … "

"Again, it's Kendra to you, not 'Honey', not 'Babe', not 'Dear,' not any form of endearment. Just Kendra! Or better still, Mrs. Rite to you."

"Yeah, yeah, yeah…Kendra…Mrs. Rite, I got it," Ian mocked her dismissively. "Anyway, I didn't say I was going to kidnap her. I was just stating her schedule. Since when that become a crime?"

"You insinuated kidnapping her, stop playing mind games with me, Ian."

"No, you let your mind go there."

"I'm not going to let you blackmail me, Ian. This conversation is over."

"Okay, okay, okay, wow, you take things too seriously for your own good! If it'll make you feel better, instead of asking you for money, I'll just have to find another way to earn it."

"Now you are sounding more reasonable," Kendra said, relieved.

"I'll just apply for a job at her school. I believe it is called Dunn's Preparatory School, right? Maybe they could do with an extra physical education teacher. I have applied for a job in many schools but I haven't tried Dunn yet. What do you think Kendra? Do you think they have vacancies? I think…"

"Wait! How much do you need?" Kendra asked in desperation. She did not want Ian near Liana. She would not forgive herself if anything happened to her.

"Now we are talking. How about we go with fifteen grand?" Ian asked as though he was negotiating a business deal.

"What??? Where do you expect me to get that type of money?"

"You are one smart cookie, figure something out…I know for a fact you can afford it."

"Ok, look, I'll think of something, just don't go near Liana."

"Stop stressing, I won't hurt the kid…I just asked for a monetary favor, that's all," Ian sounded amused. He enjoyed making Kendra squirm.

"I don't trust you…just don't go near my daughter."

"Sure thing, Kendra…anyway, I need the money in cash by next week." his tone was back to business.

"Where should I meet you?"

"I know where you work, I can meet you there to pick up the money."

"I don't want you hanging anywhere near my office or my daughter's school," she said in a hard condescending voice.

"Gee, Ms. High-and-Mighty. What? You think I am not worthy to be seen near where you work?"

"Your words, not mine."

"Whatever woman. We can meet at Starbucks on 72 Street and Broadway at 6 PM in the evening on Tuesday."

"Fine."

"And Kendra?" Ian paused dramatically for effect.

"What now?!!!" Kendra yelled into the mouthpiece. One of her colleagues, Collins Meed, who just happen to be passing by as she was yelling at him on the phone paused for a moment at her doorway with raised eyebrows but quickly moved on as Kendra glared at him with a look that said, 'mind your own damn business!' She walked over to her door and closed it while the phone was still glued to her ear.

"Baby," Ian said, "I just wanted to remind you not to be late. You know how I've always hated tardiness."

"You'll get your money. Goodbye, Ian," Kendra said coldly before hanging up the phone shaking.

Chapter 23

The next day, everyone in the Rite household went about their usual weekday routine. As usual, Peter had risen at five-thirty in the morning to go for a quick jog. When he returned home an hour later, he took a shower, got dressed and went to their underground garage to turn on the engines of his and Kendra's cars to warm them up. Liana and her twin siblings were up at six-thirty and by seven-fifteen, everyone was dressed and ready for school and work.

Observing her family go about their usual activity made Kendra even more determined not to involve Peter in Ian's shady demands. Though she felt she was making a deal with the devil, she loved her family more than anything in the world. She did not want to put them through the nightmare that was Ian. She would battle him alone.

Chapter 24

Kendra always got up after Peter and the children in the mornings, yet she always managed to get ready before any of them. As like most mornings, after she woke up, she used the treadmill for 45 minutes and then made her way to the kitchen to make breakfast for Peter and their children before they left the house. Luckily for her, today, it was Peter's turn to drop the kids at school, so they left the house half an hour before Kendra left for work. After they left, she went to her bedroom to make sure that the money she had withdrawn a day earlier was in order for Ian. She had taken the money from the family account with the intention of replacing it before Peter noticed it was missing. He generally handled the family finances. She counted the money again, put it in an envelope and then put the envelope of money inside one of the kids' old knapsacks that she had planned to donate to Goodwill. After that, she had a quick breakfast of friend eggs and black sugarless coffee before leaving the house for work.

***

Kendra arrived at work a few minutes before nine in the morning trying to act as normal as possible. She was grateful that no one wanted to engage in small talk before starting work for the day. She knew how the rumor mill worked in the office especially after her colleague, Collin, heard her talking with Ian on the phone the other day when he called demanding money. All she wanted to do now was to give him his money, forget him and go about her life. Nothing was more important to her than the family she made with Peter. They were her life. They accepted her for who she was and she did not want that to change because of Ian's messy reappearance in her life.

***

Not Quite Imperfect

As soon as the clock struck five, Kendra was out of the door. She did not want to be late. She would be waiting for Ian to give him his money. All day, she had texted Liana at school every chance she got. She wanted to be sure that she was okay. Liana had sounded a little impatient with her when she texted her for the sixth time that day, and had turned off her cell phone, which Peter had given her in case of emergency, after taking her mother's latest call to check on her.

***

Kendra arrived at Starbucks at five minutes before six and immediately ordered a strong cup of black coffee before finding a seat by the window at the right corner near the front of the cafe. After thirty minutes, Ian came strutting in with that cocky confidence that Kendra remembered like the back of her hand. Kendra was annoyed that he had insisted that she should be on time, yet, he had taken his time arriving. Despite her irritation at his tardiness, she, like a couple of other women in the café, could not help but notice his sex appeal as they watched him through the windows walk toward the café.

Ian recognized and spotted Kendra almost immediately when he entered the café. He smiled at her as he approached her. She did not return the smile. Kendra observed him some more as he walked toward her, noticing subtle changes in his appearance since the last time she saw him several years ago when they were still together. He was wearing a pair of beige khaki pants, a light blue shirt and well-worn, navy-blue Converse sneakers. He looked thinner from the last time she saw him. He had also started to grow a beard. Though, he had sprinkles of gray on his hair, they made him look even more attractive and younger in a funny sort of way. And judging from the way the other women inside cafe kept glancing at him without trying to be obvious, Kendra knew he was still a female magnet. And for a millimeter of a second, she actually felt an attraction to him until she quickly remembered why she was meeting him and a scowl took over her expression.

"Hello Sweetness, still very beautiful I see. Long time no see," Ian said attempting to kiss Kendra on the cheek when he reached her table.

"Not long enough for me," she retorted as she backed away from his kiss.

"Boy, are we friendly," Ian said sarcastically, not at all offended by her rejection of his gesture as he took the seat opposite her. The thought of money in his hands put him in a really good mood.

"Here is your money," Kendra said, coldly, as she pushed the knapsack of money across the table toward him.

"Should I count it?" Ian asked, happily as he grabbed the bag.

"Suit yourself," Kendra replied, rising up from her chair. He was annoying her to no end.

"I trust you but just to be sure, I'll count it when I get home just in case a dollar is missing. After all, a dollar can buy me two apple pies from McDonald's," Ian said, chuckling at his joke.

"Whatever. I don't want you to ever contact me again or attempt to reach my daughter," Kendra responded disgustedly, wishing she could smack him silly and make him disappear into oblivion.

"Our daughter."

"No Ian, my daughter. Now lose my number and forget I ever existed," Kendra said in a voice so vicious that Ian flinched. A first.

"I see you've grown some backbone," he said.

"Best believe I'll do anything when it comes to my family."

"Yes, ma'am. And I thank you for the gift, Daaaaaaaarling."

"It was not a gift, Ian. Just so we are clear, you blackmailed me for the money."

"Honey, that's just semantics so I won't be offended by your choice of words. Anyhow, today is a good day."

"I am sure it is a good day for you in your sorry little world."

"Despite your rudeness, I'll be the polite one and say thanks again," responded Ian in an annoyingly cheerful voice. Nothing was going to ruin his mood after this!

"You are so not welcome," Kendra hissed as she got up to leave. Liana Rite was the apple of her eye. This man did not deserve to be her father. She took a couple of steps in the direction of the exit before Ian stopped her with sudden softness in his voice.

"Kendra?" Ian said as he got up to stand very close behind her. Kendra could feel his breath on her back but she did not move away or turn around to face him.

"What Ian?"

"You still look really good, and believe it or not, thank you for the money, my Kennie."

"I am not your Kennie," she replied with little conviction. Damn! She hated the way he could still resurrect the way her body responded to him after all these years. She loved Peter, damn it! And damn Ian for still affecting her in more ways than one. She loved Peter, she loved Peter, she loved…

"You'll always be my Kennie, Kendra Mercury," he whispered into her right ear unaware of her internal conflict. "You are mine. I know it and I know you know it too. We are one. Always have been, always will be, despite the distance, despite other people, despite the time, me and you, you and me, forever, my Kennie."

"You blackmailed me for money using my daughter. I gave you what you wanted. Now leave me alone. I have to go back to my life with my husband, Peter, whom I love very much and our children," she responded in a low voice before walking away from him, out of the café and to the street to catch a cab. As she jumped into a cab, she was surprised and confused as to why Ian still pressed all her buttons and affected her on so many levels after so many years. She had moved on. She was very much in love with Peter. Ian no longer did anything for her. The only feelings he aroused in her was anger because he was blackmailing her, and fear, because he might take Liana from her. There were no other unresolved feelings regarding what they had in the past. Or so she convinced herself.

***

Ian stood watching Kendra from inside the café until she entered a cab before slumping back into his seat. He had expected to take the money from her and then just go merrily away. Yet, for some reason, seeing her again in person had had an unexpected effect on him. During their time away from each other's lives, he had thought about her many, many times, but had willed himself to move on. And he had done such a good job of moving on that he had convinced himself that he no longer had any romantic feelings for her. He was so sure he would just take the money from her and continue with life. That is until he her saw her again for the first time in years. And after all these years, what was it about this woman, Kendra, that raised so many complex emotions in him? She was like a drug he couldn't quit.

Chapter 25

It was only just 10 AM on this August Friday morning but it was already hot, muggy and sticky as was typical in the summer. Peter and Kendra had the day off work because they had planned a three-day family weekend at Lake George. They planned to drive upstate today to start their holiday. Kendra, dressed in a simple white tank top and a knee-length dark-blue skirt was in the kitchen busily putting the last of the sandwiches and snacks she had prepared for their trip, into a big bag in the kitchen. Just as she was putting the last of the sandwiches into the bag, Peter walked into the kitchen. He was wearing black khaki pants and a gray short-sleeve polo shirt. He gave Kendra a kiss on her lips and then walked toward one of the top cabinets behind Kendra to pick out a glass tumbler. He rinsed it and then turned to the large stainless double-door refrigerator next to the cabinet to get some cold water, with his back turned to Kendra.

"Hey Babe, did you take out fifteen thousand from the joint account a few days ago?" Peter asked Kendra without suspicion as he poured the water from the refrigerator faucet into his glass.

"Actually yes, I meant to tell you...I needed to borrow money unexpectedly to help Piper out of a bind...I will replace it next week," Kendra responded casually not turning around to face him as she silently berated herself for forgetting to replace the money as she had intended. A month had passed since she had given Ian the money that he had demanded from her. She had planned to replace it by borrowing the money from her sister with some excuse about doing something special for Peter, and then repay her sister in two installments before Peter noticed the money was gone and start asking questions. Unfortunately, between stress from work and taking care of the kids and Peter, she had simply forgotten.

"Honey, I thought we agreed to have a discussion whenever either of us needed to withdraw such a large amount from the joint account?" Peter turned around to look at his wife quizzically, wondering what was really up with her. She had been acting odd these last few weeks. He had tried to talk to her before to find out if anything bothering her but she just brushed him off claiming it was his imagination. He and Kendra were usually very open about everything and the fact that she was shutting him out when something was clearly up with her, worried him.

"Darling, I simply forgot to tell you, ok? I already said I would put the money back. It's not a big deal!" Kendra snapped more harshly than she intended to. Peter was the bookkeeper in the family and was usually meticulous about balancing the books. Regardless, she had hope that Peter would not check their account before she replaced the money. Kendra silently caused Ian for what he was doing to her family.

"It had to be really important for you to forget to talk to me about this," Peter said calmly refusing to be annoyed by her tone. He wished Kendra would confide in him about what was really going on.

"Well, my sister is family. She needed my help so I gave it to her. I simply forgot to tell you I borrowed the money. So now you know. Besides, like I said, I'll put it back. I am not stealing it…now are we ready to go?" Kendra forcefully shut the bag she was putting the food in, and glared at Peter who was still looking at her strangely.

"Babe, I am not accusing you of stealing. I'm just wondering what's really going on with you. This is not really about the money. Something else is going on. We always talk about everything. We've never had a communication issue," Peter responded trying to be patient with wife. He refused to get into a fight with her over this. He had always held the notion that a couple should never be angry at each other at the same time. Today, he was giving Kendra the luxury of venting her annoyance though he did not know what he did wrong to deserve her attitude. He knew she did not steal the money. He never thought she did. He never doubted his wife's honesty in that respect but something serious was going on with her and Kendra was a bad liar. The story about her sister, seemed, well, not so true…

"Peter let's just drop the issue. It's nothing. I'll put the money back. Trust me it's nothing serious. I'm sorry I snapped at you," Kendra responded more contritely walking up to Peter and then putting her arms around him to give him a quick kiss and a hug while hating Ian for causing this argument between her and Peter. She quickly changed the topic in a breezy voice. "So, Love, are we ready to go? Did you put enough bottles of water in the van? The way the weather is going, we are going to be drinking like camels all the way to Lake George."

"Yes, I put enough water in the van, we are just about ready to go," Peter replied, not at all buying Kendra's sudden happy mood. He knew his wife too well. Something was clearly bothering her and it was serious. He intended to get to the bottom of this. He wished she would open up to him about it. They never kept anything from each other. This was a first. "Kennie, Honey, you know I love you. You are my world and I have your back no matter what, you can…"

"Hey, are we still driving to Lake George today? Are we ready to go?" Liana interrupted Peter loudly. She was dressed in ripped jeans and a white t-shirt. Her backpack, which contained an iPad and several of her favorite snacks, was firmly strapped to her back. Her earphones, plugged to her ears, were attached to her iPhone, which was in one of her jeans' pockets. She was listening to Justin Beiber's music while speaking to her parents at the same time.

"We can hear you without you shouting, you know," replied Peter irritably.

"I'm sorry, what?" yelled Liana. Kendra reached out and yanked Liana's earphones off her ears.

"Yes, Ms. Liana, we are ready to go. Make sure Ryan and Easton are ready and, in the car," Kendra said glad that Liana had interrupted her conversation with Peter. She turned to Peter who was still wondering about Kendra's attitude, "look, Honey, I am sorry. I should have told you about the money earlier. I was wrong. I didn't mean to snap at you either…I love you from now to eternity. I know you got my back."

"Ok. Love, you know that if something is bothering you, we can always talk about it right? I love you more every day and there's nothing we can't work through together. You know that, right?" Peter was not convinced that Kendra was all right but for now he would drop the topic.

"Yes, I know, Love. I am fine. Just itching to get out of here. Let's go enjoy Lake George."

Chapter 26

Today, Saturday was Liana's tenth birthday party. The party was expected to begin at 6.00 PM. It was currently 3.30 PM in the afternoon. Peter was out running errands for the party; Liana was on the phone with one of her friends excitedly talking about what to expect for her birthday while her twin siblings played all over the place and basically got in the way.

Kendra was in the kitchen putting finishing touches to the meat pies she was making for the party when she heard the gate bell buzz in the living room. She went to the living room doorway to answer the buzzer.

"Who is it?"

"Ty from Special Gifts' Corp. I have a delivery for a Liana Sharp," mumbled a bored, low-gruff voice through the buzzer.

"Liana Sharp?" Kendra was confused. Everyone knew Liana as Liana Rite.

"Gift for Liana Sharp, Ma'am," Ty now sounded just a tad impatient while trying to remain polite. He had many more deliveries to make...

"Hold on a sec," responded Kendra wondering who would address Liana as Liana Sharp. Ian did not cross her mind because she had not heard from him since she gave him money over a year ago. She opened the front door and the deliveryman, a tall, lanky, dark-haired white guy in his twenties did indeed hand Kendra two big, gift-wrapped boxes addressed to Liana Sharp, a huge bouquet of flowers, ten colorful balloons and two cards. Kendra tipped Ty generously and he left with a polite smile of appreciation. Kendra checked the flowers for the gift tag to see who had sent them to Liana. To her annoyance and slight panic, the gifts were from Ian. The last time that she heard from him was when he demanded money from her and promised to go away after she gave him what he wanted. But he clearly did not intend to go away. He just took time off from being the bane of her existence! Kendra felt a tight knot in her stomach as she tried to figure out how to deal with Ian. Why couldn't he just leave her alone? Why was he rearing his ugly head back in her life? No wonder, the gifts were addressed as Liana 'Sharp' instead of Liana 'Rite.' He was trying to send a message. Damn Ian! She had given him the money he had asked for, so what the hell did he want from her now??? She was quite sure she had gotten rid of him for good along with a big chunk of her savings. He said he would go away and he did for a short while, only to show his presence in the form of gifts on her daughter's birthday. She would be damned if she was going to let him ruin the perfect life she had built with Peter.

Just as she was contemplating tossing the flowers, balloons and gifts in the trash, the phone rang. Kendra walked over to the phone and picked it up.

"Hello?"

"Hello Kennie. Thanks for the money you gave me a while ago. It was good to see you again by the way," Ian's deep raspy voice filtered through the phone.

"Why are you calling me, Ian? What now?" Kendra rolled her eyes as she spoke evenly. She refused to let him ruin her day, on Liana's birthday no less.

"Well, my love, did my baby girl like her present? I told you I know things about you and my kid. I remembered her birthday! So did she like the presents?" Ian sounded pleased with himself.

"How dare you, Ian? How dare you contact my daughter after I paid you off and you agreed to leave me and my family alone?" Kendra shouted at him through the through the phone, already forgetting her promise to herself not to let Ian piss her off today.

"Well, it is my kid's birthday. What's a daddy to do?" Ian sounded amused, making Kendra even madder. Gotta live up to my fatherly responsibilities and all that. You know how it is. Why are you so worked up, anyway? Technically speaking, I have not bothered you at all since you gave me the money but it did dawn on me to do something nice for the kid on her tenth birthday. They are just gifts for my daughter's birthday, what's the harm in that?"

"First of all, she is my daughter not yours. Second of all, you said you would leave us alone if I gave you the money you wanted. I gave you the money, Ian. Leave us alone!

"I haven't bothered you since we met at the café a little over a year ago, Kendra. This is an exception. This is a special day…our little girl's tenth birthday. That's a milestone. Come on, you should understand that" Ian repeated his point of view.

"Wow, Ian. You really do have some nerve. You never wanted her in the first place. You've never even met her. All of a sudden, you are daddy of the year? Do you want an award for that?" The venom and sarcasm in her voice was hard to ignore, even for Ian who was usually really good at ignoring people's sarcasms.

"Oh my, all these years after we split seem to have made you a very bitter woman," Ian commented, somewhat nonchalantly. "Did I do that to you, Kennie? Did I make you so bitter and angry? I hope not."

"You think I'm bitter? Especially when you decided to rear your ugly head back into my life? You are really full of yourself. You really need to crawl back into the hole you came from, Ian. That will make my day. That will make me less bitter, how about that?"

"Sorry I made you this way and no I can't crawl back into my 'hole' as you put it. My little girl needs me, her father … "

"She has a father…a really good one. His name is Peter, my husband. He's the only one she's ever known. Legally and emotionally."

"Kendra, why do we have to go through this again? Whether you like it or not, she is my flesh and blood. She and I share the same DNA. I am her biological father, that will never change, deal with it."

"You are just a sperm donor. Just a donor, my dear!" spat Kendra.

"Suit yourself with the name-calling if it makes you feel better. As a matter of fact, since you are being so rude, I have decided I want to be in her life from now on."

"Ian, please leave us alone. I gave you what you wanted. Please. Liana is happy, don't upset her life now," Kendra pleaded as panic set in. The thought of Ian taking Liana away from her was too much for her.

"I just want her to know who her father is. I want to be in her life Kendra," Ian was calm, serious.

"At the spur of the moment because you don't like the way I am responding to you; you want to take her away from me?" Kendra's tone changed from pleading to anger. Why was he doing this to her?

"I did not say I was taking her away from you. I just want to be in her life. That is my daughter too, why can't you understand that?"

"What I understand is that you blackmailed me for money to go away but clearly, you are not the type of man that keeps his word!"

"Ok, look, Kennie, you can make this all go away. Things have not been easy for me lately…" his voice trailed.

"What are you trying to say? What exactly is this all about?"

"Umm, uh, er, well, you know…it's like this…"

"Oh, I see what this is really about. You want more money, don't you?" It suddenly dawned on Kendra.

"I don't know what you are talking about," Ian replied innocently.

"All right, since you don't know what I am talking about, this conversation is over."

"Don't you dare hang up on me, Kendra!" Again, the sudden switch in mood and tone that had been so typical of Ian in the past. This time, it was a tone that demanded and commanded respect. A tone, which made Kendra hesitate…and obey…for whatever reason.

"What Ian? What do you want?" she asked evenly.

"My daughter. I have rights." Ian's tone softened slightly.

"Really? We'll see about that now, won't we? And by the way, how did you even know today was her birthday?" Kendra was so angry with him that she could kill him.

"Hon, she is still my daughter. You can deny it till you are blue in the face but fact is fact," he stated calmly. "Besides, I have my ways…anyone can find out anything these days if they really want to…I can be resourceful, you know."

"Why did you send those gifts to Liana and why did you really call, Ian?" Kendra demanded again. She knew that Ian was not sending Liana birthday gifts out of the goodness of his heart.

"Well, since you asked, I'm kinda running low on funds…"

"So, I was right then. You want more money."

"Well, you know money goes fast even when spent wisely … "

"I already gave you fifteen thousand dollars…in cash!"

"It's not polite to cut someone off when they are speaking," Ian chided Kendra. "Anyway, as I was saying, money goes fast and I am low on funds again. I have bills to pay, you know, rent, travel and miscellaneous bills. Besides, that was a while ago."

"Exactly. By now, you should have sorted yourself out."

"Things haven't worked out as planned."

"How is that my problem?" hissed Kendra coldly. Even as she spoke, she knew what was coming next.

"What I am saying Kendra, is that I need more money…soon," Ian said with authority as though he had the right to ask.

"Shouldn't you be working by now?" Kendra could not help being condescending.

"In case you have been living under a rock, the economy still stinks and most of us who are not as fortunate as you are, are still in the job market. I get by with temp jobs here and there but right now, I am going through a dry spell."

"I don't think the current state of the economy has anything to do with you being unemployed. I think you are just lazy and happy to extort money from a woman…how very manly of you!" Kendra snorted cruelly. God, how she despised him! She could not believe that she had wasted so many years of her life with him. She could not even believe that she was once so in love with him, she could not see straight. At this particular moment today, she really hated him.

"Now, now, Dear, let's not be mean. Being cruel wears ugly on you," Ian commented without emotion. He had a goal and that was to get more money from Kendra. He would not let her nastiness get to him, he decided. If anything, Ian was very good at separating his emotions. Right now, getting money from her was purely from a business standpoint. At the moment he was desperate for funds.

"Ian, you do not deserve any compassion from me. Please just leave me and mine alone," Kendra pleaded.

"I don't want your family; I just want more money. Who else can I turn to but you, Babe?" he smiled to himself. She had the nerve to actually leave him years ago and did not look back. Well, payback was a bitch. If she had listened to him when he tried to reason with her, perhaps they would still be together. He might even have caved and put a ring on that finger. Oh well, she made her own bed...he needed money now and that was that.

"Ian, I don't have any more money for you. I gave you most of my savings! I have my life and my family to take care of. Just go away," Kendra said before hanging up on him. She expected him to call back but thankfully he did not.

After Kendra hung up on Ian, she took the gifts that Ian had sent to Liana before she had a chance to see them and dumped them in a large trash bag without bothering to open the gifts to see what they were. Then she took the trash bag outside for the pickup van to take away in the morning. Thankfully, when she got back inside the house, no one had come to the kitchen where Liana's balloons had flown up against the ceiling with the strings down. There were ten of them to represent each year of her life. With aggressive determination, Kendra got out a pointed knife from a cabin drawer, pulled out one of the chairs surrounding the kitchen island, climbed on the chair that she pulled out so she could reach the balloons, began yanking each of the balloons down furiously and then began punching each of them to let out the air. After she was done and they all lay on the kitchen floor in a pile, she stepped down from the chair, pulled out another large garbage bag, gathered the deflated balloons and then put them all in the bag along with the flowers before taking the bag out and setting it down next to the other garbage bag containing the gift boxes. She refused to let Ian ruin her and her child's day.

Chapter 27

Whenever the weather was nice, Kendra would have her lunch in Bryant Park, a couple of blocks from her office, with Taylor Myers, a pretty, dark-haired, slender, Caucasian woman in her mid-forties. Taylor was also a fellow co-worker at the company where Kendra worked. They started working in the company the same day and had eventually evolved from co-workers to casual friends. Today, two weeks after Liana's birthday, Kendra and Taylor were taking advantage of the nice weather to enjoy their lunch at the park as usual. They had both ordered chicken Caesar wraps and bottled water from Au Bon Pain. Taylor, who was sitting opposite Kendra with a small round table between them as they chatted and ate had just taken a bite from her wrap when she suddenly stopped chewing and smiled widely as her eyes wandered off in the direction behind Kendra.

"Hello, Taylor, are you listening to what I am saying?" Kendra asked, noticing that Taylor was suddenly distracted.

"Now, Who. Is. He???" Taylor wondered aloud in her slight high-pitched voice, nodding discretely in the direction of the object of her admiration. She had seductive glint in her eyes as talked.

"He, who?" Kendra asked curiously as she started to turn her head in the direction of Taylor's discrete nod.

"Don't look now! He'll know we are watching! He's walking toward us! Gosh, what a sexy walk…" Taylor's voice trailed off as she drooled. A minute later, Kendra heard a familiar raspy voice behind her. It was a voice that she had come to detest and dread since the owner of that voice re-entered her life.

"Hello pumpkin. Funny, running into you here!" Ian said charmingly as he placed a hand around Kendra's shoulder to give her an unexpected kiss on her cheek and a squeeze. Kendra immediately shook him off, flinching as she dramatically rubbed her cheek as if a bee had stung her.

"How the hell did you know where I'd be lunching today? Are you stalking me?" she demanded angrily.

"Relax, Kendra, stop being so dramatic. I am not stalking you. You are not that special. The last time I checked, I was free to go anywhere I wanted…seeing you here, is merely a coincidence, my dear," Ian replied, feigning innocence as he stood behind here. "Anyway, what does it matter?"

"Ian, please leave, you are not welcome here!" snapped Kendra, turning around to face him.

"Come on, Kendra, be nice. By the way, won't you introduce me to your beautiful friend?" Ian asked as he turned his attention to Taylor with his signature smile. Kendra knew that smile. It was the one that charmed every woman Ian encountered and the one that usually got him out of life's many binds. It was also the same one that won her heart several years ago when they first met. And even now, knowing what she knew about him, for a nanosecond, she was surprised to find her heart actually warming toward Ian before she snapped back to reality knowing Ian's visit was not for a pleasant reason and hating herself for letting him still get to her after all these years and everything, he did to hurt her.

"Yes, Ken, introduce us," chimed Taylor eagerly, interrupting Kendra's thoughts. She noticed the tension between Kendra and Ian but she was not deterred. He was a hottie! Perhaps this was her lucky day after all. Lord knows how many times she had prayed for Mr. Right before going to sleep many nights. Even if he turned out not to be her Mr. Right, he could at least be her Mr. Right Now. From the look of things, Kendra certainly could not stand this Ian guy, which means she could have him.

"Ian meet Taylor, a friend of mine. Taylor, this is Ian," Kendra said stiffly, trying to be polite for the sake of Taylor. She did not bother to mention that Ian was her ex-boyfriend. No need for trivial details.

"Nice to meet you Taylor," Ian said, taking Taylor's hand and kissing it softly as he poured on the charm. This Taylor was an eager one. Yep, he planned to get laid soon. It had been a while since he had had a woman in his bed anyway. Taylor was easy on the eyes and she appeared to like him. Things would definitely happen between both of them, soon.

"Nice to meet you too, Ian," responded Taylor, wondering what was going on between Kendra and Ian. Kendra definitely did not look happy to see Ian. She knew Kendra was married to Peter whom she had met a few times. They seemed very happy together. So, who was Ian to her? Anyway, since she was single and free to mingle, then Ian just might be her catch of the day ...

"You seem like a lovely lady, you and I should have coffee or something, soon. What do you say?" Ian interrupted Taylor's thoughts.

"Well…" Taylor hesitated, glancing at Kendra who looked royally pissed at the audacity of Ian to flirt with Taylor right in front of her. Not that she wanted him back, oh no! She just did not want him damaging her friends the way he did to her. She did not want them to go through the same crap she did with him. "I am not sure." Much as she was digging Ian and already fantasying about being with him, she respected Kendra and did not want to step on her toes so she waited for her to say something. Hopefully, something good.

"Come on, it's just coffee and maybe desert," Ian persuaded charmingly before Kendra could say anything.

"I don't know if it's a good idea," Taylor replied wisely, though she really wanted to get to know Ian. She glanced at Kendra again, who finally shrugged and nodded that it was okay. Taylor was a grown woman and it was not her place to tell her whom she should or should not date. Taylor was perfectly capable of making her own decisions. They were friends but it was not like they were besties. On the bright side, maybe Ian would finally leave her and her family alone.

"I won't bite, I promise," Ian said, smiling at Taylor as though she was the most beautiful woman in the world.

"Well, if you insist," Taylor happily relented after reading Kendra's expression of approval.

"Great! Here is my number," Ian said as he gave her his number and took hers. "I'll call you to set something up."

"Sure," responded Taylor. "Anyway, I have to excuse myself and let you two talk. I'll see you later at the office, Kendra," she added as she got up, gathered her purse and empty lunch container, and smiled at Ian one more time before leaving Kendra alone with him. He immediately took the seat that Taylor had vacated. He made himself comfortable, leaning against the back of the seat. He looked at Kendra with a smug smile. She scowled back at him in return. She was no longer hungry. Ian's arrival had killed her appetite.

"So how are you these days, Kendra?" Ian smiled at her as though they were best buddies sharing a private joke. Kendra was so irritated at his presence that instead of responding to him, she closed the container of her half-eaten lunch, put it in the brown paper bag that it came in, gathered her purse and got up to leave. She did not even want to engage with him. He was annoying her to no end and ruining her lunchtime.

"What, are you leaving me to sit here all by myself?" Ian asked, amused.

"You are a big boy, I'm sure you can handle being at the park by yourself."

"But I need your company, Sweetie," Ian responding, still smiling in amusement.

"I don't have time for you today, Ian."

"Can you just sit for a minute?" Ian suddenly became very serious, catching her off guard but not really surprised at his mood change. After all, this was Ian and some things never change.

"Why are you here, Ian?" Kendra demanded as she sat back down, not sure why she was obeying his request to sit down.

"I decided to come and visit you in person since you would not talk to me on the phone the other day," replied Ian seriously.

"So, you are stalking me now?"

"Calm down, Kendra. I am not stalking you. Like I said, it is just a coincidence that I bumped into you," Ian insisted on sticking to his lie. "Why are you being so unreasonable?"

"Unreasonable? Unreasonable, Ian???" Kendra tried not to raise her voice at the audacity of him. He always managed to get a rise out of her.

"Yes, Dear. All I was doing was asking the mother of my child for some financial support the other day and she went all nuclear on me ... "

"Really????" Kendra cut him off. "You blackmailed me for money, which I gave to you and then had the nerve to contact me again for more after you blew it all? On my daughter's birthday no less and I am the one that's unreasonable????"

"I wanted to wish our daughter a happy birthday but then I thought why not kill two birds with one stone and ask you for more money? If you ask me, that's being considerate because I won't have to nag you on another day."

"Ian, please just get out of my life. I am not a bank nor am I a millionaire. You stole a good part of my self-worth when we were together. You never wanted a child and quite frankly, you were never even that great a partner...it took me a while to get myself back together. I will not let you destroy me again, Ian. Just leave me alone."

"Baby, you know I loved you. Yes, there were other women but I only slept with them when you made me mad so it is really your fault. And let's be honest Babe, nobody can ever love you like I do and you know that," Ian responded as if he made perfect sense.

"Hah! Funny how that nasty line would have made me feel so tiny many years ago when I still cared about you. Now, you are so insignificant to me that what you just said doesn't even faze me. Not even a little bit," Kendra responded disdainfully as she tossed her half-eaten lunch into the dustbin near her.

"Whatever," Ian responded. At the moment, he could care less what she thought of him. What he needed, was more money from her. He needed to cover this month's rent and maybe even take that Taylor woman for a date or two so they could come back to his place and make love later. And then there was that pesky overdue Con Ed bill that he needed to pay by next week or else they would turn off his electricity. The money Kendra gave him was long gone toward bills and everyone that he had owed money to. At least he was debt-free in that respect...except of course the recurrent utilities and rent.

"Whatever? Ok then. So, I guess our conversation is over then..."

"It is over when I say so. Just have five thousand dollars ready for me by next week. After this, I won't ask you for any more money again. I am in a bind at the moment. My rent and utility bills need to be paid urgently, plus since your friend gave me her number, she and I might be hitting it soon. So as a gentleman, I might as well take her out on a date. You know what I am saying?"

"Basically, you want me to pay your bills and cover your love life and you promise never to bother me again...promises, which you are not good at keeping by the way," Kendra scoffed. This was unreal. She always knew Ian was cheap during their relationship but this was a new low.

"Damn, Kendra, you don't have to say it like that," responded Ian, clutching his heart.

"Well Ian, you are not a man, much less a gentleman. Real men do not blackmail their ex-girlfriends to pay for their current love lives and their monthly bills. Heck, a real man would want to know about the welfare of his children without blackmailing the mother of his child. So, Ian, you are a poor wretched, lost specimen of human waste. You. Are. Not. A. Real. Man," Kendra spat out the words with such venom, Ian was momentarily lost for words. All the years that they had been together, he had never known Kendra to be capable of such feistiness. Interestingly enough, deep down inside of him, a teeny, weeny part of him actually liked this feisty part of her. It turned him on. Kendra still pressed his buttons in more ways than one. For a moment he wondered whether he should try to win her back for real this time. He had never really known Kendra to be this feisty when they had been together. This part of her personality was definitely an exciting prospect to be discovered further. Hmmm.

"What Ian, you lost your tongue?" Kendra's sneer snapped him back from his thoughts.

"Wow! Such feistiness…I think I like it! But anyway, now that you've let me know how you really feel, I still need the money by next week. Same spot we met the last time at the café…our special place, please. See? I even said 'please,'" he said with a wink and a smile that pissed Kendra off even more.

"Go to hell, Ian and stay there, please," Kendra responded before getting up for the second time to leave.

"Sit down, Kendra!" Ian commanded forcefully. Kendra sat down again without a word, hating herself for obeying him yet feeling tired of fighting Ian.

"I want five thousand dollars by next week or the next person you hear from will be my lawyer giving you notice that I will be filing for custody of Liana," Ian said in a very low but serious voice leaving Kendra without a doubt that he would carry out his threat.

"You'll get your money, Ian," she replied quietly with resignation. Ian smiled with satisfaction as he crossed his hands behind his head and leaned further back against his seat. Kendra got up and walked away without another word and without so much as a glance at him.

Chapter 28

The following week, Kendra went to Starbucks to meet Ian. He was already at the café sipping coffee. He had chosen a table by the window. He got up when he saw her, expecting her to take the seat opposite him. Kendra walked up to him without a smile or a word. She did not sit down. Instead, she took out a large envelope with the money from her purse and put it on the table in front of him. This time, she had taken the money from her own personal savings and not the family account.

"Hello Kendra. Thanks for coming," Ian said politely with a smile as though he was talking to a close associate.

"You can count it. It's all there," Kendra said without emotion, still standing. Ian sat back down when he saw that she made no attempt to sit down.

"I trust you today," he said as he grabbed the envelope from the table and put it in his knapsack. Kendra watched him without any expression. After he had the money safely tucked in his bag, he smiled again at her and made another attempt at conversation. "Won't you have a seat and have coffee with me?"

Kendra just looked at him for a few minutes longer wondering how she could possibly have ever loved this person before stalking away without another word to him but with anxiety in her heart knowing that sooner or later, Peter was going to sense something was wrong again. She wanted to keep him out of this Ian mess but she knew he was going to start asking questions very soon because Ian was affecting her normal behavior. She couldn't hide the situation with Ian from Peter much longer, and Ian was not going away anytime soon.

Chapter 29

It was a quiet Sunday evening and almost a year since Kendra's last encounter with Ian. Liana was finishing up her homework in her room, the twins were playing video games in their room, Peter was doing some work in the study and Kendra was alone in the kitchen preparing a dinner of baked Ziti for the family. She was putting the casserole dish in the oven when phone extension in the kitchen rang. She let the phone ring, hoping someone else would pick up one of extensions somewhere else in the house, while she close the oven door and set the temperature. Of course, as usual, no one picked up the phone. Everyone, except Kendra generally ignored the house phone whenever any of the extensions rang because everyone except the twins, had cell phones so they could not be bothered with the house phone. This was a constant source of irritation for Kendra. Today was no different. After she was satisfied with the level of temperature that she had set the oven to, she picked up the phone, which was still ringing.

"Hello?"

"Hello Babe," Ian's raspy voice filtered through the phone happily. He was clearly in a good mood. Kendra tensed immediately at the sound of his voice. She was just beginning to relax because she thought he had finally left her alone and now he was back...yet again.

"Please, please just don't. Not today, Ian, I'm not in the mood for you," Kendra said tiredly. She was at her wit's end on how to handle him. For once, she was thankful that no one else had picked up the phone when it rang.

"Don't what, Kennie? I haven't even said anything yet."

"Don't call me again. Don't ask me for money. Don't call me Kennie. Don't bother me. I don't have any time or money for you anymore."

"Is that why you think I called?"

"Well, if you didn't call to demand more money and threaten me, why are you calling me yet again? What do you want now? You said you would leave me alone after I gave you another five thousand the last time… so bye, Ian." Kendra hung up. Almost immediately, the phone rang again.

"I keep telling you to brush up on your phone manners. It's rude to hang up on people," Ian's hard, angry tone filtered through the phone as soon as Kendra picked up the phone again.

"You are someone who deserves to be hung up on!" retorted Kendra without missing a beat. "Why won't you leave me alone? I told you I don't have anything left for you, Ian."

"I called because I want to have face time with my daughter," replied Ian in a normal sensible voice, no trace of the anger he had in his tone a minute ago.

"Not again…are you really going back there again?" she sighed in exasperation.

"What do you mean?" he asked innocently.

"What do you mean, 'what do I mean???'" demanded Kendra, panicked.

"What? Did I stutter? I said I want to see my daughter. I want her to know her real daddy," Ian retorted, his tone back to being hard, leaving Kendra with no doubt that he meant what he was saying.

"So, we are back to it again, more money, more threats. How much more this time Ian? Kendra was scared. There was something about his tone that made her feel like this time, this was more than money. He was not playing games anymore. He wanted to get back at her for whatever reason his warped mind had come up with.

"After the nasty things you said to me when we were at the park months ago, I went home and thought about it. I want to show you what a real man is. I've decided I want to be part of my daughter's life. I deserve to know my daughter. I have rights."

"Ian, I was angry at you for blackmailing me for more money. You never wanted a child in the first place. Hell, you encouraged me to abort my child and when that was not an option, you wanted me to give Liana up for adoption, do you remember that??" Kendra reminded him yet again.

"Well, I've grown up since then. I want to spend time with my kid. I want to be responsible."

"Ha! That's a laugh. You crawled out of the hole you had been hiding in for years, to bully and blackmail me and then demand to see my daughter; the one you never wanted in the first place…the reason we broke up. Now you proclaim that you've changed? Tell me, Ian, what is your real face? Because so far, I can see many faces, the cunning one, the lazy one, the mean one, the liar, the blackmailer … "

"Ok, ok, ok! Kennie, Baby, no need to call me names. I get that I have been going about this the wrong way. But I really want to know my daughter. Please, I want back into your life…and Liana's too…our love child. Yours and mine," Ian said switching to the charmer, his tone now soft and tender.

"Again, it's not Kennie or Baby to you, Ian. It's Kendra."

"Ok, ok, ok, Kendra, I got it," Ian held his free hand up as though he was defending himself against Kendra even though they were not physically in the same place. "Anyway, as I was saying, I'm going to show you that I am a changed man now. I am not a bad person. I am still the guy you fell in love with many years ago."

"Except since you resurfaced, I have not seen a hint of that person I used to know when we first started dating. Besides, I am madly in love with Peter, my husband. Even better, Peter and I have made a wonderful family together," Kendra responded calmly wondering what angle Ian was playing from this time. She would rather he just left her alone.

"All right, I get it!" Ian was now irritated seeing that his charm was not having any effect on Kendra. Any other woman would have let him have his way without any hassle but Kendra always had to make him work for what he wanted…such a pain in the ass…yet she was Kendra, his Kennie…she always managed to get to him…even after all these years, damn! "Can't blame a guy for wanting to see his child and maybe get the gal back," he drawled lightly as though he was joking in the first place.

"Well, now that we have cleared that up, goodbye, Ian…"

"Wait! There's something else…" Ian paused dramatically for effect.

"Get to it, I have to go! Why else are you calling me?" Kendra demanded; annoyed, still quite certain he was going to ask her for more money. Since he resurfaced back to her life, it's had all been about money.

"Can't I just call to say hi? We have history, you know, you and me. And we have an eternal bond," Ian said deliberately.

"So, you also called to tell me we have a past…jeez, like I don't know that?" Kendra asked sarcastically, refusing to bite.

"My, my, such sarcasm," commented Ian.

"You called my house for crying out loud. I am busy at the moment," she snapped angrily in a low tone, trying not to be loud for fear that Peter or any of the kids might walk into the kitchen and overhear her end of the conversation.

"Would you rather I called your cell phone at a later time when you are less busy? I have that number too, you know."

"I'd rather you just don't call me at all." Only her close circle of friends and family had her cell phone number. She did not think that Ian would have it too, but by now she was no longer surprised by his antics and did not bother asking him how he found her cell phone number.

"Well, something came up, perhaps you can help me."

"Let me take a wild guess…I was right before…you want more money and if I don't give it to you, you will take Liana, correct?"

"Well, I did not call for more money…"

"So, what else do you want?" Kendra cut him off impatiently.

"My, my, Kennie, can you just let me finish what I am trying to say instead of interrupting me?"

"Ian, please stop calling me Kennie, thank you. Now what do you want? Why did you call me yet again?"

"Actually, I kinda need a loan."

"So, this is about money. I knew it. You just said it was not about money but of course, it is."

"Well, not in the way you mean."

"Really? You kinda need a loan??" Kendra mocked.

"Well, actually, yes…from you."

"Do I look like a bank to you?"

"You are more likely to give me the money than a bank. No paperwork. Just a loan between friends."

"Let's get one thing straight, Ian. You and I are not friends. Friends do not blackmail friends for money or otherwise. Like you said, we once had a past. A past. There is a reason that things are left in the past. We are the past. Exes. Nothing more."

"Except we made a child together, who bonds us for life," Ian could not help the dig even though he was the one requesting a favor from her.

"Whatever," Kendra replied dismissively. "Get to the point of the money you are demanding from me this time."

"I won't ask you for any more after this." His tone was now serious again but without malice.

"Sure, you will. You never stop. Why should I believe you this time? You said that before…twice, actually," responded Kendra disbelievingly. "Why is now any different?"

"Because I finally got another job at a big institution. A reputable one. It is a good career opportunity with benefits and everything. A regular job," he said proudly.

"The more reason why you shouldn't even be asking me for money anymore." She could care less whether he got a job or not as long as he left her alone.

"Well, there is just one glitch…"

"But of course, Ian…isn't there always a glitch with you?"

"No, really," Ian said ignoring her tone. He was focused on getting this money. "My start date was delayed. I was supposed to start this month but the powers that be at the company pushed my start date to next month instead."

"What has that got to do with me? I don't have any more money to give you. Borrow from your friend, Julian, go to the bank and borrow, do a 'Go fund me page' online, something…anything, just leave me the hell alone!" Kendra was so angry, she forgot to keep her voice down but she was not shouting either.

"Kendra, I don't have anyone else to turn to. I have borrowed more than enough from Julian…I still owe him money as a matter of fact. Look, I'm sorry I threatened and blackmailed you before, but I really need this money. This is really the last time I'll ask you for money…ever."

"I don't believe you, Ian, you said this before but you came back anyway. You just won't leave me alone. I am not a bank. I have a family and a life to take care of. Just go away."

"Not until you agree to lend me this money, just to tide me over for the month or I will get evicted. Believe it or not, I am really starting a new permanent job as a Master Trainer at Tyler's Gym at their Fifth Avenue location. I am sure you've heard of Tyler's Gym; they are one of the largest sporting facilities in the country," Ian said seriously. "I'll also manage other trainers."

"Yes, I've heard of Tyler's Gym. Good for you Ian. Still, that doesn't give you the right to blackmail me and then demand a loan. Good luck with your new job, I'm making dinner for my family." Kendra was tired of talking to him.

"Kendra don't hang up, please. I am trying to be nice about this but now you are making me go back to my old ways," Ian said, sounding like he was being forced to do something, he did not want to do.

"You mean you are back to blackmailing me? Well, the polite Ian did not last long!"

"Loose the sarcasm, Kendra. Meet me tomorrow at our Starbuck at 6.00 PM with three thousand dollars," Ian said authoritatively like a boss giving orders.

"Our Starbucks?"

"You know what I mean," Ian said, annoyed.

"No, I don't, Kendra said deliberately. If this was the one tiny thing, she could do to piss him off, she was going to do it, however petty it might seem.

"Ok, since you are a bit slow at figuring things out, "Ian came back bitingly, "meet me at the Starbucks on 72 Street and Broadway where we met before and don't be late."

"Or what?" You'll take Liana?" Kendra challenged him, quite sure that that was the next thing that was going to come out of Ian's mouth.

"Or nothing, Kendra. I told you I am starting work next month. I am getting my act together. Believe it or now, I will pay you back but right now even if I have to twist your arm to get this loan, then that's what I will do."

"I'm not sure whether you are threatening me or begging me for a loan, all the while insulting me."

"I need this money and I will pay you back," Ian said evenly instead. He would not let her goad him again. He planned to pay her back, well, after this loan. He had his reasons. One being that he had unexpectedly started to have feelings for Kendra again, so maybe he might really want her back again once he explored those feelings within himself. If and when, he decided he wanted her back, the battle to win her back would be a very long, tough, uphill one starting with repaying her all the money she ever gave him, loan or not, and getting her to forgive him for the methods he used to get the money from her.

"I see," Kendra responded quietly, breaking into his thoughts. His tone was different. Maybe he was telling the truth this time…

"In fact, I'll do one better after I start working again, I'll start paying you back all the money I ever took from you…in installments of course," Ian said, matter of fact.

"What's gotten into you Ian?" Kendra could not help but wonder aloud, not daring to completely believe him until she saw a change in his behavior and he actually returned her money but more importantly, left her and Liana alone.

"Because it is the right thing to do, Kendra. I have been through some rough times since we broke up and I was desperate for money at some point," Ian said candidly.

"So, your next best option was to blackmail the woman you once loved?"

"Well, you left me!" Ian said with a twinge of bitterness, which he could not help.

"After the way you treated me or are you still not able to see that what you were asking of me was a bit much?" Kendra responded also with bitterness.

"Look, let's not rehash the past," Ian replied with sudden lightness, refusing to acknowledge that he did anything wrong. There would be time to talk about the past later. Right now, he needed this money. There was hope in his voice as he added, "so will I see you tomorrow?"

"I'll see what I can do."

"No, Kendra, I'll see you tomorrow, right?" he insisted, almost pleading.

Kendra was taken aback by his tone. Now, this was a tone she had never heard from Ian before. He was usually too proud to beg. Maybe, he really needed her help…maybe he was taking steps to change…dare she hope he would keep his word this time? Maybe…

"Kendra?" Ian paused, questioning, tentative.

"Yes, Ian, I'll see you tomorrow," Kendra replied as she hung up. She was not sure what to make of her conversation with him. Whether she liked it or not, they had history, good, bad, ugly and complex. He had been her first true love. She buried her feelings for him many years ago. She moved on with Peter. She loved Peter and Peter loved her. She did not need Ian to mess up the balance of her life, yet she felt she could not turn her back on him despite it all.

Chapter 30

The next day after work, Kendra met up with Ian at Starbucks. Just like the last time she met him here, he was sitting at the back of the café, sipping ice-coffee. He happened to glance up the moment she walked inside the café. He smiled at her and stood up to greet her as she walked up to him. She did not smile back but she was not in a bad mood either.

"Hello Kendra," Ian said giving her an unexpected kiss on her left cheek while expecting her to flinch or insult him dramatically like she did at Bryant Park. He had come to expect that from her but surprisingly, Kendra did not react negatively. In fact, he could have sworn she almost smiled at him.

"Hello, Ian," Kendra said instead of acknowledging the kiss on her cheek. She sat down opposite him before he resumed his seat. He took another sip of his drink before speaking.

"How are you?" Can I get you something to drink?" he asked politely, not sure what he thought of this quiet version of Kendra.

"No thanks. I just came to give you the money," she replied quietly, as she fished for the standard white envelope that she had put a cashier check in from her bag. She found the envelope with the check and handed it to Ian.

"Thanks for coming and thank you for the money. I know I've been a jerk to you; blackmailing and threatening you," he said wistfully toying with his coffee cup, not looking at her, still trying to gauge her mood. He was suddenly feeling ashamed of his past behavior toward her.

"Yes Ian, you've been a jerk to me in more ways than one," she replied. She was not going to disagree with him on that.

"Ok, then…quiet sass," Ian smiled, deciding that this was her mood at the moment.

"Anyway, I have to go." Kendra stood up to leave.

"I promise to pay you back. I really will." Ian stood up with her.

"If you say so, Ian," she said, tired of fighting him. It took her a long time to get over him. Once she finally made the decision to move on, she had been doing quite well and Peter, God bless him, was her Godsend. Ian being back in her life was making her increasingly uneasy especially as the familiar stirrings of something other than hate for him, was slowly resurfacing. She needed to distance herself from him in order to figure out exactly her feelings for him …whatever they may be. She loved Peter. She buried her feelings for Ian away many years ago. They were not supposed to pop up again especially as he had been nothing but a mean jerk to her since he resurfaced back into her life. She liked her life with Peter and she was not going to let Ian ruin that.

Chapter 31

Ian was confused by the resurrection of his feelings for Kendra. He thought he could control how he felt about her. Lord knows he had tried everything in his power to fight his growing feelings for her. He had convinced himself that he only wanted to see her again because he just needed to bug her for money. After all, he had navigated through life fairly well without her since they broke up years ago. Yet, as he watched her walk into the café earlier, he had been suddenly overwhelmed by how deeply she still affected him.

How could she still affect him so much after all these years apart? It had taken him a long time to get over her after she left him, or at least he thought he had gotten over her…until he saw her again for the first time in years. Even then, he had convinced himself that it was normal to feel that away after not seeing an ex for a long time. Yet, after their last encounter at Starbucks a few days ago, those feeling became stronger than ever and he was not sure what to do with all these feelings for her. He felt like he had no control.

Ian wondered about the possibility of seriously getting Kendra back despite the way things had ended between them. Pity she was now married. But then again, the way they loved each other in the past gave him hope that all could not possibly be lost between them. Surely, she must still feel a tiny something for him? He definitely heart Kendra. Perhaps he and Kendra might happen again? He always did know how to charm the women. Take for instance, Kendra's friend, Taylor, he didn't even have to try hard with her. One casual coffee date and boom, she was in his bed. She was not even that good of a lay but more importantly, she was not Kendra. Since the first stirrings of his feelings for Kendra began coming back, he compared every woman he met to Kendra whether consciously or unconsciously. She was the standard. And so far, none of the women had measured up. Instead, they only served to intensify his feelings for her and forced him to acknowledge to himself that he wanted her back 100%, even if it means taking responsibility as a father in every way that matters with his daughter, well, their daughter. He thought he never wanted to become a father, but having a child with Kendra was certainly giving him second thoughts about fatherhood. Their daughter was a piece of Kendra and a piece of him. Therefor they were linked for life. He would just have to figure out a way to overcome that tiny issue of her married status.

The bigger problem now, was how to go about winning her heart back. He did in fact notice that she was a changed woman. This new Kendra was actually more physically beautiful than she ever was before and she was more confident and feistier. She definitely knew how to assert herself. He liked that strong personality. The docile, pushover woman, he once knew when they were together, was nowhere to be found. The way she had been standing up to him and challenging him at every turn, really turned him on. She still pushed all his buttons but this new Kendra was complicated. This Kendra was a mystery, a puzzle he wanted to unravel. This Kendra was confident and collected. This Kendra definitely knew who she was and commanded respect. He definitely liked this Kendra more than the one he knew when they had been together. He wanted this Kendra back in his life. Their years apart had done her good. She was a smart, mature, intelligent woman, no longer a girl. She occupied his thoughts all day, every day, much as it annoyed and delighted him at the same time. It was like meeting someone new and loving her with twice as much emotion as he did in the past but this time it was a more adult love. He wanted to make her happy but not obsessively and not selfishly like he did in the past. However, he knew it was going to be one hell of a fight to win her back.

Chapter 32

One night, as Ian lay in bed, he decided that he was going to do anything he could to get Kendra back. That night, he silently admitted to himself that Kendra was all the woman that he had ever wanted, and still wanted despite their history, and despite the time that has passed between them. He would not let her be 'the one that got away.' She was the mother of his child but more than anything else; she was his one true love, for better or for worse. He finally realized that after all these years, after all the women, and despite the way he treated her, Kendra was, is, and always will be the love of his life. He knew this when he first laid eyes on her in California, he knew this when he took her for granted during the course of their relationship and he felt it after she left him and he bottomed out. Ian knew it all along but this was the first time that he was willing to admit to himself that he was the one that messed up with Kendra. He had finally come to realize the errors of his ways. He realized he treated her badly during their time together. He missed her terribly but he had too much pride and had been too much of a coward to come begging for her forgiveness until so much time had gone by. He tried to get over her with other women but they were not Kendra. When he finally had the courage to contact her because he could not get over her, he went about it the wrong way. Instead of begging for forgiveness and trying to win her trust again, he had threatened her with their child because he was desperate for money. Yet, despite all the years that had passed between them, he was still madly, hopelessly and crazily in love with her.

As Ian thought about how to win Kendra back, he knew it would be the biggest fight of his life. Yet he was willing to try because she represented his ultimate happiness. He knew women of all ages and statuses fell for his charisma. All he had to do was smile his signature, charming smile and talk the talk, and he owned any woman, well, except for Kendra who no longer seemed affected by him. So, he knew if he wanted to get her back, he had to step up his game.

However, to win her back, he had major obstacles to overcome she was happily married, she was madly in love with her husband, she could not stand Ian's guts, he had strong-armed her into giving him money, and she did not believe a damn word he said when he told her he would pay her back. Yet, despite all these obstacles, the fact still remained that he wanted her back. And to win her back, he knew he had to be the man that Kendra needed and a better man than the one she once knew even if it meant stepping back for a while to give her some space.

Chapter 33

Peter and Kendra knew each other to a 'T.' After many years of marriage; they still did not take each other for granted. Usually, when they had a fight, which was rare, each of them would sulk and then hash things out until one person or the other apologized regardless of who was wrong. Throughout their married years, they had never once gone to bed angry at each other. They plucked each other's nerves and snapped at each other on occasions when one or the other was in a bad mood but they usually got over their bad moods before the day was over. Apologies were usually followed by explanations, which were then followed by PDAs, which sometimes grossed their children. The unspoken rule in the Rite household was that no one was allowed to go to bed angry. Not even the children. Kendra and Peter were a perfect example of how to communicate in a relationship. Nothing was off the table. They were secure in the love that they had for each other and their children and so were not afraid to talk about anything. Everyone knew what a tight-knit family they were. That is until Ian slithered his way into their lives.

***

The bond between Kendra and Peter began to crack after Ian first started blackmailing Kendra. For the first time since they had been married, things were strained between them. Unfortunately, this was also the first time that they were not sure how to fix what was off between them. It was unchartered waters for them especially since the strain was not due to an outright argument.

***

The oddness started the weekend of their family trip to Lake George after Peter brought up the issue of the missing money from their joint account, and Kendra's response had been a snappy, lame one, which was followed by an awkward conversation, a quick stiff makeup hug and an even more awkward kiss while the unfinished, unresolved missing money issue hung in the air. Peter had not been satisfied with Kendra's explanation at the time, and Kendra had not been in the mood to be honest since she was determined to handle Ian herself. As a result, their weekend trip felt more like an effort to play 'happy' for the sake of their children. It did not occur to Kendra at the time that Peter would notice the missing money before she had had time to replace it. He usually went over their accounts the third week of the month but as luck would have it, for some inexplicable reason, he had reviewed the accounts much earlier than she had anticipated. If Kendra had thought about it properly, she would have taken the money out of her own personal savings account instead of their joint account but of course the thought only occurred after Peter started asking questions, which forced her to lie because she did not want him involved in the mess that was Ian. She had replaced the money shortly after their weekend trip but by then it was too little too late. Peter had already noticed the discrepancy and more importantly she knew that he knew that she had not been honest about the reason why the money was missing in the first place. She could tell from the disappointed looks that he surreptitiously gave her throughout their stay at Lake George. And knowing Peter, sooner or later, he would want to get to the bottom of the issue at a more appropriate time. Since the weekend of their Lake George trip, every time Kendra caught that disappointed look on Peter's face, she cursed Ian silently. To make matters worse, he had had the nerve to ask for more money after that!

Kendra put on a 'happy' face for the family after Ian demanded more money the next couple of times but the strain of dealing with him on her own while trying to keep Peter out of the fray was wearing on her. Her moods had swung from up to down and vice versa. She had also become very short-tempered and less patient with the rest of her family, something that had not gone unnoticed by Peter. Even Liana had noticed her change in behavior and had once asked Peter "what was wrong with mummy?" A couple of times, Peter had unexpectedly caught her crying in the kitchen when she thought she was alone at home because she had been feeling overwhelmed not just because of the stress of dealing with Ian's demands for money but also because she did not understand why she was redeveloping some 'kind of feelings' for him when he was not even nice to her, and more importantly, while she was still very much in love with Peter. Kendra had brushed off Peter's concern for her with the excuse that she was just overwhelmed with the stress of a project related to work. Peter did not buy the excuse at the time but he had accepted it because he had recognized that she just needed comfort at that particular moment and not probing from him.

***

Kendra knew she was doing a bad job of hiding her situation from Peter. But because she was still convinced, she could handle Ian on her own, she continued to lie to her husband each time he asked her what was really troubling her. As a result, she and Peter walked on eggshells around each other, with him trying not to probe and her doing a bad job of pretending everything was okay.

However, knowing each other the way they did, Kendra and Peter both knew that sooner or later Kendra would have to open up to Peter, and Peter being Peter, would deal with Ian in the appropriate manner in order to protect his family.

Chapter 34

Kendra had not heard from Ian since their last meeting eight months ago. Not a phone call, not an email, not even a text. She was thankful but nevertheless still wondered about him every now and then, and deep down, if she was completely honest with herself, she even missed him a little, which was annoying.

Quite unexpectedly, Kendra found herself trying to understand why she was feeling the way she did for Ian despite her deep love for Peter. She wasn't even sure why or when she started feeling soft toward Ian again. He certainly did not give her any reason to. Besides, she was happy with her life with Peter. He was as steady as a rock and so very loving toward her and the kids. And Ian? Ian had an edge to his personality, which could be quite erratic. He could be the most charming, sweetest, seemingly harmless guy in the planet…or the devil incarnate. Ian also had this air about him, which screamed 'take me or leave me but not knowing me is your loss, not mine.' It was a part of his character, which Kendra had always loved and hated at the same time…that cockiness packaged in a box of charm. And even though Ian was generally not a loud person per se, there was always some kind of drama surrounding him, just by being Ian. Kendra knew that there was no way in hell that she should even be feeling anything other than disdain for Ian especially after the way he had treated her since he bulldozed his way back to her life in such a disrespectful manner. In fact, she still harbored disdain for him. Of that she was certain, except now, there was an added layer of something that was not quite hate or negative…it was more like the creeping of old feelings that she had buried a long ago but this time, it came with an added layer of something unfamiliar, complex, and confusing, and it was throwing her for a loop.

The first couple of years Kendra and Ian were together and so happily in love, he had been a really sweet, simple and romantic guy. Quite the charmer, quite the lover, that is, until the mention of babies. Kendra's heart suddenly did a flip and whatever softness she was beginning to feel, whatever stirrings of emotion she was starting to feel for him suddenly hardened again as she thought about what she went through when she was pregnant with Liana, what she had to do to keep Liana and how Ian had dumped her because of Liana, their child born out of love. Ian did not turn out to be the man she had thought he was when she fell in love with him after she told him she was keeping Liana. He was definitely not father material but if Kendra was honest with herself, she knew that she should not have been surprised at his attitude after she told him she was keeping Liana since he had made it clear to her right from the beginning of their relationship that he was cut out to be a father. But Kendra being a woman, thought that she could change how he felt about children with her love. Instead, he ended up resenting her because she refused to give up Liana and felt that she was forcing him to be a father against his will. But as far as Kendra was concerned, Liana was worth every heartache, torment, and abuse. Liana was her joy and her imprint to the world. She blamed herself for falling in love with Ian but at least he gave her the greatest joy of her life, whether or not he meant to. What she had to do now was to try and control whatever these renewed feelings she was beginning to have for him because he complicated her life in more ways than one. And yet, even as Kendra was talking herself into fighting her feelings for Ian, just a tiny part of her was irritated at him for not contacting her and she was not even sure why.

Chapter 35

Today, mid-morning, as Kendra was settling into her work, Alex, a thirty-something, brown-haired, chubby, Caucasian man of average height who worked at the mailroom of her company knocked on her half-opened office door before coming inside to hand her a regular-size envelope and another slightly bigger one.

"Thanks, Alex," Kendra smiled at him.

"Sure thing," Alex, smiled back before moving on to the next person that had mail on Kendra's floor.

Kendra looked at the envelopes that Alex had given her, trying to gauge for a brief moment who sent her mail before proceeding to open them. The first envelope, the regular-size one, contained a hand-written letter from a client who was very happy with the work that she had done for his company a couple of months ago and was wondering if they could schedule some time to meet so they could discuss another big project. Kendra was happy about the request. Whenever clients extended work with her or acknowledged her previous work with them, it always made her day, especially when they took time to hand-write a letter, a missing art form in itself. Everything was so impersonal these days with technology, she mused as she finished reading the contents of the letter before moving on to the bigger envelope. She opened it to discover a folded note and another smaller envelope tucked inside it. She wondered if it was junk mail. She retrieved the smaller envelope first and opened it. It contained a certified check. She read it carefully. Sure, enough it was a check addressed to her in the amount of $1,000 from Ian. Kendra was surprised, not sure what to make of it. He had actually kept his word this time and was paying her back. She took out the folded note from the large envelope and read it. It simply said: I will pay you back every cent I took from you. I am sorry I used unsavory means to get you to give it to me in the first place. I will send the next installment next month. Thanks for your help, Kennie. His writing was exactly the way Kendra remembered it: very neat and beautifully written. Ian always did have beautiful handwriting and even once considered selling his handwriting as a font, if working in the fitness industry did not pan out for him.

Kendra shook her head as she stared at the note. Since Ian messily re-entered her life, for once, she was not even irritated that he had addressed her as 'Kennie,' instead of her full name when he signed off on the note. As Kendra resumed work with an unconscious smile on her face, her mind drifted back to when she and Ian first met many years ago. Deep down, she was glad to finally hear from him.

Chapter 36

Peter, dressed in a wool hat, thick brown sweater, dark blue jeans, gloves and waist-length black puffer jacket walked in through the front door. It was 6:00 PM in the evening on Saturday in December. It had been snowing outside for the last couple of days and it was cold with temperatures in the low thirties. Peter had just come back from dropping off Liana and her siblings at each of their friends' houses where they were all having sleepovers.

As soon as Peter got inside the house, he made a beeline for the mudroom on the left side of the front door. He took off his gloves and hat and stuffed them in the pockets of his jacket before taking off the jacket to hang it on one of the jacket hooks in the mudroom. He sat down for a moment on the only wooden bench in the room on the opposite side of where the hooks were, to take off his boots, which still had a little snow at the bottom of them. He shook off the snow into the nearby dustbin, knowing how Kendra liked everything neat, before walking into the living room on sock-covered feet to find Kendra. She was dressed in jeans and a yellow hooded sweater and was relaxing on the sofa with a cup of tea and eating raspberry scones that she had bought from a nearby bakery the day before. She had her hair, which was done in tiny braids tied in a ponytail. She was watching HGTV in the living room when Peter walked in. She looked up at her husband with a smile when he entered the living room. He smiled back at her and gave her a kiss on her lips before plopping down next to her on the sofa. She snuggled close to him.

"Hi Honey," Kendra said after the kiss. "How are you? Bet the kids are happy to be with their friends today."

"They are, and I am happy to have some alone-time with my wife," Peter said mischievously.

"Yes indeed. So, what's that I hear?" Kendra cocked her ears smiling broadly and winking.

"Ah! Silence! A rare moment of peace at home…just you and me…me and you…you and me…hmmm…whatever are we going to do about that my love?" Peter asked, pulling Kendra into his arms.

"Well, I could think of a few things," replied Kendra as she began to kiss him again. As they started to get romantic, Peter's belly growled. He had not eaten lunch and had forgotten to have a snack before driving the kids to their friends' houses. Kendra smiled between kisses as she heard his stomach growl.

"Sweetie, can I get you something to eat?" she asked him.

"Not yet," Peter said as he continued to kiss her. His stomach growled again.

"I think you should probably eat something now." Kendra stood up. "We have all day to ourselves since the kids are out, but first let's feed you."

"Ok, thanks my love," Peter responded smiling back at his wife as she started to make her way to the kitchen. He reached for the control while Kendra was in the kitchen. The program she had been watching, and then abandoned when she and Peter started to get affectionate had just ended so he changed the channel to CNN. A few minutes later, Kendra came back with a mug of cappuccino and a plate of more scones. She handed Peter the cappuccino and then put the plate of scones on the coffee table next to him before proceeding to sit back and lean against him again. Peter took a sip of the cappuccino before setting the cup down on the coffee table next to the plate of scones. He took a scone and ate it before taking several more sips of cappuccino. After a while, he set the cup down again next to the rest of the scones so he could put his arm around Kendra as she snuggled more comfortably against him to watch the news with her. Kendra loved it whenever Peter wrapped his arms around her. She always felt safe and loved.

Peter saw Kendra's relaxed mood as an opportunity to talk to her again about what was really been bothering her. Despite the fact that it had been a while since his initial inquiry about their account, Peter was still troubled by Kendra's odd behavior since then. She had become a different person since then and even more troubling was that she had become secretive.

"Kendra, Honey, we need to talk," Peter said lightly after a few minutes of comfortable silence.

Kendra was puzzled. She glanced at him. Though his tone was light, he looked worried. She turned off the television to pay him her full attention. After switching off the TV, she turned to face him fully. His arm dropped from around her shoulders as she did so.

"Peter, what's wrong?" she asked worriedly, though deep down she already knew what this conversation was going to be about. She had been expecting it.

"Kennie, you are my heartbeat. You know that I love you very much," he said, gently taking both her hands in his and staring at her with loving eyes.

"Of course, I know you love me and I love you to infinity, Peter," Kendra replied quietly with a small smile. "Tell me what's got you so worried."

"Us. Whatever is going on between us that we are not addressing. It's time for us to talk about it."

"Yes, I know." Kendra averted her eyes slightly and turned her face away from him. Peter let go of her hands for a moment to gently turn her face back to him before taking her hands in his again. This time she did not turn away. Peter knew when she looked at him directly and that closely, it would be hard for her to lie to him again.

"There's this strange disconnect between you and me. I'm sure you've sensed it too." His tone was quiet, non-confrontational.

"We've both been busy with work, the kids, you know…the usual stress," Kendra replied lightly, not wanting to believe that she and Peter might be growing apart because she was trying to protect him from Ian's shenanigans at all costs.

"That's not what I am talking about but I'm sure you already know that," Peter responded.

"So, what are you talking about, Peter?" Kendra asked trying to stall.

"The weekend we took off for Lake George when I asked you about our account balance. I think there was more to it than the explanation you gave me. I don't think you were helping your sister out. You have not been yourself since that weekend, Kennie."

"Why would you say that?"

"I know you, Kendra. Even right now, I can see that I've hit a nerve. Your tone, your body language, your attitude has shifted. There's something more going on."

"What more could there be? Do you want to call Piper and ask her yourself?" Kendra demanded defensively as she tried to shift from Peter but he would not let go of her hands. He knew his wife too well. He knew when she was not being completely honest but he also sensed panic in her defensiveness. Something was definitely going on but she was afraid to share it with him. He was perplexed. They had always been comfortable talking about anything.

"Kennie, Baby, I know you better than that. I know something is wrong. I am not going to call Piper because you are going to tell me the truth. I am your husband. We've never hidden anything from each other. I love you and I will stand by you no matter what. Talk to me," Peter said firmly but gently. He would not let her back away this time. He needed her to feel safe in telling him what was going on.

"Does it really matter anymore? I've already put the money back. Let's just move on," Kendra responded nonchalantly. She wished he would just let it go. She was handling Ian on her own. Things seem to be going smoothly for now. It had been over a year since she last heard from him when he sent her the first repayment check with a note. After that, he had steadily sent her a check each month. By her estimation, the next repayment was small enough to be the last and she was expecting it in the next month. He had promised to pay her back and then leave her alone for good. So far, he had kept his promise. He had not bothered her in over a year. After the first check that came with a note…there was no other form of communication. All she got was a simple check each month with no additional attached notes. The funny thing was that while she was relieved by his silence, and the normalcy that had returned to her household, somewhat, at the same time, despite herself, she actually missed him a little. She was not exactly looking forward to receiving his last check next month because that would mean there would no longer be any reason for him to keep in contact with her.

"Actually, it does matter. It's not about the money and you know it. Why won't you tell me what's going on?" Peter was trying not to let his frustration show in his voice as he broke into her thoughts.

"Ok, it was not for Piper. I needed to help a friend out. She was in a jam," Kendra lied again. She knew Peter knew she was lying but she desperately needed to keep her family away from her issue with Ian. In a month it will all be over. No more Ian, no more debt to hold them together. She believed him this time when he said he would leave her alone, so no more expectations of him returning to her life for any more reason.

"Well, what kind of jam was she in? Who is this friend?" Peter persisted.

"You don't know her and it's not something I want to talk about anymore. Let's just enjoy our time alone," Kendra said without conviction. She was a really bad liar; she knew she did not sound convincing at all.

"Really, Kendra? Please, don't give me that! When did we stop telling each other the truth? Are we really keeping secrets from each other now?" Peter was beginning to lose his patience with Kendra. One way or another he was going to find out what she was up to. If she planned on leaving him and was taking steps, he wanted to know. He felt their marriage was quite fine, they had always talked about everything or so he thought until Kendra started disconnecting.

"Peter, please don't be angry with me," Kendra said. It was suddenly all too much. Even though it was only a month left before she stopped hearing from Ian completely, albeit by means of a check, at this particular moment, as she looked at Peter's hurt expression, it suddenly dawned on her that she had dragged him into her issue with Ian even though she had been trying to do just the opposite. Clearly, her behavior had changed toward her family and Peter had noticed. Looking at Peter, Kendra realized, she no longer wanted to deal with Ian alone anymore. The worst part of it was that Ian was turning her into someone she did not recognize. It was bad enough that she was beginning to feel soft toward him again, despite his bad behavior but lying to Peter? She had never lied to Peter until Ian slunk back into her life uninvited.

"Then talk to me, Babe. We are a team. Whatever it is, we will handle it together," Peter said, drawing Kendra closer into his embrace. She was the best thing that ever happened to him. She was his everything. He did not want to lose her and he did not want her to be unhappy.

"Okay, Peter. It was all about Ian," said Kendra in a resigned voice.

Chapter 37

"Ian? What about Ian?" Peter sat up straight thoroughly confused. The mere mention of Ian put a bad taste in his mouth.

"He was blackmailing me for a while but things are better now."

"Blackmailing you about what???"

"Liana. He said he would fight to get Liana if I didn't give him money. He demanded fifteen thousand at first…that's where the money from the family account went. And when I thought it was over, he came back asking for more. So, the other times he asked for more, I took the money from my own savings account instead of the joint account so you wouldn't notice. But the last time he demanded money, he said it was a loan and that he would pay me back with interest. He sounded contrite. I did not believe him at first, but one day, last year, the first of many repayments came in the form of a check and an apology for what he did. I am expecting the last payment next month and then he will be out of our lives for good."

"We need get a lawyer; he can't do this to you. He never wanted Liana in the first place," said Peter, angrily. Peter was generally an even-tempered person and it took a lot to make him angry. Ian definitely made him angry. Especially when he threatened his family.

"Peter, I think, it's really over this time."

"Yes, until he comes back asking for more yet again, so don't give me that crap, Kendra. He is a scumbag and you know it."

"Peter, the last time we spoke when he asked for the loan, he actually sounded different. I haven't spoken to him in over a year since then but he has kept his word. He's been sending checks through my office to pay me back…a little bit more than he owed actually. He added a 7% interest. The last repayment is due next month. It is all very impersonal. Other than the first time when he attached a note to the first payment, there has been no other form of communication; no phone calls from him to make sure I got the checks he sent, no additional notes…nothing. I just get a cashier's check and that's it. I think it's really over, this time, Peter."

"Are you sure, he won't bother you again? I still think we need to seek legal counsel and get a restraining order against him for harassment," Peter said, rubbing his chin thoughtfully. He wanted to make sure Ian did not bother them again, and if he tried, he wanted them to be ready.

"Peter, I think we should just leave it alone. It is over. Besides, I don't know how Liana is going to take all this if she ever finds out that Ian used her to blackmail me. I don't plan to tell her what he did but you never know how things will change in the future. Despite everything he did to me, I don't want him to look bad in her eyes. You saw how she reacted when she found out she was adopted."

"We need to take this seriously, Kennie. It's putting a strain on our marriage. For over a year, I've watched you pull away from the kids and I because of Ian. You have become withdrawn. I miss you. I know you felt the distance between us as much as I did. You left me out, Kennie. I thought we were a team." Peter was hurt that she did not trust him enough to talk to him about what she had been going through with Ian.

"I'm sorry for lying to you, Love. I was only trying to shield you from the nonsense with Ian. I really thought that once I gave him the money the first time, he would go away for good. The Ian I once knew was no saint but he would never have blackmailed me either."

"People change over the years, Kendra," Peter said chewing his bottom lips. He needed Ian away from their lives completely. Besides, while I appreciate the fact that you were trying to protect me, I am the one that should be protecting you and the kids. You are my family.

"I know. I am sorry for leaving you in the dark about this, I thought I was doing the right thing," Kendra said wistfully.

"I love you. I am sorry you had to go through all on your own," Peter said, pulling his wife to him for a hug. Kendra felt his strength in the hug. She was happy to be able to unburden herself to him. After a short while, she pulled back slightly while still holding him before speaking again.

"Honey, in my heart and in Liana's heart, you are Liana's father in every way that matters but at the end of the day, she is biologically related to him. When she turns eighteen, I won't be able to prevent her from seeking him out if she wants to. She is already asking questions about him."

"She is?" Peter was surprised. You never mentioned this to me before."

"Yes, she is. I just prefer to pretend that she does not think about him sometimes. Just the other day, while we were in the kitchen making dinner, out of the blue, she asked me what he was like when we were together before I met you," Kendra said as she recalled a conversation, she and Liana had last year. She remembered telling Liana that Ian was a charming man, and she and Ian were once happy together before quickly changing the conversation to avoid discussing him any further.

"Really?" Peter asked curiously. As far as he knew, Liana had not shown any more interest about Ian after she found out that Peter was not her biological father.

"Yes. I just didn't want to think for a second that Liana might want to meet Ian on her own accord, one day."

"I see. Has she talked about him again since your conversation that day?"

"Not is so many words but a couple of weeks ago, she asked me if I had any pictures of him," Kendra said in a small voice.

"What did you tell here?" Peter asked. "Did you show her the pictures of him that you have being saving for her?" Kendra once told Peter that she had kept a few pictures of Ian for Liana, not ever dreaming that Liana would in fact ask.

"I told her that I had a few pictures of him for her and she seemed satisfied though she did not ask to see them."

"Ok. But we still need to get a lawyer to send him a cease and desist letter and a restraining order. He was harassing our family, and it might not be the end, despite what he told you.

"Peter, I don't want to do that right now. I don't want to do anything that will jeopardize Liana being with us or make her resent us because of Ian."

"I don't think that will happen. Liana doesn't even have a relationship with him."

"I know that but she may want to in the future. I don't want her to hate you or me because of how we handled Ian. Please, Peter, he said he would pay me back all the money and leave us alone, and he has been doing that. He even admitted that he was wrong to blackmail me," Kendra said looking at Peter with imploring eyes. She did not add that she was having mixed emotions about Ian too. There was not need to complicate matters.

"Kendra, I'll respect your wishes for now but If Ian contacts you again to threaten you, please, Honey, talk to me. At that point we will have to take legal action, agreed?" Peter asked with quiet determination. He wanted to deal with Ian legally but he also understood where Kendra was coming from. He loved Liana like his flesh and blood and did not want to do anything to push her away. Whether he liked it or not, Ian was actually her flesh and blood and there was nothing he could do about that fact.

"I will, Love, I promise," Kendra said relieved that the air was finally cleared between her and Peter.

"I love you Kennie," Peter pulled her closer and kissed her lovingly before they made love passionately, lovingly and with pure abandon on the sofa, both of them relieved that the burden that had being weighing them down for so long had finally been lifted. They felt closer again. Peter would not let Ian destroy his family. Not in a million years.

Chapter 38

One evening, as Kendra was getting ready to leave her office for the day, she received the last payment from Ian through the office mail. True to his word, he paid Kendra all the money that he had blackmailed her for, including the 'loan' he 'borrowed' from her the last time they spoke.

The last check was accompanied by a note from him that said, Kennie, sorry again for my bad behavior and thanks. Love always, Ian. Kendra was not sure whether she was relieved or disappointed by the simplicity of the note. She did notice however that he said, 'Love always,' wondering if she was reading too much into that.

Kendra read the note one more time, kissed it and then pressed it against her chest before tucking it in her purse as she silently resolved yet again to push her growing feelings for him aside and refocus wholly on Peter. She was glad that she married Peter. In the years that they have been married, he had proven himself to be the man any woman would be glad to call her husband. He made her feel safe, he was responsible, he was even-tempered and he was a good father to the children. Peter was her rock but there was also that 'something' about Ian that was now toying with her love for Peter. She wondered whether it was possible to love two men at the same time. Whatever the case, she decided that she was not in love with Ian again. She was in love with Peter and for this reason, she chose to believe that whatever feelings she was redeveloping for Ian, it would eventually fade away.

Chapter 39

It was a crisp cool October morning and daylight had not yet broken. Fall weather was already showing signs of a very cold winter to come later in the year. Lately, Ian had been having trouble sleeping because he was consumed with thoughts of how to win Kendra back. Now was one of those times. He had tossed and turned for most of the night and by 3.30 A.M, he gave up trying to get any decent sleep. He tossed aside the bed covers and paddled bare feet to the bathroom to brush his teeth and wash his face. After that, he went to the kitchen to make a mug of green tea with lemon and grab an apple from the fridge. He leaned against the counter as he ate and drank standing up, trying not to think about Kendra.

He had not heard from her in a year. Not even after he repaid her all the money that he owed her. Not that he was expecting to hear from her again but still, he kind of hoped that she would at least call to say she got the last payment…and just so he could hear her voice. Surely, she must still feel a little something for him? They had history and even shared a daughter. They were bound together for life by that every fact. Kendra was in his blood. All he ever did these days was think about her. He thought about her all the damn time! Other women, time, and distance certainly did nothing to quench his feelings for her. Maybe he had not treated her well when they had been together but that was in the past. He was a changed man now. He was doing very well at his job, he was healthy, he was reading books on how to treat women with respect and how to be a good father to a teenage daughter he had never met. He was going to therapy to help him understand and overcome his fear of fatherhood, and how to deal with his feelings about his how his father treated him when he was a kid. Hell, he was even taking yoga classes in addition to his usual health regimen so he could be more centered. And God knows he hated yoga. But he would try anything to become the man that he wanted Kendra to be proud of, and the father he hoped, perhaps one day in the future, that his daughter might want to know…if that was at all possible. And yes, also because he still hoped Kendra would give him a chance despite the fact that she was married to another man. He wanted her back. She consumed his being and it had become an uphill battle to get her out of his head.

By the time Ian was done eating in the kitchen, it was still only 4.15 AM so he went back to the bedroom to change into some workout clothes before heading outside for a run. He had been too stupid to see it before but now he realized that Kendra was the best thing that had ever happened to him. He was a better version of himself with her in his life. He did not want her to be the one that got away.

Chapter 40

One Saturday afternoon in April, Kendra was shopping for groceries at a Key Food grocery store when she got an unexpected call on her cell phone. Her heart skipped a beat when she saw Ian's name on her caller Id. She had not heard from him in since he sent the last of her money to her, and even then, it was still not the same as actually speaking to him. She wondered what he wanted.

"Hello Kendra, how are you?" Ian's familiar raspy voice filtered through the phone pleasantly.

"I am well, thanks. Yourself?" she asked politely making sure to put a distance between them by her tone. She was not sure if she was glad to hear his voice after such a long time or she was nervous that he was about to start asking her for money all over again. She had been doing quite well trying to put her confused feelings for him aside since he re-entered her life, until, well, now. Just hearing his voice again…

"I am very well…you know, just working and staying healthy," Ian's voice broke into her thoughts, unaware of how she was feeling.

"Glad to hear that. So, what's up? Why are you calling me? You don't owe me any more money…you paid me everything back and then some ... thank you by the way, for keeping your word."

"I told you I would pay you back. I want to do right by you, Kendra."

"Well, thank you, nevertheless for keeping your word. I am surprised that you actually did after all the drama."

"I am a man of my word despite what went down between us. Life is good to me again. I was wrong to treat you the way I did when we were together and after I came back to your life. Again, I am sorry," said Ian, honestly.

"Apology accepted." This was the first time that Kendra actually felt his sincerity. It warmed her heart to think that the man that she first fell in love with so many years ago was still there somewhere deep inside. However, on the other hand, all the effort that she had been putting into forgetting about him and refocusing on Peter disappeared just by hearing his voice. "So did you call to apologize or was there something else?" asked Kendra without malice though her voice was still formal.

"I'm not calling to harass you or to threaten you, I promise. I just thought I'd say hello, you know, and check in on you."

"I see. Well, I'm fine. Things are going well."

"Good to know," Ian said, his tone indicating there was something more on his mind.

"Look, Ian, it was nice of you to call, apologize, check on me, and all that, but I have to go," Kendra said, correctly reading his tone but not sure if she wanted to know where he was going with his comments.

"Oh, I understand. I just needed to tell you something important."

"What is it, Ian?" Kendra asked, wondering if he was sick or dying.

"Look, Kendra, I know I said I won't bother you again," Ian said seriously.

"Yet, here you are, calling me again," replied Kendra, as a matter of fact.

"Believe me, I tried to stay away from you. I spent last year trying to figure out my feelings for you since we became, hmmm…re-acquainted, shall we say?"

"I see. And?" prompted Kendra, not sure where he was going with this declaration but a part of her was curious to hear.

"Well, I still have very strong feelings for you, believe it or not," Ian said, suddenly getting emotional. "I am still very much in love with you, Kendra. Days go by with thoughts of you in my mind, and I've asked myself, 'what is happening'? I've tried to stay away from you. But it is hard. You are in my head, on my mind, in my thoughts, in my heart, all the time. I can't help it. I miss you. Despite the possibility that you will reject me again, which I know I deserve by the way, my heart said I should follow it to where it leads me, 'cause it is always true to me. I know you are married. I know you are happy. And I know you probably hate me after what I did to you and I don't blame you. But the heart wants what it wants and I go where it leads. Kendra, my heart keeps leading me to you. Nothing has changed despite the years gone by. You still own my heart."

"Ian, I don't know what to say…" This was typical dramatic Ian, throwing her in for a loop. Since he reappeared in her life, he had never been clear about how he truly felt about her. He blackmailed her, and then he was sorry. Then the next minute, he appeared to still have feelings for her, but then, he gave the impression that he still harbored a lot of resentment toward her for leaving him. And when he claimed he still wanted her, he immediately brushed it off lightly as though he was not really serious but just wanted a reaction from her. And yet, despite all that, deep within her, if she was honest with herself, a part of her was relieved, maybe very glad to hear him say this to her aloud in a serious and sincere tone. In a twisted kind of way, though unbeknown to Ian, she was glad that her feelings, though undeclared to him, were not isolated or invalidated.

"Kennie, Kennie, Kennie, I just can't quit you!" Ian said more boldly, breaking into her thoughts. He sensed that she was not fighting him but absorbing what he was saying. Otherwise, she would have shut him down with a quick caustic retort.

"Ian, I have to go. I am doing some grocery shopping," Kendra said instead. Suddenly, she did not want to continue this conversation any further. It was becoming quite dangerous. He was affecting her more than he should and she was feeling guilty entertaining any unholy thoughts about him when she was happily married to Peter. And no, she was not about to tell him how she was feeling about him or that she had been somewhat annoyed that he had actually stayed away from her despite the fact that she had demanded that he leave her alone.

"Kennie, Babe, did you hear what I said? I am trying to tell you that I still love you…I want you back…and I want Liana too," Ian's voice broke into her thoughts.

"Ian Sharp, I am happy with my family and my life now. But I'll say this to you, thank you for giving me Liana. She is the best thing that ever happened to me."

"I am a changed man, Kendra. I'll prove it to you, Just you wait and see," Ian's voice was heavy with emotion.

"Still doesn't change the fact that I am happily married to Peter, Ian."

"Kennie, I mean Kendra ... " Ian paused, winning her back and showing her that he was a new man was going to take a lot of patience and determination. He had already re-entered her life on the wrong foot but he was willing to put in the work to regain her trust. He needed her back in his life. He was only half a man without her in his life.

"Ian, I have to go home to my family, Peter expects me to be on my way home by now."

"I just need you to understand where I am coming from...I still, I still, still..."

"Still what, Ian???" She was not interested in listening to him anymore...she did not want to be inadvertently pushed into revealing how he was affecting her. "Ian, please, you've already taken a lot out of me. Besides, now is not the time for this type of conversation."

"I understand. It's just that..."

"I need to finish shopping and go home. Peter is waiting."

"Ok, Kendra," Ian said quietly. Damn this Peter. He had his family, the one that he could have had with Kendra if only he had not messed up. No man should ever ask a woman to choose between him and her child. The woman would always pick her child. It was not even a contest. He had been too stupid to think she would do that for the fourth time just to be with him. Everyone had a breaking point. She reached hers when he demanded that she get a fourth abortion or lose her relationship with him...the one he still wanted with her. The one that he was now willing to go to any lengths for, to have her back in his life again. As far as Ian was concerned, Kendra was still his woman and Liana was their daughter. He wanted Kendra and Liana. He wanted what Peter now had; the family and the love of his life, and he was willing to fight for it no matter what it took.

"Have a good life," Kendra's voice interrupted his thoughts as she hung up the phone, not waiting for his response.

"Have a wonderful day my love until we are back together," Ian said quietly into the dead phone line. This time, he would wait for her to come to him no matter how hard it was for him to stay away.

***

Kendra waited a few minutes for Ian to call right back to demand why she hung up on him. Surprisingly, he did not. She shook her head as she tried to make sense of the conversation. As she finished shopping, she wondered again what was up with Ian before paying the cashier at the register and heading out to her car. Could she dare hope that he had really changed? He sounded honest. And even if he was sincere, there was nothing she could do about it. She was not ready to open up about her feelings for him or explore it any further. She was not about to hurt Peter or break up her perfect family.

Chapter 41

Kendra did not tell Peter about her conversation with Ian despite her promise to him that she would if he ever contacted her again. These days, she was not even sure how she was feeling about Ian anymore. She felt like her heart was in an invisible tug of war between Ian and Peter.

Ian had been an important part of her past; he was her first true love. And whether she liked it or not, he was the biological father of Liana, a constant and admittedly, wonderful reminder of a life that she had once shared with him. If there was one thing that she did not regret, it was Liana. Ian had been horrible to her when she told him that she was pregnant with Liana. He left her with the difficult choice of leaving their relationship because of Liana but she was grateful to him nevertheless for bringing Liana into her life.

Indeed, Ian owned Kendra's heart in more ways than one. When she and Ian were together in the past, they had loved each other passionately and fought each other equally hard. Sometimes they could not stand each other but at other times, they simply could not get enough of each other. Frankly, they had a lock on each other's hearts, in spite of the other women that Ian had cheated on Kendra with, when they had been together. Much as they tried to deny it to themselves and to the world, the fact was that time, distance and other women did nothing to break the hold that they had on each other...not even when they tried to shake it off. It just was. So, despite the years gone by, and Ian's unpleasant behavior since he had unexpectedly and messily invited himself back into Kendra's life through blackmail, there was still something that she felt for him that wasn't hatred or anger. While a part of her did indeed resent him for rejecting their daughter and blackmailing her, Ian was still the drug that she simply couldn't resist.

This was not to say that she did not love Peter because she did. She loved Peter fiercely, protectively. Peter exuded quiet confidence. He was safe, he was responsible, he was a good father and he was a good husband. Not once did she regret marrying him. But Ian? Ian was, well, unpredictable. Once upon a time, he had been her mad, crazy love. He had pulled her in and turned her into a woman. In the past, they lived in their own universe with their own special language. And from the way things were going now, Ian was still an adventure; you never quite know what to do with him, yet you can't quite let go.

After Ian's declaration about his feelings for her a few days ago, something changed in Kendra. She felt his sincerity. He was different on the phone. His declaration of his feelings for her was clean, simple and unloaded. He wanted her back even knowing that she and Peter were a family. Ian, the complicated, great first love of her life who knew her like no other, still wanted her back after all these years and despite everything that had happened between them. For Kendra, this meant that getting rid of Ian in order to preserve her marriage to Peter was not going to be as easy as she thought it would be because in spite of what she had told herself, despite all outward appearances, and notwithstanding her great love for Peter, Kendra knew that if she was completely honest with herself, she had always wished that Ian would come back and claim her and Liana. And finally, he did just that.

So, for the first time since Ian resurfaced back into her life, notwithstanding her great love for Peter and the fact that she wanted to go back to the safe, comfortable life she shared with Peter and their family, Kendra silently admitted to herself that she still had a soft spot in her heart for Ian and maybe, just maybe, even more than a little love left for him. In spite of everything that Ian had done, he was still her Ian…

Chapter 42

Peter and the rest of the family had just returned from a ten-day vacation in Spain and Morocco. A few days after they arrived from vacation, Kendra and Peter enrolled the twins, Ryan and Easton, in summer camp to occupy them for the rest of the summer. As for Liana, who was now seventeen, she was growing up to be a very responsible young adult. She had just graduated as the valedictorian from her high school and was set to study medicine in the fall at Stanford University in the West Coast. She wanted to become a neurological surgeon. This summer, before heading off to college, she was going to be working in one of the medical research labs at New York University helping out the PhD students as an intern. Though Peter and Kendra were nervous about Liana going off on her own to college far from them, they were nevertheless extremely proud of the woman she was becoming. As Kendra watched her family blossom and grow, she was filled with gratitude and happiness…except when she had quiet moments alone and thoughts of Ian crept into her mind.

She had not heard from him since their last phone conversation when she was grocery-shopping two years ago. After that phone call, she had resolved yet again to put distance between herself and Ian, more especially so, because of her increasing feelings for him. Kendra had expected that the complete dissociation from Ian would do the trick and free her mind of any more thoughts of him as she forced herself to concentrate on her life with Peter, which had returned to normalcy in every way that counted; the kids were being kids with growing pains and Peter was, well, still Peter; steady as a rock and unwavering in his unconditional love for her. She had everything many women wanted, a wonderful core family, a flourishing career, wonderful friends and support of her extended family. Kendra knew she was supposed to be content about life and for the most part, she was. She certainly did a good job of acting content. She just needed Ian to be out of her head and her heart.

Unfortunately, much as she tried, Kendra was not winning the internal battle of forgetting about Ian. Every day since she last spoke to him, she thought of him. She could not believe that he actually just stopped reaching out to her especially after he had made it clear how much he still cared about her. Since they last spoke there was not a word from him. Not a whisper, not a hang-up call, not a text…just nothing. It bothered her more than she cared to admit to herself. She was even somewhat unhappy about it. The nerve of him to disappear just like that after he claimed to still love her. Liar! Not that she expected anyone to do anything about it. And of course, she was not going to speak to Peter or any of her friends and family about it. She wouldn't dare! She was not even supposed to feel conflicted. After all, she wanted him to leave her alone. Well, he did. Even though she had sensed from the tone of Ian's voice when they last spoke that something was different, she was surprised by her own emotions; she was not quite ready to let go of Ian. And since she couldn't very well reach out to him unless she was prepared to lose everything, she was determined to continue life as usual with Peter and her family, minus Ian.

And so, Kendra went about putting on the act of her life, not showing even a hint of the inner conflict she was feeling about Ian. And nobody suspected a thing because Peter never mentioned Ian again since the last time, he and Kendra discussed him. Even Liana no longer inquired about Ian. Ian was now a non-factor in everyone's lives. Everyone but Kendra, that is. And of course, she was not going to admit that to herself, much less to Ian. Too much was at stake. Clearly, he had come to terms with letting her go when they last spoke. So, if anything was ever going to happen between them again, it would be because she, Kendra, initiated it, at the expense of Peter and the rest of her family. The next move was clearly hers. It was complicated. She had too much to lose. Without being present in her life, Ian was still very much in her space …still taking up a piece of her heart and she was not quite ready or willing to let go of him.

Chapter 43

Ian was doing well professionally and personally. He no longer owed anyone money, his social life was thriving, he had reconnected with good friends and he was feeling alive again. He still dated but it was never anything serious because his heart still belonged to Kendra. However, he was slowly coming to terms with the fact that perhaps he and Kendra would never be together again and maybe it was time to make peace with that and try to move on. After he had made one final honest plea to her for them to get back together, she had not flat-out reject him but she had not been annoyed at his declaration that he wanted her back either, nor did she respond with her usual caustic remarks. In fact, she had sounded almost receptive. This had given him hope that maybe there was still a chance for them however far-fetched it might seem. But as the days turned into weeks, which turned into two years, that hope had slowly faded until it no longer consumed him. He still thought of her often but he knew he needed to let her go for his sanity and peace of mind. Maybe one day, he would find someone else who could restore his faith in love and make him feel the way Kendra had made him feel. Maybe one day, he would be able to remove Kendra from his system completely. Maybe. Just maybe.

And then there was their daughter, Liana. Ian thought of her all the time. Not knowing his daughter openly but knowing she was alive left a hole in his heart. This was a strange feeling. This was something he could not explain, considering that once upon a time, he did not even want to be a father, not even to a child conceived with Kendra in spite of his love for her. Yet, something changed along the way over the years. He was not sure how deeply his emotions ran, until one day, when he and Julian were at the home of a mutual married friend, Paul, for a barbeque. During their visit to Paul's house, one of Paul's kids, Amber, who was five years' old, accidentally spilled juice on Ian's pants. Ian had not been offended but had laughed it off as "kids being kids," causing Julian and Paul to look at him strangely knowing how he felt about children. At that point, Ian had confessed about feeling very attached to Liana even though he had never met her. All he knew was that he felt responsible and protective of a child that he had never met and loved her fiercely in a strange kind of 'I'll do anything for her' way. He was just as surprised by his feelings for his daughter as his friends were. Unexpectedly, fatherhood had done a number on him and he liked the feeling of being a father.

He wondered what Liana looked like now at seventeen. He knew her birthday and celebrated it each year either with his best friend, Julian or by himself even though he had no relationship with her. He had respected Kendra's wish to keep his distance from Liana. He had promised Kendra that he would stay away, and he did in order to prove to her that he was indeed a changed man and no longer a threat to her. Not knowing Liana was the biggest struggle of his life, as he had had to talk himself over the years into not pursuing a legal avenue, which would have allowed him to have contact with his daughter. So, he did the next best thing he could; he had paid investigators to give him regular information about Liana as she grew up over the years. He had also watched her at school during breaks and on other occasions. But he did so from a distance without the knowledge of Kendra or Liana. It was the only way he felt he could be a part of Liana's life. He stopped using investigators last year and had not seen his daughter since. His daughter was now old enough to decide whether she wanted to meet him on her own. He hoped one day, they would be reunited and actually get to know each other.

Ian knew for sure was that he would be eternally grateful to Kendra for fighting him hard against giving up Liana when she was pregnant with her and when he was adamant that he did not want a child. At the risk of losing everything, she fought for their daughter when he was not willing to. For that alone, he would always respect Kendra and she would always be the woman that he measured other women against. As for his daughter, Liana, he was so grateful to have her even though they did not know each other. Just knowing she was on this earth due to the love he and Kendra once shared was a blessing in itself. For both their sakes, whether they realized it or not, he would continue to better himself. He lived for the day he got to know his daughter and they had a real relationship.

Chapter 44

Peter's brother, Kenneth Rite and his wife, Julia, were throwing a big Christmastime holiday party on Saturday, the week between Christmas and New Year. They had invited the extended Rite family and their spouses to London to spend the week with them. Also in tow for the London holiday trip were Kendra's sister, Piper and her husband, Cain, as well as their parents, Leon and Kate Mercury. Everyone was in a festive mood and looking forward to a much needed holiday break in London. Family gathering complete with the usual bickering, harmony and all-around love that came with it were part of the deal. It was a time to breathe and relax.

Peter and his family were the last to be leaving the United States for London to join his brother and the rest of the family, who had all arrived in London three days earlier for the party. The time to travel could not come fast enough, especially for the twins, now thirteen, who had been looking forward to spending time with their cousins in London. They had been impatiently asking Kendra and Peter every chance they got "why they were not traveling the same time as Grandpa and Grandma or Aunty Piper and Uncle Cain???" Kendra had explained to them several times that they had to wait for Liana to come home from school so they could all travel to London together. She had made sure that everyone's schedules were coordinated so that they could travel together as a family. Liana had declared during a phone conversation with Kendra that she was "an adult now and could travel alone," and would catch up with everyone in London, but Kendra had insisted that she travel with them. As far she as concerned, Liana would always be her 'little girl.' And so, Liana indulged her and agreed to travel with the family.

***

Thursday, travel date, finally arrived. They were flying out to London later that evening at 8.45 PM via JFK airport and were scheduled to arrive in London at 8.45 AM London time. Kenneth would pick them up from the airport. Liana arrived home for the holidays from college the day before and was also looking forward to the trip. While she was just as excited as her siblings about spending time with her extended family, she was equally excited about meeting up with two of her friends who lived in London and hanging out with them.

By 6.30 PM Kendra was hurrying everyone into the car. She knew how long security checks could be at the airport and wanted them to be there on time in order to avoid missing their flight. She had helped the twins and Peter pack the night before. Liana of course did her own packing at the last minute.

After a lot of yelling and nagging, by 6.45 PM everyone had piled into their SUV. It had heavily snowed two days before so certain spots on the road were still quite slippery, though effort had been made by the agency in charge to clean up the roads. As predicted, within twenty minutes of the trip to the airport, members of the Rites had gotten into an argument. Ryan and Easton started arguing about a game they were playing until Liana, fed up with their yelling, quieted them down by promising to take them with her to shop for sneakers when they got to London. That did the trick, and within minutes they were back to their game until they nodded off to sleep, allowing Peter and Kendra to listen to music in comfortable silence, on Kendra's favorite rock station while Peter drove. As they drove, Liana busied herself on her iPhone texting, taking selfies and snapchatting with her friends.

"Liana, please wake up Easton and Ryan, we are going to arrive at the airport in fifteen minutes," Peter said over his shoulders to Liana as he made a turn to the right side of the road.

"Ok, Dad," Liana said, and shook her siblings until they groggily woke up.

"Are we there yet?" Ryan asked sleepily.

"Almost," Kendra answered as she fiddled with the music button in the car to turn off the music.

Just as Peter was about to make another turn, he noticed a truck bearing down on them a split second before it hit their car from his side of the car. The next thing Peter knew, their car was somersaulting several times in the air until it finally crashed upside down to a stop. Peter felt severe burning sensations all over his body as he tried to look around for Kendra and the kids. He was barely conscious and could not open his eyes nor could he move his head much. Part of their car was completely damaged and he was pinned inside. More importantly, he could not hear any sound from the twins, Liana or Kendra. He needed to know they were okay. He needed to hear his family's voices. He heard what sounded like a leak of water from the car and felt drips of what turned out to be fuel on his body from either the truck that struck his SUV or from his SUV. In his near unconscious state, Peter could vaguely hear cars screeching to stops around him, sounds of footsteps, strange voices and screams as people yelled.

"Somebody call 911 quick!! Let's try to pull them out, there is a lot of smoke coming from the car!!" a man's deep voice shouted.

"Shit! There are children in the car!!!" screamed another hoarse male voice.

"Two children and a male driver pinned to their seats," another person said urgently. "We can't wait for the emergency crew, let's try to get them out now!!!"

Peter felt his SUV rattle and shake in an apparent attempt by people trying to turn the car to an upright position.

"Let's try to pull them out," huffed another deep male voice to three other drivers who had stopped to help as they managed to get the car to an upright position with Peter still pined inside by his seat belts and the car door from the impact of the truck that had hit the SUV. The twins were still inside unconscious.

"Hurry! I got one kid; somebody get the other kid…and the driver…we got to get the driver…I smell fuel on the guy…oh crap!!! Oh shit…everyone RUN NOW!!!!" said the person as the other truck that hit the Rites burst into flames a short distance from them and Peter's car started sparking flames. The four helpers, one holding Easton ran as fast as they could from Peter's car. They heard a loud boom. They barely made it toward a safe distance as they fell to the ground. After a few minutes, a couple of the good Samaritans turned around to see that Peter's car had burst into flames with him and Ryan still trapped inside.

***

By some miracle, Liana and Kendra were flung out of the SUV as it somersaulted. Liana landed a short distance from her family's SUV where Peter and her sister, Ryan had been burned to death. She hit her head against a small rock on the roadside when she landed on the ground and was knocked completely unconscious. She suffered internal injuries including severe kidney damage, a broken right hand and leg, broken ribs, burns from the heat intensity of the burning SUV nearby and several cuts on her body from flying metal pieces and glass from the shattered windshield of their SUV. She was bleeding everywhere. She was barely alive by the time the paramedics got to her and whisked her quickly to the nearest hospital, St. Anne's hospital in Queens, where she was immediately prepped for surgery.

***

Kendra was thrown several feet from Liana but much closer to the burning truck that had hit their SUV. She suffered a deep gash on her back, several wounds on her body and face, a broken right leg, dislocated right shoulder, broken ribs, several cuts on various parts of her body, smoke inhalation from the fumes of the burning truck and severe burns. One of her kidneys was also completely damaged. She landed near a small pile of ice, hitting the left side of her head, which led to a gash. By the time the paramedics got to her, she was already unconscious. They rushed her in another ambulance to Pacy Hospital, another nearby hospital, which was ten minutes from St. Anne's, where she was taken to the emergency ward.

***

Easton, who was also taken to Pacy Hospital, the same hospital as Kendra, was in better shape than the other members of his family. Thanks to Jeffery, one of the random strangers that had rescued him just before the SUV exploded in flames, he was the least hurt of everyone. He had suffered from slight smoke inhalation, which thankfully, was not as severe as the other members of his family, a broken left arm and mild concussion. He was treated for smoke inhalation and his arm was put in a cast.

***

Peter was barely conscious as his car burst into full flames with him and Ryan in the car. The last thing on his foggy mind as smoke inhalation and severe burns overwhelmed him was Kendra and his children as he tried to scream 'my family' but no sound came out of his mouth as death finally claimed him and Ryan in a gulf of flames. The charred bodies of Peter and Ryan were transported to the Coroner's Office for processing and identification.

Chapter 45

Kenneth Rite, a chartered accountant by profession, was a tall man; six feet and three inches in height. Like his younger brother, Peter, he had an athletic built, was dark-skin in complexion, wore wire-rimmed glasses and preferred his hair very closely shaven, almost bald. Facially, they looked very much alike and one could not deny they were related. Kenneth and his Caucasian British lawyer wife, Julia, a tall, slender, brunette, lived with their two children, Brea, who was ten years old and Jude, who was eight years old, in a cute low-rise, two-story, five-bedroom, Victorian house in the suburb of Fulham, a middle class neighborhood in London, which was about fifty minutes by car from Heathrow airport. Kenneth was scheduled to pick up Peter, Kendra and their kids, from the airport. They had opted to stay with him and Julia at Kenneth's insistence. As he had mentioned to Peter when they had spoken on the phone a few days ago, they had plenty of room in the house, and Julia and the kids would love it. His in-laws and parents, who had arrived three days earlier, were already settled at Hotel Novatel London West.

***

Julia was sound asleep and tucked under the blankets when Kenneth woke up at 6.30 in the morning to take a shower and get dressed. Both he and his wife had taken two weeks' vacation time from work to spend time with the family. Brea and Jude who were on holiday from school were also sound asleep. Julia, Kenneth, and the kids had spent most of the last two days showing their extended family much of London and just having a good time while they all waited for Peter and his family to arrive.

By 7.00 AM, Kenneth was in the Kitchen having a cup of sugarless green lemon tea. He planned to leave the house at 7.30 AM to pick up Peter and the others. As he stood drinking his tea by the kitchen island, he glanced out the window and noticed it was drizzling outside as was typical of the British weather. His mind briefly drifted to a time when he and Peter were kids playing soccer outside in the rain when they lived for a time in the Bahamas as army brats. Kenneth smiled to himself. He missed the simple days just hanging out with his younger brother. They had been very close growing up but as they grew older, the business of life and geographical distance made it harder to stay in daily contact. As a family, they still tried to maintain close ties by phone, Facetime, Skype and many visits but it was not the same as being in the same country much less the same city. Though Kenneth spoke to Peter often, he had not seen his brother in person in almost eighteen months, a particularly long stretch for them and so he was looking forward to seeing him this year. He took another sip of his tea and glanced at his watch. It was 7.28 AM. He set his half-finished tea down on the counter, searched the small dish on the island where he or Julia usually dropped their house and car keys, and retrieved the keys to his black Audi.

As he was turning the keys on door from the kitchen, which led to the garage where his car was parked, the phone rang in the living room. Kenneth hesitated. He glanced at his watch again. It was 7.35 AM. He had planned to leave the house five minutes ago. He wanted to be at the airport on time to pick up Peter and the others. The phone continued ringing insistently and Kenneth could see that Julia, who was the heavier sleeper of the two of them, was not going to pick up the extension in their bedroom so he hurried back to the living room and picked up the handset.

"Hello?" asked Kenneth in his deep measured voice, while standing, hoping this was going to be a very short call.

"Good morning is the Rite residence?" a female voice with an American accent asked gravely.

"Yes, it is. Who is this?" Kenneth's asked quietly, partly suspicious about this being a marketing call, and partly concerned by the serious tone in the person's voice. Why would someone call so early in the morning?

"My name is Dr. Grant from the Coroner's Office in Queens, New York, I understand that you are listed as a secondary emergency contact for a Peter Rite…"

"Dr. Grant, why are you calling me?" Kenneth cut her off more out of anxiousness than out of rudeness, suddenly wishing with a sinking feeling, and perhaps even irrationally, that he had just ignored the ringing phone and let whoever was at the other end leave a message on the voice mail.

"There's been a car accident that led to two fatalities and severe injuries involving…"

"I'm sorry, did you just say fatalities??" Kenneth asked in a shaky voice barely able to maintain his balance standing up as the impact of her words sunk in.

"I'm sorry, Mr. Rite, we were not able to get in touch with his wife … "

"Is my brother alive?" Kenneth asked, though instinctively, he knew the answer to his question as he sat clumsily on the edge of the nearest sofa next to the side table where the phone base was.

"Is Peter Rite your brother?" asked Dr. Grant.

"Yes," Kenneth whispered, getting up and then sliding to the floor in despair.

"I'm sorry to do this on the phone but … "

"Is Peter alive?" Kenneth asked again. He needed to hear the words. He needed to be sure. His brother had always been a fighter. This Dr. Grant, whoever she was, must be mistaken.

"I'm sorry, Mr. Rite. I wish I could say otherwise but he is dead," responded Dr. Grant, painfully. She did not mention Ryan to him. It was bad enough that this difficult conversation was taken place over the phone several miles away.

"My brother is dead?" he repeated as though he did not quite understand her.

"Yes," Dr. Grant said, quietly.

"What about Kendra? Is she all right?"

"Who?" asked Dr. Grant, confused. The emergency vehicles had brought in the charred bodies of a young teenage girl and an adult male. Debris from the car wreck, which revealed barely visible prints on the identification cards, showed that the adult male was a Peter Christian Rite and the young teenage girl was a Ryan Emerson Rite, not a Kendra Rite.

"His wife, Kendra Mercury Rite," said Kenneth.

"No, no body belonging to a Kendra Mercury Rite was brought in," Dr. Grant said carefully. She had purposely not mentioned the second body of Ryan Rite that had been brought in along with the body of Peter Rite. She was hoping to give him the rest of the horrible news in person. She could feel the pain of this man through the phone.

"You said fatalities, Dr. Grant...plural," Kenneth said in a pained voice breaking into Dr. Grant's thoughts, "I don't understand...how many people died in the accident?"

"I'm sorry, Mr. Rite, we need a family member here for body identification," Dr. Grant said instead. "You are the secondary emergency contact we have."

"I will take the first flight out there today of course but Kendra Rite, his wife, is the primary contact," Kenneth prayed that at least she was okay. "Have you tried to reach her?"

"We were unable to get in touch with her, that's why we called you, sir," replied Dr. Grant patiently.

"Are my nieces and nephews, okay?" Kenneth asked, hoping for some positive assurance.

"Your nephew and nieces?" Dr. Grant asked.

"Yes, Liana, Easton and Ryan. I spoke to my brother a few days ago; he gave me his itinerary. He was supposed to be travelling with the whole family. I was on my way to the airport to pick them up when you called," Kenneth said sadly.

"I see. I'm sure the hospital they were taken to would give you a call, Mr. Rite,"

"So that means they are all ok, right?" He desperately needed to know that Kendra and the children were alright. He knew the full pain of losing his brother, and telling the rest of the family the devastating news would hit everyone really hard, especially his parents.

"Mr. Rite, I'm so sorry but I can only confirm that the body a Ryan Rite was also brought in from the same accident," Dr. Grant said. She was hoping to tell him the rest of the sad news when he arrived in New York but this would not be the case.

"Oh, God, no!" Kenneth could not help the tears. The thought of not seeing his beautiful niece broke his heart. She had been so full of life. She had been the extrovert of the twins. He also knew Easton was going to miss his twin sister terribly. They had been very close.

"I'm so sorry, Mr. Rite," Dr. Grant said again, sad for him.

"Thank you for informing me, Dr. Grant. We, the family will be in New York with the first available flight." Kenneth said before hanging up.

Chapter 46

Kenneth went to the living room and sat on the floor with his head on his hands crying for a long time for the loss of a brother that he had loved and protected his whole life. He could not imagine his world without Peter. And then there was his sweet niece, Ryan. It was all just too much. How in God's name was he going to break the news to his parents and the rest of the family?

"Oh God! No! No! No! No! No!!! God, why???!!! Why did this have to happen to my family? Why? Oh, why???" he screamed loudly, tears running down his cheeks as he clutched his head and made loud gulping, hiccupping sounds.

"Ken, love, what's wrong??" Julia, dressed in a dressing gown, asked as she came rushing down the stairs in a panic. She had woken up a few minutes earlier and was brushing her teeth upstairs when she heard her husband's cries. She rinsed her mouth hurriedly and ran downstairs, making sure to check the kids' rooms momentarily to be sure that they were safe and sound before running downstairs to the living room.

Kenneth looked at his wife sadly. He had not heard her come down the stairs in his grief. He looked at her, unable to speak, tears streaming down his eyes.

"Honey, you are scaring me. What's wrong?" Julia asked him again, taking her husband in her arms as she sat next to him on the floor and cradled his head while he sobbed unto her chest.

"Ken, what happened?" Julia asked worriedly. She had never seen her husband like this before.

"Peter and Ryan…they are, they, they are gone!!"

"What do you mean, gone?" Julia asked incredulously.

"They are dead!" he sobbed. "I just got off the phone with the Coroner's office in Queens. They need someone to officially identify their bodies."

"What!" Julia cried. She could not believe what she was hearing.

Ken looked at his wife sadly and she saw the truth in his eyes and they both began to cry again in each other arms.

"Oh my God, I am so sorry, baby. I know how close you and Peter were," Julia as she cried with her husband. She felt his pain.

***

Two hours later, Julia and Ken were still seating on the floor, spent from crying when the phone rang again. Julia picked up the phone. It was from Piper, Kendra's older sister. She was a slender, beautiful dark-skin woman, five feet six inches tall with the same similar eyes and nose as Kendra. She had turned fifty earlier in the year. She wore her hair in tiny braids. Like, Kendra, people often thought she was several years younger than her age. Her husband, Cain, a Caucasian man from Lyon, France, was eight years her junior but people often thought he was older. Piper was often the calm one the family and the voice of reason whenever the family had any arguments.

"Hello, Piper, how are you?"

"We need to go back home, now!" Piper sounded like she had been crying.

"I understand," said Julia sadly.

"So, you got the news?" Piper asked.

"Yes. Kenneth is devastated. He is sitting here with me. I can't believe Peter and Ryan are both gone…"

"Wait! What???!!" Piper screamed.

"Wait a minute, you didn't know?" asked a puzzled Julia.

"Oh, no!" Piper replied sobbing on the phone as she spoke. "I got a call from Pacy Hospital telling me that Kendra was in serious condition from a car accident…I didn't know about Peter and Ryan!"

"Oh, my goodness," Julia said. "This is just terrible. Any news about Easton and Liana?"

"I haven't heard anything yet. Can I speak to Kenneth?" asked Piper, tearfully.

"Yes, hang on a moment," Julia responded and then handed the phone to Kenneth who was still sitting on the floor beside Julia with his head bowed down and his hands on both cheeks. "Honey, it's Piper on the phone."

"Hi Piper," Kenneth said hoarsely.

"Kenneth, I am so, so sorry about Peter," Piper said soothingly, despite the loss of her niece, her worry about her sister, and her anxiousness about the status of her nephew and other niece.

"Thank you, Piper," Kenneth responded to his in-law. "Any news about Kendra?"

"Yes, I was just telling Julia that Pacy Hospital contacted me about her. I don't know anything about Easton and Liana yet."

"Please God, let them be ok, two deaths in one family on the same day is more than enough," Kenneth said, sadly.

"Yes. I pray they are ok," Piper added.

"What about your parents?"

"We were together, getting ready to come to your place when I got the call. We are making plans to go back to the US on the first flight tomorrow," Piper said, unhappily.

"Yes, of course. I have to speak to my parents after I hang up with you and then make arrangements for the earliest flight to US as well…if not today, then tomorrow," Kenneth said in a tired voice. He felt spent from crying. He knew he needed to be strong for his parents and everyone else. Their beloved Peter and sweet Ryan were gone…just like that.

***

Peter's family was in a lot of emotional pain after hearing about the deaths of Peter and Ryan. They had been a very close family and could not wrap their heads around the fact that their son and his daughter were gone and the rest of his family were fighting for their lives when they should all be celebrating the holidays and family time. Kenneth was in charge of his parents' emotional well-being even though he was also in pain himself. Julia did her best to support her husband the best way she could.

Not Quite Imperfect

***

Kendra's parents, Leon and Kate Mercury, were beside themselves with worry for their daughter and overwhelming despair over the loss of their son-in-law, Peter and granddaughter, Ryan. Overnight, they had aged ten years as a result of the tragedy that happened to their daughter's family. Piper had the extra job of making sure that they were okay after receiving such devastating news. She was grateful for the support of her husband, Cain, since she had the burden of being in charge of her parents' welfare and making sure that Kendra and her surviving kids were okay.

***

Liana's Uncle Kenneth and his wife cancelled the holiday festivities that they had been planning and flew to the US the next morning on Virgin Airways at 7.15 AM, which was the earliest available flight they could find. Piper, her husband and the rest of the extended family had flown back to the US on two other early flights. Their moods were decidedly somber.

***

The Rites and Mercury families arrived in the United States within an hour of each other. They all met at the baggage station at JFK. They greeted, hugged, consoled each other, picked up their suitcases and then huddled for a few more minutes to decide how to split themselves between the hospitals where Kendra and her kids were admitted.

Piper, Cain, Kate, Peter's father, Andrew and Peter's step-mother, Samantha went directly to Pacy hospital where Kendra was admitted, while Kenneth, Julia, Liana's grandfather, Leon, his mother, Laura and her husband, Ellington, went straight to St. Ann's hospital to see Liana and Easton.

Kenneth and Piper planned to go the Corona's office in the next couple of days to identify Peter and Ryan's bodies.

They both knew no one else in the family could handle that horrific task, so it was up to them.

Chapter 47

Piper and the others arrived at Pacy Hospital within forty minutes. It was an average sized, brick building hospital three blocks from a busy freeway. Several medical personnel were buzzing in and out helping people. Others were taking short breaks. Piper went to one of the six receptionists' desks in the main areas. Each desk was attached to the next and separated by a glass partition. The others waited anxiously, a short distance away from the receptionist while Piper tried to find out more information. There was an agitated, Caucasian, woman in her mid-seventies, dressed in a pair of wool pants, a thick gray sweater and a wool coat, already talking to the receptionist trying to get information about her grandson who had been admitted for a gunshot wound the day before so Piper had to wait until the receptionist was done with her. After the receptionist, a Chinese woman, in her mid-fifties, finished helping the woman, she gestured for Piper to come forward before turning her attention to a note pad on her desk to jot something.

"Yes?" she asked Piper without preamble while pushing stray strands of gray and black hair from her face. She looked tired and somewhat annoyed and did not even bother to look up as she spoke to Piper in a slight Chinese accent, while she finished jotting what she was jotting.

"There was an accident yesterday and my sister, Kendra Mercury Rite was admitted here. We got a call from a Dr. Logan Dean from this hospital concerning her. Can you tell me what floor she was taken to, please?" asked Piper, choosing to ignore the receptionist's bad attitude. She was too concerned about her sister to care about this receptionist and her nasty demeanor.

"We had three accidents come in yesterday, all very serious, all emergencies," the receptionist said without emotion. "I need more information."

"Look, there was a family that was involved and two vehicles: a truck and an SUV. The family driving the SUV was the Rite family. My sister, Kendra Mercury was in the SUV along with her family. The driver, her husband, Peter, and my niece, her daughter, Ryan all died and so did the truck driver. I was told my sister was badly injured and brought here last night. Someone, a Dr. Logan Dean from Pacy Hospital, this hospital, from this address, called me. So, I am asking you again, what floor is my sister???" Piper asked authoritatively. She was becoming impatient. She wanted to see her sister and a doctor who could explain her condition. She was not in the mood to deal with some bored, robotic receptionist who was clearly, in her opinion, in the wrong profession.

"Hold on a second," the receptionist said as she checked her computer screen and then dialed a number on her desk phone. After the call, which took a few minutes, she turned to Piper. "Please take a seat, the doctor will be out in a moment."

After a few minutes, one of the doctors came to meet Piper and the rest of the family. She was a medium built, light skin, African-American woman in her mid-forties, about five feet seven inches tall with a pretty face. She spoke briefly to the receptionist behind the partitioned glass window before coming out to the lobby on the other side to speak to Piper.

"Hello, I am Dr. Logan Dean, the doctor on call when the patient was brought in last night," she said politely with a kind smile while extending her hand to Piper for a handshake. "I was the doctor that called you about Kendra Mercury Rite."

"Good morning, Dr. Dean," replied Piper shaking her hand. "How is my sister? Can we see her?" Is she going to make it?"

"She suffered severe degree burns, a completely damaged kidney, internal injuries, broken ribs and broken limbs. She will have to undergo a series of surgeries. We may also need to remove part of her spleen. In order to perform these surgeries, we need authorization from the family for the go-ahead," said Dr. Dean.

"When is the first surgery?"

"We need to do a partial splenectomy this afternoon and remove the damaged kidney and then schedule the other surgeries. As for her broken limbs, specifically her leg, after we work on that, we will put her on a cast. Eventually she will need physical therapy after the cast is removed. We might also need to perform plastic surgery to cover the effects of burns on her body but that will be up to her. Luckily, her face was spared of burns but there are scars on her face from debris when she landed on the ground after she was flung from the car. There was also a gash that ran from her left ear to her neck, which we have stitched up."

"My poor sister. I know Kendra. She is a fighter. I know, she'll pull through," Piper said hopefully, glancing furtively at her mother and the other family members as they hovered anxiously in the background while waiting for Piper to come back with news from the doctor. Piper wondered how she would relate the news without worrying her mother more than she already was.

"She is lucky to be alive," said Dr. Dean. "We will take good care of her and give her the best treatment possible," she added reassuringly.

"Can we see her please?" asked Piper holding tightly to her purse as though it was a source of comfort.

"She is still in intensive care unit, so at this time, as per the hospital policy, we cannot allow you into the room but you can visit her through the room next to the one she is in. It separated from her room by a glass partition. I advise that you be very quiet and very brief, and not more than two people at a time," replied Dr. Dean. "She is on the third floor, ward 3C."

"Thank you, Dr. Dean."

"You are welcome. I will give you a few minutes to consult with your family and then the receptionist will tell you how to get to the ICU where your sister is."

"Thanks again, Dr. Dean," said Piper. "What about my nephew, Easton Rite?"

"He was treated by my colleague, Dr. Oliver Blue," said Dr. Dean just as a tall, thin, blond haired Caucasian man in his thirties approached them. He looked a little frazzle, as he ran a hand through his full hair. He wore glasses and had kind green eyes. "Speaking of which, here he is, he'll fill you in on your nephew," she smiled kindly at Piper, touched her arm in a comforting manner and then walked away. Piper watched her say something to Dr. Blue as she walked past him, before disappearing through a set of double doors down the hall.

"I'm Dr. Blue, I'm sorry, I didn't come out here to see you sooner, I was in surgery," he said in a calm, cool voice, which belied his outward frazzled appearance. He shook Piper's hand.

"I'm Piper, my nephew, Easton Rite was admitted here yesterday from an accident," she said as she shook his hand.

"Yes. He suffered a mild concussion, smoke inhalation and a broken left arm. The good news is that they brought him to us before irrevocable damage could be done to his system. Plus, since he is young and in good shape, he will recover well. We put a cast on his broken arm to help him heal. The cast will remain in place for the next six weeks, after which we will prescribe physical therapy. We prefer that he remain in the hospital for the next couple of days for observation."

"Thank you. When can we see him?" asked Piper, relieved that at least Easton would be fine. She hoped the same for Liana. She planned to see her after they leave Pacy.

"You can see him now, he is on the second floor, room 202B. The receptionist will give you directions on how to get there when you are ready."

"Thank you, Dr. Blue."

"You are welcome," he said before leaving her.

Chapter 48

St. Ann's hospital where Liana was receiving treatment was just a short distance from Pacy hospital where Kendra and Easton were. It was a much larger hospital than Pacy. There were many patients-care activities going on when Kenneth Rite and the other members of the Rite and Mercury family, arrived. Like Pacy hospital, there were several receptionist desks in front of the visitors' lobby. People were pacing, seating and/or milling around with anxious, worried, happy and/or tired expressions on their faces. New patients were brought in while others were leaving. A husband was rushing his pregnant wife who was about to give birth into the hospital just as Kenneth and the others arrived. After the commotion surrounding the arrival of the pregnant woman calmed down, Kenneth walked up to the first empty receptionist desk he saw while the others waited anxiously as he spoke to the receptionist. The receptionist was a thin, mustached, dark-skinned, African American man, not more than his mid-twenties. He looked up with a smile as Kenneth approached him.

"Good morning, my name is Kenneth Rite, my niece, Liana Rite, was admitted here yesterday. She was injured in a car accident."

"Ok. Do you remember who called you?" asked the receptionist, Sheldon, in a deep pleasant voice, which did not match his looks.

"Dr. Abbot Reed called my sister in-law, Piper Mercury Roche. She is my niece's aunt. Her mother, Kendra Mercury Rite is Piper's sister. Kendra and her husband, my brother, Peter Rite were also involved in the accident and could not be reached, so he called Piper Roche. She is not here because she is at St. Ann's inquiring about her sister, Kendra. I am here to see about my niece, because my brother, Peter died in the accident. My name is Kenneth Rite. Here is my ID card," explained Kenneth as he fished into his right pocket to bring out his wallet and pull out his ID card, which he handed to

Sheldon, hoping that it was enough to talk to the doctor in charge and see his niece.

"Ok, please give me a moment," said Sheldon as he took the ID card, examined it and then handed it back to Kenneth. He clicked a few keys on his computer, scrolled down the screen, paused for a few moments, pressed a button on his phone and then said something into the handset before looking up again to address Kenneth. "Dr. Abbot Reedberg was the doctor on call for that case yesterday. He will be with you shortly, please take a seat."

"Thank you," responded Kenneth and then went back to join the other family members who were pacing back and forth anxiously as they waited for news about Liana.

Finally, after about ten minutes, Dr. Abbot Reedberg, the doctor in charge of Liana's case walked in. He was a partially bald, Jewish man, clean-shaven and in his mid-sixties. He had kind green eyes, was about six feet tall and a little on the chubby side. He was wearing a white coat and a stethoscope around his neck. He glanced at Sheldon as he approached the lobby area and Sheldon nodded in the direction of Kenneth and the rest of the family.

"Mr. Kenneth Rite?" he asked as he reached the group.

"Yes, that's me," Kenneth replied stepping forward to shake Dr. Reedberg's hand as everyone else immediately gathered around Dr. Reedberg, anxiously.

"Hello Dr. Reedberg. How is my niece? How serious are her injuries?" asked Kenneth, trying to sound strong for the sake of the family while inwardly he was in as much a bag of nerves as the others.

"Will she make a smooth recovery?" asked Leon, Liana's maternal grandfather, before Dr. Reedberg could respond.

"How soon will she be released?" asked Julia, Kenneth's wife just as Dr. Reedberg was about to say something.

"When can we see her? Where is she? How serious are her injuries? Everyone was speaking at once, until finally, Dr. Reedberg put up both his hands to silence them. He understood, how they felt. He was used to these types of reactions from families inquiring about loved ones.

"The good news is that she is alive even though her condition is graded as 'touch and go,'" Dr. Reedberg said calmly, soothingly.

"What exactly do you mean by 'touch and go' Dr. Reedberg?" asked Kenneth trying not to sound pessimistic. He did not like the sound of 'touch and go.' That did not sound like good news to him.

"We had to operate on her immediately even without family consent. We finished operating on her three hours ago. She is in intensive care unit at the moment recovering. We managed to repair major damages to her system, however…"

"Well, that's good news, Kenneth, right Dr. Reed?" interrupted Laura, Liana's paternal grandmother, with a hopeful glance at her son, her shoulders visibly relaxing. She was still in shock about losing Peter so she needed to know that a part of him, Liana, her granddaughter was still alive.

"However," continued Dr. Reedberg, pausing for a moment, she…"

"However, what, Dr. Reedberg? She's what?" This time it was Kenneth who interjected tensely as Laura held tightly unto his arm, holding her breath.

"Well…"

"Yes, Dr. Reedberg?" It was Leon's turn to interrupt him. Again, more out of anxiety than rudeness.

"One of her kidneys was completely destroyed from the accident. We took it out of her body. The other one was severely damaged and is barely functional to her body," said Dr. Reed patiently. He did not take offense to their interruption when he spoke because he could see that they were worried.

"What exactly does that mean for my niece? What are you trying to say, Dr. Reedberg?" Kenneth asked pointedly.

"She is going to need dialysis or a transplant," Dr. Reedberg said gravelly.

"I don't want my grandchild to depend on dialysis for the rest of her life. She has suffered enough loss and pain," Leon said in a broken voice.

"I understand," said Dr. Reedberg, "but there is also the option of a kidney transplant to consider."

"How does the transplant process work?" Julia asked crossing and uncrossing her arms, and then fiddling with strands of her hair, unnecessarily. She understood why Leon did not want Liana to go through dialysis at such a young age but she was also realistic enough to know that it might also be the only option if they did not find a match for Liana.

"Well, she will have to go through a match process for compatibility if you decide to go with the transplant option. We will run several tests, which will include the blood test type, tissue typing, cross-matching, antibody screenings, urine and a bunch of other tests. For women potential donors, we will also include gynecological screening as well. The process will be very thorough to ensure that a right match is selected and that her body does not reject the transplant. Of course, it is advisable to list her on the National Kidney Registry."

"I understand, Dr. Reedberg. Please let me speak with my family members to see decide what route to take. I am sure we all want to help Liana."

"Of course. Please also assure them that people can live a long, healthy, normal life span with just one kidney so if they choose to donate, they should not be concerned about that. Most patients usually prefer to undergo the kidney transplant option but the choice is up to the family and if they get a donor match. Also, best to check family members and relatives for a donor before searching outwards."

"Yes, I understand," Kenneth replied, chewing his bottom lip.

"My poor granddaughter. Dr. Reed, is she awake? Can we go see her now?" asked Laura sadly. She felt her heart reaping at the immense pain her grandchild was going through.

"Has she spoken since she was brought in?" asked Julia.

"She was unconscious when she was brought in, yesterday. She woke up briefly before we prepped her for surgery and said "Dad," before the anesthesia took effect."

"Well, how long before we can go see her…can we see her now?" inquired Laura again.

"Not at this particular moment since she is still in intensive care. In a few hours, you will be able to visit with her but not more than two people at a time. The nurse will come and take you to her."

"Thank you," said Kenneth, trying to sound calmer than he felt inside.

"And please, do think about what route you want us to take with the Kidney situation…it is important that we move on this quickly."

"Ok. I will discuss the issue of kidney donation with my family and tell you what we decide," Kenneth said again, putting his arm around his mother as she held unto him for support. He could feel the weight of everything that's happened to the family within the last couple of days taking its toll on her. She lost a son and a granddaughter, and the other granddaughter was in serious condition. Kenneth knew he needed to support his mother as best as he could. He was all she had now.

"Please note that I have not had a chance to talk to Liana about this as she is not yet in stable condition. It is also rather too early to tell her about her the details of the accident. We don't want to discourage her healing process with any tough news just yet. Let's give it some time before telling her what happened that led her to the hospital," advised Dr. Reedberg referring to what happened to her family.

"Of course. We plan to wait for a while," Kenneth responded as the others nodded their heads in unison.

"I will discuss this with her after I get a decision from the family and then you can all consult again with her to be sure you are all in agreement with the next course of action. Again, it is important that I know sooner rather than later so we can begin a method of treatment quickly," Dr. Reedberg stressed.

"I understand, Dr. Reedberg," Kenneth replied, completely understanding the need to keep Liana in the dark for the moment about Peter, Ryan and her mother, as well as the kidney replacement decision.

"The mental road to recovery is going to be a very long one and she is going to need a lot of support and patience. If you have any further questions, I am reachable," Dr. Reedberg added as his beeper went off.

"Thank you," everyone said.

"Excuse me, please, I have to tend to another patient," Dr. Reedberg said, nodding politely to the group before walking away.

"Well?" asked Leon immediately after Dr. Reedberg walked away. "What do we do now? Do we agree that it is best to go with a kidney donor? I am happy to get tested."

Yes, that's best. At least one of us should match, don't we agree? I am happy to test first." Everyone but Kenneth was speaking simultaneously in both hopeful and anxious tones, as they immediately volunteered to be tested.

"Calm down everybody," Kenneth eventually said in a soothing voice. "I do agree that a kidney replacement is probably the best option for Liana, but we also have to discuss this with the rest of the family, Piper and the others before making a concrete decision.

***

After a family meeting, everyone agreed to withhold the news of Peter and Ryan from Kendra and Liana until they were safely on the road to recovery. Kenneth and Piper were also chosen to handle important decisions for the rest of the surviving Rite and Mercury family.

Chapter 49

Peter's family were staying at his home in Brooklyn Heights while Kendra's family were staying in New Jersey with Piper. For the most part, everyone hovered around St. Anne's and Pacy hospitals, splitting time between both hospitals where Liana and Kendra were admitted. As many of them as the hospital staff would allow, slept in the waiting room while praying and hoping that Liana and Kendra pull through.

***

Easton who was treated and released from the hospital after a couple of days was at home with Andrew, his paternal grandfather, while Kate, his maternal grandmother was at the hospital. They were taking turns taking care of him whenever Piper, who had taken some time off work, was at the hospital or funeral making arrangements. It was Piper who broke the news to him about the accident and the deaths of his dad and sister. He volunteered to test for a kidney for Liana. Dr. Reedberg agreed that it was safe for him to test. Unfortunately, he was not a good match, as he did not meet all the criteria that would have made him a perfect kidney donor for Liana.

When Piper told Easton about Peter and Ryan, she also explained to him in the kindest way possible that it was best not to mention what happened to his father and sister to his mother and Liana until they got out of the hospital. He tried not to cry in front of the adults but eventually the thought of never seeing his father or sister again became all too much for him. He became more quiet than usual and barely ate or spoke to anyone. He missed his twin, Ryan and his dad, Peter, terribly, and he desperately wanted his mom and Liana to be back to normal and well again. He wanted the familiarity of how things were before they went to London. He wanted to play and squabble with Ryan and speak the secret language that only he and his twin sister knew. She had been the more extroverted one of the two of them and she was extremely protective of her Easton, even when they fought. They had that special twin connection that only twins understood.

Piper and Kenneth took Easton to the hospital a few times to see his mother and Liana, but he was only allowed to briefly visit each time because everyone was concerned about how seeing his mother and sister is such serious semi-conscious conditions, would affect him.

Chapter 50

Between visitations, Kenneth, Julia and Piper were also running around making funeral arrangements for Peter and Ryan. The combined funeral services of Peter and Ryan were expected to take place in three days at Pittman Funeral Home in Brooklyn. A few of Peter's former clients and a few close friends were invited. The plan was for everyone to wear white since it was agreed that they would remember Peter and Ryan's lives as gifts that the surviving family members were lucky to have enjoyed while they were alive and so instead of mourning their departure, they would celebrate them at the funeral.

***

The funeral took place without a hitch. Everyone invited was in attendance. The only ones not in attendance were Liana and Kendra because they were still at the hospital and were not yet informed of Peter and Ryan's deaths for fear that it would hamper their recovery process. Easton tried to be strong without the presence of his immediate family during the funeral but his pain was obvious to everyone, nevertheless.

Chapter 51

Unfortunately, though everyone agreed that a kidney transplant would be the best option for Liana, the search for the perfect donor match was harder than they had anticipated. None of them were considered good matches to donate a kidney to Liana without possible complications. Kendra was out of the question because she only had one good kidney. Besides, the family had decided not to tell her about Liana needing a kidney until she was in stable condition and on the way to recovery.

Chapter 52

Today was the first time that Kendra had been fully conscious since the accident. Before today, she had been in and out of consciousness for very short periods of time. At such times, she was usually very groggy and unable to make full sentences. The doctors had performed a series of surgeries on her since she was admitted more than a week ago. Her scars were healing slowly but nicely, and her brain and memory functions were almost back to normal. The doctors had put her broken leg in a cast after fixing it and they told her family that she would need mental and physical therapy after she was released from the hospital. Dr. Amita Davis, the doctor on call, was checking her vitals when she woke up.

"Where am I?" Kendra asked, using her left hand to rub her bandaged head as she tried to orient herself to her environment. She could not lift up her right hand properly and she felt pain in every part of her body.

"Hello, Kendra, you are at the hospital, how are you feeling today?" Dr. Amita Davis responded, turning her full attention to Kendra as she pushed her glasses to the top of her head. She spoke in a clear, pleasant voice with a hint of Indian accent. She was a tall, slender Indian woman in her mid-thirties with long black hair, which she tied in a bun. She was dressed in a white coat over her slacks and a checkered shirt.

"The hospital?" Kendra asked slowly. Her speech was still weak but the doctors had warned her family that when she regained full consciousness, this was to be expected for a short time mostly because she was still in pain and had not had a proper conversation with people in days since she had been in and out of consciousness, until now.

"Yes," said Dr. Amita Davis gently. "Do you remember what happened?"

"Not really," Kendra replied, trying to jog her memory.

"You were in an accident," Dr. Davis was said carefully struggling for the right words. She and the other doctors in charge of Kendra's case had decided to wait until Kendra was out of the woods before informing her about the full impact of the accident that led her to the hospital because they wanted to make sure that she was fully stabilized first.

"Yes, yes, the accident, Kendra said tiredly struggling to remember the details, "well, no, not really…I vaguely remember that … that I was in the car with my husband, Peter, and our kids, fiddling with the music when Peter suddenly swerved the car avoid a truck that came from nowhere and then…then…nothing. I don't remember anything after that." One minute she was adjusting the music in their car while Peter was driving, and the next minute she was sailing in the air and then nothing. Just blackness.

"You are lucky to be alive. You are very lucky," said Dr. Amita. She did not want traumatic news about the accident to hamper Kendra's recovery. "You've been in and out of consciousness since you were admitted but I think you will make it through.

"How long have I been at the hospital?" Kendra asked in a soft voice.

"You been here for a little over a week now."

"Oh my God!" cried Kendra, weakly, her body racked with pain as she tried to speak louder. "Where is my family? Are they ok? Peter, the kids…I need to see them … I want to see my…"

"Kendra, please try not to worry too much, your daughter is recovering at St. Ann's hospital," replied Dr. Davis.

"Wait, what do you mean, she's at St. Ann?" Kendra implored slowly in a quavering voice, afraid of what she might hear.

"Well," Dr. Davis hesitated, "first we need you to get better, you have been responding well to treatment, we'll…"

"What about the rest of my family? Peter, Easton, Liana, Ryan?" asked Kendra again, fear gripping her heart. Peter and her kids were the foundation of her existence. She could not stand it of anything bad happened to them.

"Kendra, I am going to give you dosage for your pain, you have to let yourself heal," interrupted Dr. Amita, firmly but kindly. She wanted to reduce Kendra's stress level and get her to focus on her healing before anyone told her more about her husband and child.

"I need to know about my family!" Kendra said anxiously, wanting to get up from her bed to find out about her family but still too weak and in pain to move.

"I understand but first we need to take care of you," replied Dr. Amita as she injected the IV that was hooked to Kendra's arm with some medicine. After a few minutes, as Kendra was still struggling to seat up, the medicine took effect and Kendra collapsed back on her bed and dozed off.

Chapter 53

Usually, on most days, if the weather was good, Ian would wake up between 4:30 AM and 5:00 AM to go for a morning run before getting ready for the day. After he got back from his run and got dressed, he would have a cup of sugarless green tea lemon and grab a piece of fruit for breakfast before heading to work. Once the train, on his way to work, he usually read about sports on his iPhone or listened to music. In some ways, he was simple in the daily choices that he made. Ian lived by the mantra; the less choices you have, the less complicated life was.

Unfortunately, in the last nine days, Ian did not keep his routine. He virtually disappeared from society because he had been home, sick with the flu and was basically shut out from the rest of the world. Julian and a couple of his other friends had called to check on him when they did not hear from him during the first two days of his sickness. He told them that he was sick with the flu and just needed to rest without disturbance. He did not want visitors or any calls. No TV, music, radio, games or Internet-surfing either. He needed complete rest. And rest he did. During this time, all he did was sleep, rest and drink as much fluids as he could per doctors' orders, until he was finally recovered enough to resume work and get back into the swing of things.

Finally, today, Ian was happy to be going back to work again. He was walking to the train station three blocks from his apartment building when his cell phone rang. He glanced at the caller's name. It was Julian. He hadn't spoken to Julian in such a long time.

"Hey, Bro, how are you feeling today? Ready to get back to the real world?" asked Julian jovially in his deep voice. Julian, an only child was of mixed race with a Caucasian father, a retired engineer, whom he was very close to, and a deceased African-American mother. Julian was two years younger than Ian. He and Ian met when they were teenage boys of fourteen and sixteen at a pick-up basketball game on West Fourth Street in the Village in Lower Manhattan. They hit it off immediately, becoming more like brothers as they grew up. Like Ian, Julian, an employment lawyer, was athletic and tall at six feet three inches. And like Ian, he had always been a 'chick magnet,' even now at 50 years old. Again, like Ian, he did not care for the marriage part of a relationship with even with the right partner. However, unlike Ian, Julian had no reservations about settling down with his girlfriend of ten years and their son, Rusty, who was eight years old. He knew he was very lucky to have met the right woman, Adrianne, who like him, did not want to be married but was happy to settle down in a relationship without marriage papers.

"I am much better…eager to get back to the grind of things!" Ian responded as he walked briskly to the train station narrowly avoiding bumping into a young, black, slender woman with workout outfit and earphones attached to her ears as she was jogging with her dog in the opposite direction of him but on the same side of the sidewalk. She gave him a quick apologetic smile but did not slow down her pace. Ian turned around for a minute to appreciate her butt as she jogged away, while still on the phone with Julian, this time with a slight smile on his face as they chatted.

"Listen, Ian, I know I should have mentioned this to you a few days ago when I first saw the news on TV, but you've been out of it with the flu and I was not even sure if it mattered to you anymore, one way or the other," Julian said, his voice suddenly serious, "but Bro, I was wondering if…"

"What are you yammering about, Jules?" cut in Ian as he reached the subway station on 125th Street to catch the number 2 train. He was using the nickname everyone close to Julian addressed him with.

"Sorry, my man. Anyway, so I know you said you and Kendra no longer keep in touch."

"Kendra? Why are you bringing up Kendra out of the blue?" asked Ian, perplexed. Since he told Julian that he was respecting Kendra's wishes and keeping his distance, they basically stopped talking about her. Ian believed that the less he talked about her, the easier it would be to stop thinking about her.

"So, when was the last time you heard from Kendra?" asked Julian, ignoring Ian's question about why he was suddenly talking about Kendra.

"It's been quite a long time since Kendra and I last spoke. I stopped counting after a year. As I told you before, I promised her that I would respect her wishes and keep my distance and I have," Ian replied, trying to sound unaffected by not having Kendra in his life. Lord knows it took a lot of will power to stay away from her. She had been pretty clear to him the last time they spoke that she preferred he stayed away from her and Liana. He wanted to prove to her that he was a changed man and do as she requested even if it meant not having her or their daughter in his life…sort of. He still planned to resume seeing Liana again from a distance, unbeknownst to Kendra. He had not checked on Liana since she turned seventeen, but lately for some reason, he had been having an overwhelming urge to see how his daughter was doing. He planned to see her sometime this week…from a distance of course, and in secret. Kendra did not need to know about it and neither did Liana. "Jules, why are you asking me about Kendra all of a sudden?

"Did you see the news last week?"

"There's news all the time but you and I both know that I have been out of commission because of the flu. And you know as well as I do that, I don't even watch television much, except to catch the weather or watch sports. I only listen to the news briefly in the morning before work…if I have a little time…too much negative information for my taste," Ian said as a matter of fact. "Better to stay away from all the crap."

"Well, there was an accident just over a week ago," Julian said slowly. He heard the rumbling noise of the train on Ian's side of the phone as he spoke.

"And?"

"It involved Kendra's family," said Julian in a low voice.

"You are going to have to speak louder, Bro, I can't hear you…the train, which I just missed, is drowning your voice,"

Ian said loudly as the train picked up passengers and then left while Ian was still standing by the clerk's booth to finish speaking to Julian. He needed to add value to his MetroCard anyway. "The next train will here in eight minutes so talk fast. What were you saying?"

"I was saying Kendra and her family were in a bad accident last week."

"What!!?" Ian asked in a shocked voice, his good mood turning serious. What did you just say?"

"Kendra and her family were in an accident. Check the news almost two weeks ago…they admitted Kendra to Pacy Hospital and Liana to St. Ann's."

"Liana and Kendra…are they ok?" Ian asked in a low voice, with a sinking feeling, his heart skipping a beat. He was almost afraid to hear Julian's response.

"I am not sure but she lost her husband and…"

"Actually, I need you to call my job and tell them I can't come in today, after all because of a family tragedy," Ian said feeling distraught.

"No problem. What else can I do for you?" asked Julian, concerned. He knew Ian and Kendra's history. He also knew his friend enough to know how much he still loved Kendra. Even when Ian was not particularly nice to Kendra, Julian knew without a doubt that she was special to Ian, so he knew that her accident was affecting him more deeply than he was letting on, on the phone.

"Nothing…what hospital did you say they were admitted to?"

"The papers said that Kendra was admitted to Pacy and Liana to St. Ann's in Queens," said Julian as he searched for more information about the accident on his laptop at work. "Here is the address."

"Hold on a minute," Ian said as he fished for something to write on from his leather backpack while wedging his cell phone between his left shoulder and ear so he could free both hands.

"Sure," said Julian.

"Ok, what's the address?" asked Ian again. He scribbled the addresses of the hospitals on the back of a magazine that he had in his bag as Julian dictated them to him over the phone. "Thanks. I am on my way there now."

"Ok, Bro," Julian said. "Let me know when you get there. My schedule is light today…I can leave work early today and meet you later if you want. Call me when you get to the hospital and let me know where I can meet you."

"Thanks Jules," Ian said and hung up.

Chapter 54

After Ian hung up with Julian, he quickly went online on his phone while he waited for his train and typed in the keywords: 'Rite, Mercury, Kendra, accident,' for news about Kendra's accident. Several headlines regarding the accident resulted back. Ian read the first item on the list of results: a delivery truck driver from a private company called Logan's Warehouse who was traveling between Boston and New York on a triple shift, had apparently drifted off to sleep at the wheel of his truck and hit the Rite family, killing Peter Rite and his daughter, Ryan Rite. His wife, Kendra Rite and other daughter, Liana Rite were badly injured in the accident and were rushed to Pacy and St. Ann's hospitals respectively as ambulances from both hospitals arrived on the scene within minutes of each other. Their son, Easton Rite, Ryan's twin brother was the luckiest of the victims as he managed to escape with just a broken arm and slight smoke inhalation, thanks to the brave heroes who were driving by when the accident occurred. The heroes had immediately stopped and pulled Easton out of the car just before the truck and the SUV exploded. Unfortunately, the driver of the truck, described as a hard-working father of three from Poland, also lost his life. The Rite family had been on their way to JFK airport where they were set to travel to London to begin a family vacation. Peter Rite was...

Ian felt a jolt in his heart as he read about the death of Peter and his daughter, Ryan. When Julian told him that Kendra lost her husband and daughter, the impact of the news did not sink in until now after reading about it online. He did not know Peter. He had only spoken to him once on the phone many years ago, and it was not a pleasant conversation. Hell, he had been jealous and resentful of the guy when he was alive because Kendra had moved on with her life, with this guy. Nevertheless, this same Peter seemed to have been a good man and a good husband and father. Because of this, Ian was strangely sad that his romantic rival, whom he did not know, and his daughter, Ryan, also Kendra's daughter, were now dead. Ian ached for Kendra. He felt her loss. He wanted to comfort her. He wanted to make her pain go away. His heart hurt for her. He wanted to bring her back to happy even if not with him.

And as he thought of his daughter, Liana, the daughter that he had never officially met and was slow to love but finally did love wholeheartedly from a distance, Ian felt even more overwhelmed with gratefulness because she survived but also sad for her because she lost her sister and Peter, the man that raised her as his daughter, when he, Ian failed to step up. He thought about the first time he spoke to Liana on the phone many years ago. He had not been particularly nice to her but then he had also been a different person too. Perhaps this was a second chance for him to do right by his daughter as a father if she would let him. Ian looked up at the overheard electronic screen board at the station that displayed the train schedules; the next train would arrive in two minutes. He refilled the value of his MetroCard at the clerk booth, swiped the MetroCard through the turnstile and then climbed up the stairs, two at a time just as the train arrived.

***

The journey to Pacy hospital took Ian about an hour. He took the number 2 train to Times Square Station, got off and then used the shuttle train to Grand Central Station where he transferred to the M train, which took him to Queens. He planned to take a cab from Pacy hospital to St. Ann's hospital to see Liana after he visited Kendra. As Ian sat in the train by the corner, near the conductor's area, he felt an overwhelming grief for Kendra, anxiety for Liana, the daughter he did not have a relationship with, and regret for the way he had treated Kendra in the past. Further complicating matters was the fact that all his feelings for Kendra that he had worked so hard to suppress, came rushing back stronger than ever after her learnt about her accident. This was the woman he had truly ever loved and would truly ever love till the day he died regardless of whether they ended up back together or not. He simply could not imagine his world without her existing in it. Even if she never took him back, he would be happy just knowing that somewhere in her part of the world, she was happy and healthy with her children and even with someone else, painful as that would be. He wanted Kendra to be all right. He wanted their daughter, Liana to be all right too. He wished he could help in some way. His happiness depended on Liana and Kendra's happiness.

Chapter 55

Ian arrived at arrived at Pacy Hospital, still feeling fraught with worry. As usual, the hospital was busy. He made his way to one of the receptionists to inquire about Kendra.

Good morning, can you tell me what room Kendra Mercury is?" Ian asked Sam, the receptionist on duty, politely.

What's your name sir?" Sam asked brightly, glancing at him briefly, and then clicking a few keys on her computer to look up 'Kendra Mercury.' She was a twenty-three-year-old, slender, blond-haired, Caucasian woman with green eyes, dimples on both cheeks and a pretty smile. The old Ian would not have hesitated to flirt with her and secure a date regardless of the purpose of his contact with her but this Ian was too busy being worried about Kendra and Liana to even notice her appearance. All he saw was someone who could hopefully provide him with the information he needed.

May I ask what your relationship to the patient is? Are you family or Friend?" inquired Sam, pausing, hands hovering over her keyboard as she glanced up at him.

"I'm, I'm, I'm...well...I'm...practically family," Ian struggled for the right words. He knew Pacy hospital had a reputation for being very cautious when it came to the security of their patients, especially after a previous incident two years ago when a woman claiming to be a sister of a patient that was recuperating from surgery, managed to gain access to the patient in the recovery room and kill him. It turned out to be a scorned ex-mistress of the man.

"How are you related sir?" asked Sam quizzically, raising an eyebrow, thinking it was strange that Ian did not seem to know how he was related to Kendra, considering that it was a straight-forward question.

"Well, we used to live together a few years ago."

"Ok," said Sam, "but I am going to need more information than that. What is your name?"

"My name is Ian Sharp. Kendra Mercury and I were in a long-term relationship once upon a time. We have a daughter together. I just heard about the accident that brought her here. I would like to see her, please," Ian responded as calmly as he could, trying not to sound agitated. He needed to present a calm front so that he would be allowed to see Kendra.

"May I see your ID?"

"Sure, Ian replied, immediately sliding his leather knapsack from his shoulder, unzipping the front pocket of the knapsack and retrieving his driver's license from it. He slid it under the narrow slot of the glass partition to Sam.

"Thank you," she said as she examined it, clicked a few more keys on her computer before handing it back to Ian through the slot with a skeptical look on her face.

"So can you tell me what room she's in?" asked Ian hopefully.

"I'm sorry but you are not on the list of visitors allowed to see her."

"Look, I am practically family. We were close once. We have a daughter together," Ian said with a pleasant, charming smile, which he hoped would get her to allow him to see Kendra. He had not anticipated that visiting Kendra would be complicated.

"I understand but I'm sorry…these are hospital rules. The welfare of our patients is our first priority," replied Sam, seemingly impervious to Ian's charms, a first for him, causing him to wonder for a vain moment if he was losing his charms.

"Like I said, we have a child together and that makes me family. Please, I have to see her."

"Well…" Sam hesitated. After all, the fact that this guy, Ian, was a handsome man, was not lost on her, despite her professional air.

"Thank you, Sam, that's a pretty name by the way…goes with the face," Ian turned up the charm a notch, as he noticed her name tag.

"Thank you," Sam smiled back. "Now, maybe, I can let you see her, but very briefly…I don't want to get in trouble, you know," she added falling for Ian's charms.

"Thanks, Sweetie, very kind of you…"

"Excuse me, he is not family!" spat out Piper from nowhere as she practically shoved Ian aside to talk to the receptionist. She had come to pay Kendra a visit and was about to make her way to the elevators when she suddenly noticed a vaguely familiar figure from the side of her eyes, speaking to a receptionist a short distance from her so she walked closer to the figure. As she got closer, it suddenly dawned on her that the vaguely familiar person was Ian, whom she had met just a handful of times in the past when he was dating Kendra before Kendra cut the family off from her life in order to preserve her relationship with him. Piper had always resented Ian because of how he treated her sister when they were together in the past and even more so when Kendra cut off the rest of the family to please him. As the years went by, she simply tolerated Kendra's choices regarding Ian, choosing to put her feelings of dislike for him aside because he was her niece's biological father whether she liked it or not, and because she knew that despite everything, and regardless of her sister's marriage to Peter, she suspected that Ian would always have a soft spot in Kendra's heart. And so, in order to keep the peace in the family, it was best to let Kendra make her own choices and support her regardless of her bad decisions because she was her sister and she loved her.

"Excuse me, I was talking to the lady!" snapped Ian, who was momentarily taken by surprised by the sheer rudeness of this person.

"I'm sorry?" asked Sam, confused, wondering if she needed to press the security button for help.

"He is not family," repeated Piper with authority, ignoring Ian, her back to him as she spoke to Sam.

"Look, do I know you?" asked Ian, still not recognizing Piper, quite annoyed at her behavior and especially more so because she was getting in the way of him trying to persuade the receptionist into letting him see Kendra.

"Maybe if you hadn't forced my sister, Kendra, to cut us off when you two were together, you might recognize me," muttered Piper sarcastically, still not even bothering to turn around to address Ian properly.

"Piper?" It suddenly hit Ian. That biting sarcasm. Of course, it was Piper! Kendra's older sister, whom he did not care much for back in the days. He had met her few times her when he and Kendra first started dating, and tolerated her for the sake of Kendra, but had not appreciated how close Kendra and Piper were at the time because, as far as he was concerned, that had meant that Kendra had less time and attention for him. So of course, naturally, he had 'suggested' that Kendra make 'certain choices' after they moved to New York in order for their relationship to grow. Basically, it meant that it was either her family or him.

"Oh, I see, you remember me now," hissed Piper, finally turning around to face Ian.

"How are you, Piper? Long time, no see." said Ian pleasantly, determined to win her over so he could see Kendra. Besides, he was a different person now.

"Not long enough as far as I am concerned," replied Piper rudely. All the resentment and anger she felt against him all these years plus the added stress of what happened to Kendra and Liana, came bubbling out.

"You two clearly need a moment to sort this out," interjected Sam who was watching the exchange curiously. "You can talk in the lobby floor or outside while I tend to others."

"Of course," answered Ian before speaking to Piper again.

"Do you mind if we talk for a few minutes, please?" he asked.

"Why? We don't have anything to talk about. I am here to see my sister."

"As a matter of fact, we have a lot to talk about…Kendra for one, and Liana, my daughter, your niece, whom we both care about," Ian said firmly but politely. He was determined to be pleasant to Piper. He needed her to help him gain access to Kendra.

"Look," said Piper, stubbornly, "I…

"Please?" asked Ian in his most charming voice, the one that made every woman want to indulge him even when he did not deserve it. He hoped it would work on Piper. After all, even the receptionist was falling for it, until Piper got in the way.

"Well, ok then but make it fast," Piper said reluctantly, succumbing to his charms as he guided her to one of the chairs in the visitors' lobby so he could make his case about visiting persuading Piper to put his name on Liana and Kendra's visitors' lists at both hospitals.

Chapter 56

After Ian convinced Piper to put him on the list of visitors for Kendra and Liana, they went to see Kendra together, though Ian would have preferred to visit Kendra alone. Dr. Amita had just finished attending to Kendra and was leaving her room just as Piper and Ian were approaching. They bumped into her just short off the doorway to Kendra's room.

"Good morning, Dr. Amita, how is my sister doing today?" Piper asked pleasantly while Ian stood by awkwardly since Piper, who was normally a polite person, could not be bothered to introduce him. As far as she was concerned, he should be grateful that she even let him anywhere near her sister.

"Good morning. Kendra is recovering nicely. We expect to release her soon," replied Dr. Amita.

"That's fantastic!" exclaimed Piper. "Finally, some good news! Can we go see her now?"

"Actually, she is asleep at the moment. I just gave her some medication. Give her a couple of hours to rest and then you can see her," she replied just as her pager went off. She glanced at it briefly and then back at Piper, "I'm sorry but I am needed. I have to go," she said before walking away.

"Do you mind if I just see her anyway?" Ian asked Piper after Dr. Amita left them. He did not want to ruffle Piper's feathers anymore.

"Well, you were standing right here when Dr. Amita said to wait a couple of hours, weren't you?" Piper snapped at him. Despite the good news from Dr. Amita, she was still not interested in being nice to Ian. Hell, no! She did not know if Kendra ever forgave him for the way he treated her in the past, but as far as she was concerned, there was no law that said she, Piper, had to forgive him for treating her sister badly, however long ago that was. So, whatever.

"Yes, I heard her," Ian responded, ignoring her sarcastic tone as he broke into her thoughts. He was this close to seeing Kendra with his own eyes after two years.

"Ok, then," Piper said beginning to turn away from the direction of Kendra's room to go back to the lobby. "I guess you will just have to come back later."

"Please Piper, I just want to look at her for a few minutes. I promise not to wake her up."

"Well, the doctor…"

"Please? I'm already here. I'll just stand at the doorway of her room. I just want to see her with my own eyes for a few minutes and then I can go see my daughter. I will still come back later when she is awake, if you don't mind," Ian gently insisted. Piper was really plucking his nerves. She had already agreed to let him be listed as a visitor for Kendra so at this point, as far as he was concerned, Piper was being a mean bitch just for the hell of it. Oh well, as long as he got his wish to see Kendra and Liana, then that was all that mattered. So, he would put up with Piper's shitty attitude for now.

"Ok but make it quick," responded Piper. "And remember, if she happens to wake up while you are here or when you visit her later, don't talk about the accident to her or Liana when you see Liana. We have not told them about the loss of Peter and Ryan yet," she added before walking away in a huff.

"All right," Ian smiled while inwardly patting himself on the back for patiently putting up with Piper's condescending bad attitude. Besides, he had achieved his end result with her; unrestricted access to Kendra and Liana.

Chapter 57

Ian stood at the doorway watching Kendra for a few minutes. She looked so fragile. God, how he still loved her! He wished he could take away all the pain she was going to feel once she learnt about the loss of Peter and her daughter. That was definitely worse than any physical pain. He felt a strong desire to wrap his arms around her but he knew better than to actually do that. Ian glanced around to make sure that Piper was out of sight. As soon as Piper turned around to the corner where the elevator banks were, he stepped inside Kendra's room and walked to the foot of her bed, not taking his eyes off her.

He stood at the foot of Kendra's bed looking at her with tenderness. Even in her fragile state and all the scars and tubes hooked to her body, he thought she was the most beautiful woman he had ever met. If only he had been good to her. If only he had appreciated her when they were together. If only. Once again, regret and sadness about the way he had treated her in the past coupled with the impact of the tragedy that happened to her and her family washed over him. He wished he could have protected her from the accident however irrational that seemed. After a few minutes, he moved to the side of her bed still not taking his eyes off her. He reached out to touch her hand but stopped himself just as he was about to make contact. Ian promised himself that when he finally touched her again or wrapped his arms around her, it would be with her consent, when she was conscious and aware of him, and more importantly, it would be because she wanted him to. In the meantime, he would do his best to comfort her anyway he could however way she wanted. It was the least he could do. Ian looked up for a brief moment, and for the first time since he was a small child at his grandmother's house, he said a silent prayer for Kendra and Liana, looked at Kendra again for a few moments longer and then left.

Chapter 58

Ian arrived at St. Ann's to see Liana around mid-afternoon. He was glad that he was able to persuade Piper to let him see his daughter without any more hassle. She had contacted St. Ann about him right after their conversation while they were both at Pacy. He sent Julian to let him know that he had seen Kendra briefly but planned to go back again after his visit with Liana. There was no need for Julian to meet him. He would fill him in on his visit later.

Ian made it through security and reception at the hospital without incident. He entered an empty elevator and pressed the ninth floor button where Liana's room was. Just as the elevator doors were about to close, a hand stopped it much to Ian's annoyance. He hated when people did that but that annoyance quickly turned to surprise as he instantly recognized Kendra's and Piper's father, Leon. Of all the people to enter this elevator in a fairly large hospital, why did it have to be Mr. Mercury? Ian did not say anything but nodded politely to Leon as he shifted aside to let him inside the elevator properly. Leon returned the nod as he glanced at Ian. A brief expression of recognition and then confusion passed Leon's face but he said nothing while Ian stared straight ahead praying that they either reached the ninth floor in record time or somebody else joined them in the elevator on the way up before Leon said anything. He was certainly not in the mood for any type of awkward conversation. He hoped Leon did not recognize him but he saw Leon's expression and he immediately knew what Leon was thinking; Ian looked vaguely familiar from somewhere. He had met Kendra's father two, maybe three times while they were dating and only for a very short time since he had not been particularly keen on meeting her parents when they were together. But the brief times that they had met, Ian remembered being slightly uncomfortable in Leon's presence. Leon had been polite but nevertheless intimidating. Perhaps it had been because Leon was a man who had always carried himself with an air of confidence and in a way that commanded respect wherever he went.

Ian eyed Leon surreptitious from the corner of his eyes. The years have been kind to the man. He had clearly been taking good care of himself. He had not changed much since the last time that Ian saw him many years ago. Apparently, neither age nor the stress of his daughter's painful situation had taken much of a toll on him physically. The man was now in his seventies but looked more like a man in his early sixties. And if anything, Leon looked physically better than the last time Ian saw him. The elevator stopped on the fourth floor but relief was short-lived. Apparently, whoever was waiting to enter the elevator changed their minds. The elevator doors closed again.

"I guess whoever was waiting decided to use the stairs," Leon commented.

"Yes," said Ian feeling obliged to respond, staring in front of him at the elevator doors as they rode to the ninth floor.

"Pardon me, but don't I know you from somewhere?" Leon finally asked turning to look at Ian fully.

"I'm sorry?" Ian said pretending not to know what Leon was talking about.

"Have we met?"

"I don't think so."

"Are you sure?"

"Sir, respectfully, I would have remembered," Ian replied firmly but politely just as the elevators reached the ninth floor and they both got out, turned right and walked in the same direction down the white sterile-looking hospital hall.

"Wait a minute," Leon suddenly stopped walking, "are you the man who hurt my daughter many years ago?

"Sorry?" Ian continued with his little charade of innocence.

"Do you know my daughter, Kendra Mercury?"

"Hmmm…yes … we dated many years ago…ah! Now I remember! You are Kendra's father. I'm sorry I did not recognize you earlier!" Ian stopped and turned to Leon, faking sudden recognition as he stretched out his hand for a handshake. Might as well get this over with. They were both going to end up in Liana's room, anyway.

"I thought you looked familiar," Leon grunted, not accepting Ian's handshake.

"I am Liana's father, Ian Sharp," Ian said politely, dropping his extended hand.

"You mean you are the man that hurt my daughter." Leon had never been one to mince words.

"I am sorry about how I treated Kendra in the past. I was immature and foolish, and I sincerely regret causing her pain," Ian said putting his right hand on his chest as he spoke and looking directly at Leon. "I am also sorry for indirectly hurting your family by hurting your daughter, Sir."

"Yes, you hurt my family deeply by hurting my daughter but I will accept your apology. However, my daughter and granddaughter, your biological daughter, are the ones you need to apologize to," replied Leon as they resumed walking toward Liana's room, which was at the end of the hall opposite a small ward.

"Yes sir, I understand that I have to earn their respect and trust," said Ian, silently appreciating Leon for acknowledging that he was Liana's father, if only by DNA. He was not sure if Leon realized that he had referred to Liana as his biological daughter but he was glad that he did regardless of whether the comment was deliberate or not.

"So, you are here to see Liana, I take it?" asked Leon non-confrontationally but with slight measure.

"Yes, Mr. Mercury. I saw Piper at Pacy hospital earlier this morning when I went to see Kendra. We talked about me visiting Liana and we came to an understanding," said Ian, feeling the need to provide some sort of explanation to Leon. For some reason, Ian who was not usually easily intimidated felt like he was a teenager meeting the parent of a girl that he liked for the first time. He always felt that way with Leon in the past.

"So, I take it that you have seen Kendra already then?" quizzed Leon, one hand rubbing his chin thoughtfully, wondering how Kendra felt about seeing Ian again after all this time, quite unaware that this was not exactly their first contact since they broke up years ago.

"Very briefly," Ian replied deciding not to mention his progress on the apology front with Kendra, which started way before the accident. Apparently, her family, except maybe Piper, did not know much about his on and off re-connection of sorts, with Kendra since they broke up years ago. He would leave it to Kendra to divulge as much or as little as she wanted about their 'relationship' when she got better.

"Uh-huh," replied Leon, not giving Ian any indication, one way or another, how he felt about it. "How did she take seeing you?"

"She was asleep when I visited. I plan to go back again after I see Liana."

"I see. When you go back, be gentle with her. She is in a very fragile state and will need even more support once she knows the full situation of the accident that put her in the hospital," Leon said, his voice heavy with emotion.

"I understand. And I am deeply sorry for the loss of your son-in-law and granddaughter. I heard about it in the news today."

"Thanks for your condolences," replied Leon as they reached Liana's room and walked in.

Chapter 59

Liana was awake when Leon and Ian arrived at her room. She was propped up on her bed and had her earphones on, listening to Pink's Glitter in the air song on her iPhone. Her right hand was hooked to an IV. Her legs and her face were still heavily bandaged. The doctors were going to remove the casts on her broken leg and arm in a few weeks. Though, the doctors had determined that she was in fact healing from her wounds to a casual observer, she looked very helpless with all the bandages and visible scars on her body.

"Hey Grandpa!" Liana smiled brightly at Leon when he walked in with Ian. She removed her earphones from her ears and turned off the music on her phone.

"My baby girl, how are you doing today?" Leon smiled at his granddaughter as he bent down to give her a kiss on her cheek before sitting next to her on her bed, while Ian hovered near the doorway unsure of what to do or say. He was suddenly glad that Leon was here to ease any potential tension since he was not sure how Liana was going to react to him. This was the first time that Ian was formally meeting his daughter. This time he did not have to spy on her or have investigators provide him with updates on her. He was actually in the same room with his flesh and blood. As he looked at Liana, a sudden wave of emotions overcame him. He felt a strong need to protect her and take away her pain. He wished the effects of the accident had happened to him instead of his daughter. He felt embarrassed and ashamed that he had stayed away from her for so long. He could not believe that he wanted Kendra to abort her or give her away. He wondered what kind of person he was then. He had missed so much by not being in his daughter's life. He was grateful that Kendra had stood up to him and fought to have Liana. For the first time in his life, Ian understood the wave of protection and love that Kendra felt for their daughter. He felt the instinct of a parent. He would gladly give up his life for Liana.

"This is my daughter," he thought. He was still overcome with emotion as he continued to watch Leon and Liana. 'My daughter, Liana. My own daughter. This is my daughter. Mine.' The words kept running through his mind.

"I am feeling better Grandpa. I'm not in as much pain as I was two days ago though the doctors said that I would be here for a while longer," she replied, not yet acknowledging Ian even though she saw him walk in with Leon.

"It is good to hear that you are getting better, Sweetie."

"I can't wait for the doctors to send me home. They said I was responding well to treatment even with the kidney transplant stuff that I still have to go through," Liana said optimistically, refusing to even think that a donor might not be possible. She and her family had decided that she would undergo a kidney transplant, should they find a donor match for her. Unfortunately, so far, everyone in the family that had been tested were not cleared as a donor for one reason or the other, not even her brother, Easton who had a higher percentage of being a good match since he was her sibling. Nevertheless, Liana, who had always seen the glass half-full, growing up, was hopeful. She knew that everyone was doing everything they could to find a kidney donor. So as far as she was concerned, there was hope. Being on dialysis was not an option as far as she was concerned.

"You have to be patient. In no time you will be back to a 100%. We are all rooting for you."

"Yeah, I guess. But I am mad at Daddy and Ryan though. Why aren't they here yet? You said they were not admitted to the hospital so that means they must not have been seriously hurt. Did I do something wrong? Why won't Daddy even speak to me on the phone?" Liana sounded hurt. Like her mother, Kendra, Liana had not yet learnt about the faith of Peter and her sister, Ryan, though she recalled the accident vaguely. Family members gave her the run-around whenever she asked about them.

"Listen to me, sweetheart. You did not do anything wrong. The main concern is for you to get better first and then we can talk about everything else," Leon replied vaguely. His heart broke for his granddaughter knowing that she would never see Peter or Ryan again but at the same time recognizing that the time was fast approaching for the family to tell her the truth.

"Easton comes with Aunt Piper all the time, why can't Ryan and Dad come see me too?" Liana asked again with a frown, "and why does Easton always look so sad every time I ask him about mom, Dad or Ryan? And Mom, I want to see Mom…what is really going on, Grandpa?"

"Sweetheart, I want you to concentrate on you. Your mom would want that," said Leon instead, carefully masking his own heartbreak.

"Hmmm, I better get well faster then!" pouted Liana before glancing at Ian again. He was still standing silently by the door as he observed the interaction between Leon and Liana. Without question, they were obviously very close; there was love and trust between them. Liana clearly loved her grandfather. "Who is he?" Liana finally asked Leon, as she nodded in the direction of Ian.

"Lili, this is Mr. Ian Sharp," Leon said to Liana as he glanced at Ian and then back at Liana. He took her left hand, which was not hooked to the IV, smiled at her warmly and added, "Mr. Sharp is here to see you. I'll go get a cup of coffee from the cafeteria downstairs while you two talk. I'll be back soon." He kissed her on her forehead, got up, nodded at Ian and then left the room. Ian took that as his cue to come forward and introduce himself properly to Liana.

Chapter 60

"**Who** are you and why are you here?" asked Liana eyeing Ian curiously before he could say anything.

"Well, my name is Ian..."

"Yes, I got that already from my grandpa. What do you want to talk about?" Liana interrupted slightly impatient. She wanted to see her mother, Peter and Ryan, not a stranger. Besides, she did not feel like having polite conversation with this person, whoever he was. And why did her grandfather leave so she could speak with this man alone?

"Wow, you sure do know how to cut to the chase, don't you?" Ian said, marveling at her take-charge attitude. She was a feisty one, just like her mother but he liked that. 'His' girls had 'fire' in them, which meant they did not take crap from anyone. He pulled the only seat in the room closer to the side of Liana's bed but at a respectable distance, set his backpack on the floor next to the chair and then sat down. Seating at the foot of her bed would have annoyed her, he decided. He was here to begin the process of earning her respect and hopefully love.

"Well?" What do you want to talk about?" asked Liana again staring at him without flinching. She had a feeling she had spoken to him before but was not sure. There was something vaguely familiar about him. There was also something about this man that she did not care for.

"Well, I am not quite sure how to say this to you but did your mother mention me to you at any time in the past?" asked Ian hopefully.

"What do you mean? And why would she?" She was not giving him any indication one way or another, that she knew him. Liana's expression showed no emotion toward him.

"Hmmm...how do I put this? I...umm...I was the man that spoke to you on the phone a few years ago," Ian said slowly.

Liana just stared at him blankly so he continued. "If you recall, I was not very nice to you that day. I asked about your mother and I identified myself as a good friend of hers. I was rude to you when you asked me for my name. I am really sorry about that. I also said that I..."

"That you were my father..." Liana's voice trailed off as she recalled the day that Peter told her he was not her biological father after this man called. Now she knew why he felt familiar and why he rubbed her the wrong way.

"I was really nasty to you and I spoke to you in a very unkind way. I am sorry," said Ian again, apologetically. What she thought of him meant more to him than he even realized.

"So, is it true? Are you my biological father?" asked Liana without malice and with a slightly shaky voice.

"Yes, it is true. I am your biological father," Ian said slowly. He wanted to get to know his daughter properly. More than anything, he prayed that Liana would accept and forgive him for being absent from her life. He also hoped that she would forgive him for how he treated her mother though he was not sure how much Kendra had told her about her relationship with him. But more than ever, he hoped that she would give him a chance to be a father to her, especially now that the man that raised her as a daughter, the one she knew as her father, Peter, was gone.

"I see," said Liana, not quite sure what to feel. She loved Peter. Peter was her father no matter what this man said to her and yet she still wanted to know what this man was about. She had always been somewhat curious about him over the years after she found out that Peter had adopted her but she did not really press the issue out of respect for Peter. He loved her unconditionally and she loved him back unconditionally. They had always been very close. He was her daddy. The best father in the world as far as she was concerned so she never really missed a father figure even though a small part of her wondered every now and then about the man that shared her DNA as she got older. Well, now, she did not have to wonder anymore. His name was Ian and he was right here in front of her.

"I know you have many questions?" asked Ian, anxious to know what she was thinking.

"Well," said Liana still looking at him intently as though she was studying him, "I am not sure what to think to be honest. You say you are my father but you have not been around. When I asked my mom about you in the past, she did not say mean things about you but she always had a sad look on her face when the topic of you came up. Why is that?"

"Hmmm," said Ian taking a deep breath. He appreciated Kendra not revealing details of their relationship to their daughter or why he had been an absent father, even though it was probably to spare Liana's feelings but he felt that he owed Liana some version of the truth. "I was not very nice to your mom when we were together. I was immature and unpleasant. My behavior toward her when she was pregnant with you was selfish. If I could turn back time and treat her better than I did when we were together, I would. By the time I realized the errors of my ways, it was too little too late."

"So, because your relationship did not work out with my mother, you decided to abandon your child too?" Liana grilled him. She wanted answers. She was a smart college student practically a grown-up now. She did not feel the need to be sheltered from the truth.

"It was more complicated than that. Like I said, I was very immature and selfish. I hope that one day you can forgive me for being absent from your life."

"I have a father already so you don't have to worry about that," Liana said sarcastically, wanting to take a dig at him and not sure why. Perhaps, because she felt abandoned by him even though she did not know him and despite the fact that she had Peter.

"I am sorry, nevertheless," said Ian hurt at her response but recognizing how she felt. But even more so, he was especially sad for her because she still thought Peter was alive.

"What for?" demanded Liana. She was fine, or so she wanted him to think. Never mind how profound this moment was that she meeting her biological father for the first time.

"Just sorry that I was not present in your life or a good man to your mom," said Ian softly.

"Hmmm," said Liana, looking away from him. "I don't know what you want from me. I have been doing fine all these years. My Mom, dad and the rest of my family love me so I'm quite fine, thank you."

"I see. So, is it ok for me to come back and visit you again?" Ian asked hopefully.

"Why?" asked Liana, not trying to make it easy for him to get to know her now.

"Just to see how you are doing," Ian replied.

"I don't know. I have a lot of thinking to do," she replied just as Leon came back to the room.

"How are we doing?" Leon asked, glancing first at Liana then at Ian and then back at Liana.

"Grandpa, your coffee sure took a long time," Liana commented; glad to see a familiar face.

"I wanted to give your two enough time to chat. Did you two talk?" asked Leon.

"Yes, we did," replied Ian standing up and picking up his backpack. He did not want to over-stay his welcome. He looked at Liana and addressed her. "I know this is a lot to absorb. Please give me a chance to get to know you."

"I'll think about it but thanks for visiting," said Liana politely throwing him a bone. She was confused and somewhat upset. She needed time to understand how she was feeling. Maybe she might want to see Ian again and get to know him or maybe not. For now, she just wanted to adjust to meeting him and how she felt about it.

"Thank you for speaking to me. I am happy that you survived the accident," Ian said, stepping closer. He really wanted to hug his daughter but was afraid of upsetting her. "Would you mind if I gave you, my number? You don't have to use it if you don't want to." Liana hesitated, looked at her grandfather who was watching protectively, he gave a perceptible nod. It wouldn't hurt for her to know her father. She was going to need all the support she could get, especially after the family told her about the severity of the accident and the loss of Peter and Ryan.

"I supposed," she responded and gave him her phone to key in his number. Ian entered his cellphone number, email, office number and home address...just in case, and then handed her phone back to her.

"Is it ok if I came back to see you tomorrow?" he asked again, hopefully.

"I have a lot to think about. So not tomorrow."

"Oh, okay," Ian said, feeling deflated.

"I'll let you know when you can come," Liana said. She needed a little space to think and she wanted to talk to her parents first. She really wanted to see Peter. He would advise her on what to do.

"Of course, no pressure. Please don't hesitate to call me at any time." Ian said with a smile. "I am happy to finally meet you, Liana." Technically, it was the first time, though he had watched her from a distance in the past, this was different. He was officially meeting her in the open and speaking to her. His heart was full of joy that his daughter survived a terrible accident. Hopefully they might have a future as father and daughter. Liana did not respond to his comment but nodded.

"Nice to meet you again, Mr. Mercury," Ian said to Leon as he held out his hand for a second time for a handshake. This time, Leon shook his hand politely and then Ian left, feeling like he made a little headway with Liana and Leon.

Chapter 61

After Ian left St. Ann's hospital, he did not go back to see Kendra as he had planned. Instead, he decided he would go back and see her the next day before he went to work in the morning. Besides, he knew Piper would tell Kendra that he stopped by, which was just as well since it would mentally prepare her for when he came back the next day.

***

Later that afternoon, when Ian got home, he called Julian at work to let him know how it went with Liana.

"I actually met my daughter for the first time in the open," was the first thing he said to Julian as soon as he picked up the phone.

"That's good news!" Julian said. He was genuinely happy for Ian. "How do you think it went?"

"To be honest, I am hopeful. Her grandfather was also there. I think his presence might have helped in a way."

"Ah, that's good. How's your girl doing?"

"My heart just broke seeing her in all those bandages and stuff. I hope she can forgive me for being a sorry excuse for a father. And now that I have met her properly, I don't have to sneak around anymore to check on her like I did in the past."

"That's right. What about Kendra? How is she doing?"

"I was glad to see her with my own eyes. She was asleep when I went there to the hospital this morning. I'll go back and see her again tomorrow before I go to work."

"I am glad they are alive, Bro."

"Yeah, me too. I'll do anything to win my daughter's trust and support Kendra."

"I hear you. One day at a time, one step at a time. Take it slowly so you don't push them away though," said Julian, knowing how Ian could get when things don't go as quickly as he wanted.

"Yes, I get you," replied Ian understanding exactly what Julian was saying. "I'll talk to you tomorrow, Jules.

"Sure, thing."

After Ian hung up with Julian. He called the office from his bedroom to check on work and inform them that he would be late coming in tomorrow. Afterwards, he went to the kitchen, opened one of the drawers that had various take-out menus, selected an Italian menu, and called the restaurant to order shrimp quesadilla and fried calamari. After he ordered the food, he made his way to the living room, flopped down on the sofa and then turned on the television to watch sports while he waited for his meal to arrive. He felt strangely calm as he tried to digest spending time with Liana and seeing Kendra again. He would be their rock in every way going forward. Somehow, he felt they were going to need him and he planned to be a good support system for them.

Chapter 62

Kendra had been making considerable progress since she had been at the hospital. The scars on her back and the burns on her cheeks and forearms were also healing well. The doctors had removed the damaged kidney from her body leaving her with one good one to function normally. They told her that the visibility of the burn effects on her cheeks and arms would eventually fade to become barely visible but if she felt too conscious of them, she could have plastic surgery to make them disappear completely. However, that could be done later down the road. The doctors also told her that they would remove the cast from her leg in six weeks, which would be followed by weeks of physical therapy. All and all, she was on the path to recovery.

***

It was 10.00 AM in the morning today. Kendra was awake and had just been cleaned by a nurse. She was awkwardly reaching for the TV remote control on the left side table, which was so she could turn on the TV in the room when she heard a knock on her half-opened door. She looked up to see Ian clumsily knocking on her door with one of his elbows while at the same time trying to hold steady a basket of fruits and a large bouquet of gardenias, her favorite flowers. Piper had warned her yesterday that Ian would be coming to see her and that he had refused to take 'no' for an answer so she hoped that Kendra was not upset with her for adding his name to the list of people permitted to visit her. Kendra said it was 'ok,' knowing that Piper was not privy to the fact that she and Ian had somewhat reconnected in the last few years since they broke up and were no longer hostile to each other even though they were not exactly friends either.

"Hello, Kendra, may I come in?" asked Ian with a hopeful smile.

"Hi, Ian, yes, please come in. Piper told me you stopped by yesterday. Thanks for checking in on me."

"Of course, Kennie ... Kendra," Ian replied, correcting himself quickly before he annoyed her. She had warned him not to use the name he called her when they were together a long time ago. He wanted to respect her wishes though it was quite easy to fall back to old ways. "These are for you," he said as he searched for where to put them.

"Thank you...how thoughtful of you," said Kendra, as a brief flash of the first few months they were dating many years ago, flashed through her mind. This was a glimpse of the Ian that had knocked her off her feet many years ago as she fell madly in love with him. "You can put them over there." She pointed weakly to the bay window on her left. Though she was getting better, she still felt weak and the aches and pains on her body, intensified, whenever she moved. She tried not to wince as she pointed but it showed on her face. Ian saw the look on her face and he wanted to cradle her in his arms but he did not dare.

"Ok. I'll do that," he said as he walked to the bay window and set the flowers and fruits down."

"It's very nice of you to brings me gifts," she said with feeling. It was not lost on her that he remembered her favorite flowers.

"It's the least I could do. How are you feeling?"

"I am getting better and bored by the day."

"That's normal after being in the hospital for so long," Ian said as he took one of the two chairs in the room and moved it closer to the side of her bed to a respectable distance. He did not want her to think he came here to support her in any capacity other than as a friend, even though he wanted more. He sat down and gazed at her tenderly. Even with the scars on her face and body and even with the cast still on her arm and leg, she was still the most beautiful woman he ever met. She was his 'Kennie.'

"I can't wait to be released."

"How long do you think you'll be in the hospital? Are the doctors going to let you go soon?"

"All they said was that I was on track to recovery but it is still too soon to release me."

"It is probably for the best."

"I guess, but I would feel much better after I see Liana, Ryan and Peter with my own eyes. I saw Easton for the first time since the accident two days ago. My little boy has changed, Ian. He is no longer a happy kid. He told me he saw Liana at the hospital but when I asked him about his dad and sister, Ryan, he became very quiet and then started crying. My sister had to take him away. I am worried about him."

"I am sorry for what you and your family are going through Kendra. Truly, I am. I care about you and I want you to be happy no matter what. I am glad you survived," Ian said. He could not imagine her pain once her family told her about the deaths of her husband and child.

"Thanks, Ian," Kendra said without malice. She was actually glad he came. She felt comforted by his presence.

"Kendra, no matter what has transpired between us, I'll always care about your welfare. That's a given," Ian replied, and then hesitated before adding, "Kendra, please don't get mad at me but…umm…eh … "

"Ian, what is it? What did you do?" Kendra was alert. What was Ian up to now?

"Well, I kinda…I went…"

"Ian, spit it out already," said Kendra, impatiently.

"I went to visit Liana yesterday," he blurted out.

"My Liana?" Kendra adjusted her bed with a side button on the bed so that she was in a half-seating position. She winced again at the sudden movement of the bed after she pressed the button. Ian bolted out of his seat to help prop her.

"Can I get you anything? Should I call the nurse? Do you need me to pour you a glass of water?" he asked, worriedly.

"No, I'm ok. How is Liana doing?" Kendra asked.

"She is getting better. I met your dad at the elevator on my way to see her. We went to her room together and then he let me spend some time with her," he said honestly as he sat down again.

"Really? I'm surprised he didn't give you a little tongue lashing first."

"Well, he did let me know in a few words that he recognized me as the cad that mistreated his daughter."

"Now, that's the dad I know and love," Kendra smiled. "So how is Liana doing? Did she look ok to you? Was she in pain?"

"She seemed to be doing well under the circumstances. So, you are not angry at me for seeing her?"

"Under previous circumstances, I would have been mad at you but she is a young adult now. I can't legally stop her from seeing you. Besides, it was big of you to seek her out after what happened."

"I can't take away the past. I was immature and badly behaved. I am sorry to have been such a lousy absentee father. I am sorry for rejecting you because of her. I missed out on seeing her grow up and I couldn't be prouder of the job you have done with her without my help. I am so very thankful you fought me to keep her. I don't deserve your forgiveness and I don't deserve her forgiveness but I am asking for it anyway. I hope to get to know her and earn her respect. I will not force myself on her or pressure you about talking to her about getting her to know me but I will do everything I can to have a relationship with her going forward," Ian said emotionally as he looked straight into Kendra's eyes.

"Thank you for saying that, Ian. I forgave you a while ago. I had to do so in order to relieve myself of the burden of resentment. Liana will do what she wants regarding you at her own pace. Did you tell her who you were?"

"Yes."

"How did she react?"

"She said she needed time to absorb everything I told her and my presence in her life. I gave her my contact information and told her to call me whenever she felt up to it. I don't want to push her but I would like to see her again today. If she wants me to."

"Give her time. She is a very forgiving person but please also be respectful of the fact that she acknowledges Peter as her father."

"I understand," said Ian, painfully aware of the fact that Peter was dead yet he knew it was not his place to tell Kendra.

"So how are you doing otherwise?"

"Very well. Work is going fine, and Julian and the others are fine as well," he said.

"I am happy for you," Kendra said and then added, "Can you do me a favor?"

"Sure, what is it?"

"Yesterday was the first time the doctors thought I was strong enough to learn about Liana. I was able to speak with her on the phone for a few minutes…but I can't wait to see her for myself though."

"Did you try to Facetime her?"

"No, the phone Piper gave me is very basic with no Internet access…one of those cheap temporary phones. I told her to get me my old iPhone. She said it was damaged in the accident."

"Oh, I see," replied Ian. He suspected Piper's real reason was so Kendra could not access the Internet to find out more details about the accident especially as her memory of it was somewhat foggy.

"So anyway, as I was saying, I need you to do something for me."

"What is it you need me to do?"

"Actually, can you find out how Peter and Ryan are doing for me? Where they were admitted and what their condition is?"

"Kendra, first things first. Why don't you try and concentrate on getting better so you can be there for…" Ian caught himself and quickly added, "are you sure you want to do that? I'm sure Piper can easily talk to you about them."

"I did ask her the last time she came with my mom and son but before she could respond, the nurse came in to check on me and somehow the conversation stirred toward how everyone was looking forward to me getting better. I have a feeling that she's keeping me in the dark about how badly Peter and Ryan were hurt."

"Maybe she just wants you to concentrate on getting better."

"I am getting better and would be ten times more at ease once I see every one of my family with my own eyes and speak to them. So please can you help me check on them, Ian?"

"Kendra, it's more complicated than that," Ian said, rubbing his chin. This was a very painful conversation because of what he knew and she didn't.

"Why is it complicated? I am asking you for a small favor ... find out about my husband and kid."

"Piper already hates me. When I start asking questions and digging…well, you know how your sister can be," Ian replied trying to wiggle his you of this line of conversation. He recognized that it was not his place to tell Kendra what he had heard and read about Peter and Ryan. He also knew Kendra well enough to know that she would not drop this conversation until he agreed, and so if her family did not tell her the truth sooner rather than later, somehow, she would find out herself. He just hoped that he was around to comfort her when she did.

"Ian, please…they won't tell me where they were admitted or how they are doing. I need to know."

"Kendra, it's not that I don't want to help but…"

"Ian, please? If I ever meant anything to you, help me with this little favor?" Kendra implored as she touched him with her left hand. Ian closed his eye tightly for a moment. He was at a loss. It was time she knew the truth but he could not tell her.

"Kendra, when is your sister coming to visit you again?" he asked instead.

"She will be here sometime tomorrow or the day after," Kendra said looking at him curiously. "Why?"

"Just asking. So, in answer to your question, I'll see what I can do."

"Thank you. I am glad you came."

"Me too," Ian said tenderly. He planned to reach out to Piper after he left the hospital to persuade her that it was time to tell Kendra the truth. It was not going to be easy but she needed to know. "So, now that we have the serious stuff out of the way, how about some bad TV?" He asked as he reached for the remote control and turned the TV on. He browsed on the various channels until they settled for Channel 9 where People's Court was playing.

Chapter 63

By the time Ian left Pacy hospital in the afternoon for work, he was feeling happy about the time he spent with Kendra but also very burdened by what she wanted him to do. By 4.30 PM, as he was finishing some paperwork before heading home, he was still mulling over how to get her family to break the news about the deaths of Peter and Ryan to her. He checked his phone for the third time in half an hour to see if Liana had had sent him a text him. Still nothing from her. He would have liked to go see her again, today, before going home but he knew that he had to be patient. The ball was in her court. By 6.00 PM he was done with work. He checked his phone again just in case. Still no word from Liana. He picked up his knapsack and left the office.

When Ian got home, he checked his mailbox in the area of the main lobby of his apartment building where the mailboxes were, for any mail, before bounding up the stairs to his second floor apartment. He dropped his mail on the dining table, took off his jacket and then threw it over one of the dining chairs before going to his bedroom to change into his pajama's pants. His upper body was bare. Like many times before, the apartment was extremely hot even though it was thirty-three degrees outside, which was not unusual for December in New York. The overheating in the apartment had been bone of contention for Ian with the building management for years; they could never do anything in moderation and so like many times before, he made yet another mental note to search for another apartment though he had not done anything about looking for a new place either. Ian cracked open the windows in the living room to counter the heat in the apartment and then went to the bathroom to wash his hands before going to the kitchen to rummage for something to eat. He settled for half-eaten, three-day-old Chinese food that he found in the refrigerator, which he had actually forgotten about. He smelt it, decided it was still good to eat and then transferred the contents from the box the food came with, to a microwave-safe dish, before putting the dish of food in the microwave to warm up. As the food warmed up, he brought out a glass of wine and poured himself a glass, deciding he was going to need it to celebrate Kendra and Liana surviving a terrible accident and to calm his mood when he spoke to 'Piper, the bitch,' later. He took the glass of wine, his cellphone from the pocket of his jacket, and his mail, and set them on the center table in the living room in front of the TV. A minute later, he heard the microwave beep in the kitchen so he went to retrieve his food before coming back to the living room with his food. He checked the wall clock in the living room; it was 7.45 PM. He decided to eat and wait till it was about 8.15 PM to call Piper, convincing himself that he was not stalling.

Ian took his time eating and sipping his wine thinking about the last couple of days and all that had transpired. In two days, he had officially met his daughter and spent time with her, and he had reconnected with Kendra again in a truly good way. After finishing his meal, he took the dirty dishes and wine glass to the kitchen and washed them. Then he took out a bottle of Poland water and took a gulp. He took the half-emptied water bottle with him back to the living room and settled into the couch with his legs crossed over each other on the center table. He glanced at the wall clock again. It was 8.25 PM. He took a deep breath, picked up his cell phone, reminded himself not to get mad at Piper when they talked, no matter what she said or how she said it, and then called her number.

"Hello Piper," he said politely while mentally preparing himself to be nice to her.

"Who's this?" was the first thing she said instead of "hello."

"Come on, Piper, I'm pretty sure you can see my name on your caller ID," Ian said in a friendly tone.

"How did you get my number?" she demanded, annoyed.

"A little bit of sleuthing," he replied without apology.

Piper harrumphed, grunted and then was silent long enough for Ian to wonder if she was still on the phone.

"Piper?"

"What??"

"Oh, I thought you hung up on me."

"Believe me, I am tempted," she shot back, not mincing words. "What do you want, Ian??"

"Well, I saw Kendra today. We had a nice long visit. I have to thank you again for making it possible," Ian said overly sweet. Truth be told, there was no way he would have let Piper stop him from seeing Kendra. One way or another, he would have figured out a way to see her.

"Oh, ok," responded Piper, her tone a little softer. "Is that why you called? To thank me?"

"Actually, there's another reason. I learnt about the details of the accident through the news and a friend. As a matter of fact, the day that I saw you at the hospital was the first time I was actually hearing about it ... "

"Ok, so what do you want? An apology because we did not contact you?" Her tone changed back to unfriendly.

"Well, as a matter of fact…"

"Because if that's why you called, you will not be getting one from me or any of my family members. After all, you were the one who chose to disappear when my sister was pregnant with your child!"

"Wow! Tell me how you really feel!" Ian said calmly, determined not to get angry. He deserved her wrath but now was not the time. Besides, he had already apologized to the people that matter. He was not going to spend the rest of his life apologizing. He could only move forward and make up for past bad behavior.

"Well?" Piper's sharp tone interrupted his thoughts.

"Well, what?"

"Isn't that why you called?" she wanted to know.

"Actually, no. I am trying to get to it but you keep interrupting me?" Ian said condescendingly. He was getting fed up with her nastiness but once again, he had to remind himself that he would not be goaded. His plan was to convince her to tell Kendra about Peter and Ryan.

"Well get to it," she said impatiently.

"I think it is time to tell Kendra about the loss of her husband and child."

Irene Ayo Asuen

Chapter 64

"What do you know about Peter and Ryan?" demanded Piper in a hard voice.

"Only what I've read and heard on the news, online and through my friend, Julian. Clearly, Kendra does not remember much about what happened, just bits here and there. I get that she has been through a traumatic experience and is still recovering but I think it's time she knew that her husband and child died and have been buried."

"What exactly did you tell Kendra when you visited her?" Piper asked brusquely.

"All I know is what I've read and heard. I know that they are both dead, Liana is still in a different hospital from her mother, and she and Kendra are asking for Ryan and Peter," said Ian. "Obviously, Liana is also not aware that her sister and father are both dead either but she is going to go online sooner or later and find out more details about the accident. I suspect the only reason why she is not digging yet is because she assumes Peter and Ryan are just badly hurt and not dead," he added, recognizing out loud for the first time that Peter was his daughter's legal father in a moment of self-honesty.

"Did you say anything to Liana?" asked Piper, suspiciously.

"No, of course not…I was meeting her for the first time under intense circumstances and at the same time telling her that I am her biological father…do you think I am stupid enough to add such devastating news at the same time?" He shook his head incredulously at the audacity of her question.

"Well, one never knows with you," Piper shot back rudely, unapologetic.

"Look, I'm not going to get into an argument with you about what I talked to my daughter about. There's no need for you to be so rude!" Ian came back sharply. She was really testing him. He took a deep breath and waited for her to say something.

"Ok, I'm sorry, you don't deserve that," Piper said, clearly not sorry for what she said. "Anyway, what did you say to my sister when she asked you about Peter and Ryan?"

"I kept trying to skirt the issue but you know your sister. She can be quite determined when she wants something. Right now, all she wants is to see every member of her family. Especially Peter and Ryan," said Ian.

"She is not strong enough to handle the news," Piper's voice broke as she thought about the brother-in-law and niece that she lost. She also felt her sister's impending pain at the loss of her family members.

"She is stronger than you give her credit for," Ian's voice broke into her thoughts. "She knows something is off. She is going to find out sooner or later."

"I gave her a basic phone so she won't find go online to find out more about the accident," said Piper

"Well, I don't think that's going to help matters. Kendra is a smart woman, that basic flip phone you gave her only raised her suspicions…she has asked me to find out where Peter and Ryan are. She wants to know how they are doing."

"I don't want her to lose her will to live," Piper said softly.

"From my humble, non-medical opinion, it is time to tell her. She is awake and making good progress and quite determined to see the rest of her family."

"It's been a very rough couple of weeks…it's a lot to tell her and to top that, neither she, nor the rest of us can donate a kidney. None of the family members that tested are a match…Kendra only has one good one, which automatically disqualifies her…so Liana has to…" Piper rambled all over the place, her voice trailing off.

"Wait! What are you talking about?" Ian asked, taking his legs off the table and sitting up, very confused.

"Didn't you hear what I just said? I don't know how to help Kendra. I don't know how she can survive the news of Peter and Ryan, and then not being able to help Liana with a kidney!" snapped Piper before she could help herself.

"What do you mean about helping Liana with a kidney?" Ian asked in a low voice.

"Liana is still on the waiting list for a kidney transplant, both her kidneys were damaged from the accident," Piper said.

"This is my daughter, I want to help her," he said, more to himself than to Piper. He was overcome with emotion.

"Yes, the same daughter that you wanted my sister to give up," Piper could not help the bitterness even during dire circumstances.

"I cannot begin to tell you how sorry I am about that. I want my daughter in my life. Kendra knows that and I also made it very clear to Liana," he replied gruffly.

"I am not sure my sister will let you anywhere near Liana and quite frankly, I won't blame her except for the fact that Liana has the right to know you and it is up to her to make that decision."

"Actually, Kendra knows that I saw Liana and she is ok with it. She is also ok with whatever decision that Liana makes regarding me. Kendra and I are in a good place now," he said smugly despite his anxiety about learning about Liana's condition.

"Hmmm! She is a better woman than I am then."

'You got that right!' he thought but did not voice that out loud. Instead, he asked, "does Liana know that she needs a kidney?"

"Yes, of course but Kendra does not. We told Liana not to say anything to Kendra so as not to worry her."

"I see a lot of secrets are being kept in this family," he observed loudly. "So, when next are you going to see your sister?"

"Next tomorrow. I don't think the doctors will keep her much longer in the hospital, anyway."

"Ok. So, this is what we are going to do," Ian said in a take-charge tone, "the next time you visit her, don't go by yourself. Go with other family members. "

"Why? Who are you to tell me how to visit my sister?" Piper was immediately argumentative.

"Because you are going to break the news her then and she is going to need all the support that she can get," Ian replied with authority.

"No, I am not,"

"Yes, you will."

"'It's gonna break her,"

"The Kendra I used to know, will be sad, depressed and angry at the universe. That Kendra will probably lash out at everyone but eventually she will fight to get better and stronger for her surviving children."

"I'm not ready to tell her the bad news."

"I hate to break it to you but it's not about you or what you want."

"I'll visit and talk to her about Liana but not Peter...not yet."

"If you don't tell her, I will," Ian said firmly. Piper had no doubt that he would by the tone of his voice.

"I see. Can we at least tell her on the day she gets released from the hospital?"

"If it is within a week as you think, then I suppose I can stall until then. I do plan to see her tomorrow. Please let me know when you are about to tell her...I'll like to be there for her too."

"Fine. Like you said, she is going to need all the support she can get."

"Yes. Now about Liana, I want to help her too."

"Sure, you want to help!" she scoffed.

"Of course! I am not a monster, you know. Just a man who made a mistake. I am still her biological father and yes, I do care about her whether you believe it or not."

"Hah! You appear in her life for a minute and suddenly you care."

"I am going to ignore that comment." He did not feel the need to tell her that he had watched his daughter grow up from a distance in secret. It was none of her business.

"Whatever, Ian."

"Anyway, I want to get tested to see if I can be a kidney donor for Liana. I am in excellent health and we share the same DNA, so I just may be what the doctor ordered," Ian said calmly.

"Thanks, but no thanks. I am sure we will be able to find a match somewhere else," Piper said unreasonably.

"With all due respect, you are not in a position to tell me not to help my own daughter! I will get tested," he said forcefully, a flash of the old Ian coming back but for the right reasons. Piper flinched at her end of the phone but she also recognized his desperation to help Liana and respected that determination to help, in spite of herself.

"Well, ok then," she said grudgingly. He was the only other viable option left at the moment anyway.

"Good...see? We can come to a resolution against all odds," Ian smiled. "I will call you tomorrow for more details and everything I need to know before I reach out to her doctor."

"Ok." Piper said tiredly. She was exhausted by the weight of this conversation with Ian.

"And Piper?"

"Yes?"

"Please don't say anything to Liana. I want to see if I am a match first."

"Ah, I see. Hmmm, Ian...somewhere, deep, deep, deep, deep down in there, there is a heart," Piper said without malice. There was still hope for him to be the man he could have been after all. Who would have thought?

"Good night, Piper," Ian said, amused by her backhanded compliment.

"Good night, Ian."

Chapter 65

The next day before she went to her shift at work as a nurse, Piper called her parents and Kenneth, and told them about her conversation with Ian, the night before. Even though they all had reservations about Ian, their main objective was the welfare of Liana and Kendra so they were able to see the bigger picture. Regardless of how any of them felt about Ian, they agreed that it was time to speak to Kendra about the accident but they would do it after she was discharged and back home. They were also hopeful that Ian would be a match for Liana because they were running out of options other than dialysis, which nobody wanted. Leon commented that it was funny how the last person any of them could ever imagine they would rely on, was the very person they were counting on to help Liana. In the grand scheme of things, he was the one taking a leadership role in the welfare of Kendra and Liana.

***

After Piper talked her family, she called Dr. Reedberg, the doctor in charge of Liana's case, before calling Ian during her first break. He picked up after a few minutes.

"Hello, Ian, this is Piper."

"Yes…I saw your name on my phone so I know it's you," he said shading her in reference to his call to her the day before when she pretended not to know who was calling.

"Umm, well, I called Dr. Reedberg's office earlier to make an initial appointment for you to start the assessment process to see if you are a donor match for Liana," she said, ignoring his dig.

"Dr. Reedberg?" Ian asked confused.

"He is the doctor in charge of Liana's case."

"Oh, I see. So, when do I get tested?"

"The earliest date they said the lab attached to the hospital could give you is in three days. Are you ok with that?"

"Of course! I have more than enough sick and vacation time…I will make arrangements to take time off, and if I am a match, I'll take a short-term disability leave. I'll do whatever I need to do."

"Ok…thanks for doing this," she said matter of fact.

"You don't need to thank me. She is my daughter; I'll do anything for her."

"Ok, if you say so," she said with disbelief.

"Believe what you want…anyway, I'll be there for the donor test," Ian replied knowing he deserved whatever Piper threw at him.

"So have you spoken to Kendra today?"

"I plan to go visit her again today after work. "

"I see. Just so you know, we plan to talk to her after she is released from the hospital. The doctors said that they would probably discharge her next week if she kept making the progress that she is making. So don't say anything to her yet."

"Ok, I won't. I told you that yesterday."

"Well, just making sure."

"And don't say anything to Liana about me trying testing to be a donor."

"I won't. You told me that yesterday," Piper threw his words right back at him.

"Good. Just making sure we understand each other," Ian said. After a moment, he asked, "so are you going to give me the details of the appointment…address and stuff, or are we going there together?

"We don't need to go together. I'll text you Dr. Reedberg's phone number. They are actually expecting you to call. You can call them to give you the address. They'll also tell you what you need to do to prep," she said.

"Sure, not a problem."

"My break is over; I have to get back to work."

"Have a good day, Piper," Ian said pleasantly, determined to eventually win her over. In response, he heard a click as she hung up the phone.

Chapter 66

Ian called Dr. Reedberg's office the next day, during his lunchtime.

"Good afternoon, this is Madison, you have reached Dr. Reedberg's office," a female administrator's voice with a slight southern accent answered the phone.

"Hello, my name is Ian Sharp, my sister-in...umm, my fri ... sorry, I mean my ex-girlfriend's sister, Piper Mercury Roche, said you would be expecting a call from me regarding the possibility of donating a kidney?" Ian fumbled through the introduction unsure of how to refer to Piper. What the hell was she to him? In-law? Nah, he was foolish enough not to marry Kendra when he had the chance. Aunt of daughter he just met? Not quite...after all, he and Liana had to develop a comfortable father-daughter relationship for him to even feel Piper was related to him in a round-about-sort-of way. Hostile sister of ex-girlfriend? That could work because she was certainly not a friend...well, at least not yet but she was hostile to him, so that seemed like the right description of Piper's relationship to him, Ian mused. He also wondered how Piper described him when she called Dr. Reedberg's office to set him up for this phone appointment.

"Sorry, can you repeat your name?" Madison's polite voice broke through his thoughts.

"My name is Ian Sharp, I wanted to confirm my appointment to come in next tomorrow for a kidney donor match assessment," Ian said more confidently. "I was told that he would be expecting my call today," he added without mentioning Piper's name this time.

"Dr. Reedberg is performing surgery today at St. Ann's but I can help you. Would you mind if I put you on hold for a moment?"

"No problem," responded Ian.

"Thanks," said Madison and put him on hold. Classical music played while he waited on hold. After about five minutes, Madison was back on the phone.

"You are set to come in at 10 AM for pre-assessment and counseling."

"Pre-assessment? I thought I was just coming to see if I would be kidney donor match for my daughter?" he asked confused.

"It's not as simple as that. It is a process but Dr. Reedberg and his colleagues who are also specialists will go into the details with you."

"Wait a minute, I thought I was meeting with only Dr. Reedberg?"

"You will meet with Dr. Reedberg and a group of other specialists equipped to answer any questions you might have. Dr. Reedberg will head the process and he is the doctor in charge."

"Hmmm, I see. So, what's this pre-assessment about then?" Ian asked curiously, still determined to help Liana, regardless of the inconveniences and hoops he had to jump to get it done.

"An informational season…what to expect, the process, how long it will take…Dr. Reedberg will fill you in on the details and after that we will contact you to set the dates and times for the donor match assessment."

"Ok then. Thank you," he said and hung up. He checked his phone. He had still not heard from Liana. He was tempted to go to the hospital to see her but he knew he had to wait for her to invite him. He did not want to do anything to push her further away. So, he called Kendra.

"Hi Kendra, how are you doing today?"

"I feel stronger. The doctors are discharging me on Monday. I'll just have to wobble around the house until the casts on my leg and arm are taken off.

"That's excellent news," Ian said happy for her. "So how is Liana? I would love to go and see her after work but I don't want to push her away…I already did enough damage to her, well, to both of you," he said contritely.

"I spoke to her on the phone just before you called. She mentioned you but didn't say much…just that she was still a bit confused. She wanted to speak to Peter first before deciding how to deal with you. Give her time, Ian."

"Yes, I know," he agreed, his heart breaking knowing that neither Kendra nor Liana would ever see or speak to Peter again. "So, is it ok for me to come back and visit you again, later today?"

"You've been here every day for the past three days since you found out about the accident. I think that question is sort of redundant by now, don't you think?" Kendra teased before adding, "and by the way, I do appreciate your visit…I am a sour patient but company does me good."

"So, it's fine then. I'll bring some food so you don't have to eat that hospital crap they feed patients."

"With all the food and sweets that I've been receiving from you, my colleagues and my family, I'll probably be the first patient to gain weight from being at a hospital by the time I am discharged," she laughed.

"Nice to hear you laugh again, Kendra," Ian said seriously, his mind flashing back to their early days of courtship many years ago. They fought, yes, but they also had a lot of laughter together.

"I am getting better so it is easy to laugh again. Plus, I spoke to Piper, I saw Easton and my parents today, and Kenneth called from London so I am feeling good so far even though I still have this nagging feeling of incompleteness…by the way, have you been able to find out where Peter and Ryan were admitted? Are they ok? I asked my family again today and they are still giving me the run-around…maybe you can tell me what you've found out on them…"

"Ken, slow down," Ian said, knowing it was his turn to give her the run-around.

"Sorry. Liana was asking me today and I didn't have an answer for her. She wants to know why Peter and Ryan still haven't come to see her or if they are ok from the accident. I want to know too… so have you been able to find anything about them yet?

"Kendra, I am still looking," he lied. "But you know me, I'll find out soon enough."

"Thanks," she said, sounding deflated. She wanted to know if they were badly hurt, how they were doing, what hospital they were admitted to. Most importantly she wanted to hear their voices even if she was stuck at the hospital. It did not occur to Kendra even once, that they did not make it out alive from the accident.

Chapter 67

"Is this what absentee fathers do???" The text from Liana was sarcastic with an angry undertone. Ian read it as he was lying down on his bed around 10 PM the following night. Despite the unfriendly tone, he was glad to finally hear from her. Anything was better than silence. Plus, now he had her number, which he did not have before.

"What do you mean?" Ian texted back, puzzled. Though her text was biting and unfriendly, just hearing from her calmed his anxiety about his appointment with Dr. Reedberg tomorrow.

"Appearing from nowhere, making a big claim about being my biological dad and then disappearing!"

"I did not exactly disappear again," he texted back not wanting to admit he was waiting for a signal from her before he reached out again.

"Really?? Hmmm!" Another angry response.

"So how are you doing kiddo?" he asked, ignoring her tone while stirring the conversation toward a less argumentative direction. He would work to build a relationship with her no matter what it took. In fact, he had decided that regardless of what Kendra had advised him or his 'sensible' advice to himself regarding waiting to hear from Liana before he contacted her again, he was going to see her anyway if he did hear back from her by the end of the week. Luckily, he did albeit via an angry text. Ian knew he had to man-up and fight for his daughter. Her finally reaching out to him after he visited her was a positive sign as far as he was concerned. It did not matter that her tone was quite angry…one step at a time. In fact, her anger was a good thing. It meant she cared. It was definitely better than nonchalance, which meant she didn't care.

"I'm not a kid, I am nineteen, stop calling me 'kiddo'" came back a scold a minute later.

"Sorry, I didn't mean to imply that. How are you feeling?"

"Better."

"I would love to come see you again...that is, if it's ok with you?" Ian texted back. He might as well throw it out there.

No response from her. After five minutes, he texted her again.

"Are you still there?"

"Yes...thinking," she texted back.

"Would you mind if I visit you tomorrow?" he re-phrased the question.

"Umm...if you want...I guess."

"Ok. Then it is settled. I will come by tomorrow."

Silence.

"I am happy to hear from you, you know," Ian tried again five minutes later.

More silence.

"Still there?" asked Ian, after a few more minutes.

"Yes. Tired. Going to sleep now."

"Ok, Liana. I'll see you tomorrow. Sleep well," Ian said. Awkward conversation but at least it was a small step forward. He was not one for prayers but before he slept that night, Ian thanked God again for sparing Liana and Kendra, prayed that they would be strong enough to go through the grieving process for the loss of Peter and Ryan, and more importantly that he would be the perfect match to donate a kidney for his daughter.

Chapter 68

Ian fiddled with his hands in the waiting room of Dr. Reedberg's private practice as he waited for his name to be called for his appointment. Dr. Reedberg's practice, which was on 21st Avenue in Queens, was affiliated with St. Anne's hospital where Liana was admitted. After a few minutes, Ian glanced around. The office looked like any other medical practice; sterile-looking, white wall paint, magazines on side tables as people waited, coffee and water machines for conveniences, two receptionists busy with phones and paperwork, and a couple of nurses and other staff aides coming in and out of the rooms to the waiting areas as they led people to see the medical personnel they came for when their names were called. There were three other people waiting as well; a middle age African-American man reading one of many Time magazines provided by Dr. Reedberg's office, a tall skinny teenage Spanish boy, probably eighteen or nineteen years old who had large earphones on his ears as he played a video game on his phone, and a plump Caucasian woman in her mid-sixties, flipping through one of many AARP magazines also provided by Dr. Reedberg's practice. Ian was trying not to be nervous about what he was going to learn about the donor matching process. Hospitals or anything to do with them always made him nervous.

Finally, after twenty minutes, Madison, a tall, pretty, slender Caucasian woman with short blonde hair called his name. She was the same person he spoke to on the phone before. She told him to fill out and sign a set of forms concerning his medical history, ability to pay should his insurance not cover the process and his agreement not to sue regarding certain aspects of the process. She also told him to return the forms to her with his insurance ID after he was done completing them. Ian completed the forms and returned them to her. She looked them over to be sure he filled them out correctly and then told him to take a seat again. Dr. Reedberg would see him is a few minutes.

After several minutes, Madison called Ian again and introduced him to one of her colleagues, Andy, who had just come out of one of the inner rooms to the general waiting area. Andy, a slender African-American woman in her early thirties, with short brown hair was a Physician's Assistant. Andy smiled at Ian and then led him to another room, where he met with Dr. Reedberg.

Dr. Reedberg explained to Ian that he would undergo a series of psychological, general and physical assessment to establish if he was fit and healthy to donate. After all of the tests were completed, and he was cleared to be a match, the surgery would be scheduled three to five weeks in advance. He explained to Ian that typically, a living kidney transplant donor spend two days to three days in the hospital after the surgery and will have an additional four to six weeks of recovery time.

"Do you have any questions?" Dr. Reedberg asked after he explained the process to Ian who was seated across his desk from him.

"What about my daughter? How long will it take for her to recover from the transplant operation?"

"Her recovery will be 5 to 10 days if there are no complications. However, she will spend 24-48 hours in intensive care immediately after the surgery."

Dr. Reedberg went on to explain the physiological and emotional expectations, the monitoring process after the surgery should Liana and Ian, match, and the medication they would need to take.

"Hmmm, I see," said Ian thoughtfully as he tried to absorb and understand what Dr. Reedberg just told him.

"So, before you meet with my colleagues who are specialists in various related fields and who will provide consultation in the process, given what I've told you, are you sure you still want to undergo the testing process?"

"Absolutely," Ian said without hesitation. He had to do this for Liana. He would take one for the 'team.'

"Ok. The next step is to meet with my colleagues, sit through informative seasons with them and then the receptionist will schedule you for the various tests you need to do. If it's possible, you should be able to do the blood work today after the informative seasons, and then Madison can schedule you for the other tests as soon as possible if you like," Dr. Reedberg said standing up from behind his desk. Ian stood up with him.

'Shit just got real,' he thought, as he followed Dr. Reedberg out of his office.

***

By 2.30 PM, Ian was finally done with the informative season and the blood work at Dr. Reedberg's office. He told the receptionist that he would call tomorrow to schedule the other tests after he worked out his schedule with his job. Then he called Kendra and spoke to her for few minutes. She was getting discharged very soon. He asked her what Liana's favorite desert was, and she told him red velvet and cocoanut chocolate cake. After he spoke to Kendra, he texted Liana to tell her that he was coming to see her. Liana did not respond to his text so he took that as a 'yes,' given their awkward conversation the night before. St. Anne was about twenty minutes from Dr. Reedberg's office so he decided to walk. He bought sixteen yellow roses and a dozen cupcakes: six red velvet and six cocoanut chocolate flavors. He hoped it would put a smile on her face.

Chapter 69

"**Knock,** knock…can I come in?" Ian knocked on Liana's opened door as he stood on the doorway. She looked up from her iPhone, gave him a smile, which was barely noticeable but enough to make Ian feel like he was making headway with her.

"Hello," Liana said politely. No anger, no annoyance. Just politeness.

"How are you feeling today?" asked Ian.

"Bored and ready leave here," she replied honestly. She was seating comfortably on her bed. Her right leg, which was in a cast, was propped up on several pillows.

"These are for you, I hope you don't mind," Ian said nodding at the flowers and cupcakes that he was holding. She acknowledged them with a more expressive smile than the first one she gave when he knocked on her door.

"Thanks. You can put them over there." she pointed to a small high table standing by the right corner of her room.

"You mom told me what your favorite cupcakes were, so I took the liberty…a little sugar here and there would not hurt once in a while," Ian smiled. He was a health nut but one of his vices, which he absolutely refused to give up, was red velvet cake. So, he was pleasantly surprised to learn that it was also one of Liana's favorites as well. At least they had that in common.

"Yeah, my dad is always telling me to cut down on sugars but they taste so good!" she volunteered.

"I know," Ian smiled as he took the only seat in the room, moved it closer to her bed at a non-intrusive distance and sat down. "I have a piece at least once a week but I try to make up for it by working out often."

"Me too…I eat what I want but I am on my college track team and we practice all the time," she said conversationally.

"Really? That's great. What race do you run?" He was excited to learn that athletics another thing they had in common.

"Sprints...100 meters and 200 meters. I plan..." Liana suddenly stopped.

"What is it, Liana?" Ian was happy that she was beginning to feel comfortable talking to him but he also understood her sudden hesitation. He expected it.

"Nothing...I don't know you," she blurted. "I have to make sure my dad is ok with me talking to you."

"You can ask me anything...you should be able to decide for yourself who you want to talk to, you are an adult remember? You told me that when you texted me," he smiled. He wished it was him that she referred to as 'Dad' instead of Peter. He realized that the journey to win her trust, respect and even love would be an even bigger battle now that Peter was gone.

"Of course, I know I can make my own decisions as an adult!" she scoffed at him, breaking into his thoughts. "I meant I don't want to hurt my dad's feelings," she added, seriously. Ian nodded. He remembered that Kendra had told him that Liana really wanted to talk to Peter about him first before she even gave him a chance. Except that she was never going to talk to Peter again because he was dead. It made Ian wonder why she went ahead and communicated with him again anyway since she had not heard from Peter. Maybe her curiosity and impatience about him got the best of her or she wanted to gauge him further before mentioning him to Peter.

"Well, first, I want you to know that I am not trying to replace your dad in any way," Ian said honestly, looking at her seriously.

"Ok, because no one can replace my dad even if they tried," she replied. Ian felt a jab at his heart even though he recognized that she did not mean to hurt him. She was just brutally honest, which could sometimes be hurtful.

"Well, now that we've got that out of the way, feel free to ask me anything you want," he invited.

"For starters, what should I call you?" Liana asked looking at Ian without flinching.

"Well, you call me Ian if you are comfortable with that..."

Not Quite Imperfect

The next few hours Liana grilled Ian about his life, where he had been all this time, why he broke up with her mother, what he did, why he finally decided to reach out to her. Ian did his best to be as honest as possible. He also asked Liana to talk to him about her life and school. He assured her that it was okay if she was not yet comfortable telling him certain things. She could talk to him about whatever she was comfortable about.

It ended up being a long but very productive day for Ian. He felt closer to Liana. Despite the circumstances, things were actually looking up. He asked her if it was ok if he came back to see her or call her sometimes and she said yes. Ian left the hospital feeling happy and even more determined to go through with the process of testing for a kidney match for her. He promised himself that even if he ended up not being the right kidney donor for Liana, he would do whatever it took to find a donor for her.

The next day before Ian left work, he told his bosses without revealing too many details what he was going through and requested flexibility in his schedule. He gave them advance notice that he would need some time off in the event that he was a match. They granted his request and wished him the best. After he spoke to his bosses, he called Dr. Reedberg to schedule the required tests.

Chapter 70

Kendra had been looking forward to this day. It was the day that Kendra was finally getting discharged from the hospital. She was more than ready to go home. She had made considerable progress since she was admitted more than two weeks ago and the doctors were pleased with her recovery process. The scars from the accident remained on her body though some were more visible than others. Dr. Amita told her that they would all but disappear in a few weeks but the ones on her face, neck and back might require minor plastic surgery to completely go away and she could have the surgery later if she wanted.

***

The nurse on duty had already helped Kendra get cleaned up and dressed by 10 in the morning. The crutches that the doctors gave her to aid her movement until she no longer needed them, were propped up against the wall by her bed. She was sitting on her bed with her right leg, which was in a cast, propped up on some pillows when Piper, Kate, Leon and Easton entered her room. She expected them to be here to take her home after she was released from the hospital and of course they were. As, usual, Kendra was happy to see her parents, son and sister. She smiled at them as she hugged each of them in turns. They had serious looks on their faces, which they tried to mask as they hugged Kendra but it was not before she noticed.

"What's with the glum faces? I thought you would be glad that they are finally releasing me from the hospital today," Kendra joked.

"Of course, we are happy to see you get released, don't be silly," Leon said with false brightness as he hugged his daughter.

"Then why the seriousness? What's up? Is it Peter? Ryan?" Kendra knew her sister and parents well enough to know that something was up.

"Sweetie, we are just glad you are finally coming home," her mother said, avoiding Kendra's questions.

"Ok, Mom," Kendra replied still puzzled. "Anyway, so I just spoke to Liana. I told her I would stop at the hospital to see her first before going home. She is eager to see me though still asking about her dad and sister. Speaking of Peter and Ryan, they are not here with you, which means they are probably admitted at a hospital, except you still won't tell me which hospital or how they are doing, am I right? Were they badly hurt and you don't want to tell me? How are they doing?" Kendra asked pointedly, looking at her father while her mother turned away and started getting busy opening the closets in Kendra's hospital room to take out her daughter's few belongings and put them in the small suitcase that she had brought with her to pack Kendra's things to take home. Piper joined her mother in helping her pack for Kendra. She was feeling anxious and she did not want Kendra to notice. She was not as ready as she thought she would be to break the news to her sister. She knew just how painful it was going to be for Kendra yet even she could not deny that it was just not something the family could postpone any longer. It was time Kendra knew the truth. And in a few hours, when she got home, they would have to tell her what happened to her husband and daughter.

"Baby, we'll talk when you get home. First, let's get the doctor to sign you out," her father said instead of responding to Kendra's inquiry.

"They are ok, right? I hope they were not as badly hurt as I was," Kendra said worriedly.

"Hmmm, honey, one step at a time. First, we get you out of here." Leon said.

"Dad why are you avoiding my question?" asked Kendra as she pulled Easton who was now sitting next to her on the bed, closer to her. Ian was supposed to come through for her with any information about Ryan and Peter but still no results from him either. Somewhere deep down inside, she knew something was terribly wrong. She sensed it. Maybe she was in denial. She had had a feeling from the moment she woke up from unconsciousness that something was not quite right. She could not explain the emptiness she felt or that nagging feeling of despair that would not go away even now. The only thing she was sure that would make her feel better would be to have every member of her family with her at home, under one roof. She wanted Peter. Peter always knew how to make things better. Peter was her comfort zone. The problem was that she has not spoken or seen Peter since the accident. It was not like Peter not reach out to his family no matter where he was or how inconvenienced he was…meetings, work, business trips…it didn't matter…unless he was in such bad shape from the accident…or was he in a coma? And Ryan…where was her baby girl? Even Easton had developed a new personality. He was now a very quiet child, not talking much, moody but still always happy to see her and Liana. He would not open up to her when she asked him how he was doing after the accident or if he wanted to talk about it. At the mention of his twin, he would withdraw even further and just stare into space. Kendra was worried about him. Piper told her that the doctors that treated Easton had recommended that he see a therapist to help with the emotional trauma from the accident and she was already taking him to see one since Kendra was not in a position to do so at the moment. When the doctors told Piper about Easton needing a therapist, she remembered thinking that the whole family actually needed therapy after what they went through.

"Kendra, I'm not avoi…"

"How are you feeling, Kendra?" Dr. Amita asked as she walked in, interrupting Kendra and Leon. Leon smiled politely at Dr. Amita, grateful for her unwitting interruption, as he moved away from Kendra's bedside to take one of the visitors' seats near the door.

"Good, now that I am going to be released," Kendra replied turning her attention to Dr. Amita.

"Our patients usually say that on their last day at the hospital," Dr. Amita smiled as she walked over to Kendra to stand next to her bed. Easton got up from his sitting position on the bed next to his mother to stand next his grandfather so the doctor could examine Kendra. "Do me a favor, open your eyes wide for me." Kendra opened her eyes and Dr. Amita took out a small otoscope from the pocket of her scrubs and pointed it at Kendra's pupils, one eye at a time. When she was satisfied, she put it back in her pocket and then removed the stethoscope hanging around her neck from her neck and used it to feel and listen to Kendra's heart. Just as she was finishing up, a nurse came by with a sphygmomanometer, gave it to Dr. Amita and then left. Dr. Amita used it to take Kendra's blood pressure. When she was satisfied, she smiled at Kendra.

"Everything looks good. Your cast will be taken off in six weeks, and as I mentioned before, if you need to move around, use the crutches the way we taught you. After we remove the cast from your leg, you might need a walking cane for another two weeks and of course you'll need physical therapy for a while too. The hospital can also provide you with a wheelchair to use at home if you like, should you need one instead of the crutches. Please follow the instructions I gave you regarding your medication."

"I'll be a good girl," Kendra joked. She liked Dr. Amita. She had been a good doctor to her.

"Ok, then," said Dr. Amita.

"Thank you for everything, Dr. Amita," Kendra said, touching the scars on her face. She was conscious of them.

"You know, you can fix the scars on your face through minor plastic surgery at a later date," Dr. Amita reminded her.

"Yes, you said so."

"Ok, good. I wish you the best. You know how to reach me if you need anything. Let me sign your release papers and someone will be here to wheel you out," said Dr. Amita with a smile. She nodded to Kendra's family politely, touched Kendra's arm lightly and then left the room to officially release her.

Chapter 71

Peter's brother, Kenneth, and his wife, Julia were in the US for a week. Kenneth, Julia and his parents, Andrew and Laura were at St. Ann's hospital visiting Liana when Kendra and the others arrived. Kendra was on a wheelchair, which her father helped roll her in. Liana was ecstatic to see her mother. Even though they had spoken several times on the phone from their hospitals, it was the first time that they were seeing each other since the accident. Liana wanted to jump out of her bed to hug her mother but she was not strong enough to move about that quickly, yet so Kendra's father pushed Kendra's wheelchair as close to Liana's bed as he could so they could hug.

"Mom!" Liana cried happily immediately feeling a sense of comfort and a familiar safety net upon seeing her mother.

"Baby!" Kendra cried hugging her daughter. After they finally pulled away from each other, Liana hugged the rest of her family and then her mother again, before speaking.

"How are you, Mama? Are you feeling better? I am so, so, so happy to see you."

"I know baby. I am happy to see you too. How are you? I missed you, Lili. When is the doctor releasing you?" Kendra asked worriedly. Looking at the cast, the scars and the obvious pain in which Liana moved just to hug her. She wished she could take away her daughter's pain.

The doctor said by next week, I should be able to go home but…" Liana hesitated.

"But what, Lili?" asked Kendra.

"I didn't want to tell you while you were still at the hospital because I didn't want you to worry," said Liana, shifting her gaze to grandfather, Leon, for encouragement. She had told him the day before when he came to visit her that she was going to tell her mother about needing a kidney today.

"Lili, talk to me. What did you want to tell me?" asked Kendra anxiously.

"Well, the doctor said I was going to need a new kidney because they had to take out the one that was damaged from the accident, and the other one I have left is failing fast."

"Wait, what does that mean?" Kendra was shocked that Liana was even more hurt from the accident than she thought. "Why didn't you tell me this before…all this time we have been talking on the phone?" Why didn't anyone tell me? Kendra glared around accusingly at her family members, who suddenly would not look at Kendra.

"I didn't want to worry you, Mom. You were still in the hospital," Liana replied, removing the heat from the rest of the family.

"Baby, I am your mother…I'll always worry about you even when you are a hundred years old. So, what does this mean for you? Just how badly damaged is your remaining kidney?"

"Well, the doctors said I am going to need a new kidney otherwise I might have to be put on dialysis," Liana said, looking at her mother with concern.

"Oh my God, my poor baby!" Kendra hugged Liana again. "What can we do? We need to have everyone we know get tested. You will not be on dialysis. We will find a match for you…listen, I'll talk to the doctor … "

"Mom!" Liana interrupted, watching her mother go into panic mode in her delicate condition was not a good thing. "Mom, it will work out, you'll see. I am already registered on the national list of people needing a donor."

"What do you mean already registered? Why can't the family help?" Kendra demanded looking around at everyone again, her expression demanding an immediate answer.

"We've all gone through the matching process, Kennie, the doctors said we were not suitable. Even Easton offered to get tested and he was not a donor match," Piper ventured, stepping forward and putting a comforting hand on her sister's right shoulder. Kendra shook it of angrily and glared at Piper as though she had the solution but was refusing to help.

"Then I should be tested. I am her mother after all. There is a good chance I might be the right match…maybe they can use mine," replied Kendra in a take-charge attitude. Then turning back to Liana, she added, "Lili, sweetie, you have your whole life ahead of you, you will not be on dialysis. We will find the right donor for you. Turning her chair around to face everyone again, Kendra demanded, "how do we start?" Let's get the doctor in here to talk about the process."

"Kennie, sweetie," Kendra's mother, Kate, said soothingly as she stepped forward to wrap her arms around her daughter, "you only have one good kidney, which you need. Remember the doctor also took out your damaged kidney."

"I don't care! They can use it. I'd rather be on dialysis than Lili...she's my daughter, I am supposed to protect her!" Kendra said, tears already falling down her face. Her mother wiped them with her hand. Liana was Kendra's daughter but Kendra was her daughter. No matter how old she was, Kendra was still her baby. She felt helpless. She wished she could help her daughter and granddaughter.

"The doctors won't let you do it."

"Then we need to find out who can. I have to see Peter first. I need to know where he is. Where is my husband, Mom? Dad? Piper?" Kendra demanded looking at each one of them pointedly. No one said anything so she turned to Kenneth who had been standing by quietly.

"Ken, do you know where your brother was admitted? I want to see my husband. I want to see Peter...he always knows how to handle complicated situations. He'll know what to do," Kendra said as she shook off her mother's embrace and moved her chair again close to Liana's bed and took her hand for comfort.

"Well, umm, Kendra...the thing is...umm...well, Peter is...umm," Kenneth hesitated to look at Piper who nodded. Now was the moment but he could not bring himself to say the words...it would also mean that he, too, would have to accept that his brother was really gone. He was still grieving. Despite the fact that they had already buried Peter and Ryan, Kenneth and the rest of the family were still in deep mourning and accepting the fact that Peter and Ryan were both gone was still a bit much. But they all recognized that Kendra and Liana had the right to know, no matter how painful and sad it was. They also recognized that though they had planned to do it when Kendra got home, the time was now.

"Uncle Kenneth, where is Dad? I also asked everyone, Mom, and no one would tell me anything," Liana said, interrupting Kenneth's thoughts.

Everyone gathered around Liana's bedside, huddling around her and Kendra, as Kenneth took a deep breath and spoke again.

"Liana, Kendra, there's something we need to tell you," he said emotionally. "The reason why you haven't heard from Peter or Ryan is because, well, you know, the accident was really, really bad. We were lucky that Easton and both of you survived..."

"Kenneth, where is Peter and Ryan??? Kendra whispered, instinctively knowing his response before he replied.

"Kendra, Liana," Kenneth said looking from one to the other, "Peter and Ryan did not make it out of the accident alive. They are both gone."

Chapter 72

"**What** do you mean gone???" demanded Liana shaking her head from side to side in denial, tears already streaming down her face from her eyes.

"I'm so sorry but they didn't make it. They died at the scene of the accident," said Kenneth painfully, not sure how to comfort Liana or Kendra.

"Noooooo!!!!" shrieked Kendra and Liana in unison.

"I want my daddy!!! I want to see him now!!!" Liana wailed as Kendra gathered her in her arms in an awkward position since Liana was on her bed and Kendra was on her wheelchair. "Baby, I am so sorry," Kendra said even though she was in pain as well. She turned to her father, Leon, not quite believing that Peter and Ryan were indeed gone, "Dad, tell Kenneth, he is wrong! Tell him he made a mistake! Tell him, Dad!"

"Honey, I am so sorry but it is true," said Leon, putting his arms around his wife who was now crying.

"Listen to me, Kendra, Liana," said Piper sitting on one side of Liana's bed, "they are both gone. They died from the accident."

"No! No! No! No! No!" screamed Liana, "stop lying! Aunt Julia, Grandma Laura, Grandpa Andrew, one of you tell me Uncle Kenneth is lying. Tell me Aunt Piper is lying!!" Tell me where my dad is! Tell me where Ryan is! I want to see my dad and sister now!!!"

"Honey," said Peter's mother, tearfully, trying to rub away Liana's tears but Liana's turned her face away, "he is really gone and so is Ryan." Her heart broke again over Kendra and Liana's pain, and for the loss of her son. Every day since she got the news she had missed Peter so much. The pain she felt as a mother over the loss of a son was unbearable. It was a loss she would live with for the rest of her life.

"Prove to me that they are gone!" shouted Kendra at her family while still clinging to Liana. "Where is Peter's body? Where is Ryan's body? Where is my baby Ryan?" she asked sobbing.

"Sweetheart, I am so sorry," said Leon sadly, wishing he could take away his daughter's pain.

"I don't believe any of you! I want to see their bodies!"

"Mom, are they really gone? They are lying right?" asked Liana tearfully. "I want to see Dad! I want him to write something on my casts. He makes everything all right. Ryan can't be gone! I need her, Easton needs her, Mom."

"Oh Liana," said Kendra tearfully, "I am sure they are ok. Maybe they are just in another hospital. Right, everyone?" Kendra asked no one in particular. Everyone looked helpless, feeing the loss of Peter and Ryan even more so now, than ever before.

"Kendra," Piper attempted to get her to acknowledge the truth, "they have been…"

"Piper, unless you are going to tell me that this is just a cruel joke and that they are fine, I don't want to hear what you have to say!" Kendra said forcefully.

"Kendra!" Leon said more harshly than he intended, "You've got to face the truth! Peter and Ryan died at the scene of the accident. They never made it out alive."

"What are you saying to me, Dad?" asked Kendra still in shock. "Are you telling me that I'll never see the love of my life and my precious Ryan again? Is that what you are saying to me?"

"Honey, I am afraid so. We held their funerals a few days after the accident," he replied just as Ian walked in through the open doorway.

Chapter 73

Ian took one look at the scene in Liana's hospital room and knew immediately that they had told Kendra and Liana the truth about her husband and daughter. The expressions and tears on their faces said it all. His first instinct was to walk up to Kendra and Liana and wrap his arms around them but he stopped short as Kenneth who had never met him before took a couple of long strides to block his path. They stood within an inch of each other, both tall handsome men, both feeling a strong sense of protection for the same people.

"Do you work here?" asked Kenneth in a commanding, polite manner. He did not notice a name-tag or hospital uniform of any sorts on Ian, who was dressed in dark jeans and a thick, short, heavy, unzipped winter jacket, which revealed a black sweater beneath.

For a minute, Ian was taken aback by Kenneth's gesture. His one singular focus at the moment was to comfort Kendra and Liana even though he was unsure of what to say or how to comfort them. He eyed Kenneth for a few seconds before responding firmly.

"My name is Ian, I'm…"

"Ian! Please tell me you found out where Peter! Tell me you found Ryan! Tell me they are alive!!!" wailed Kendra shaking off everyone hugging and comforting her and trying to get up from her wheelchair but unable to because she was not in a condition to do so without help. Though Liana was confused by her mother's inquiry of the man she recently met as her biological father, she was nevertheless hopeful and looked imploringly along with her mother at Ian for the answers they both wanted to hear.

"Kendra," Ian said sadly, as Kenneth, recognizing that Kendra knew Ian, stepped aside to let Ian walk up to Liana and Kendra to console them, "I'm so sorry. So very sorry but they are gone."

"No! No! No! No! No!!!!!" Liana and Kendra began screaming and crying again until their voices were hoarse as everyone stood helplessly by. A nurse passing by their room knocked on the open door and poked her head in.

"Is everyone ok? Should I get the doctor?" the nurse asked.

"I'm sorry about the noise," Piper said walking up to her. My sister just learnt about the deaths of her husband and child."

"I'm so sorry to hear that," the nurse said sympathetically, "I was concerned about the noise, which might be affecting our other patients nearby."

"I'm sorry," said Piper, "we will be leaving soon. I'll close the door."

"All right. I understand. Again, I am sorry for your loss," the nurse said.

"Thank you," said Piper before the nurse walked away. Piper closed the door and turned back to her grieving relatives.

Chapter 74

As Kendra and Liana cried holding each other, Ian hugged them both. He was tentative at first but when they didn't push him off, he hugged them more comfortably. He wished he could take away their pain. After crying for a while, Kendra suddenly shook off Ian and glared at him.

"Did you know about this time the whole time I have was asking you about them? You were stalling from telling me the truth, weren't you?" she demanded angrily.

"Yes, Kendra," Ian said honestly, bracing himself for the fallout he knew was coming.

"Really, Ian? Why didn't you tell me?" she demanded angrily glaring at him while Liana looked confused amid her tears. Easton was also in tears beside her. Clearly there was still stuff going on between Ian and her mother.

"You needed to hear this type of news from your family," he replied reasonably, not adding the fact that he was the one that insisted that they tell her as soon as possible. There was no point alienating Piper or the rest of the family again.

"After all we've been through? You couldn't even tell me the truth? So much for being a changed man!" she shouted.

"Kendra, please…"

"No, Ian. Get out!!!"

"Kendra," he tried again. She needed someone to lash out at and he understood that. "Let me help you…"

"Help me do what exactly?" she glared at him, "help me bring Peter back? Help me bring Ryan back? Reverse time and be the man you were supposed to be all these years? Just how are you going to help me, Ian???" Kendra asked bitterly and irrationally. She wanted him to hurt as much as she was hurting. She wanted everyone to feel the pain that she, Liana and Easton were feeling.

"I'm sorry for your loss. I wish there was something I could do," Ian tried again.

"Well, what I want you to do is bring Peter and Ryan back!" she cried hoarsely.

"I wish I could do that but I can't. I'm sorry."

"No, you are not! You are probably glad they are gone, aren't you? Aren't you Ian? Now, you don't have Peter in the way!" she said angrily, not caring that Liana was hearing any of this, not caring that Easton was hearing any of this, not caring that she was hitting below the belt, and not caring that it was an unfair thing to say to Ian, especially in front of her family. She was in so much pain from her loss that she almost wished that she had died along with Peter and Ryan, except that that would have been too much for Easton and Liana to handle. Oh, how she wanted Peter back. How she wanted to hug Ryan. How was she going to go on now without them in her life? How was she going to be strong for Easton and Liana? It was all too much.

"Kendra, you know that's not true," Ian said trying to reason with her despite the painful things she just said to him.

"Isn't it? Get out, Ian!!!"

"Kendra…"

"You heard her, Ian," said Piper from where she was standing.

"You too, Piper, get out! You are just as bad as him for not telling me the truth all this time." Kendra said now directing her anger at Piper, who dared to speak.

"I was trying to protect you, Kennie," said Piper, mournfully.

"Protect me from what exactly? The fact that Peter and Ryan are gone?"

"Kennie," her father interjected, "we were all…"

"You too, Dad, please leave me alone!" Kendra said to her father, her eyes blazing. "In fact, all of you leave! Leave me alone. I just want to be with Liana and Easton! Get out!!! Everyone just go!" She started to cry again as everyone slowly left Liana's room.

***

Everyone, including Ian waited in the lobby quietly. They planned to wait for as long as it took for Kendra to allow them to take her home to finish recuperating. They did not want this news to be a step back in her or Liana's recovery. Liana still had the kidney transplant surgery to go through if they could find a donor.

As they waited in the lobby silently, each person was deep in thought about Kendra, Liana and Easton. Each person was feeling the loss of Peter and Ryan in different ways and for different reasons. After many hours of waiting, everyone, except Kendra's parents and Ian eventually left for the day, each person hoping to see Kendra at home at a later time.

***

As Ian sat silently in the lobby, he could not help but feel the pain of Kendra's loss even though he had never met Peter when he was alive and their one phone conversation was a hostile one. Still, he would rather Peter was alive for Kendra, and he lost any chance of ever rekindling a relationship with her, than to see her in so much pain. He also wished Ryan was alive because he could only imagine the pain, he would have felt had it been Liana who died in the accident that faithful day instead of Ryan.

Chapter 75

It was way past visiting hours at Liana's hospital, and Kendra still showed no signs of leaving Liana's side even though she, herself, had just been released from the hospital. Eventually, doctors at Liana's hospital insisted that Kendra and Easton go home so Liana could get some rest. It was only then that Kendra allowed her parents to take her and Easton home. She promised Liana that she would come back to see her the next day despite the fact that she was not in the best mobile condition to do so.

***

As for Ian, despite Kendra and her parents' protests, he had taken it upon himself to spend the night in the main lobby of the hospital. He refused to leave Liana alone at the hospital after such devastating news. One way or the other he intended to be there for his daughter however awkward it could be.

***

After Kendra, Easton and Kendra's parents went home, Ian texted Liana to tell her that he was spending the night at the hospital lobby downstairs. He told her that she could call him or text him at any time during the night if she needed him. He also told her that he would see her early in the morning before going home to shower and get ready for work. He did not expect a response from her but he wanted her to know that she was not alone, nevertheless. He was pleasantly surprised when she replied with a simple "OK." That was enough for him. He took off his jacket to use as a makeshift cover and made himself as comfortable as he could with three adjoining vacant armless chairs near a corner, which he used as a bed. He used his leather knapsack as a pillow. Just as sleep took over, he hoped that Kendra would be more receptive of him when he went to see her at home soon. He planned to keep checking on her, Liana and Easton whether they liked it or not. As far as he was concerned, they needed all the support they could get.

Chapter 76

Ian turned and repositioned himself several times during the night trying to be as comfortable as he could in order to get some sleep. As a result of a restless sleep, he woke up, cramped and uncomfortable. When he woke up, he forgot for a moment where he was until memories of yesterday's events came flooding back. He looked around. A couple of visitors who had also spent the night in the waiting room were still sleeping awkwardly. Though it was only 6.20 AM in the morning, the hospital was already bustling with staff going about their routines, patients being admitted and agitated visitors and relatives coming in and out of the hospital.

After Ian was oriented, he got up and walked outside across the street from the hospital where a small number of mobile food trucks were already selling breakfast of assorted bagels, doughnuts, sandwiches, pastries and beverages. The chill in the air was undeniable. Though he was wearing his thick winter jacket and his sweater from yesterday, he still felt the brutal New York cold. It was eighteen degrees outside today and winter was generally not one of his favorite seasons in New York. He bought a large cup of sugarless coffee with cream and then hurried back to the hospital. He took his coffee with him to Liana's floor hoping no one would stop him on his way there considering it was still too early for visitors. Thankfully, he made it to her room without any hassle from anyone. He knocked gently on the door but no one responded so he opened to the door slowly and gently so as not to startle her. Instead of stepping in, he took a peek inside first, once the door was slightly ajar. Liana was still asleep. Ian watched her for a few minutes before going back downstairs to wait in the waiting room.

Back in the waiting room, he sipped his coffee while he checked his phone for any messages. His battery had about 33 percent of battery time left and he did not bring his charger. He texted Julian to let him know where he was and the then left a message at work to tell them he was not coming in today.

Next, he texted Kendra to tell her that he would come by to see her and hoped she had forgiven him for not telling her about Peter and Ryan. He did not expect a response but he wanted to reach out to her anyway. He checked the time…it was just 6.59 AM so against his better judgment, he called Piper.

"Good morning, Piper, this is Ian," Ian said politely, not really expecting a response and preparing to leave a voicemail. "I was…

"Good morning, Ian," she responded almost immediately, much to his surprise.

"Sorry to bother you so early in the morning. I was wondering if you've spoken to Kendra since you left the hospital yesterday?"

"Actually, I went to her place last night. My parents and I spent the night with her. I actually got home twenty minutes ago." Her usual biting tone whenever she and Ian spoke was absent. Instead, she sounded a little tired.

"Oh good!" said Ian, "how is she doing? I texted her but she has not responded yet."

"Well, she's not doing well. It was a lot for her to take in yesterday about Ryan, Peter and Liana but I am glad she knows the truth now," Piper said acknowledging without directly saying it that Ian was right about them telling Kendra the truth sooner rather than later.

"Yes. It is a lot for anyone…I plan to go see her later today."

"She is still lashing out at everybody, so be prepared," Piper warned.

"Wow! Is this Piper warning me the 'no-good guy'?" Ian asked surprised at her change in attitude.

"Whatever, Ian," Piper replied not offended. It was the least she could do for him not telling Kendra that she had wanted to hold off telling her the truth about Peter and Ryan for as long as possible. "Anyway, my family and I have made arrangements for someone to always be around her for the next few weeks. My parents are staying with her for a couple of weeks before going back to California, and Kenneth and his family would be going back to London next week.

"That's good. I plan to check on her regularly too. I intend to keep coming to see her, Liana and Easton before or after work in the following days, and help out in any way that I can," he offered by way of information while they were still being courteous to each other. He decided that regardless of what anyone said, he would just do what he could to support Kendra and her children. He expected a protest from Piper but she continued to surprise him this morning with her responses.

"I supposed that would be fine. After everyone leaves, you and I are the closest ones to my sister... me being in New Jersey and you right there in New York City."

"Yes," said Ian glad she did not put up a fight. She had finally accepted that they had a common interest in the welfare of Kendra and the kids.

"By the way, how is the donor matching process coming along?" Piper asked.

"I expect to finish all the tests I need to do to see if I am the right kidney donor within a couple of weeks, according to the doctors."

"Great. I hope you end up being the right match. Liana needs this and my sister needs to know that her daughter will be fine. They both could do with some good news."

"Believe me, Piper, no one wants to be the right match more than I do," he stressed. After the pain he saw Liana and Kendra go through yesterday, every single fear he had about hospitals, surgeries and the whole transplant process went out of the windows. Any shred of doubt he ever felt disappeared. More than ever, he was determined to complete the process and hope that he was a match for his daughter.

"I actually do believe you care," Piper said, truthfully.

"Again, please don't say anything to Kendra or Liana until the tests are completed and it turns out positive."

"I won't."

"Thanks." Only after he got the results would he talk to Kendra and Liana about donating a kidney. He had decided that if he was not a match, he would not say anything at all to them because there was no point in doing so.

"Sure."

"Sorry again for calling so early in the morning but I'm glad we had this conversation," Ian said feeling like he had crossed some kind of bridge with her.

"Yes, glad we spoke too."

"My phone is about to give up on me so perhaps we can talk another time."

"Ok. Have a good day," Piper said before hanging up.

***

By the time Ian hung up with Piper, it was about 7.40 A.M. He checked his texts. Got a response from Julian wishing him well and saying he would call him later. There was still no response from Kendra. He checked his emails. There was a notification from Dr. Reedberg's office confirming the dates for three other tests he needed to do in order to see if he was eligible to be a donor for Liana. After reading his emails, he sent a text to Liana to ask if it was okay for him to come up to check on her. Within a few seconds, she replied with a "Yes."

Ian was not sure what Liana liked to eat for breakfast so before he went back to her room, he went outside again to get her some pastries, bagels, egg and bacon sandwich, hot chocolate and coffee so she could have a variety to choose from.

Chapter 77

Liana was awake and texting one of her friends on her phone on her bed when Ian knocked on her half-opened door for a second time that morning.

"Hi," said Ian gently, "may I come in?"

Liana turned her head to see Ian and almost imperceptibly at him when she saw him. She nodded for him to come in. She looked so sad. Ian wished there was something he could do to console her.

"I brought you some breakfast," he said, setting the packages of food on the side table next to her and then pulling one of the chairs in the room next to her bed to a respectable distance.

"Thank you," she replied showing no interest in the food.

"How are you feeling?"

"I miss my dad so much. I miss my sister too," she said in a small voice and then started sobbing. Ian instinctively got up from his chair to wrap his arms around her gently as she sobbed. He let her cry for a long time. He was glad to be here with her. After a long while, Liana, pulled away looking slightly embarrassed.

"I'm sorry," she said.

"Why? Don't be sorry. You suffered a great loss. You are allowed to feel how you feel. I know I haven't always been there for you growing up but I am here now…whatever you need…I wish I could bring back your dad and sister but I can't. Take comfort in knowing that they are in a better place. They are in a better place now."

"I just miss them so, so, so much."

"I understand. Tell me about your sister and dad…whatever you are comfortable sharing," Ian said.

Liana, looked at Ian, unsure at first, but after a few minutes, started talking about Peter and Ryan, sometimes crying between stories of her father and sister, and sometimes laughing as she recalled some funny moments she shared with them while Ian listened and comforted her as best as he could, nodding in-between and sometimes telling a silly joke to tear her from her sadness if only for a few seconds as she talked for a long time, sometimes repeating herself.

They were together for hours until the doctor came in to check on her. Before Ian left the hospital in the afternoon, he promised Liana he would be back the next day.

***

Later that evening, Ian went to see Kendra. Her mother was in the kitchen making a meal of grounded turkey, steamed cauliflower and roasted potatoes when he arrived. Kendra was in the living room with her father, Leon. She was seating on the long sofa with her leg propped up on a bunch of pillows speaking to Liana on Facetime. Clearly, she was still upset with Ian as she barely acknowledged him when he entered the living room because she did not pause her conversation with Liana to say 'hello' or even look at him. Leon gestured for him to take a seat and then got up to join his wife in the kitchen.

Ian fiddled with his phone while Kendra took her time talking to Liana. Finally, after about twenty minutes, she finished talking to Liana, and put her iPad on the center table, which had been moved closer to her for easy reach, and then she glared at Ian.

"Why are you here?" she demanded.

"Come on Kendra, you know I came to see how you are doing," Ian replied, glad that at least, she did not throw him out again.

"Why? What do you care?"

"I do care about you."

"Sure, you do! Just like you cared about Peter…hmmm," she replied unkindly.

"Kendra, don't be like that…you know as well as I do that it was not my place to tell you such devastating news."

"Whatever, Ian."

"Are you taking your medicine? Is there something you would like me to help you with?" asked Ian tactfully stirring the conversation. He knew she was still hurting but there was nothing he could do about that.

"Can you bring Peter and Ryan back?" Kendra looked at him. The glare on her face had turned to sadness.

"Kendra…"

"I just miss them…my heart hurts so much from missing them," Kendra said, her voice breaking as she spoke and tears rolling down her face.

Ian got up from where he was seating across from her, to crouch next to her. He took her hand, which she did not resist, before speaking. "Kendra, I am truly sorry for your loss. I know I was not pleasant to Peter the time we spoke when he was alive but believe me when I say, I am sorry that you lost him, and I am also sorry you lost your daughter. Really, I am."

"Thank you," she said mournfully. "I don't know how to be strong for Liana and Easton. I don't know how to do this without Peter."

"Kendra, you are not alone. You have your family and you have me…in however way you want…to cry on my shoulders, to vent to, to run errand, tell stupid jokes…even to listen when you want to talk about Peter and Ryan…I'll be that guy for you…anything you want."

"Wow…who are you and what have you done with Ian?" Kendra asked mirthlessly despite her sadness.

"He's here … the improved version, I hope," Ian laughed, glad to see she still had her wits about her despite her sadness.

"Thanks…I'll take you up on your offer."

"Good."

"I couldn't go to the hospital today but I really want to go see Liana tomorrow."

"I'll be happy to take you there if you want."

"That will be nice," she smiled at him for the first time since he arrived.

Chapter 78

Liana was discharged from the hospital, a week after Kendra. Ian offered to bring her home the day she was discharged because Kendra was not in a position to do so. Dr. Reedberg had given Liana instructions and medication to take, and a schedule for regular follow-up visits so he could monitor her closely. Dr. Reedberg also told Liana and her family that if they find the right kidney donor, Liana should be prepared to come back for the transplant surgery within days.

Liana decided to defer college for a year because of all she was going through and was even considering transferring to a school in the East Coast to be closer to Kendra and Easton, though she and Kendra both agreed to make that decision much later.

Chapter 79

The days that followed were not easy. Between Kendra and her kids, everyone was moody. They were angry, sad, depressed, nonchalant, non-cooperative, sullen or not in talkative moods. At any given time, someone would fly of the handle because even the slightest thing could set that person off. It turned out that Kendra had the toughest time dealing with the deaths of her husband and child and worrying about the possibility of Liana not finding a kidney donor, which could result to her being on dialysis for the rest of her life. It was all too much for her.

As a result, she fell into a deep depression and went through mood swings. One moment, she was calm, strong and collected, and then the next moment, she was in tears and inconsolable. Some days, she was not interested in eating or speaking to anyone and other times, she was talking as if everything was normal; chatting about Peter and Ryan, and saying things like "when Peter gets home, we are going to get away from it all," "let's make Peter's favorite meal today," "Lili, please call your dad at work and remind him that he needs to check up on the time for Easton's and Ryan's PTA meetings," and "Easton, where is your sister? Go get her for me, please." On other days, all Kendra would do, was sleep. Further, she did not care enough to keep up with her regular physical therapy appointments or take her medication on schedule.

It was quite challenging for Kendra's family, in-laws and Ian to pull Kendra out of her funk as they alternated between forcing her and pleading with her to eat, take her medication, keep her therapy appointments and generally take care of herself for the sake of her remaining children. Sometimes she cooperated with them but other times, it was a struggle. She was mad at everyone for treating her like a baby and was generally angry for being alive. She lashed out at her family for having the funeral without her present even though she was not in a condition to be there at the time. Ian and Piper in particular, bore the brunt of Kendra's negative moods whenever they came by as she lashed out at them more harshly than other family members and even unreasonably blamed them for the accident though they had nothing to do with it. At some point, though Piper understood what her sister was going through, she could not tolerate Kendra's behavior any longer and decided to visit less often but check on her more regularly by phone.

***

Liana tried to be strong for her mother and brother but sometimes it was just a bit too much for her as well. She also fell into depression but handled it in a different way; she barely ate, kept to herself a lot, and cut off contact with her friends.

Easton seemed to do a better job of taking care of his mother and sister at his age than they did of him. The doctors had taken off the cast on his arm and he appeared to be as good as new. Physical and mental therapy seem to be working for him although everyone knew it would take a very long time for him to be completely healed from the trauma of the accident if ever at all. He had lost his dad and best friend, Ryan, the one person who understood him like no other. He came into the one with Ryan and now he felt lost without her. Yet, he had to put up a front and help Liana and his mother heal from a tragedy they all went through.

Suddenly, he was the 'man' of the house, growing up overnight since the accident. He was making effort in his own way to take care of his mother and his sister, while putting his own needs aside by checking on them several times a day and threatening to "go away and live with his grandparents if they did not take care of themselves." Some days, it was enough to scare Kendra and Liana because they did not want to lose Easton in any way.

***

After Kendra's parents went back to Los Angeles, and Kenneth and his wife went back to London, Piper and Ian were left to take care of Kendra and her family. They made sure to make Easton aware that the burden of responsibility of Liana and Kendra's welfare was not only on him. At some point during their joint mission to help Kendra and Liana heal, Easton and Ian bonded.

***

Whenever, Ian visited, he was careful to assure Easton that he was not replacing Peter or taking over his position as the 'head' of the family. Anything he did to help them in terms of moving on and healing, he made sure it was ok with Kendra and her kids. He wanted to earn their respect on their own terms. During this time, Liana and Easton eventually became closer than they had been before the accident. They had even managed to accept Ian who had become their pillar of strength and had essentially taken up where Peter had left off, though in their minds, Peter would always be their father. Ian had also gotten to know Liana better and they had become somewhat close though it was still a relationship in progress. Though they were working on their relationship, tragic circumstances had help to draw them closer. Their one undisputed common goal, whether they liked it or not, was the welfare of Kendra. Everyone was determined to make sure she got better and somehow begin the healing road to recovery.

***

At some point, the burden of taking care of Kendra, Easton and Liana fell on Ian as everyone else eventually fell back into their lives and routines. He still came to see Kendra and her family before or after work and it was not easy to say the least. Sometimes, when he visited her, she still refused to speak to him, let him feed her or take her medicine. Ian took all the blows that Kendra sent his way, refusing to be deterred. He also took Easton to school and therapy seasons, cleaned Kendra's house, made her appointments and ran errands for them before going home each day. On occasions, he invited Easton to the gym with him to keep his mind of the pain of his loss. He also made sure to engage Liana in everything he did or touched in the house. He took Liana and Kendra (sometimes forcefully) to their doctor's appointments and physical therapies, made sure that Kendra's office knew she was still sick and had all her extended disability leave papers brought over to her house for her to sign. Without realizing it, Kendra and her family had come to rely heavily on Ian.

***

Between taking care of Kendra and her family, Ian completed all the donor tests he needed to do. After that, all he could do was wait for the results and hope that it came out right. The only person he told after he completed the process was Piper. The funny thing that happened was that Piper saw how hard Ian worked to help Kendra and her family, and how determined he was to see them get better. Amid the whole troubled circumstances, despite his past with her sister, she grudgingly came to respect him and all he was doing for her family.

Chapter 80

It took a while but the Rite family was finally beginning to accept the fact that Peter and Ryan were gone. Ian noticed it in the little things that Kendra, Easton or Liana said or did. They no longer cried every single time Peter or Ryan's names were mentioned but the sadness was certainly still there. They now referred to Peter and Ryan in past terms and talked mostly about fond memories of them. Both Kendra and Liana were now taking better care of themselves, of each other and of Easton. It was as if they realized in the last few weeks that they needed to be strong for each other in order to push through the mourning phase. They had now become diligent about taking their medication and going to physical therapy. The doctors told Liana and Kendra that their casts would be taken off the following week. Liana was still closely being monitored to see how well she was holding up until a kidney donor could be found while Ian anxiously waited to hear the results of his tests any day from now.

***

Ian was in the bathroom taking a shower when someone from Dr. Reedberg's office called him. He did not hear his phone ring so they left him a message to call the office. After he had showered, dressed and made a cup of coffee, he listened to his voicemail. Ian called Dr. Reedberg's office back immediately.

"Good morning, may I please speak with Dr. Reedberg? My name is Ian Sharp, he left me a voicemail," said Ian anxiously as soon as a female staff picked up his call at the other end.

"Yes, one moment please." Classical music played while he was put on hold. A few minutes later, Dr. Reedberg came on the line.

"Hello Ian," said Dr. Reedberg pleasantly.

"Good morning, Dr. Reedberg…I am assuming the message you left me on my phone to call you back concerns the results of the test?" Ian asked, skipping the chitchat and getting straight to the point.

"As a matter of fact, that's why I called. The test came out positive. You are an excellent donor match for your daughter."

"Fantastic!" Ian said with a sigh of relief unaware that he had been holding his breath until now. "Wow, now I can actually help my daughter!"

"Yes," replied Dr. Reedberg.

"This is such good news…she could use a bit of good news! We all can. So, what now, Dr. Reedberg?" he asked as he silently thanked God for his healthy lifestyle, which may have contributed to him being able to help his daughter.

"Well, we've already worked you through the whole process and what to expect. You and Liana will need to come in at some point for another counseling season together and then we can schedule a time to perform the transplant surgery. We've been monitoring her and so far, she has been holding up but it is good to know she has a donor."

"Yes, indeed, Dr. Reedberg. Thank you for the news," Ian said before hanging up. After he hung up with Dr. Reedberg, he called Piper and gave her the news. She was ecstatic. He told her that he preferred to give Liana and Kendra the news himself and she agreed. Who would have thought that of all people, Ian was the one who would end up being there when it counted the most?

Chapter 81

Today, Saturday, Kendra, Liana and Easton decided it was time to talk about giving away Peter and Ryan's things and keep what they wanted. By afternoon, they had boxed up things to give away and Kendra had called Goodwill to pick up what they were donating. She kept Peter's leather watch and a couple of Ryan's baby clothes. Liana and Easton also kept a few things from their father and sister. Later, Piper called Kendra to check on her. When they spoke, Kendra asked her for the details of Peter and Ryan's funeral and where they were buried. It was the first time that they had spoken at length about it. Piper was worried at first but Kendra assured her that she had accepted the fact that he was gone but she needed to know certain things concerning the accident and how her husband and child were hurt and buried in order to heal properly. After she hung up with Piper, she called Ian. He asked if he could stop by on his way to see Julian but Kendra did not want anyone other than her children around her today.

"You know, Ian, you don't have to stop by today. There's somewhere I would like to go alone with the kids," Kendra said as they spoke on the phone.

"Are you sure you don't need my help, today? You know that's not a problem for me. I could drive you to where you want to go today." Ian offered generously.

"I'll be fine, Ian. We are just days from taking off our inconvenient casts. I am more mobile than I was a few weeks ago. Besides, there's always Uber."

"You are sure?" Ian asked worriedly.

"I am positive. It's something I have to do alone with my kids. Just us."

"Hmmm…I see," Ian said, feeling slightly left out. "Can I call you later? I don't mean to smother you or anything. I know you are fine…but just to check."

"I promise we are fine today. I, well, myself, Liana and Easton need to do this alone. We are going to see Peter and Ryan at the cemetery…to say goodbye. Liana and I have not said goodbye…we need to do this on our own. We need to let them go. Peter and Ryan would want us to let go and move on. They would want us to live life fully and be happy," Kendra shared with Ian.

"Of course. I understand, Kendra," Ian replied, feeling guilty and selfish for feeling left out. He understood why she wanted to do this alone. She needed to do this alone. "Remember, I am just a phone call away."

"I know. Thanks, Ian. I'll talk to you tomorrow," she replied before hanging up.

"Have a peaceful day today," Ian replied. He decided that the news about him being a match for Liana could wait for now.

Chapter 82

Ian did not see Kendra until three days later and he didn't call her because he didn't want to crowd her space. He felt she needed to start adjusting to life normally without her husband and one of her children. He missed not speaking to her practically every day since the accident. He also missed Liana a lot. They were building a respectable relationship and she was slowly beginning to trust him. He hoped that despite the three days' break, they would continue on that path. He knew he could never replace Peter in her life so he was happy that she even accepted him in any form. He had even formed a connection with Easton whom he considered to be a sweet kid. He hoped to continue to bond with Kendra and her family in a good way.

***

He was watching a football game between the NY Giants and Los Angeles Rams with Julian at Julian's house on Saturday afternoon when Kendra finally called him.

"Hello, Ian," said Kendra, "how are you?"

"Hi Kennie...Kendra," Ian replied quickly catching himself before falling back to familiar ways. She did not comment on his slip. In the past when she hated his guts, she had insisted he not call her anything other than Kendra. "I'm fine...how are you feeling?"

"Actually, ok."

"I'm sorry that I haven't called you since we last spoke. I didn't want to smother you. I know you needed time."

"Ian, I am fine. You are right, I needed time alone to say goodbye. We...me, Liana, Easton...we needed to be together...just us. We needed to say goodbye in our own way without anyone else but I felt your support nevertheless," she said sounding resigned and sad.

"Kendra, I am sure Peter and Ryan would want you to accept that they are in a better place. No pain, just peace. They are watching over you and your kids. They would want you to be happy and move on in life. It doesn't mean that you will forget them.

"Yes," she replied tearfully, her voice breaking despite her attempt to sound calm. She was in the living room alone sitting on the couch as she spoke to Ian.

"Kendra, by the way, I have some news that could cheer you up. Is it ok if I stop by later?" Ian asked. She could do with some good news. He did not like how she sounded on the phone...vulnerable.

"Yes, you can come by, especially if you are bringing good news...we could all do with some positive news."

"Ok. I'll see you all soon. Tell Liana I'll see her soon. She is going to be interested in what I have to say."

"Wow, ok then," Kendra said sounding more cheerful by the time she hung up. Whatever he had to say, as long as it carried a touch of good news, she was okay with it.

Chapter 83

By the time Ian arrived at Kendra's place in Brooklyn around 3:00 PM, the cloudy skies had turned to pouring rain. It was also chilly at forty degrees. Ian wore a pair of jeans, a thick sweater and thick leather jacket. He used the subway to go to Kendra's pace because he did not want to deal with looking for parking space today even though it was a Saturday. When he arrived at Kendra's brownstone, he rang the bell and Easton let him in.

"How are you feeling, my man? Your mom was expecting me," greeted Ian as he shook Easton's hand. To Ian, Easton appeared to have grown several inches taller since the last three days when he last saw him.

"I am fine, Ian. Come in," Easton said politely as he opened the door. He walked into the living room with Ian, where Kendra and Liana were chatting. After a few pleasantries and greetings between Liana, Kendra and Ian, Easton made an attempt to leave them.

"What, you are not hanging out with us?" asked Ian as Easton started to walk away. He wanted Easton to be part of the news.

"Nah, I have things to do," Easton said.

"Well, ok then...I wanted to share some good news with your mom and sister regarding your sister's health."

"Oh, ok then. In that case, I guess I want to know what's up," Easton said and then sat down next to Liana on the couch. She was looking at Ian curiously wondering what this was all about but said nothing. She wanted to hear what he had to say first.

"So, Ian, what news do you want to share with us?" asked Kendra after they were all seated.

"Well, the good news is," he said looking at Liana, "I completed all the requirements for donor eligibility and it turns out that I am a perfect match for you, Liana."

"Wait, what?" asked Kendra stunned.

"First of all, how did you know that I needed a kidney donor? I never told you about that," Liana said, glad that he was a match but curious to know how he knew about her kidney issues. She was still getting to know him and she purposely did not tell him about her condition because she was not yet comfortable enough with him to tell him all her business.

"Lili, I think the first thing you should be saying is you are glad to hear that and thank you," said Kendra to her daughter.

"I am glad to hear that but I still want to know. Did you tell him Mom?" demanded Liana glaring her mother, not sure how she should be feeling. She was suddenly confused and scared. First, here was a man she had just gotten to know as her biological dad, and then he tells her that he was a donor match for her, which meant he might be the one to give her a part of himself so she would not need to depend on dialysis anymore but worse of all, her father, Peter was not here to help her navigate all these feelings of confusion. She was glad, of course that Ian was a match and he seemed nice enough since she had gotten to know him but did, she want to feel like she owed him for the rest of her life? It was a bit much. Yet she did not want to seem ungrateful.

"Actually, I didn't learn about your situation from your mom," responded Ian truthfully, breaking into her thoughts. He was confused by her reaction. Even Kendra was not as elated as he thought she would be. Perhaps it was a mistake. Maybe he had been getting ahead of himself in his quest to help his daughter.

"How did you know?" asked Liana.

"Well, I found out from your Aunt Piper.

"Aunt Piper?" asked Liana, surprised.

"My sister of all people?" asked Kendra, surprised. She thought she was the one who told him when they first talked about it during one of his visits to her in the hospital. He never showed any indication that he already knew, and it never even occurred to her to have Ian test if he might be a match. It actually made sense that he was the right donor. He was her biological father after all. They shared the same DNA.

"Yes," said Ian breaking into Kendra's thoughts and then proceeded to tell them how he knew about Liana, and why he decided to see if he was a donor match. "I insisted she tell me about Liana after I read about the accident. I didn't want her to say anything to you until I knew for sure that I was in a position to help."

"Wow," said Kendra looking at Ian with renewed respect. He was certainly a changed man.

"I want to help our daughter. I want to do what I can to help you, Liana," he added looking at her.

"Why do you want to help me?" Liana asked suspiciously. "You don't owe me anything."

"When I found out how badly you were hurt, what you lost, I felt your pain just as though it was me. I realized at that moment that I would do anything to help you and to lessen your mom's anguish ... maybe part of me also felt guilty for being such a horrible person to your mom in the past and for being an absentee father to you, I don't know," Ian said thoughtfully.

"Hmmm," was all Liana said, turning her face away so Ian could not see how confused she was. Was he really going to help her or was he just trying to buy her love and replace Peter?

"Look, I don't expect anything in return from you or your mom. I'm not trying to replace your dad, and I am not trying to buy your love or your mother's for that matter. It's what I want to do. I want to be your donor. Please let me help," Ian said reading Liana's mind and then looking from Kendra to Liana to Easton, who had been silent all this time.

"I don't see the harm in Ian helping you, Liana. He is a match and you get to live life normally. Plus, Ian is a good man. It takes a long time for people to find donors and everyone in the family that could test out, already did, except for you mom because you can't. You only have one, remember?" It was the first time that Easton had said anything. Ian smiled at Easton. He appreciated his vouch of acceptance.

"Actually, you are right, Easton. You are a smart kid," Kendra smiled at her son as it finally hit her that Ian had eased a major part of her burden! "Thank you, Ian! Thank you so, so, so much!"

"I'll do it many times over if I could but I need to hear from Liana if she wants to do this," Ian replied glad to finally get the reaction he was expecting from Kendra but understanding nevertheless, that for process to go forward, Liana acceptance was key. Everyone looked at Liana.

"So, I won't need to rely on dialysis if you give me a kidney?" Liana asked again.

"According to the doctors, no," said Ian.

"Thank you so much," she said tearfully, finally letting it sink that Ian sincerely wanted to help her without any conditions. She hobbled over to him and gave him a hug. It was the first time that they had hugged since they met. Easton joined in the hug and Kendra joined in as well. Ian could not have felt fuller in their embrace. It was the first time that he felt he belonged anywhere.

Chapter 84

The following week, the doctors took off Kendra's cast but increased the schedule for her physical therapy. Everything had healed nicely. Kendra was grateful that her body had recovered except for the few scars on her face, which was barely visible but she was conscious of, nevertheless. She found herself touching the scars ever so often. She was still toying with the idea of plastic surgery to conceal them completely. To her, the scars were more than a reminder of what happened. They also made her feel guilty for surviving the accident while Peter and Ryan died. Physically, she also felt ugly with the scars on her face, however indiscernible they were. Ian and her family members had assured her many times that she was still beautiful but Kendra knew that at the end of the day, it was what they represented to her emotionally that mattered. One or two times, she had spoken to Liana and Ian about how they made her feel. Ian had suggested that maybe she should think about going to a counselor to deal with the trauma of the accident. Easton was still seeing one and maybe it was time that Liana and Kendra do the same, individually and as a family. Kendra did not immediately warm up to the idea but promised to think about it.

***

The week after the doctors took off Kendra's cast, Liana's doctors also took hers off from both her arm and her legs. She was ecstatic that her wounds were healings well.

***

Piper and Ian finally convinced Kendra to go to therapy to deal with the trauma of their accident. It took a lot of persuasion but she finally agreed to go. She set up sessions for her and Liana individually. Easton continued to go to his sessions. Kendra also set up family therapy for the whole family. She wanted her family to heal and learn to live again without Peter and Ryan.

Chapter 85

A month after Ian revealed to Liana that he would be her kidney donor, she went with Kendra to see Dr. Reedberg for her scheduled follow-up checkup. During her checkup, Dr. Reedberg gave her the news that she had been expecting yet dreading; her damaged kidney could no longer hold up and was shutting down rapidly despite the medicine and diet she was on. He advised her that it was time to go on dialysis…unless of course, her living donor still wanted to give her a kidney. He already knew that Ian was a donor match for her but since he told Ian that he passed all the eligibility requirements to be a donor, he had not heard back from him.

Though Liana and Kendra had been expecting this news from Dr. Reedberg sooner or later, nevertheless, it still rattled them when he told them. At the same time, they were glad that Ian had taken it upon himself to see how he could help Liana. As luck would have it, he turned out to be the right donor for the daughter he was still getting to know. Kendra thanked her blessings that Ian never gave up on her or Liana. He may have been a shitty boyfriend in the past, and their relationship may not have been a bed of roses but at the lowest point of her life, when it counted the most, he showed up to be the man she always hoped he would be. For that, she was extremely grateful.

***

The next day, Kendra called Ian at work to tell him about Liana's checkup visit with Dr. Reedberg.

"Hello, Ian," said Kendra after Ian picked up her call on the second ring.

"Hi, Ken, how are you?" Ian asked pleasantly as he shuffled clients' fitness schedules on his desk. He had been planning to stop by her place after work. So far, things were going well between him and Kendra. They had settled into a friendly relationship and he was getting along very well with

Easton and Liana. His love for Kendra had remained steadfast but he knew that if they were to move forward in their relationship, it would be up to Kendra. So far, she had given no indication that she wanted to be more than friends with him, so he had to be patient. He also knew that she still needed time to mourn the loss of Peter at her own pace.

"I'm fine. Has Liana called you today?" asked Kendra.

"No, why?" Ian asked. Though Liana now called him, sometimes, on her own accord, it was still not as often as he would have liked but he was not pushing it. Their relationship was still growing and the fact that she was even calling him at all was enough to make him grateful. They were making progress; she was no longer nonchalant or angry with him. Now, she accepted him as her biological father and her mother's friend. Maybe one day, she would accept him as her second dad. For now, he was happy at the pace of their relationship.

"Well, Liana and I went to see Dr. Reedberg for her follow-up visit."

"And?"

"Well, I am worried," said Kendra.

"Why? What did he say? Did something happen? Is Liana, ok?" Ian asked more sharply than he intended to because he was anxious. Kendra had been through enough…no more bad news, please.

"She needs to do the transplant surgery as soon as possible or begin dialysis. I can't handle this, Ian. She's been through enough. She is too young to depend on dialysis for the rest of her life." Kendra's voice began to crack on the phone.

"Kendra, listen to me…it is going to be ok…as I said before, I'm ready to give her a kidney, remember? She does not need to depend on dialysis."

"Will it really be ok, Ian? When are we all going to start feeling normal, again?" Kendra started to cry. She could not help it as her emotions overwhelmed her. She wished she could spare her children any more pain or discomfort. She would rather be the one in need of a kidney and undergoing a transplant surgery instead of Liana.

"Kendra, you are a strong woman and so is Liana. She will be all right. You both will. And I am here for you…all of you."

"You promise we'll be ok?"

"Yes, you will be ok, Kendra. In fact, more than ok. I don't know anyone stronger than you that can handle everything you've been through."

"I want to be sure you are still okay with helping Liana…you will be giving her a part of yourself…literally."

"Of course, I am ok with this. I told you I would help her. I haven't changed my mind. I want to do this for Liana…for you," Ian said bravely. Scared as he was to undergo any kind of surgery, he was prepared to do this for Liana.

"Thank you, Ian…for everything you've done for us since, well, since…" Kendra could not bring herself to say the 'deaths of Peter and Ryan.' She had accepted that they were gone but saying the words was still too painful, nevertheless.

"I understand what you are trying to say, Kennie. I will come over after work and we … you, me and Liana, will talk about the next steps; call Dr. Reedberg's office and schedule the surgery," Ian said in a take-charge manner. He wanted Kendra to know that he was in her corner. He was all in. "Now, I want you to stop all that crying, go out to the park and enjoy this very beautiful, cold day that you are blessed to enjoy, you hear me? Before you know it, your disability leave will be over and you are back to the work grind. So go have a nice, lazy day and don't worry about a thing. We got this, girl!"

"Yes, Ian." Kendra sniffed, feeling the comfort and strength in his voice. He made her feel safe … just the way Peter used to.

Chapter 86

The following week, on the day of the surgery, Ian went to Kendra's place very early in the morning so they could all go to St. Ann's hospital together with an Uber. Ian, Easton and Kendra sat in the back seat of the car while Liana sat in front on the passenger side next to the driver. They dropped Easton off at school on their way to the hospital. His Aunt Piper had agreed to pick him up and have him sleep over at her place in New Jersey, after school.

The driver, a heavy-set, Polish man in his fifties, put on pleasant Polish music from some random radio station while Ian, Liana, and Kendra sat silently in the car, absorbed in their own thoughts.

Kendra's thoughts were focused on Liana. She worried about anything that could possibly go wrong during the surgery. What if Liana never woke from surgery because the doctors gave her too much anesthesia? What if her body ended up rejecting Ian's kidney? What if there were complications during the surgery and God forbid, Liana died on the operating table? She could not survive the loss of another child. Her heart simply would not take it. Loosing Liana would just about kill her…and that in itself, would destroy Easton. He would not want to be left alone in this world without any of his parents or siblings. She wished Peter was alive to make things right. She wished they had not decided to go to London at all and then the accident would never have happened. Kendra prayed silently that God would make everything go smoothly. She squeezed Ian's hand tightly without even realizing that she was doing it until he covered her hand with both of his. He gave her a reassuring smile.

"It is going to be fine, Kendra, I promise you. Liana is going to come out fine and so will I," Ian said, reading her mind.

"Of course, we are going to be ok," said Liana turning her head slightly to the left in the direction of her mother who was sitting directly behind the driver. "Dad and Ryan are watching over us from heaven. Besides, if Ian says we are going to be ok, then we are going to be ok."

"See? Liana and I are going to be fine," added Ian, reassuringly. He also appreciated the confidence that Liana had in his words.

"Yes," said Kendra in a small voice, still worried as she turned to look through the half-opened window on her side of the car.

"Good," said Liana, before turning back to face forward. As she gazed through the windshield of the car, she thought about Ryan and Peter and just how much she missed them. Peter would have made them feel better. He always knew how to make things better in times of challenges. Ryan, along with her partner in crime, Easton, would have been plucking her nerves as usual but she would have secretly loved bossing them around and telling them to behave. Her mom, who had become a different person since the accident, would have calmly assured her that she was going to be okay because they had Peter. Unfortunately, since the accident, her mom had become a bag of nerves; always anxious and no longer as confident as Liana once knew her to be. Liana took another glance backwards over her shoulders at Kendra who was still looking through her side window with a worried look on her face. Liana reached out and touched her mother's knee and gave it a reassuring squeeze. Kendra turned to give Liana a small smile trying to mask her worries but Liana knew her mother too well. Nevertheless, she smiled bravely at Kendra without saying anything before turning back to adjust herself again so that she was facing the front, once again. She was anxious too but she also believed that she would be ok. She had to be strong for her mother and brother. Plus, now, she had Ian. Over the course of the last few months since he first introduced himself to her in the hospital, she had slowly begun to trust him and even like him. He could never replace Peter of course, but at least, he was trying to be a good second father. She could even tell by the way he treated her mother that he was still in love with her. She even suspected that her mother might be returning the same feelings for him but she could not be quite certain. And from the way Ian and Easton interacted, Liana knew that there was mutual respect between them. They went for talks, played ball together, sometimes just sat silently in the Kitchen or living room together sipping beverage, watching TV or just doing nothing. Liana was glad that Ian had stepped in to support them. Without even being aware of it, they had all come to depend heavily on him. After a short while, as they neared the hospital, Liana felt a hand on her shoulder from the back of her seat.

"You are going to be okay, you hear me, Liana?" Ian's voice was calm, reassuring and completely belying how he was feeling.

"Of course, I am! I am a tough girl!" she replied with false bravado.

"I know that's right!" Ian smiled at her braveness. This was his girl. "You are going to be as good as new before you know it…guaranteed."

"Yes. And, Ian?" Liana craned her neck awkwardly to half-face him, "thank you for giving me a kidney," she said sincerely.

"Please ... I am the one that's grateful that I am able to do this. I'll do this for you again in a heartbeat without question I know it is too soon to tell you this, but I really do love you. Peter was your daddy and you loved him. I understand that so I'm not trying to replace him. However, I will try my best to be a second best father to you," he said sincerely. "Besides, who needs two kidneys, anyway?"

"Well, I am glad you are here now," Liana said before turning back to the front. Ian was touched. Another big step had just been taken between him and Liana. As they fell back into silence, Ian tried not to think about what was ahead of them by thinking pleasant thoughts; from the first time he met Kendra many years ago in Los Angeles to the first time he hugged his daughter and the gratefulness he felt that Liana did not push him away. In his heart he knew he was doing the right thing and this put his own anxiety and fears about the impending transplant surgery to rest.

Chapter 87

When they arrived at the hospital, Ian, Kendra and Liana were advised again by Dr. Reedberg and his team about what to expect after the surgery and told to fill and sign a bunch of forms. Before Ian and Liana went to get prepped, Kendra huddled with both of them in the main area of the hospital, told Liana how much she loved her and Ian how grateful she was that he was doing this. Liana told her mother she loved her and told Ian that she was happy he was her donor, this way they will always be connected. Ian was touched. Then they all hugged and then a couple of nurses led Ian and Liana to get prepped for surgery.

Kendra waited anxiously in the waiting room, playing with her phone, going for a short walk, calling Piper, her parents and in-laws to while away the time. Since her parents were in the West Coast, Piper, who was the closest in NJ, offered to take off work and come and wait with her but Kendra had insisted that she not take any more time off work for her this week. However, Julian had taken off work to come to the hospital to wait with Kendra. He wanted to be there to support Ian. It was the most time that Julian and Kendra had spent together since Ian had reconnected with Kendra. They got a chance to know each other again while they waited.

***

The doctors discharged Liana and Ian from the hospital two weeks after the surgery. Liana and Ian were instructed to follow certain protocols for the rest of their lives. Kendra was relieved that the surgery had gone smoothly. She could not be more grateful to Ian for what he had done for Liana. He showed her the true heart of a father; he showed up when she needed him the most. Everything he did in the past to hurt her, he had made up for with this single act of selflessness. The daughter he once rejected, was the one he ended up giving a whole new life to.

The kidney transplant surgery also turned out to have a positive effect on the relationship between Liana and Ian as it brought them closer together. It may also have been the tipping point for Liana in terms of accepting Ian without any more reservations.

One day, six months after the surgery, Liana called Ian and said she wanted to have lunch with Ian at Cafe D'Alsace, a French restaurant near 88thStreet and Second Avenue, her treat. Ian was pleasantly surprised. Though they had become closer since the accident and surgery, they were still getting to know each other.

They met a little after 1:00 PM and sat by a corner table near the window. While they were eating their meal, they chatted about this and that, until eventually, Ian asked Liana why she had invited him for lunch.

"So, Liana, what's the occasion?" ask Ian curiously before he took a bite out of his food.

"What do you mean?" asked Liana.

"Well, I know, we've come a long way in our relationship but I also know we still have ways to go, so why are you treating me to lunch today? What's going on?"

"Well," said Liana, just as the waitress arrived to take their empty plates away. She waited until the waitress took their dishes away, presented them with the dessert menus, and then leaving them to make a choice of desert, before speaking again.

"Today marks six months since you gave me a kidney so I decided to celebrate it with you, Dad." she said, looking up from the dessert menu. Ian immediately understood what she was saying, Liana had invited him to lunch to let him know that she was accepting him as her father. He had been waiting for this moment for many years.

"Ah, that's true but more importantly, this is the first time, you've ever called me 'Dad,'" Ian said, trying not to become emotional.

"Well, you are my dad. I am lucky to have had two dads. One is in heaven watching over me but the other is here with me, taking care of me and making sure that I have all that I need…even a kidney," she said, her voice cracking a little as she spoke.

"Thank you, Lili, you don't know how happy I feel to hear you acknowledge me as your dad."

"It took me a while to accept you. I was angry that you did not want me even though I had Peter. I was resentful about the way you treated my mom…she did not give me the full details of your relationship but I can put two and two together…the family's attitude toward you; little things here and there that they said. I was also confused about whether to hate you for not wanting me or be glad you want to be part of my life now. But more than anything else, I am grateful that you saved me from being on dialysis. It showed me that you care enough to do this for me. I can also see that you love Easton and I know you still love my mom. Best of all, I know you don't only love my mom, Easton and me, I know you actually like us, Dad," Liana finished the speech that she had been rehearsing in her head for a long time. By the time she was done speaking, Ian actually had tears in his eyes. He was so happy that Liana was his daughter. This was the best gift that God could have given him: the gift of Liana.

"I love you, Liana, daughter of mine," he said getting up from his seat across the table from her to give her a tight hug.

"I love you too, Dad," said Liana as she hugged Ian back.

Chapter 88

A little over a year later, By all accounts, everyone was adjusting to life without Peter and Ryan but in their hearts, Peter and Ryan would always live on. They also knew that Peter and Ryan would have wanted them to go on with their lives and be happy.

Kendra resumed had work a month earlier and was adjusting to her new 'normal,' which entailed a life without Peter and Ryan, but one with Ian as a constant presence either by media or in person, though still not in the capacity that Ian wanted. Despite all that had happened, Kendra was grateful, nevertheless, that Liana and Easton had survived the accident. She was also extremely thankful that Liana's body had adjusted to her kidney from Ian without any complications.

***

Liana ended up not transferring to a college in the East Coast. Instead, she planned to resume classes in Stanford in the summer so she could catch up on the classes that she had missed the previous year while recovering. She had also recently started dating a guy called Mark Bjørn, a tall Danish boy, who was the same age as her. Mark was studying chemical engineering in Stanford. Liana met Mark before the accident when they both attended a class that all majors were required to take. They hit it off immediately but he did not ask her out until a few months ago. Of course, Ian warned Mark not to hurt Liana or he'll have him to answer to.

***

Easton, who would be finishing high school in two years had become very close to Ian. Ian was extremely proud of him and the man he was becoming. He had been guiding him through manhood since Peter died, all the while taking care not to give Easton the impression that he was trying to replace his father. One Saturday in April, as Ian and Easton were playing basketball in a public outdoor court on Bleecker Street in the village, Easton suddenly stopped the game and said he wanted to speak to Ian about something important.

"Easton, what's up?" asked Ian wondering what was bothering him.

"I want to talk to you about something important to me."

"Sure thing…is this about Brina?" asked Ian, referring to the girl that Easton had a crush on, in his school.

"Nah, we are good…I finally asked her out like you suggested…we are going bowling next weekend," Easton smiled as he wiped sweat off his eyebrows with the swipe of his forearm across his forehead. "It's something else."

"Let's seat for a moment," Ian said. They walked toward the bleachers and sat down. "So, what's going on?" Ian asked, after they sat down.

"Well, I've been thinking about this a lot and I talked to my mom and Lili about it already," said Easton, a bit nervously.

"Ok, what is it?"

"Is it all right if I called you 'Dad'?" he asked, looking at Ian with a serious expression on his face.

"Are you sure about this, Easton?" asked Ian, caught off guard but very touched.

"Yes, I am. I'll never forget my real dad of course, and I still miss him a lot but you have been there for my mom, my sister and I, since the accident. You've been taking care of all of us. I respect you and I love you, and I know that I can talk to you about stuff. I asked Liana if I could share you with her and she said "yes" but I had to ask you too. I see you as another dad…so if it's ok with you, can I call you 'Dad'?" Easton looked at Ian with sincerity.

"Yes, of course you can call me 'Dad.' I can never replace your real father and I don't intend to try, but I will do my best to be a good second father to you. So yes, I will be very honored if you called me 'Dad,'" said Ian, emotionally. He was incredibly touched by Easton's request. Easton was the son that he never even imagined he could have. First Liana, now Easton. He now had two children. He felt fulfilled.

"Good," said Easton. "Thanks, Dad."

"No, thank you, Son," Ian said as he and Easton hugged tightly. This was one of the best days of Ian's life.

Chapter 89

It was the weekend. Ian, Kendra and Easton had just escorted Liana to the airport so she could catch her 4.30 PM flight back to Stanford. She was due to resume school on Monday so she wanted to get situated ahead of time. Ian was especially glad that he was able to go with Kendra and Easton to the airport, not just because he wanted to see his daughter off but also because he knew that everyone would be feeling somewhat sad on the way to the airport because it would bring back memories of the last time that they had driven to the airport on their way to start a holiday that never was the day of the faithful accident that changed their lives forever.

After Kendra, Ian and Easton got home to Kendra's place at 5.30 PM, Easton grabbed a packet of chocolate chip cookies from the pantry and a bottle or grape juice from the fridge and then went upstairs to his room to talk to his friend, Steve, on FaceTime. Kendra and Ian were left alone in the kitchen. Kendra asked Ian if he wanted to stay for dinner before going back to his place. He said "yes," since this would be an opportunity for him to talk to her about something that had been on his mind since he made a decision a week ago. He asked Kendra if she wanted help preparing the meal. She said "no," so he got himself a bottle of water from the fridge, sat on one of the stools by the kitchen island and then proceeded to watch her bring out frozen ground-turkey and diced vegetables from the fridge, put a pan on the stove, light up the burner, pour a little olive oil in the heated pan, stir in the diced vegetables, add some spices and then the ground turkey into the pan. She adjusted the stove so that the turkey did not burn before it was done, and then brought out green plantains from the pantry, which she cut to small sizes after peeling off the skin. She rinsed the plantains, put them in a pan of water, put the pan of plantains on another burner next to the ground turkey, and then light the burner. She adjusted the fire and then washed and dried her hands with a kitchen napkin. As Ian watched Kendra cook, he could not help but remember the time that they lived together many years ago and wish for that again. While everything was cooking, Kendra got herself a bottle of water and sat next to Ian with a small smile. She liked having him around. She took a couple of sips from her bottled water before Ian spoke.

"So Kennie, I've finally come to a decision."

"About what?" asked Kendra, curiously.

"Well, the head honchos at my office offered me a great opportunity to head their newest branch in Culver City. It's a chance to advance on the corporate level. The benefits and salary bump are fantastic. I am excited about this opportunity. Imagine, I started out as a trainer, then a manager, and now I'll have even more responsibilities as a director. It's the perfect opportunity for me especially since I am getting older, more office stuff, less physical stuff. My body is not as young as it used to be,' he smiled. "I've being thinking about it about it for a while and I've finally decided to accept the promotion. They'll set me up with temporary housing until I find my own place and they'll cover the relocation expenses."

"Ian, that's fantastic! I'm so happy for you!" Kendra said, excitedly and then it hit her; "wait a minute…did you just say Culver City, as in California???"

"Umm…yeah," Ian replied, quietly, "that California on the West Coast."

"Ian, are you saying you are moving to California?"

"It sure looks like it." he replied slowly as he gauged her reaction. Kendra seemed happy at first, but now…not so much.

"But why does it have to be so far?" whined Kendra. She had grown used to seeing him almost every day and speaking to him all the time. Their relationship had evolved over the years to something even better than they had the first time. Kendra had gotten to know Ian on a more mature level. He had become her Ian again; someone she could trust, talk to and depend on. He made her feel safe. She just never imagined that one day he would just not be around anymore, and by choice.

"Kendra, this is not something I can turn down. I told them 'yes.'"

"Well, maybe I come too," interjected Easton who had walked into the kitchen as Ian was speaking. Neither Kendra nor Ian had noticed him come in because they were engrossed in their conversation. .

"What do you mean, 'I could come too?'" demanded Kendra glaring at her son, "don't you have school to finish in New York?"

"Well, I could transfer to a school in Culver City, and live with Ian or maybe grandma and grandpa since they live in Highland Park. That's not far from Culver City, you know," replied Easton, thoughtfully, as he grabbed a raspberry yogurt from the fridge. He took out a spoon from one of the drawers, made himself comfortable on another stool next to Ian and began eating, apparently unconcerned by Ian's news.

"You are not going to have any room left in your stomach for dinner if you keep eating snacks just before dinner, " Kendra admonished her son.

"Don't worry, Mom, I'm a growing boy…there's going to be plenty of room in my stomach left for dinner, trust me," Easton replied and took another mouthful of yogurt before turning to Ian and asking, "so, Dad, is it cool if I come and live with you in California?" One way or another, he was going to be where Ian was. He was sixteen now and a big boy. Besides, since Peter died, he no longer had any desire to be in New York. He just never said it out loud to anyone. He figured that if his mother insisted that he stay in New York to finish school, and he had no choice but to stay, then once he turned eighteen and graduated from high school, he was going to go to college, anywhere but New York.

"That would depend on your mother, my man," Ian said, looking at Kendra. He wondered what exactly she was thinking.

Instead of responding, Kendra got up and went to check on the food that she was cooking. She did not want Ian to see how upset she was that he was not just leaving but he was leaving her again. She stirred the ground turkey source, saw that it was done, and then turned off the stove. After that, she checked the plantains. There was still a little water left in the pan but it was also done, so she drained it off and went about setting plates in front of Ian, Easton and one for herself.

"Do you need me to help you set up the dishes?" asked Ian, watching her carefully. He knew that she was upset that he was leaving but he wished she would talk to him properly. He did not want to be far from Kendra and Easton but he knew he needed to take this transfer. He would be a fool to turn down an opportunity like this.

"I'm ok!" Kendra snapped, upset with herself for feeling so angry that Ian was leaving. She knew he had to accept the promotion yet she the selfish part of her was not happy about it. He was leaving her.

"So does that mean that I can move to California too?" asked Easton, not helping matters, as he polished off his yogurt and then got ready to dig into his meal, which Kendra had dished out. Kendra shook her head at him again; sometimes she could not believe the appetite of teenage boys.

"I don't think so, Easton," she said.

"Why not?" demanded Easton before he took a bite out of his food.

"You've got school to finish…besides, what about that girl you like, Bri…something?'

"Her name is Brina, Mom, and we broke up…plus, like I said before, I can always transfer to a school in Culver City," Easton said, justifying his case.

"Kennie, why do you seem upset? I just told you some good news about my job but you seem, well, not quite happy about it," Ian said not yet touching his food. He knew Kendra well enough to know his news was bothering her.

"Who said I'm not happy for you? I am happy for you…just so you know."

"Oookaaay … you sure don't act like it though…hmmm," he said and started eating.

"He's right, Mom. You sound upset," said Easton between bites.

"Well, I am not upset! You are both wrong. Can we just drop the subject for now?" she asked, and without another word, she began eating slowing, not really tasting her food.

Easton and Ian glanced at each other, puzzled at her behavior, shrugged and continued eating.

***

After dinner, Easton went to his room, and Ian and Kendra cleaned up. Ian did not leave for his place immediately because he wanted to be sure that Kendra was ok before he left. As they sat on the couch in the leaving room drinking cold chocolate drinks, Ian turned to Kendra and asked, "Kennie, are you sure you are ok? Did I upset you with my news of my moving to California?"

"Of course not, Ian. I am truly happy for you. You deserve this promotion."

"Ok, so what's got you so rattled?" he asked quietly. "I know you Kennie, you are upset." Kendra turned her head away so he wouldn't see the truth in her eyes but Ian put his hand under her chin and gently turned her face back to face him. "Kendra, please talk to me."

"Ok, Ian, if you really want to know, I'm glad you got this opportunity, really I am…it's just that…" she hesitated.

"Yes, Kendra?" he asked quietly. He knew that she would miss him but he sensed it was more than that. It was no secret how he felt about her, but he had respected her request and held back these last few years. However, that did not mean that he stopped loving her. For him, it was simply impossible not to love Kendra. No matter whom he ended up with, Kendra would always be his number one girl. She would always be his Kennie.

"Well, I know I am being selfish, but I need you too. I'll always need you, Ian."

"Hey, it is just California, Kendra. Your family lives there, Liana goes to school there, and you grew up there. Heck, even Easton is ok with me leaving. A plane ride will get you there in five hours," Ian said, trying to make light of their conversation.

"It's not the same thing, Ian."

"Well, you now, you can call me at any time…I'm just a phone call and a plane ride away. We can still talk every day, Kendra."

"Ian, I'll miss you. I like having you around."

"I'll miss you, too, Kennie."

"No, Ian, you don't understand, I need you to continue to exist in my world in person, every day," Kendra said tearfully, in such a low voice that Ian had to strain to hear her.

"What are you trying to say to me, Ken?" asked Ian hopefully, his voice almost as low as Kendra's.

"I am saying that I love you, Ian Sharp. I am in love with you…more than I ever was before. I need you in my world…all of you."

"Oh, my Kennie!" Ian said, gathering Kendra in his arms. He dreamt of this moment for so long. He waited for years to hear her say this to him again. Now it was actually happening! How he loved this woman! They had been through so much together and now they had finally come full circle. "I love you so, so, so much, Kendra. You have no idea just how much I wanted to hear you say this to me again. You are my world. You've always been my world."

***

A month later, Kendra sold the house that she once shared with Peter and resigned from work. She and Easton joined Ian in Culver City, where Easton had transferred to a school there. A few months, later, Kendra found a job there as well. Liana was pleased that everyone had moved back to the West Coast even though she was in the San Francisco region while everyone was in Los Angeles area.

***

A year later, Kendra and Ian got married in the garden at the back of their house in Culver City. It was a small ceremony with just her family, children and Julian there. Kenneth and his wife also came. Kendra was glad. To her it was a sign of that they had accepted that she had found love again with someone who was not Peter. Easton stood beside Ian as his best man, and Liana stood with her mother as they said their vows.

There were tears in Ian's eyes as he said his vows. This was his woman. This was the love of his life. He could never love another woman the way he loved Kendra. That was a fact. She knew his person: good, bad and ugly, and loved him, anyway. He was happy to let go in her arms for the rest of his life because he knew she was the one he would love till the day he died.

As for Kendra, she was happy that Ian never gave up on her. He knew her like no other. After she had finally accepted that Peter was gone forever, she had allowed herself to love Ian freely again. This time around, the love she felt for him was deeper and fuller than anything she had ever experience with him in the past. They had been through so much together and apart and had finally come full circle. Though slightly imperfect, they just fitted. What she loved best about him? Well, him. All of him. Just him. Simple, human and not quite imperfect.

Books by Irene Ayo Asuen

- I Close My Eyes (Novella coming March 2024)
- Destiny's Faces (Novel)
- Destiny's Voices (Poetry)
- Destiny's Love (Lyric Poem)
- Destiny's Anguish (Lyric Poem)
- Just My Opinion, But …
- QuietlyWriting Journal series
- Nobody Told Me Five short stories
- QuietlySpeaking wall art the quotes (coming soon)

Not Quite Imperfect

"Tell your story in your own way …"

QuietlySpeaking™
www.ireneayoasuen.com
www.quietlyspeaking.com
https://www.facebook.com/iaasuen/

www.ingramcontent.com/pod-product-compliance
Lightning Source LLC
Chambersburg PA
CBHW070643180626
46817CB00006B/2225